THE MORTAL INSTRUMENTS

Book Four

City of Fallen Angels

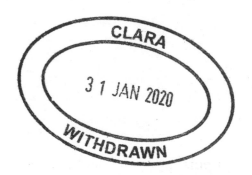

THE MORTAL INSTRUMENTS

Book Four

City of Fallen Angels

CASSANDRA CLARE

WALKER
BOOKS

This is a work of fiction. Names, characters, places and incidents are either the product
of the author's imagination or, if real, used fictitiously. All statements, activities, stunts, descriptions,
information and material of any other kind contained herein are included for entertainment purposes
only and should not be relied on for accuracy or replicated as they may result in injury.

First published in Great Britain 2011 by Walker Books Ltd
87 Vauxhall Walk, London SE11 5HJ

4 6 8 10 9 7 5

Text © 2011 Cassandra Claire LLC

Cover illustration © 2011 Cliff Nielsen

The right of Cassandra Clare to be identified as author of this work has been asserted
by her in accordance with the Copyright, Designs and Patents Act 1988

This book has been typeset in Dolly

Printed and bound in the UK by CPI Mackays, Chatham ME5 8TD

British Library Cataloguing in Publication Data:
a catalogue record for this book
is available from the British Library

ISBN 978-1-4063-2867-7

www.walker.co.uk

For Josh
*Sommes-nous les deux livres
d'un même ouvrage?*

———⬦———

Part One
Exterminating Angels

There are sicknesses that walk in darkness;
and there are exterminating angels, that fly wrapt up in the
curtains of immateriality and an uncommunicating nature;
whom we cannot see, but we feel their force,
and sink under their sword.
—Jeremy Taylor, "A Funeral Sermon"

1

THE MASTER

"Just coffee, please."

The waitress raised her penciled eyebrows. "You don't want anything to eat?" she asked. Her accent was thick, her attitude disappointed.

Simon Lewis couldn't blame her; she'd probably been hoping for a better tip than the one she was going to get on a single cup of coffee. But it wasn't his fault vampires didn't eat. Sometimes, in restaurants, he ordered food anyway, just to preserve the appearance of normalcy, but late Tuesday night, when Veselka was almost empty of other customers, it didn't seem worth the bother. "Just the coffee."

With a shrug the waitress took his laminated menu and went to put his order in. Simon sat back against the hard plastic diner chair and looked around. Veselka, a diner on the corner of Ninth Street and Second Avenue, was one of his favorite places on the Lower East Side—an old neighborhood eatery papered with black-and-white murals, where they let you sit all day as long as you ordered coffee at half-hour intervals. They also served what had once been his favorite vegetarian pierogi and borscht, but those days were behind him now.

It was mid-October, and they'd just put their Halloween decorations up—a wobbly sign that said TRICK-OR-BORSCHT! and a fake cardboard cutout vampire nicknamed Count Blintzula. Once upon a time Simon and Clary had found the cheesy holiday decorations hilarious, but the Count, with his fake fangs and black cape, didn't strike Simon as quite so funny anymore.

Simon glanced toward the window. It was a brisk night, and the wind was blowing leaves across Second Avenue like handfuls of thrown confetti. There was a girl walking down the street, a girl in a tight belted trench coat, with long black hair that flew in the wind. People turned to watch her as she walked past. Simon had looked at girls like that before in the past, idly wondering where they were going, who they were meeting. Not guys like him, he knew that much.

Except this one was. The bell on the diner's front door rang as the door opened, and Isabelle Lightwood came in. She smiled when she saw Simon, and came toward him, shrugging off her coat and draping it over the back of the chair before she sat down. Under the coat she was wearing one of what Clary called her "typical Isabelle outfits": a tight short velvet dress, fishnet stockings, and boots. There was a knife stuck into the top of her left boot that Simon knew only he could see; still, everyone in the diner was watching as she sat down, flinging her hair back. Whatever she was wearing, Isabelle drew attention like a fireworks display.

Beautiful Isabelle Lightwood. When Simon had met her, he'd assumed she'd have no time for a guy like him. He'd turned out to be mostly right. Isabelle liked boys her parents disapproved of, and in her universe that meant Downworlders—faeries, werewolves, and vamps. That they'd been dating regularly for the past month or two amazed him, even if their relationship was limited mostly to infrequent meetings like this one. And even if he couldn't help but wonder if he'd never been changed into a vampire, if his whole life hadn't been altered in that moment, would they be dating at all?

She tucked a lock of hair behind her ear, her smile brilliant. "You look nice."

Simon cast a glance at himself in the reflective surface of the diner window. Isabelle's influence was clear in the changes in his appearance since they'd been dating. She'd forced him to ditch his hoodies in favor of leather jackets, and his sneakers in favor of designer boots. Which, incidentally, cost three hundred dollars a pair. He was still wearing his characteristic word shirts—this one said EXISTENTIALISTS DO IT POINTLESSLY—but his jeans no longer had holes in the knees and torn pockets. He'd also grown his hair long so that it fell in his eyes now, covering his forehead, but that was more necessity than Isabelle.

Clary made fun of him about his new look; but, then, Clary found everything about Simon's love life borderline hilarious. She couldn't believe he was dating Isabelle in any serious way. Of course, she also couldn't believe he was also dating Maia

Roberts, a friend of theirs who happened to be a werewolf, in an equally serious way. And she really couldn't believe that Simon hadn't yet told either of them about the other.

Simon wasn't really sure how it had happened. Maia liked to come to his house and use his Xbox—they didn't have one at the abandoned police station where the werewolf pack lived—and it wasn't until the third or fourth time she'd come over that she'd leaned over and kissed him good-bye before she'd left. He'd been pleased, and then had called up Clary to ask her if he needed to tell Isabelle. "Figure out what's going on with you and Isabelle," she said. "Then tell her."

This had turned out to be bad advice. It had been a month, and he still wasn't sure what was going on with him and Isabelle, so he hadn't said anything. And the more time that passed, the more awkward the idea of saying something grew. So far he'd made it work. Isabelle and Maia weren't really friends, and rarely saw each other. Unfortunately for him, that was about to change. Clary's mother and her long-time friend, Luke, were getting married in a few weeks, and both Isabelle and Maia were invited to the wedding, a prospect Simon found more terrifying than the idea of being chased through the streets of New York by an angry mob of vampire hunters.

"So," Isabelle said, snapping him out of his reverie. "Why here and not Taki's? They'd serve you blood there."

Simon winced at her volume. Isabelle was nothing if not unsubtle. Fortunately, no one seemed to be listening in, not even the waitress who returned, banged down a cup of coffee in front of Simon, eyed Izzy, and left without taking her order.

"I like it here," he said. "Clary and I used to come here back when she was taking classes at Tisch. They have great borscht and blintzes—they're like sweet cheese dumplings—plus it's open all night."

Isabelle, however, was ignoring him. She was staring past his shoulder. "What is *that?*"

Simon followed her glance. "That's Count Blintzula."

"Count *Blintzula?*"

Simon shrugged. "It's a Halloween decoration. Count Blintzula is for kids. It's like Count Chocula, or the Count on *Sesame Street.*" He grinned at her blank look. "You know. He teaches kids how to count."

Isabelle was shaking her head. "There's a TV show where children are taught how to count by a *vampire?*"

"It would make sense if you'd seen it," Simon muttered.

"There is some mythological basis for such a construction," Isabelle said, lapsing into lecturey Shadowhunter mode. "Some legends do assert that vampires are obsessed with counting, and that if you spill grains of rice in front of them, they'll have to stop what they're doing and count each one. There's no truth in it, of course, any more than that business about garlic. And vampires have no business teaching children. Vampires are terrifying."

"Thank you," Simon said. "It's a joke, Isabelle. He's the Count. He likes counting. You know. 'What did the Count eat today, children? *One* chocolate chip cookie, *two* chocolate chip cookies, *three* chocolate chip cookies . . .'"

There was a rush of cold air as the door of the restaurant opened, letting in another customer. Isabelle shivered and reached for her black silk scarf. "It's not realistic."

"What would you prefer? 'What did the Count eat today,

children? *One* helpless villager, *two* helpless villagers, *three* helpless villagers . . .'"

"Shh." Isabelle finished knotting her scarf around her throat and leaned forward, putting her hand on Simon's wrist. Her big dark eyes were alive suddenly, the way they only ever came alive when she was either hunting demons or thinking about hunting demons. "Look over there."

Simon followed her gaze. There were two men standing over by the glass-fronted case that held bakery items: thickly frosted cakes, plates of rugelach, and cream-filled Danishes. Neither of the men looked as if they were interested in food, though. Both were short and painfully gaunt, so much so that their cheekbones jutted from their colorless faces like knives. Both had thin gray hair and pale gray eyes, and wore belted slate-colored coats that reached the floor.

"Now," Isabelle said, "what do you suppose they are?"

Simon squinted at them. They both stared back at him, their lashless eyes like empty holes. "They kind of look like evil lawn gnomes."

"They're human subjugates," Isabelle hissed. "They belong to a vampire."

"'Belong' as in . . . ?"

She made an impatient noise. "By the Angel, you don't know anything about your kind, do you? Do you even really know how vampires are made?"

"Well, when a mommy vampire and a daddy vampire love each other very much . . ."

Isabelle made a face at him. "Fine, you know that vampires *don't* need to have sex to reproduce, but I bet you don't really know how it works."

"I do too," said Simon. "I'm a vampire because I drank some of Raphael's blood before I died. Drinking blood plus death equals vampire."

"Not exactly," said Isabelle. "You're a vampire-because you drank some of Raphael's blood, and then you were bitten by other vampires, and *then* you died. You need to be bitten at some point during the process."

"Why?"

"Vampire saliva has . . . properties. Transformative properties."

"Yech," said Simon.

"Don't 'yech' me. You're the one with the magical spit. Vampires keep humans around and feed on them when they're short on blood—like walking snack machines." Izzy spoke with distaste. "You'd think they'd be weak from blood loss all the time, but vampire saliva actually has healing properties. It increases their red blood cell count, makes them stronger and healthier, and makes them live longer. That's why it's not against the Law for a vampire to feed on a human. It doesn't really hurt them. Of course every once in a while the vampire will decide it wants more than a snack, it wants a subjugate—and then it will start feeding its bitten human small amounts of vampire blood, just to keep it docile, to keep it connected to its master. Subjugates worship their masters, and love serving them. All they want is to be near them. Like you were when you went back to the Dumont. You were drawn back to the vampire whose blood you had consumed."

"Raphael," Simon said, his voice bleak. "I don't feel a burning urge to be with him these days, let me tell you."

"No, it goes away when you become a full vampire. It's only

the subjugates who worship their sires and can't disobey them. Don't you see? When you went back to the Dumont, Raphael's clan drained you, and you died, and then you became a vampire. But if they hadn't drained you, if they'd given you more vampire blood instead, you would eventually have become a subjugate."

"That's all very interesting," Simon said. "But it doesn't explain why they're staring at us."

Isabelle glanced back at them. "They're staring at *you*. Maybe their master died and they're looking for another vampire to own them. You could have pets." She grinned.

"Or," Simon said, "maybe they're here for the hash browns."

"Human subjugates don't eat food. They live on a mix of vampire blood and animal blood. It keeps them in a state of suspended animation. They're not immortal, but they age very slowly."

"Sadly," Simon said, eyeing them, "they don't seem to keep their looks."

Isabelle sat up straight. "And they're on their way over here. I guess we'll find out what they want."

The human subjugates moved as if they were on wheels. They didn't appear to be taking steps so much as gliding forward soundlessly. It took them only seconds to cross the restaurant; by the time they neared Simon's table, Isabelle had whipped the sharp stiletto-like dagger out of the top of her boot. It lay across the table, gleaming in the diner's fluorescent lights. It was a dark, heavy silver, with crosses burned into both sides of the hilt. Most vampire-repelling weapons seemed to sport crosses, on the assumption, Simon thought, that most vampires were Christian. Who knew that following a minority religion could be so advantageous?

"That's close enough," Isabelle said, as the two subjugates paused beside the table, her fingers inches from the dagger. "State your business, you two."

"Shadowhunter." The creature on the left spoke in a hissing whisper. "We did not know of you in this situation."

Isabelle raised a delicate eyebrow. "And what situation would that be?"

The second subjugate pointed a long gray finger at Simon. The nail on the end of it was yellowed and sharp. "We have dealings with the Daylighter."

"No, you don't," Simon said. "I have no idea who you are. Never seen you before."

"I am Mr. Walker," said the first creature. "Beside me is Mr. Archer. We serve the most powerful vampire in New York City. The head of the greatest Manhattan clan."

"Raphael Santiago," said Isabelle. "In that case you must know that Simon isn't a part of any clan. He's a free agent."

Mr. Walker smiled a thin smile. "My master was hoping that was a situation that could be altered."

Simon met Isabelle's eyes across the table. She shrugged. "Didn't Raphael tell you he wanted you to stay *away* from the clan?"

"Maybe he's changed his mind," Simon suggested. "You know how he is. Moody. Fickle."

"I wouldn't know. I haven't really seen him since that time I threatened to kill him with a candelabra. He took it well, though. Didn't flinch."

"Fantastic," Simon said. The two subjugates were staring at him. Their eyes were a pale whitish gray color, like dirty snow. "If Raphael wants me in the clan, it's because he wants something from me. You might as well tell me what it is."

"We are not privy to our master's plans," said Mr. Archer in a haughty tone.

"No dice, then," said Simon. "I won't go."

"If you do not wish to come with us, we are authorized to use force to bring you."

The dagger seemed to leap into Isabelle's hand; or at least, she barely seemed to move, and yet she was holding it. She twirled it lightly. "I wouldn't do that if I were you."

Mr. Archer bared his teeth at her. "Since when have the Angel's children become the bodyguards for rogue Downworlders? I would have thought you above this sort of business, Isabelle Lightwood."

"I'm not his bodyguard," said Isabelle. "I'm his *girlfriend.* Which gives me the right to kick your ass if you bother him. That's how it works."

Girlfriend? Simon was startled enough to look at her in surprise, but she was staring down the two subjugates, her dark eyes flashing. On the one hand he didn't think Isabelle had ever referred to herself as his girlfriend before. On the other hand it was symptomatic of how strange his life had become that *that* was the thing that had startled him most tonight, rather than the fact that he had just been summoned to a meeting by the most powerful vampire in New York.

"My master," said Mr. Walker, in what he probably thought was a soothing tone, "has a proposition to put to the Daylighter—"

"His name is Simon. Simon Lewis."

"To put to Mr. Lewis. I can promise you that Mr. Lewis will find it most advantageous if he is willing to accompany us and hear my master out. I swear on my master's honor that no harm will come to you, Daylighter, and that should you wish to refuse my master's offer, you will have the free choice to do so."

My master, my master. Mr. Walker spoke the words with a mixture of adoration and awe. Simon shuddered a little inwardly. How horrible to be so bound to someone else, and to have no real will of your own.

Isabelle was shaking her head; she mouthed "no" at Simon. She was probably right, he thought. Isabelle was an excellent Shadowhunter. She'd been hunting demons and lawbreaking Downworlders—rogue vampires, black-magic-practicing warlocks, werewolves who'd run wild and eaten someone— since she was twelve years old, and was probably better at what she did than any other Shadowhunter her age, with the exception of her brother Jace. And there had been Sebastian, Simon thought, who had been better than them both. But he was dead.

"All right," he said. "I'll go."

Isabelle's eyes rounded. "Simon!"

Both subjugates rubbed their hands together, like villains in a comic book. The gesture itself wasn't what was creepy, really; it was that they did it exactly at the same time and in the same way, as if they were puppets whose strings were being yanked in unison.

"Excellent," said Mr. Archer.

Isabelle banged the knife down on the table with a clatter and leaned forward, her shining dark hair brushing the tabletop. "Simon," she said in an urgent whisper. "Don't be stupid. There's no reason for you to go with them. And Raphael's a jerk."

"Raphael's a master vampire," said Simon. "His blood made me a vampire. He's my—whatever they call it."

"Sire, maker, begetter—there are a million names for what he did," Isabelle said distractedly. "And maybe his blood made you a vampire. But it didn't make you a *Daylighter*." Her eyes met his across the table. *Jace made you a Daylighter*. But she would never say it out loud; there were only a few of them who knew the truth, the whole story behind what Jace was, and what Simon was because of it. "You don't have to do what he says."

"Of course I don't," Simon said, lowering his voice. "But if I refuse to go, do you think Raphael is just going to drop it? He won't. They'll keep coming after me." He snuck a glance sideways at the subjugates; they looked as if they agreed, though he might have been imagining it. "They'll bug me everywhere. When I'm out, at school, at Clary's—"

"And what? Clary can't handle it?" Isabelle threw up her hands. "Fine. At least let me go with you."

"Certainly not," cut in Mr. Archer. "This is not a matter for Shadowhunters. This is the business of the Night Children."

"I will not—"

"The Law gives us the right to conduct our business in private." Mr. Walker spoke stiffly. "With our own kind."

Simon looked at them. "Give us a moment, please," he said. "I want to talk to Isabelle."

There was a moment of silence. Around them the life of the diner went on. The place was getting its late-night rush as the movie theater down the block let out, and waitresses were hurrying by, carrying steaming plates of food to customers; couples laughed and chattered at nearby tables; cooks shouted orders to each other behind the counter. No one looked at them or acknowledged that anything odd was going on. Simon was used to glamours by now, but he couldn't help the feeling sometimes, when he was with Isabelle, that he was trapped behind an invisible glass wall, cut off from the rest of humanity and the daily round of its affairs.

"Very well," said Mr. Walker, stepping back. "But my master does not like to be kept waiting."

They retreated toward the door, apparently unaffected by the blasts of cold air whenever someone went in or out, and stood there like statues. Simon turned to Isabelle. "It's all right," he said. "They won't hurt me. They *can't* hurt me. Raphael knows all about . . ." He gestured uncomfortably toward his forehead. "This."

Isabelle reached across the table and pushed his hair back, her touch more clinical than gentle. She was frowning. Simon had looked at the Mark enough times himself, in the mirror, to know well what it looked like. As if someone had taken a thin paintbrush and drawn a simple design on his forehead, just above and between his eyes. The shape of it seemed to change sometimes, like the moving images found in clouds, but it was always clear and black and somehow dangerous-looking, like a warning sign scrawled in another language.

"It really . . . works?" she whispered.

"Raphael thinks it works," said Simon. "And I have no reason to think it doesn't." He caught her wrist and drew it away from his face. "I'll be all right, Isabelle."

She sighed. "Every bit of my training says this isn't a good idea."

Simon squeezed her fingers. "Come on. You're curious about what Raphael wants, aren't you?"

Isabelle patted his hand and sat back. "Tell me all about it when you get back. Call me *first*."

"I will." Simon stood, zipping up his jacket. "And do me a favor, will you? Two favors, actually."

She looked at him with guarded amusement. "What?"

"Clary said she'd be training over at the Institute tonight. If you run into her, don't tell her where I went. She'll worry for no reason."

Isabelle rolled her eyes. "Okay, fine. Second favor?"

Simon leaned over and kissed her on the cheek. "Try the borscht before you leave. It's fantastic."

Mr. Walker and Mr. Archer were not the most talkative of companions. They led Simon silently through the streets of the Lower East Side, keeping several steps ahead of him with their odd gliding pace. It was getting late, but the city sidewalks were full of people—getting off a late shift, hurrying home from dinner, heads down, collars turned up against the stiff cold wind. At St. Mark's Place there were card tables set up along the curb, selling everything from cheap socks to pencil sketches of New York to smoky sandalwood incense. Leaves rattled across the pavement like dried bones. The air smelled like car exhaust mixed with sandalwood, and underneath that, the smell of human beings—skin and blood.

Simon's stomach tightened. He tried to keep enough bottles of animal blood in his room—he had a small refrigerator at the back of his closet now, where his mother wouldn't see it—to keep himself from ever getting hungry. The blood was disgusting. He'd thought he'd get used to it, even start wanting it, but though it killed his hunger pangs, there was nothing about it that he enjoyed the way he'd once enjoyed chocolate or vegetarian burritos or coffee ice cream. It remained blood.

But being hungry was worse. Being hungry meant that he could smell things he didn't want to smell—salt on skin; the overripe, sweet smell of blood exuding from the pores of strangers. It made him feel hungry and twisted up and utterly wrong. Hunching over, he jammed his fists into the pockets of his jacket and tried to breathe through his mouth.

They turned right onto Third Avenue, and paused in front of a restaurant whose sign said CLOISTER CAFÉ. GARDEN OPEN ALL YEAR. Simon blinked up at the sign. "What are we doing here?"

"This is the meeting place our master has chosen." Mr. Walker's tone was bland.

"Huh." Simon was puzzled. "I would have thought Raphael's style was more, you know, arranging meetings on top of an unconsecrated cathedral, or down in some crypt full of bones. He never struck me as the trendy restaurant type."

Both subjugates stared at him. "Is there a problem, Daylighter?" asked Mr. Archer finally.

Simon felt obscurely scolded. "No. No problem."

The interior of the restaurant was dark, with a marble-topped bar running along one wall. No servers or waitstaff approached them as they made their way through the room to a door in the back, and through the door into the garden.

Many New York restaurants had garden terraces; few were open this late into the year. This one was in a courtyard between several buildings. The walls had been painted with trompe l'oeil murals showing Italian gardens full of flowers. The trees, their leaves turned gold and russet with the fall, were strung with chains of white lights, and heat lamps scattered between the tables gave off a reddish glow. A small fountain plashed musically in the center of the yard.

Only one table was occupied, and not by Raphael. A slim woman in a wide-brimmed hat sat at a table close to the wall. As Simon watched in puzzlement, she raised a hand and waved at him. He turned and looked behind him; there was, of course, no one there. Walker and Archer had started moving again; bemused, Simon followed them as they crossed the courtyard and stopped a few feet from where the woman sat.

Walker bowed deeply. "Master," he said.

The woman smiled. "Walker," she said. "And Archer. Very good. Thank you for bringing Simon to me."

"Wait a second." Simon looked from the woman to the two subjugates and back again. "You're not Raphael."

"Dear me, no." The woman removed her hat. An enormous quantity of silvery blond hair, brilliant in the Christmas lights, spilled down over her shoulders. Her face was smooth and white and oval, very beautiful, dominated by enormous pale green eyes. She wore long black gloves, a black silk blouse and pencil skirt, and a black scarf tied around her throat. It was impossible to tell her age—or at least what age she might have been when she'd been Turned into a vampire. "I am Camille Belcourt. Enchanted to meet you."

She held out a black-gloved hand.

"I was told I was meeting Raphael Santiago here," said Simon, not reaching to take it. "Do you work for him?"

Camille Belcourt laughed like a rippling fountain. "Most certainly not! Though once upon a time he worked for me."

And Simon remembered. *I thought the head vampire was*

someone else, he had said to Raphael once, in Idris, it felt like forever ago.

Camille has not yet returned to us, Raphael had replied. *I lead in her stead.*

"You're the head vampire," Simon said. "Of the Manhattan clan." He turned back to the subjugates. "You tricked me. You told me I was meeting Raphael."

"I said you were meeting our master," said Mr. Walker. His eyes were vast and empty, so empty that Simon wondered if they had even meant to mislead him, or if they were simply programmed like robots to say whatever their master had told them to say, and were unaware of deviations from the script. "And here she is."

"Indeed." Camille flashed a brilliant smile toward her sub-jugates. "Please leave us, Walker, Archer. I need to speak to Simon alone." There was something about the way she said it—both his name, and the word "alone"—that was like a secret caress.

The subjugates bowed and withdrew. As Mr. Archer turned to walk away, Simon caught sight of a mark on the side of his throat, a deep bruise, so dark it looked like paint, with two darker spots inside it. The darker spots were punctures, ringed with dry, ragged flesh. Simon felt a quiet shudder pass through him.

"Please," said Camille, and patted the seat beside her. "Sit. Would you like some wine?"

Simon sat, perching uncomfortably on the edge of the hard metal chair. "I don't really drink."

"Of course," she said, all sympathy. "You're barely a fledgling, aren't you? Don't worry too much. Over time you will train yourself to be able to consume wine and other beverages. Some of the oldest of our kind can consume human food with few ill effects."

Few ill effects? Simon didn't like the sound of that. "Is this going to take a long time?" he inquired, gazing pointedly down at his cell phone, which told him the time was after ten thirty. "I have to get home."

Camille took a sip of her wine. "You do? And why is that?"

Because my mom is waiting up for me. Okay, there was no reason this woman needed to know that. "You interrupted my date," he said. "I was just wondering what was so important."

"You still live with your mother, don't you?" she said, setting her glass down. "Rather odd, isn't it, a powerful vampire like yourself refusing to leave home, to join with a clan?"

"So you interrupted my date to make fun of me for still living with my parents. Couldn't you have done that on a night I didn't have a date? That's most nights, in case you're curious."

"I'm not mocking you, Simon." She ran her tongue over her lower lip as if tasting the wine she had just drunk. "I want to know why you haven't become part of Raphael's clan."

Which is the same as your clan, isn't it? "I got the strong feeling he didn't want me to be part of it," Simon said. "He pretty much said he'd leave me alone if I left him alone. So I've left him alone."

"*Have* you." Her green eyes glowed.

"I never wanted to be a vampire," Simon said, half-wondering why he was telling these things to this strange woman. "I wanted a normal life. When I found out I was a Day-lighter, I thought I could have one. Or at least some approximation of one. I can go to school, I can live at home, I can see my mom and sister—"

"As long as you don't ever eat in front of them," said Camille. "As long as you hide your need for blood. You have never fed on someone purely human, have you? Just bagged blood. Stale. Animal." She wrinkled her nose.

Simon thought of Jace, and pushed the thought hastily away. Jace was not precisely *human*. "No, I haven't."

"You will. And when you do, you will not forget it." She leaned forward, and her pale hair brushed across his hand. "You cannot hide your true self forever."

"What teenager doesn't lie to their parents?" Simon said. "Anyway, I don't see why you care. In fact, I'm still not sure why I'm here."

Camille leaned forward. When she did, the neckline of her black silk blouse gaped open. If Simon had still been human, he would have blushed. "Will you let me see it?"

Simon could actually feel his eyes pop out. "See *what?*"

She smiled. "The Mark, silly boy. The Mark of the Wanderer."

Simon opened his mouth, then closed it again. *How does she know?* Very few people knew of the Mark that Clary had put on him in Idris. Raphael had indicated it was a matter for deadly secrecy, and Simon had treated it as such.

But Camille's eyes were very green and steady, and for some reason he wanted to do what she wanted him to do. It was something about the way she looked at him, something in the music of her voice. He reached up and pushed his hair aside, baring his forehead for her inspection.

Her eyes widened, her lips parting. Lightly she touched her fingers to her throat, as if checking the nonexistent pulse there.

"Oh," she said. "How lucky you are, Simon. How fortunate."

"It's a curse," he said. "Not a blessing. You know that, right?"

Her eyes sparked. "'And Cain said unto the Lord, My punishment is greater than I can bear.' Is it more than you can bear, Simon?"

Simon sat back, letting his hair fall back into place. "I can bear it."

"But you don't want to." She ran a gloved finger around the rim of her wineglass, her eyes still fixed on him. "What if I could offer you a way to turn what you regard as a curse into an advantage?"

I'd say you're finally getting to the reason you brought me here, which is a start. "I'm listening."

"You recognized my name when I told it to you," Camille said. "Raphael has mentioned me before, has he not?" She had an accent, very faint, that Simon couldn't quite place.

"He said you were the head of the clan and he was just leading them while you were gone. Stepping in for you like—like a vice president or something."

"Ah." She bit gently on her lower lip. "That is, in fact, not quite true. I would like to tell you the truth, Simon. I would like to make you an offer. But first I must have your word on something."

"And what's that?"

"That everything that passes between us this night, here, remains a secret. No one can know. Not your redheaded little friend, Clary. Not either of your lady friends. None of the Lightwoods. No one."

Simon sat back. "And what if I don't want to promise?"

"Then you may leave, if you like," she said. "But then you

will never know what I wished to tell you. And that will be a loss you will regret."

"I'm curious," Simon said. "But I'm not sure I'm that curious."

Her eyes held a little spark of surprise and amusement and perhaps, Simon thought, even a little respect. "Nothing I have to say to you concerns them. It will not affect their safety, or their well-being. The secrecy is for my own protection."

Simon looked at her suspiciously. Did she mean it? Vampires weren't like faeries, who couldn't lie. But he had to admit he was curious. "All right. I'll keep your secret, unless I think something you say is putting my friends in danger. Then all bets are off."

Her smile was frosty; he could tell she didn't like being disbelieved. "Very well," she said. "I suppose I have little choice when I need your help so badly." She leaned forward, one slim hand toying with the stem of her wineglass. "Until quite recently I led the Manhattan clan, happily. We had beautiful quarters in an old prewar building on the Upper West Side, not that rat hole of a hotel Santiago keeps my people in now. Santiago—Raphael, as you call him—was my second in command. My most loyal companion—or so I thought. One night I found out that he was murdering humans, driving them to that old hotel in Spanish Harlem and drinking their blood for his amusement. Leaving their bones in the Dumpster outside. Taking stupid risks, breaking Covenant Law." She took a sip of wine. "When I went to confront him, I realized he had told the rest of the clan that I was the murderer, the lawbreaker. It was all a setup. He meant to kill me, so that he might seize power. I fled, with only Walker and Archer to keep me safe."

"So all this time he's claimed he's just leading until you return?"

She made a face. "Santiago is an accomplished liar. He wishes me to return, that's for certain—so he can murder me and take charge of the clan in earnest."

Simon wasn't sure what she wanted to hear. He wasn't used to adult women looking at him with big tear-filled eyes, or spilling out their life stories to him.

"I'm sorry," he said finally.

She shrugged, a very expressive shrug that made him wonder if perhaps her accent was French. "It is in the past," she said. "I have been hiding out in London all this time, looking for allies, biding my time. Then I heard about you." She held up her hand. "I cannot tell you how; I am sworn to secrecy. But the moment I did, I realized that you were what I had been waiting for."

"I was? I am?"

She leaned forward and touched his hand. "Raphael is afraid of you, Simon, as well he should be. You are one of his own, a vampire, but you cannot be harmed or killed; he cannot lift a finger against you without bringing down God's wrath on his head."

There was a silence. Simon could hear the soft electrical hum of the Christmas lights overhead, the water plashing in the stone fountain in the center of the courtyard, the buzz and hum of the city. When he spoke, his voice was soft. "You said it."

"What was that, Simon?"

"The word. The wrath of—" The word bit and burned in his mouth, just as it always did.

"Yes. *God*." She retracted her hand, but her eyes were warm.

"There are many secrets of our kind, so many that I can tell you, show you. You will learn you are not damned."

"Ma'am—"

"Camille. You must call me Camille."

"I still don't understand what you want from me."

"Don't you?" She shook her head, and her brilliant hair flew around her face. "I want you to join with me, Simon. Join with me against Santiago. We will walk together into his rat-infested hotel; the moment his followers see that you are with me, they will leave him and come to me. I believe they are loyal to me beneath their fear of him. Once they see us together, that fear will be gone, and they will come to our side. Man cannot contend with the divine."

"I don't know," Simon said. "In the Bible, Jacob wrestled an angel, and he won."

Camille looked at him with her eyebrows arched.

Simon shrugged. "Hebrew school."

"'And Jacob called the name of the place Peniel: for I have seen God face to face.' You see, you are not the only one who knows your scripture." Her narrow look was gone, and she was smiling. "You may not realize it, Daylighter, but as long as you bear that Mark, you are the avenging arm of heaven. No one can stand before you. Certainly not one vampire."

"Are you afraid of me?" Simon asked.

He was almost instantly sorry he had. Her green eyes darkened like thunderclouds. "Me, afraid of you?" Then she collected herself, her face smoothing, her expression lightening. "Of course not," she said. "You are an intelligent man. I am convinced you will see the wisdom of my proposal and join with me."

"And what exactly is your proposal? I mean, I understand the part where we face down Raphael, but after that? I don't really hate Raphael, or want to get rid of him just to get rid of him. He leaves me alone. That's all I ever wanted."

She folded her hands together in front of her. She wore a silver ring with a blue stone in it on her left middle finger, over the material of her glove. "You think that is what you want, Simon. You think Raphael is doing you a favor in leaving you alone, as you put it. In reality he is exiling you. Right now you think you do not need others of your kind. You are content with the friends you have—humans and Shadowhunters. You are content to hide bottles of blood in your room and lie to your mother about what you are."

"How did you—"

She went on, ignoring him. "But what about in ten years, when you are supposed to be twenty-six? In twenty years? Thirty? Do you think no one will notice that as they age and change, you do not?"

Simon said nothing. He didn't want to admit he hadn't thought ahead that far. That he didn't want to think ahead that far.

"Raphael has taught you that other vampires are poison to you. But it does not need to be that way. Eternity is a long time to spend alone, without others of your kind. Others who understand. You befriend Shadowhunters, but you can never be of them. You will always be other and outside. With us you could belong." As she leaned forward, white light sparked off her ring, stinging Simon's eyes. "We have thousands of years of knowledge we could share with you, Simon. You could learn how to keep your secret; how to eat and drink, how to speak the name of God. Raphael has cruelly hidden this information from you, even led you to believe it doesn't exist. It does. I can help you."

"If I help you first," Simon said.

She smiled, and her teeth were white and sharp. "We will help each other."

Simon leaned back. The iron chair was hard and uncomfortable, and he suddenly felt tired. Looking down at his hands, he could see that the veins had darkened, spidering across the backs of his knuckles. He needed blood. He needed to talk to Clary. He needed time to think.

"I've shocked you," she said. "I know. It is a great deal to take in. I would be happy to give you as much time as you needed to make up your mind about this, and about me. But we don't have much time, Simon. While I remain in this city, I am in danger from Raphael and his cohorts."

"Cohorts?" Despite everything, Simon grinned slightly.

Camille seemed baffled. "Yes?"

"Well, it's just . . . 'Cohorts.' It's like saying 'evildoers' or 'minions.'" She stared at him blankly. Simon sighed. "Sorry. You probably haven't seen as many bad movies as I have."

Camille frowned faintly, a very fine line appearing between her brows. "I was told you would be slightly peculiar. Perhaps it is just that I don't know many vampires of your generation. But that will be good for me, I feel, to be around someone so . . . young."

"New blood," said Simon.

At that she did smile. "Are you ready, then? To accept my offer? To begin to work together?"

Simon looked up at the sky. The strings of white lights

seemed to blot out the stars. "Look," he said, "I appreciate your offer. I really do." *Crap*, he thought. There had to be some way to say this without him sounding like he was turning down a date to the prom. *I'm really, really flattered you asked, but . . .* Camille, like Raphael, always spoke stiffly, formally, as if she were in a fairy tale. Maybe he could try that. He said, "I require some time to make my decision. I'm sure you understand."

Very delicately, she smiled, showing only the tips of her fangs. "Five days," she said. "And no longer." She held out her gloved hand to him. Something gleamed in her palm. It was a small glass vial, the size that might hold a perfume sample, only it appeared to be full of brownish powder. "Grave dirt," she explained. "Smash this, and I will know you are summoning me. If you do not summon me within five days I will send Walker for your answer."

Simon took the vial and slipped it into his pocket. "And if the answer is no?"

"Then I will be disappointed. But we will part friends." She pushed her wineglass away. "Good-bye, Simon."

Simon stood up. The chair made a metallic squeaking sound as it dragged over the ground, too loud. He felt like he should say something else, but he had no idea what. For the moment, though, he seemed to be dismissed. He decided that he'd rather look like one of those weird modern vampires with bad manners than risk getting dragged back into the conversation. He left without saying anything else.

On his way back through the restaurant, he passed Walker and Archer, who were standing by the big wooden bar, their shoulders hunched under their long gray coats. He felt the force of their glares on him as he walked by and wiggled his fingers at them—a gesture somewhere between a friendly wave and a kiss-off. Archer bared his teeth—flat human teeth—and stalked past him toward the garden, Walker on his heels. Simon watched as they took their places in chairs across from Camille; she didn't look up as they seated themselves, but the white lights that had illuminated the garden went out suddenly—not one by one but all at the same time—leaving Simon staring at a disorienting square of darkness, as if someone had switched off the stars. By the time the waiters noticed and hurried outside to rectify the problem, flooding the garden with pale light once again, Camille and her human subjugates had vanished.

Simon unlocked the front door of his house—one of a long chain of identical brick-fronted row houses that lined his Brooklyn block—and pushed it open slightly, listening hard.

He had told his mother he was going out to practice with Eric and his other bandmates for a gig on Saturday. There had been a time when she simply would have believed him, and that would have been that; Elaine Lewis had always been a relaxed parent, never imposing a curfew on either Simon or his sister or insisting that they be home early on school nights. Simon was used to staying out until all hours with Clary, letting himself in with his key, and collapsing into bed at two in the morning, behavior that hadn't excited much comment from his mother.

Things were different now. He had been in Idris, the Shadowhunters' home country, for almost two weeks. He had vanished from home, with no chance to offer an excuse or explanation. The warlock Magnus Bane had stepped in and performed a memory spell on Simon's mother so that she now had no recollection that he had been missing at all. Or at least, no *conscious* recollection. Her behavior had changed, though. She was suspicious now, hovering, always watching him, insisting he be home at certain times. The last time he had come home from a date with Maia, he had found Elaine in the foyer, sitting in a chair facing the door, her arms crossed over her chest and a look of barely tempered rage on her face.

That night, he'd been able to hear her breathing before he'd seen her. Now he could hear only the faint sound of the television coming from the living room. She must have waited up for him, probably watching a marathon of one of those hospital dramas she loved. Simon swung the door closed behind him and leaned against it, trying to gather his energy to lie.

It was hard enough not eating around his family. Thankfully his mother went to work early and got back late, and Rebecca, who went to college in New Jersey and only came home occasionally to do her laundry, wasn't around often enough to notice anything odd. His mom was usually gone in the morning by the time he got up, the breakfast and lunch she'd lovingly prepared for him left out on the kitchen counter. He'd dump it into a trash bin on his way to school. Dinner was tougher. On the nights she was there, he had to push his food around his plate, pretend he wasn't hungry or that he wanted to take his food into his bedroom so he could eat while studying. Once or twice he'd forced the food down, just to make her happy, and spent hours in the bathroom afterward, sweating and retching until it was out of his system.

He hated having to lie to her. He'd always felt a little sorry for Clary, with her fraught relationship with Jocelyn, the most overprotective parent he'd ever known. Now the shoe was on the other foot. Since Valentine's death, Jocelyn's grip on Clary had relaxed to the point where she was practically a normal parent. Meanwhile, whenever Simon was home, he could feel the weight of his mother's gaze on him, like an accusation wherever he went.

Squaring his shoulders, he dropped his messenger bag by the door and headed into the living room to face the music. The TV was on, the news blaring. The local announcer was reporting on a human interest story—a baby found abandoned in an alley behind a hospital downtown. Simon was surprised; his mom hated the news. She found it depressing. He glanced toward the couch, and his surprise faded. His mother was asleep, her glasses on the table beside her, a half-empty glass on the floor. Simon could smell it from here—probably whiskey. He felt a pang. His mom hardly ever drank.

Simon went into his mother's bedroom and returned with a crocheted blanket. His mom was still asleep, her breathing slow and even. Elaine Lewis was a tiny, birdlike woman, with a halo of black curling hair, streaked with gray that she refused to dye. She worked during the day for an environmental nonprofit, and most of her clothes had animal motifs on them. Right now she was wearing a dress tie-dye printed with dolphins and waves, and a pin that had once been a live fish, dipped in resin. Its lacquered eye seemed to glare at Simon accusingly as he bent to tuck the blanket around her shoulders.

She moved, fitfully, turning her head away from him. "Simon," she whispered. "Simon, where are you?"

Stricken, Simon let go of the blanket and stood up. Maybe he should wake her up, let her know he was okay. But then there would be questions he didn't want to answer and that hurt look on her face he couldn't stand. He turned and went into his bedroom.

He had thrown himself down onto the covers and grabbed for the phone on his bedside table, about to dial Clary's number, before he even thought about it. He paused for a moment, listening to the dial tone. He couldn't tell her about Camille; he'd promised to keep the vampire's offer a secret, and while Simon didn't feel he owed Camille much, if there was one thing he had learned from the past few months, it was that reneging on promises made to supernatural creatures was a bad idea. Still, he wanted to hear Clary's voice, the way he always did when he'd had a tough day. Well, there was always complaining to her about his love life; that seemed to amuse her no end. Rolling over in bed, he pulled the pillow over his head and dialed Clary's number.

2

FALLING

"So, did you have fun with Isabelle tonight?" Clary, her phone jammed against her ear, maneuvered herself carefully from one long beam to another. The beams were set twenty feet up in the rafters of the Institute's attic, where the training room was located. Walking the beams was meant to teach you how to balance. Clary hated them. Her fear of heights made the whole business sickening, despite the flexible cord tied around her waist that was supposed to keep her from hitting the floor if she fell. "Have you told her about Maia yet?"

Simon made a faint, noncommittal noise that Clary knew meant "no." She could hear music in the background; she could picture him lying on his bed, the stereo playing softly as he talked to her. He sounded tired, that sort of bone-deep tired she knew meant that his light tone didn't reflect his mood. She'd asked him if he was all right several times at the beginning of the conversation, but he'd brushed away her concern.

She snorted. "You're playing with fire, Simon. I hope you know that."

"I don't know. Do you really think it's such a big deal?" Simon sounded plaintive. "I haven't had a single conversation with Isabelle—or Maia—about dating exclusively."

"Let me tell you something about girls." Clary sat down on a beam, letting her legs dangle out into the air. The attic's half-moon windows were open, and cool night air spilled in, chilling her sweaty skin. She had always thought the Shadowhunters trained in their tough, leatherlike gear, but as it turned out, that was for later training, which involved weapons. For the sort of training she was doing—exercises meant to increase her flexibility, speed, and sense of balance—she wore a light tank top and drawstring pants that reminded her of medical scrubs. "Even if you haven't had the exclusivity conversation, they're still going to be mad if they find out you're dating someone they know and you haven't mentioned it. It's a dating rule."

"Well, how am I supposed to know that rule?"

"Everyone knows that rule."

"I thought you were supposed to be on my side."

"I am on your side!"

"So why aren't you being more sympathetic?"

Clary switched the phone to her other ear and peered down into the shadows below her. Where was Jace? He'd gone to get another rope and said he'd be back in five minutes. Of course, if he caught her on the phone up here, he'd probably kill her. He was rarely in charge of her training—that was usually Maryse,

Kadir, or various other members of the New York Conclave pinch-hitting until a replacement for the Institute's previous tutor, Hodge, could be found—but when he was, he took it very seriously. "Because," she said, "your problems are not real problems. You're dating two beautiful girls at once. Think about it. That's like . . . rock-star problems."

"Having rock-star problems may be the closest I ever get to being an actual rock star."

"No one told you to call your band Salacious Mold, my friend."

"We're Millennium Lint now," Simon protested.

"Look, just figure this out before the wedding. If they both think they're going to it with you and they find out at the wedding that you're dating them both, they'll kill you." She stood up. "And then my mom's wedding will be ruined, and she'll kill you. So you'll be dead twice. Well, three times, technically . . ."

"I never told either of them I was going to the wedding with them!" Simon sounded panicked.

"Yes, but they're going to expect you to. That's why girls have boyfriends. So you have someone to take you to boring functions." Clary moved out to the edge of the beam, looking down into the witchlight-illuminated shadows below. There was an old training circle chalked on the floor; it looked like a bull's-eye. "Anyway, I have to jump off this beam now and possibly hurtle to my horrible death. I'll talk to you tomorrow."

"I've got band practice at two, remember? I'll see you there."

"See you." She hung up and stuck the phone into her bra; the light training clothes didn't have any pockets, so what was a girl to do?

"So, are you planning to stay up there all night?" Jace

stepped into the center of the bull's-eye and looked up at her. He was wearing fighting gear, not training clothes like Clary was, and his fair hair stood out startlingly against the black. It had darkened slightly since the end of summer and was more a dark gold than light, which, Clary thought, suited him even better. It made her absurdly happy that she had now known him long enough to notice small changes in his appearance.

"I thought you were coming up here," she called down. "Change of plans?"

"Long story." He grinned up at her. "So? You want to practice flips?"

Clary sighed. Practicing flips involved flinging herself off the beam into empty space, and using the flexible cord to hold her while she pushed off the walls and flipped herself over and under, teaching herself to whirl, kick, and duck without worrying about hard floors and bruises. She'd seen Jace do it, and he looked like a falling angel while he did, flying through the air, whirling and spinning with beautiful, balletic grace. She, on the other hand, curled up like a potato bug as soon as the floor approached, and the fact that she intellectually knew she wasn't going to hit it didn't seem to make any difference.

She was starting to wonder if it didn't matter that she'd been born a Shadowhunter; maybe it was too late for her to be made into one, or at least a fully functional one. Or maybe the gift that made her and Jace what they were had been somehow distributed unequally between them, so he had gotten all the physical grace, and she had gotten—well, not a lot of it.

"Come on, Clary," Jace said. "Jump." She closed her eyes and jumped. For a moment she felt herself hang suspended, free of everything. Then gravity took over, and she plunged toward the floor. Instinctively she pulled her arms and legs in, keeping her eyes squeezed shut. The cord pulled taut and she rebounded, flying back up before falling again. As her velocity slowed, she opened her eyes and found herself dangling at the end of the cord, about five feet above Jace. He was grinning.

"Nice," he said. "As graceful as a falling snowflake."

"Was I screaming?" she asked, genuinely curious. "You know, on the way down."

He nodded. "Thankfully no one's home, or they would have assumed I was murdering you."

"Ha. You can't even reach me." She kicked out a leg and spun lazily in midair.

Jace's eyes glinted. "Want to bet?"

Clary knew that expression. "No," she said quickly. "Whatever you're going to do—"

But he'd already done it. When Jace moved fast, his individual movements were almost invisible. She saw his hand go to his belt, and then something flashed in the air. She heard the sound of parting fabric as the cord above her head was sheared through. Released, she fell freely, too surprised to scream— directly into Jace's arms. The force knocked him backward, and they sprawled together onto one of the padded floor mats, Clary on top of him. He grinned up at her.

"Now," he said, "that was much better. You didn't scream at all."

"I didn't get the chance." She was breathless, and not just from the impact of the fall. Being sprawled on top of Jace, feeling his body against hers, made her hands shake and her heart beat faster. She had thought maybe her physical reaction to him— their reactions to each other—would fade with familiarity, but that hadn't happened. If anything, it had gotten worse the more time she'd spent with him—or better, she supposed, depending on how you thought about it.

He was looking up at her with dark golden eyes; she wondered if their color had intensified since his encounter with Raziel, the Angel, by the shores of Lake Lyn in Idris. She couldn't ask anyone: Though everyone knew that Valentine had summoned the Angel, and that the Angel had healed Jace from injuries Valentine had inflicted on him, no one but Clary and Jace knew that Valentine had done more than just injure his adopted son. He had stabbed Jace through the heart as part of the summoning ceremony—stabbed him, and held him while he died. At Clary's wish Raziel had brought Jace back from death. The enormity of it still shocked Clary, and, she suspected, Jace as well. They had agreed never to tell anyone that Jace had actually *died*, even for a brief time. It was their secret.

He reached up and pushed her hair back from her face. "I'm joking," he said. "You're not so bad. You'll get there. You should have seen Alec do flips at first. I think he kicked himself in the head once."

"Sure," said Clary. "But he was probably eleven." She eyed him. "I suppose you've always been amazing at this stuff."

"I was born amazing." He stroked her cheek with the tips of his fingers, lightly but enough to make her shiver. She said nothing; he was joking, but in a sense it was true. Jace had been born to be what he was. "How long can you stay tonight?"

She smiled a little. "Are we done with training?"

"I'd like to think that we're done with the part of the evening where it's absolutely required. Although there are a few things I'd like to practice. . . ." He reached up to pull her down, but at that moment the door opened, and Isabelle came stalking in, the high heels of her boots clicking on the polished hardwood floor.

Catching sight of Jace and Clary sprawled on the floor, she raised her eyebrows. "Canoodling, I see. I thought you were supposed to be training."

"No one said you had to walk in without knocking, Iz." Jace didn't move, just turned his head to the side to look at Isabelle with a mixture of annoyance and affection. Clary, though, scrambled to her feet, straightening her crumpled clothes.

"It's the training room. It's public space." Isabelle was pulling off one of her gloves, which were bright red velvet. "I just got these at Trash and Vaudeville. On sale. Don't you love them? Don't you wish you had a pair?" She wiggled her fingers in their direction.

"I don't know," said Jace. "I think they'd clash with my gear."

Isabelle made a face at him. "Did you hear about the dead Shadowhunter they found in Brooklyn? The body was all mangled up, so they don't know who it is yet. I assume that's where Mom went."

"Yeah," said Jace, sitting up. "Clave meeting. I ran into her on the way out."

"You didn't tell me that," said Clary. "Is that why you took so long getting rope?"

He nodded. "Sorry. I didn't want to freak you out."

"He means," said Isabelle, "he didn't want to spoil the romantic mood." She bit her lip. "I just hope it wasn't anyone we know."

"I don't think it could have been. The body was dumped in

an abandoned factory—had been there for several days. If it
had been someone we knew, we would have noticed they were
missing." Jace pushed his hair back behind his ears. He was
looking at Isabelle a little impatiently, Clary thought, as if he
were annoyed she'd brought this up. She wished he'd told her
earlier, even if it would have spoiled the mood. Much of what he
did, what they all did, Clary knew, brought them into frequent
contact with the reality of death. All the Lightwoods were, in
their own ways, still grieving the loss of the youngest son, Max,
who had died simply for being in the wrong place at the wrong
time. It was strange. Jace had accepted her decision to leave
high school and take up training without a murmur, but he
shied away from discussing the dangers of a Shadowhunting
life with her.

"I'm going to get dressed," she announced, and headed for
the door that led to the small changing room attached to the
training area. It was very plain: pale wood walls, a mirror, a
shower, and hooks for clothes. Towels were stacked neatly on
a wooden bench by the door. Clary showered quickly and put
on her street clothes—tights, boots, jean skirt, and a new pink
sweater. Looking at herself in the mirror, she saw that there
was a hole in her tights, and her damp and curling red hair was
an untidy tangle. She would never look perfectly put together
like Isabelle always did, but Jace didn't seem to mind.

By the time she came back to the training room, Isabelle
and Jace had left the topic of dead Shadowhunters behind and
had moved on to something Jace apparently found even more
horrifying—Isabelle's date with Simon. "I can't believe he took
you to an actual restaurant." Jace was on his feet now, putting
away the floor mats and training gear while Isabelle leaned

against the wall and played with her new gloves. "I assumed his idea of a date would be making you watch him play World of Warcraft with his nerd friends."

"I," Clary pointed out, "am one of his nerd friends, thank you."

Jace grinned at her.

"It wasn't really a restaurant. More of a diner. With pink soup that he wanted me to try," Isabelle said thoughtfully. "He was very sweet."

Clary felt instantly guilty for not telling her—or Jace—about Maia. "He said you had fun."

Isabelle's gaze flickered over to her. There was a peculiar quality to Isabelle's expression, as if she were hiding something, but it was gone before Clary could be sure it had been there at all. "You talked to him?"

"Yeah, he called me a few minutes ago. Just to check in." Clary shrugged.

"I see," Isabelle said, her voice suddenly brisk and cool. "Well, as I said, he's very sweet. But maybe a bit *too* sweet. That can be boring." She stuffed her gloves into her pockets. "Anyway, it isn't a permanent thing. It's just playing around for now."

Clary's guilt faded. "Have you guys ever talked about, you know, dating exclusively?"

Isabelle looked horrified. "Of course not." She yawned then, stretching her arms catlike over her head. "Okay, off to bed. See you later, lovebirds."

She departed, leaving a hazy cloud of jasmine perfume in her wake.

Jace looked over at Clary. He had started unbuckling his

gear, which clasped at the wrists and back, forming a protective shell over his clothes. "I suppose you have to go home?"

She nodded reluctantly. Getting her mother to agree to let her pursue Shadowhunter training had been a long, unpleasant argument in the first place. Jocelyn had dug her heels in, saying that she'd spent her life trying to keep Clary out of the Shadowhunter culture, which she saw as dangerous—not just violent, she argued, but isolationist and cruel. Only a year ago, she pointed out to Clary, Clary's decision to be trained as a Shadowhunter would have meant she could never speak to her mother again. Clary argued back that the fact that the Clave had suspended rules like that while the new Council reviewed the Laws meant that the Clave had changed since Jocelyn had been a girl, and anyway, Clary needed to know how to defend herself.

"I hope this isn't just because of Jace," Jocelyn had said finally. "I know how it is when you're in love with someone. You want to be where they are and do what they do, but Clary—"

"I am not you," Clary had said, struggling to control her anger, "the Shadowhunters aren't the Circle, and Jace isn't Valentine."

"I didn't say anything about Valentine."

"It's what you were thinking," Clary had said. "Maybe Valentine brought Jace up, but Jace isn't anything like him."

"Well, I hope not," Jocelyn had said softly. "For all our sakes." Eventually she had given in, but with some rules:

Clary wasn't to live in the Institute but with her mother at Luke's; Jocelyn got weekly progress reports from Maryse to assure her that Clary was learning and not just, Clary supposed, ogling Jace all day, or whatever she was worried about.

And Clary wasn't to spend the night at the Institute—ever. "No sleepovers where your boyfriend lives," Jocelyn had said firmly. "I don't care if it is the Institute. No."

Boyfriend. It was still a shock, hearing the word. For so long it had seemed a total impossibility that Jace would ever be her boyfriend, that they could ever be anything to each other at all but brother and sister, and that had been too hard and horrible to face. Never seeing each other again, they had decided, would have been better than that, and that would have been like dying. And then, by a miracle, they had been set free. Now it had been six weeks, but Clary wasn't tired of the word yet.

"I have to get home," she said. "It's almost eleven, and my mom freaks if I stay here past ten."

"All right." Jace dropped his gear, or at least the top half of it, onto the bench. He wore a thin T-shirt underneath; Clary could see his Marks through it, like ink bleeding through wet paper. "I'll walk you out."

The Institute was quiet as they passed through. There were no visiting Shadowhunters from other cities staying right now. Robert, Isabelle and Alec's father, was in Idris helping set up the new Council, and with Hodge and Max gone forever, and Alec away with Magnus, Clary felt as if the remaining occupants were like guests in a mostly empty hotel. She wished other members of the Conclave would come around more often, but she supposed everyone was giving the Lightwoods time at the moment. Time to remember Max, and time to forget.

"So have you heard from Alec and Magnus lately?" she asked. "Are they having a good time?"

"Sounds like it." Jace took his phone out of his pocket and handed it to her. "Alec keeps sending me annoying photos.

Lots of captions like *Wish you were here, except not really.*"

"Well, you can't blame him. It's supposed to be a romantic vacation." She flipped through the photos on Jace's phone and giggled. Alec and Magnus standing in front of the Eiffel Tower, Alec wearing jeans as usual and Magnus wearing a striped fisherman's sweater, leather pants, and an insane beret. In the Boboli Gardens, Alec was still wearing jeans, and Magnus was wearing an enormous Venetian cloak and a gondolier's hat. He looked like the Phantom of the Opera. In front of the Prado he was wearing a sparkling matador jacket and platform boots, while Alec appeared to be calmly feeding a pigeon in the background.

"I'm taking that away from you before you get to the India part," said Jace, retrieving his phone. "Magnus in a sari. Some things you don't ever forget."

Clary laughed. They had already reached the elevator, which opened its rattling gate when Jace pushed the call button. She stepped inside, and Jace followed her. The moment the elevator started down—Clary didn't think she'd ever get used to the initial heart-stopping lurch as it began its descent—he moved toward Clary in the dimness, and drew her close. She put her hands against his chest, feeling the hard muscles under his T-shirt, the beat of his heart beneath them. In the shadowy light his eyes shone. "I'm sorry I can't stay," she whispered.

"Don't be sorry." There was a ragged edge to his voice that surprised her. "Jocelyn doesn't want you to turn out like me. I don't blame her for that."

"Jace," she said, a little bewildered by the bitterness in his voice, "are you all right?"

Instead of answering he kissed her, pulling her hard against him. His body pressed hers against the wall, the metal of the mirror cold against her back, his hands sliding around her waist, up under her sweater. She always loved the way he held her. Careful, but not too gentle, not so gentle that she ever felt he was more in control than she was. Neither of them could control how they felt about each other, and she liked that, liked the way his heart hammered against hers, liked the way he murmured against her mouth when she kissed him back.

The elevator came to a rattling stop, and the gate opened. Beyond it, she could see the empty nave of the cathedral, light shimmering in a line of candelabras down the center aisle. She clung to Jace, glad there was very little light in the elevator so she couldn't see her own burning face in the mirror.

"Maybe I can stay," she whispered. "Just a little while longer."

He said nothing. She could feel the tension in him, and tensed herself. It was more than just the tension of desire. He was shaking, his whole body trembling as he buried his face in the crook of her neck.

"Jace," she said.

He let go of her then, suddenly, and stepped back. His cheeks were flushed, his eyes fever-bright. "No," he said. "I don't want to give your mother another reason not to like me. She already thinks I'm the second coming of my father—"

He broke off, before Clary could say, *Valentine wasn't your father.* Jace was usually so careful to refer to Valentine Morgenstern by name, never as "my father"—when he mentioned Valentine at all. Usually they stayed away from the topic, and Clary had never admitted to Jace that her mother worried that he was secretly just like Valentine, knowing that even the suggestion would hurt him badly. Mostly Clary just did everything she could to keep the two of them apart.

He reached past her before she could say anything, and yanked open the elevator gate. "I love you, Clary," he said without looking at her. He was staring out into the church, at the rows of lighted candles, their gold reflected in his eyes. "More than I ever—" He broke off. "God. More than I probably should. You know that, don't you?"

She stepped outside the elevator and turned to face him. There were a thousand things she wanted to say, but he was already looking away from her, pushing the button that would bring the elevator back up to the Institute floors. She started to protest, but the elevator was already moving, the doors closing as it rattled its way back up. They shut with a click, and she stared at them for a moment; the Angel was painted on their surface, wings outspread, eyes raised. The Angel was painted on everything.

Her voice echoed harshly in the empty room when she spoke. "I love you, too," she said.

3

SEVENFOLD

"You know what's awesome?" said Eric, setting down his drumsticks. "Having a vampire in our band. This is the thing that's really going to take us over the top."

Kirk, lowering the microphone, rolled his eyes. Eric was always talking about taking the band over the top, and so far nothing had ever actually materialized. The best they'd ever done was a gig at the Knitting Factory, and only four people had come to that. And one of them had been Simon's mom. "I don't see how it can take us over the top if we're not allowed to tell anyone he's a vampire."

"Too bad," said Simon. He was sitting on one of the speakers, next to Clary, who was engrossed in texting someone, probably Jace. "No one's going to believe you anyway, because look—here I am. Daylight." He raised his arms to indicate the sunlight pouring through the holes in the roof of Eric's garage, which was their current practice space.

"That does somewhat impact our credibility," said Matt, pushing his bright red hair out of his eyes and squinting at Simon. "Maybe you could wear fake fangs."

"He doesn't need fake fangs," said Clary irritably, lowering her phone. "He has real fangs. You've seen them."

This was true. Simon had had to whip out the fangs when initially breaking the news to the band. At first they'd thought he'd had a head injury, or a mental breakdown. After he'd flashed the fangs at them, they'd come around. Eric had even admitted that he wasn't particularly surprised. "I always knew there were vampires, dude," he'd said. "Because, you know how there's people you know who, like, always look the same, even when they're, like, a hundred years old? Like David Bowie? That's because they're vampires."

Simon had drawn the line at telling them that Clary and Isabelle were Shadowhunters. That wasn't his secret to tell. Nor did they know that Maia was a werewolf. They just thought that Maia and Isabelle were two hot girls who had both inexplicably agreed to date Simon. They put this down to what Kirk called his "sexy vampire mojo." Simon didn't really care what they called it, as long as they never slipped up and told Maia and Isabelle about each other. So far he'd managed to successfully invite them each to alternate gigs, so they never showed up at the same one at the same time.

"Maybe you could show the fangs onstage?" Eric suggested. "Just, like, once, dude. Flash 'em at the crowd."

"If he did that, the leader of the New York City vampire

clan would kill you all," Clary said. "You know that, right?" She shook her head in Simon's direction. "I can't believe you told them you're a vampire," she added, lowering her voice so only Simon could hear her. "They're idiots, in case you haven't noticed."

"They're my friends," Simon muttered.

"They're your friends, *and* they're idiots."

"I want people I care about to know the truth about me."

"Oh?" Clary said, not very kindly. "So when are you going to tell your mother?"

Before Simon could reply, there was a loud rap on the garage door, and a moment later it slid up, letting more autumn sunlight pour inside. Simon looked over, blinking. It was a reflex, really, left over from when he had been human. It no longer took his eyes more than a split second to adjust to darkness or light.

There was a boy standing at the garage entrance, backlit by bright sun. He held a piece of paper in his hand. He looked down at it uncertainly, and then back up at the band. "Hey," he said. "Is this where I can find the band Dangerous Stain?"

"We're Dichotomous Lemur now," said Eric, stepping forward. "Who wants to know?"

"I'm Kyle," said the boy, ducking under the garage door. Straightening up, he flipped back the brown hair that fell into his eyes and held out his piece of paper to Eric. "I saw you were looking for a lead singer."

"Whoa," said Matt. "We put that flyer up, like, a year ago. I totally forgot about it."

"Yeah," said Eric. "We were doing some different stuff back then. Now we mostly switch off on vocals. You have experience?"

Kyle—who was very tall, Simon saw, though not at all gangly—shrugged. "Not really. But I'm told I can sing." He had a slow, slightly drawling diction, more surfer than Southern.

The members of the band looked uncertainly at one another. Eric scratched behind his ear. "Can you give us a second, dude?"

"Sure." Kyle ducked back out of the garage, sliding the door closed behind him. Simon could hear him whistling faintly outside. It sounded like "She'll Be Comin' Round the Mountain." It wasn't particularly in tune, either.

"I dunno," Eric said. "I'm not sure we can use anyone new right now. 'Cause, I mean, we can't tell him about the vampire thing, can we?"

"No," said Simon. "You can't."

"Well, then." Matt shrugged. "It's too bad. We need a singer. Kirk sucks. No offense, Kirk."

"Screw you," said Kirk. "I do not suck."

"Yes, you do," said Matt. "You suck big, hairy—"

"I think," Clary interrupted, raising her voice, "that you should let him try out."

Simon stared at her. "Why?"

"Because he is superhot," Clary said, to Simon's surprise. He hadn't been enormously struck by Kyle's looks, but then, perhaps he wasn't the best judge of male beauty. "And your band needs some sex appeal."

"Thank you," said Simon. "On behalf of us all, thank you very much."

Clary made an impatient noise. "Yes, yes, you're all fine-looking guys. Especially you, Simon." She patted his hand. "But Kyle is hot like 'whoa.' I'm just saying. My objective opinion as a female is that if you add Kyle to your band, you will double your female fan base."

"Which means we'll have two female fans instead of one," said Kirk.

"Which one?" Matt looked genuinely curious.

"Eric's little cousin's friend. What's her name? The one who has a crush on Simon. She comes to all our gigs and tells everyone she's his girlfriend."

Simon winced. "She's thirteen."

"That's your sexy vampire mojo at work, man," said Matt. "The ladies cannot resist you."

"Oh, for God's sake," said Clary. "There is no such thing as sexy vampire mojo." She pointed a finger at Eric. "And don't even say that Sexy Vampire Mojo sounds like a band name, or I'll—"

The garage door swung back up. "Uh, dudes?" It was Kyle again. "Look, if you don't want me to try out, it's cool. Maybe you changed your sound, whatever. Just say the word, and I'm out."

Eric cocked his head to the side. "Come on in and let's get a look at you."

Kyle stepped into the garage. Simon stared at him, trying to gauge what it was that had made Clary say he was hot. He was tall and broad-shouldered and slim, with high cheekbones, longish black hair that tumbled over his forehead and down his neck in curls, and brown skin that hadn't lost its summery tan yet. His long, thick eyelashes over startling hazel-green eyes made him look like a pretty-boy rock star. He wore a fitted green T-shirt and jeans, and twining both his bare arms were tattoos—not Marks, just ordinary tattoos. They looked like scrolling script winding around his skin, disappearing up the sleeves of his shirt.

Okay, Simon had to admit. He wasn't hideous.

"You know," Kirk said finally, breaking the silence. "I see it. He *is* pretty hot."

Kyle blinked and turned to Eric. "So, do you want me to sing or not?"

Eric detached the mike from its stand and handed it to him. "Go ahead," he said. "Give it a try."

"You know, he was really pretty good," Clary said. "I was kind of kidding about including Kyle in the band, but he can actually sing."

They were walking along Kent Avenue, toward Luke's house. The sky had darkened from blue to gray in preparation for twilight, and clouds hung low over the East River. Clary was trailing one of her gloved hands along the chain-link fence that separated them from the cracked concrete embankment, making the metal rattle.

"You're just saying that because you think he's hot," said Simon.

She dimpled. "Not that hot. Not, like, the hottest guy I've ever seen." Which, Simon imagined, would be Jace, though she was nice enough not to say it. "But I thought it would be a good idea to have him in the band, honestly. If Eric and the rest of them can't tell *him* you're a vampire, they can't tell everyone else, either. Hopefully it'll put an end to that stupid idea." They were nearly at Luke's house; Simon could see it across the street, the windows lit up yellow against the coming dark. Clary paused at a gap in the fence. "Remember when we killed a bunch of Raum demons here?"

"You and Jace killed some Raum demons. I almost threw

up." Simon remembered, but his mind wasn't on it; he was thinking of Camille, sitting across from him in the court-yard, saying, *You befriend Shadowhunters, but you can never be of them. You will always be other and outside.* He looked side-ways at Clary, wondering what she would say if he told her about his meeting with the vampire, and her offer. He imag-ined that she would probably be terrified. The fact that he couldn't be harmed hadn't yet stopped her from worrying about his safety.

"You wouldn't be scared now," she said softly, as if reading his mind. "Now you have the Mark." She turned to look at him, still leaning against the fence. "Does anyone ever notice or ask you about it?"

He shook his head. "My hair covers it, mostly, and anyway, it's faded a lot. See?" He pushed his hair aside.

Clary reached out and touched his forehead and the curving scripted Mark there. Her eyes were sad, as they had been that day in the Hall of Accords in Alicante, when she'd cut the old-est curse of the world into his skin. "Does it hurt?"

"No. No, it doesn't." *And Cain said unto the Lord, My punish-ment is greater than I can bear.* "You know I don't blame you, don't you? You saved my life."

"I know." Her eyes were shining. She dropped her hand from his forehead and scrubbed the back of her glove across her face. "Damn. I hate crying."

"Well, you better get used to it," he said, and when her eyes widened, he added hastily, "I meant the wedding. It's what, next Saturday? Everyone cries at weddings."

She snorted.

"How are your mom and Luke, anyway?"

"Disgustingly in love. It's horrible. Anyway—" She patted him on the shoulder. "I should go in. See you tomorrow?"

He nodded. "Sure. Tomorrow."

He watched her as she ran across the street and up the stairs to Luke's front door. *Tomorrow.* He wondered how long it had been since he had gone more than a few days without seeing Clary. He wondered about being a fugitive and a wanderer on the earth, like Camille had said. Like Raphael had said. *Thy brother's blood crieth unto me from the ground.* He wasn't Cain, who had killed his brother, but the curse believed he was. It was strange, he thought, waiting to lose everything, not knowing if it would happen, or not.

The door shut behind Clary. Simon turned to head down Kent, toward the G train stop at Lorimer Street. It was nearly full dark now, the sky overhead a swirl of gray and black. Simon heard tires squeal on the road behind him, but he didn't turn around. Cars drove too fast on this street all the time, despite the cracks and potholes. It wasn't until the blue van drew up beside him and screeched to a stop that he turned to look.

The van's driver yanked the keys from the ignition, killing the engine, and threw open the door. It was a man—a tall man, dressed in a gray hooded tracksuit and sneakers, the hood pulled down so low that it hid most of his face. He leaped down from the driver's seat, and Simon saw that there was a long, shimmering knife in his hand.

Later Simon would think that he should have run. He was a vampire, faster than any human. He could outrun anyone. He should have run, but he was too startled; he stood still as the man, gleaming knife in hand, came toward him. The man said something in a low, guttural voice, something in a language Simon didn't understand.

Simon took a step back. "Look," he said, reaching for his pocket. "You can have my wallet—"

The man lunged at Simon, plunging the knife toward his chest. Simon stared down in disbelief. Everything seemed to be happening very slowly, as if time were stretching out. He saw the point of the knife near his chest, the tip denting the leather of his jacket—and then it sheared to the side, as if someone had grabbed his attacker's arm and *yanked*. The man screamed as he was jerked up into the air like a puppet being hauled up by its strings. Simon looked around wildly—surely someone must have heard or noticed the commotion, but no one appeared. The man kept screaming, jerking wildly, while his shirt tore open down the front, as if ripped apart by an invisible hand.

Simon stared in horror. Huge wounds were appearing on the man's torso. His head flew back, and blood sprayed from his mouth. He stopped screaming abruptly—and fell, as if the invisible hand had opened, releasing him. He hit the ground and broke apart like glass shattering into a thousand shining pieces that scattered themselves across the pavement.

Simon dropped to his knees. The knife that had been meant to kill him lay a little way away, within arm's reach. It was all that was left of his attacker, save a pile of shimmering crystals that were already beginning to blow away in the brisk wind. He touched one cautiously.

It was salt. He looked down at his hands. They were shaking. He knew what had happened, and why.

And the Lord said unto him, Therefore whosoever slayeth Cain, vengeance shall be taken on him sevenfold.

So this was what sevenfold looked like.

He barely made it to the gutter before he doubled over and vomited blood into the street.

The moment Simon opened the door, he knew he'd miscalculated. He'd thought his mother would be asleep by now, but she wasn't. She was awake, sitting in an armchair facing the front door, her phone on the table next to her, and she saw the blood on his jacket immediately.

To his surprise she didn't scream, but her hand flew to her mouth. "*Simon.*"

"It's not my blood," he said quickly. "I was over at Eric's, and Matt had a nosebleed—"

"I don't want to hear it." That sharp tone was one she rarely used; it reminded him of the way she'd talked during those last months when his father had been sick, anxiety like a knife in her voice. "I don't want to hear any more lies."

Simon dropped his keys onto the table next to the door. "Mom—"

"All you do is tell me lies. I'm tired of it."

"That's not true," he said, but he felt sick, knowing it was. "I just have a lot going on in my life right now."

"I know you do." His mother got to her feet; she had always been a skinny woman, and she looked bony now, her dark hair, the same color as his, streaked with more gray than he had remembered where it fell around her face. "Come with me, young man. *Now.*"

Puzzled, Simon followed her into the small bright-yellow kitchen. His mother stopped and pointed toward the counter. "Care to explain those?"

Simon's mouth went dry. Lined up along the counter like a row of toy soldiers were the bottles of blood that had been in the mini-fridge inside his closet. One was half-full, the others entirely full, the red liquid inside them shining like an accusation. She had also found the empty blood bags he had washed out and carefully stuffed inside a shopping bag before dumping them into his trash can. They were spread out over the counter too, like a grotesque decoration.

"I thought at first the bottles were wine," Elaine Lewis said in a shaking voice. "Then I found the bags. So I opened one of the bottles. It's *blood*. Isn't it?"

Simon said nothing. His voice seemed to have fled.

"You've been acting so strangely lately," his mother went on. "Out at all hours, you never eat, you barely sleep, you have friends I've never met, never heard of. You think I can't tell when you're lying to me? I can tell, Simon. I thought maybe you were on drugs."

Simon found his voice. "So you searched my room?"

His mother flushed. "I had to! I thought—I thought if I found drugs there, I could help you, get you into a rehab program, but this?" She gestured wildly at the bottles. "I don't even know what to think about this. What's going on, Simon? Have you joined some kind of cult?"

Simon shook his head.

"Then, tell me," his mother said, her lips trembling. "Because the only explanations I can think of are horrible and sick. Simon, please—"

"I'm a vampire," Simon said. He had no idea how he had said it, or even why. But there it was. The words hung in the air between them like poisonous gas.

His mother's knees seemed to give out, and she sank into a kitchen chair. "What did you say?" she breathed.

"I'm a vampire," Simon said. "I've been one for about two months now. I'm sorry I didn't tell you before. I didn't know how."

Elaine Lewis's face was chalk white. "Vampires don't exist, Simon."

"Yes," he said. "They do. Look, I didn't ask to be a vampire. I was attacked. I didn't have a choice. I'd change it if I could." He thought wildly back to the pamphlet Clary had given him so long ago, the one about coming out to your parents. It had seemed like a funny analogy then; now it didn't.

"You think you're a vampire," Simon's mother said numbly. "You think you drink blood."

"I do drink blood," Simon said. "I drink animal blood."

"But you're a *vegetarian*." His mother looked to be on the verge of tears.

"I was. I'm not now. I can't be. Blood is what I live on." Simon's throat felt tight. "I've never hurt a person. I'd never drink someone's blood. I'm still the same person. I'm still me."

His mother seemed to be fighting for control. "Your new friends—are they vampires too?"

Simon thought of Isabelle, Maia, Jace. He couldn't explain Shadowhunters and werewolves, too. It was too much. "No. But—they know I am one."

"Did—did they give you drugs? Make you take something? Something that would make you hallucinate?" She seemed to have barely heard his answer.

"No. Mom, this is real."

"It's not real," she whispered. "You *think* it's real. Oh, God.

Simon. I'm so sorry. I should have noticed. We'll get you help. We'll find someone. A doctor. Whatever it costs—"

"I can't go to a doctor, Mom."

"Yes, you can. You need to be somewhere. A hospital, maybe—"

He held out his wrist to her. "Feel my pulse," he said.

She looked at him, bewildered. "What?"

"My pulse," he said. "Take it. If I have one, okay. I'll go to the hospital with you. If not, you have to believe me."

She wiped the tears from her eyes and slowly reached to take his wrist. After so long taking care of Simon's father when he'd been sick, she knew how to take a pulse as well as any nurse. She pressed her index fingertip to the inside of his wrist, and waited.

He watched as her face changed, from misery and upset to confusion, and then to terror. She stood up, dropping his hand, backing away from him. Her eyes were huge and dark in her white face. "What are you?"

Simon felt sick. "I told you. I'm a vampire."

"You're not my son. You're not Simon." She was shuddering. "What kind of living thing doesn't have a pulse? What kind of monster are you? *What have you done with my child?*"

"I am Simon—" He took a step toward his mother.

She screamed. He had never heard her scream like that, and he never wanted to again. It was a horrible noise.

"Get away from me." Her voice broke. "Don't come any closer." She began to whisper. "*Barukh ata Adonai sho'me'a t'fila . . .*"

She was *praying*, Simon realized with a jolt. She was so terrified of him that she was praying that he would go away, be banished. And what was worse was that he could feel it. The name of God tightened his stomach and made his throat ache.

She was right to pray, he thought, sick to his soul. He was cursed. He didn't belong in the world. *What kind of living thing doesn't have a pulse?*

"Mom," he whispered. "Mom, stop."

She looked at him, wide-eyed, her lips still moving.

"Mom, you don't need to be so upset." He heard his own voice as if from a distance, soft and soothing, a stranger's voice. He kept his eyes fixed on his mother as he spoke, capturing her gaze with his as a cat might capture a mouse. "Nothing happened. You fell asleep in the armchair in the living room. You're having a bad dream that I came home and told you I was a vampire. But that's crazy. That would never happen."

She had stopped praying. She blinked. "I'm dreaming," she repeated.

"It's a bad dream," Simon said. He moved toward her and put his hand on her shoulder. She didn't pull away. Her head was drooping, like a tired child's. "Just a dream. You never found anything in my room. Nothing happened. You've just been sleeping, that's all."

He took her hand. She let him lead her into the living room, where he settled her into the armchair. She smiled when he pulled a blanket over her, and closed her eyes.

He went back into the kitchen and swiftly, methodically, swept the bottles and containers of blood into a garbage bag. He tied it at the top and brought it to his room, where he changed his bloody jacket for a new one, and threw some things quickly into a duffel bag. He flipped the light off and left, closing the door behind him.

His mother was already asleep as he passed through the living room. He reached out and lightly touched her hand.

"I'll be gone for a few days," he whispered. "But you won't worry. You won't expect me back. You think I'm on a school field trip. There's no need to call. Everything is fine."

He drew his hand back. In the dim light his mother looked both older and younger than he was used to. She was as small as a child, curled under the blanket, but there were new lines on her face he didn't remember being there before.

"Mom," he whispered.

He touched her hand, and she stirred. Not wanting her to wake, he jerked his fingers back and moved soundlessly to the door, grabbing his keys from the table as he went.

The Institute was quiet. It was always quiet these days. Jace had taken to leaving his window open at night, so he could hear the noises of traffic going by, the occasional wail of ambulance sirens and the honking of horns on York Avenue. He could hear things mundanes couldn't, too, and these sounds filtered through the night and into his dreams—the rush of air displaced by a vampire's airborne motorcycle, the flutter of winged fey, the distant howl of wolves on nights when the moon was full.

It was only half-full now, casting just enough light for him to read by as he sprawled on the bed. He had his father's silver box open in front of him, and was going through what was inside it. One of his father's steles was in there, and a silver-handled hunting dagger with the initials SWH on the handle, and—of most interest to Jace—a pile of letters.

Over the past six weeks he had taken to reading a letter

or so every night, trying to get a sense for the man who was his biological father. A picture had begun to emerge slowly, of a thoughtful young man with hard-driving parents who had been drawn to Valentine and the Circle because they had seemed to offer him an opportunity to distinguish himself in the world. He had kept writing to Amatis even after their divorce, something she hadn't mentioned before. In those letters, his disenchantment with Valentine and sickness at the Circle's activities were clear, though he rarely, if ever, mentioned Jace's mother, Céline. It made sense—Amatis wouldn't have wanted to hear about her replacement—and yet Jace could not help hating his father a little for it. If he hadn't cared about Jace's mother, why marry her? If he'd hated the Circle so much, why hadn't he left it? Valentine had been a madman, but at least he'd stood by his principles.

And then, of course, Jace only felt worse for preferring Valentine to his real father. What kind of person did that make him?

A knock on the door drew him out of his self-recriminations; he got to his feet and went to answer it, expecting Isabelle to be there, wanting to either borrow something or complain about something.

But it wasn't Isabelle. It was Clary.

She wasn't dressed the way she usually was. She had a low-cut black tank top on, a white blouse tied loose and open over it, and a short skirt, short enough to show the curves of her legs up to midthigh. She wore her bright red hair in braids, loose curls of it clinging against the hollows of her temples, as if it had been raining lightly outside. She smiled when she saw him, arching her eyebrows. They were coppery, like the fine eyelashes that framed her green eyes. "Aren't you going to let me in?"

He looked up and down the hallway. No one else was there, thank God. Taking Clary by the arm, he pulled her inside and shut the door. Leaning against it, he said, "What are you doing here? Is everything all right?"

"Everything's fine." She kicked off her shoes and sat down on the edge of the bed. Her skirt rode up as she leaned back on her hands, showing more thigh. It wasn't doing wonders for Jace's concentration. "I missed you. And Mom and Luke are asleep. They won't notice I'm gone."

"You shouldn't be here." The words came out as a sort of groan. He hated saying them but knew they needed to be said, for reasons she didn't even know. And he hoped she never would.

"Well, if you want me to go, I will." She stood up. Her eyes were shimmeringly green. She took a step closer to him. "But I came all the way here. You could at least kiss me good-bye."

He reached for her and drew her in, and kissed her. There were some things you had to do, even if they were a bad idea. She folded into his arms like delicate silk. He put his hands in her hair and ran his fingers through it, untwisting her braids until her hair fell around her shoulders the way he liked it. He remembered wanting to do this the first time he had seen her, and dismissing the idea as insane. She was a mundane, she'd been a stranger, there'd been no sense in wanting her. And then he had kissed her for the first time, in the greenhouse, and it had almost made him crazy. They had gone downstairs and been interrupted by Simon, and he had never wanted to kill anyone as much as he had wanted to kill Simon in that moment, though he knew, intellectually, that Simon hadn't done anything wrong. But what he felt had nothing to do with intellect, and when he had imagined her leaving him for Simon, the thought had made him sick and scared the way no demon ever had.

And then Valentine had told them they were brother and sister, and Jace had realized that there were worse things, infinitely worse things, than Clary leaving him for someone else—and that was knowing that the way he loved her was somehow cosmically wrong; that what had seemed the most pure and most irreproachable thing in his life had now been defiled beyond redemption. He remembered his father saying that when angels fell, they fell in anguish, because once they had seen the face of God, and now they never would again. And he had thought he knew how they felt.

It had not made him want her any less; it had just turned wanting her into torture. Sometimes the shadow of that torture fell across his memories even when he was kissing her, as he was now, and made him crush her more tightly to him. She made a surprised noise but didn't protest, even when he lifted her up and carried her over to the bed.

They sprawled onto it together, crumpling some of the letters, Jace knocking the box itself aside to make room for them. His heart was hammering against the inside of his ribs. They had never been in bed together like this before, not really. There had been that night in her room in Idris, but they had barely touched. Jocelyn was careful never to let either of them spend the night where the other one lived. She didn't care much for him, Jace suspected, and he could hardly blame her. He doubted he would have liked himself much, if he'd been in her position.

"I love you," Clary whispered. She had his shirt off, and her fingertips were tracing the scars on his back, and the star-shaped scar on his shoulder that was the twin of her own, a relic of the angel whose blood they both shared. "I don't ever want to lose you."

He slid his hand down to untie her knotted blouse. His other hand, braced against the mattress, touched the cold metal of the hunting dagger; it must have spilled onto the bed with the rest of the contents of the box. "That will never happen."

She looked up at him with luminous eyes. "How can you be so sure?"

His hand tightened on the knife hilt. The moonlight that poured through the window slid off the blade as he raised it. "I'm sure," he said, and brought the dagger down. The blade sheared through her flesh as if it were paper, and as her mouth opened in a startled O and blood soaked the front of her white shirt, he thought, *Dear God, not again.*

Waking up from the nightmare was like crashing through a plate glass window. The razored shards of it seemed to slice at Jace even as he pulled free and sat up, gasping. He rolled off the bed, instinctively wanting to get away, and hit the stone floor on his hands and knees. Cold air poured through the open window, making him shiver but clearing away the last, clinging tendrils of the dream.

He stared down at his hands. They were clean of blood. The bed was a mess, the sheets and blankets screwed into a tangled ball from his tossing and turning, but the box containing his father's things was still on the nightstand, where he'd left it before he went to sleep.

The first few times he'd had the nightmare, he'd woken up and vomited. Now he was careful about not eating for hours before he went to sleep, so instead his body had its revenge on him by racking him with spasms of sickness and fever. A spasm hit now, and he curled into a ball, gasping and dry-heaving until it passed.

When it was over, he pressed his forehead against the cold stone floor. Sweat was cooling on his body, his shirt sticking to him, and he wondered, not idly, if eventually the dreams would kill him. He had tried everything to stop them—sleeping pills and potions, runes of sleep and runes of peace and healing. Nothing worked. The dreams stole like poison into his mind, and there was nothing he could do to shut them out.

Even during his waking hours, he found it hard to look at Clary. She had always been able to see through him the way no one else had, and he could only imagine what she would think if she knew what he dreamed. He rolled onto his side and stared at the box on the nightstand, moonlight sparking off it. And he thought of Valentine. Valentine, who had tortured and imprisoned the only woman he'd ever loved, who had taught his son—both his sons—that to love something is to destroy it forever.

His mind spun frantically as he said the words to himself, over and over. It had become a sort of chant for him, and like any chant, the words had started to lose their individual meanings.

I'm not like Valentine. I don't want to be like him. I won't be like him. I won't.

He saw Sebastian—Jonathan, really—his sort-of-brother, grinning at him through a tangle of silver-white hair, his black eyes shining with merciless glee. And he saw his own knife go into Jonathan and pull free, and Jonathan's body tumbling down toward the river below, his blood mixing with the weeds and grass at the riverbank's edge.

I am not like Valentine.

He had not been sorry to kill Jonathan. Given the chance, he would do it again.

I don't want to be like him.

Surely it wasn't normal to kill someone—to kill your own adoptive brother—and feel nothing about it at all.

I won't be like him.

But his father had taught him that to kill without mercy was a virtue, and maybe you could never forget what your parents taught you. No matter how badly you wanted to.

I won't be like him.

Maybe people could never really change.

I won't.

4

THE ART OF EIGHT LIMBS

HERE ARE ENSHRINED THE LONGING OF GREAT HEARTS AND NOBLE THINGS
THAT TOWER ABOVE THE TIDE, THE MAGIC WORD THAT WINGED WONDER
STARTS, THE GARNERED WISDOM THAT HAS NEVER DIED.

The words were engraved over the front doors of the
Brooklyn Public Library at Grand Army Plaza. Simon was sitting on the front steps, looking up at the facade. Inscriptions glittered against the stone in dull gilt, each word flashing into momentary life when caught by the headlights of passing cars.

The library had always been one of his favorite places when he was a kid. There was a separate children's entrance around the side, and he had met Clary there every Saturday for years. They would pick up a stack of books and head for the Botanical

Garden next door, where they could read for hours, sprawled in the grass, the sound of traffic a constant dull thrumming in the distance.

How he had ended up here tonight, he wasn't quite sure. He had gotten away from his house as fast as he could, only to realize he had nowhere to go. He couldn't face going to Clary's—she'd be horrified at what he'd done, and would want him to go back to fix it. Eric and the other guys wouldn't understand. Jace didn't like him, and besides, he couldn't go into the Institute. It was a church, and the reason the Nephilim lived there in the first place was precisely to keep creatures like him out. Eventually he had realized who it was he *could* call, but the thought had been unpleasant enough that it had taken him a while to screw up the nerve to actually do it.

He heard the motorcycle before he saw it, the loud roar of the engine cutting through the sounds of light traffic on Grand Army Plaza. The cycle careened across the intersection and up onto the pavement, then reared back and shot up the steps. Simon moved aside as it landed lightly beside him and Raphael released the handlebars.

The motorcycle went instantly quiet. Vamp motorcycles were powered by demonic spirits and responded like pets to the wishes of their owners. Simon found them creepy.

"You wanted to see me, Daylighter?" Raphael, as elegant as always in a black jacket and expensive-looking jeans, dismounted and leaned his motorcycle against the library railing. "This had better be good," he added. "It is not for nothing that I come all the way to Brooklyn. Raphael Santiago does not belong in an outer borough."

"Oh, good. You're starting to talk about yourself in the

third person. That's not a sign of impending megalomania or anything."

Raphael shrugged. "You can either tell me what you wanted to tell me, or I will leave. It is up to you." He looked at his watch. "You have thirty seconds."

"I told my mother I'm a vampire."

Raphael's eyebrows went up. They were very thin and very dark. In less generous moments Simon sometimes wondered if he penciled them on. "And what happened?"

"She called me a monster and tried to pray at me." The memory made the bitter taste of old blood rise in the back of Simon's throat.

"And then?"

"And then I'm not sure what happened. I started talking to her in this really weird, soothing voice, telling her nothing had happened and it was all a dream."

"And she believed you."

"She believed me," Simon said reluctantly.

"Of course she did," said Raphael. "Because you are a vampire. It is a power we have. The *encanto*. The fascination. The power of persuasion, you would call it. You can convince mundane humans of almost anything, if you learn how to use the ability properly."

"But I didn't want to use it on her. She's my mother. Is there some way to take it off her—some way to fix it?"

"Fix it so she hates you again? So she thinks you are a monster? That is a very odd definition of fixing something."

"I don't care," Simon said. "Is there a way?"

"No," Raphael said cheerfully. "There is not. You would know all this, of course, if you did not disdain your own kind so much."

"That's right. Act like *I* rejected *you*. It's not like you tried to kill me or anything."

Raphael shrugged. "That was politics. Not personal." He leaned back against the railing and crossed his arms over his chest. He was wearing black motorcycle gloves. Simon had to admit he looked pretty cool. "Please tell me you did not bring me out here so you could tell me a very boring story about your sister."

"My mother," Simon corrected.

Raphael flipped a dismissive hand. "Whatever. Some female in your life has rejected you. It will not be the last time, I can tell you that. Why are you bothering me about it?"

"I wanted to know if I could come and stay at the Dumont," Simon said, getting the words out very fast so that he couldn't back out halfway. He could barely believe he was asking. His memories of the vampire hotel were memories of blood and terror and pain. But it was a place to go, a place to stay where no one would look for him, and so he would not have to go home. He was a vampire. It was stupid to be afraid of a hotel full of *other* vampires. "I haven't got anywhere else to go."

Raphael's eyes glittered. "Aha," he said, with a soft triumph Simon did not particularly like. "Now you want something from me."

"I suppose so. Although it's creepy that you're so excited about that, Raphael."

Raphael snorted. "If you come to stay at the Dumont, you will not address me as Raphael, but as Master, Sire, or Great Leader."

Simon braced himself. "What about Camille?"

Raphael started. "What do you mean?"

"You always told me you weren't really the head of the vampires," Simon said blandly. "Then, in Idris, you told me it was someone named Camille. You said she hadn't come back to New York yet. But I assume, when she does, *she'll* be the master, or whatever?"

Raphael's gaze darkened. "I do not think I like your line of questioning, Daylighter."

"I have a right to know things."

"No," said Raphael. "You don't. You come to me, asking if you can stay in my hotel because you have nowhere else to go. Not because you wish to be with others of your kind. You shun us."

"Which, as I already pointed out, has to do with that time you tried to kill me."

"The Dumont is not a halfway house for reluctant vampires," Raphael went on. "You live among humans, you walk in daylight, you play in your stupid band—yes, don't think I don't know about that. In every way you do not accept what you really are. And as long as that is true, you are not welcome at the Dumont."

Simon thought of Camille saying, *The moment his followers see that you are with me, they will leave him and come to me. I believe they are loyal to me beneath their fear of him. Once they see us together, that fear will be gone, and they will come to our side.* "You know," he said, "I've had other offers."

Raphael looked at him as if he were insane. "Offers of what?"

"Just . . . offers," Simon said feebly.

"You are terrible at this politics business, Simon Lewis. I suggest you do not attempt it again."

"Fine," Simon said. "I came here to tell you something, but now I'm not going to."

"I suppose you are also going to throw away the birthday present you got me," Raphael said. "It is all very tragic." He retrieved his motorcycle and swung a leg over it as the engine revved to life. Red sparks flew from the exhaust pipe. "If you bother me again, Daylighter, it had better be for a good reason. Or I will not be forgiving."

And with that, the motorcycle surged forward and upward. Simon craned his head back to watch as Raphael, like the angel he was named for, soared into the sky trailing fire.

Clary sat with her sketchpad on her knees and gnawed the end of her pencil thoughtfully. She had drawn Jace dozens of times—she guessed it was her version of most girls' writing about their boyfriends in their diaries—but she never seemed to be able to get him exactly *right*. For one thing, it was almost impossible to get him to stand still, so she'd thought that now, while he was asleep, would be perfect—but it still wasn't coming out quite the way she wanted. It just didn't look like *him*.

She tossed the sketchpad onto the blanket with a sigh of exasperation and pulled her knees up, looking down at him. She hadn't expected him to fall asleep. They'd come to Central Park to eat lunch and train outside while the weather was still good. They'd done *one* of those things. Take-out containers from Taki's were scattered in the grass beside the blanket. Jace hadn't eaten much, picking through his carton of sesame noodles in a desultory fashion before tossing it aside and flinging himself down onto the blanket, staring up at the sky. Clary had sat looking down at him, at the way the clouds reflected in his clear eyes, the outline of muscles in the arms crossed behind his head, the perfect strip of skin revealed between the hem of his T-shirt and the belt of his jeans. She had wanted to reach out and slide her hand along his hard flat stomach; instead she'd averted her eyes, rummaging for her sketchpad. When she'd turned back, pencil in hand, his eyes were closed and his breathing was soft and even.

She was now three drafts into her illustration, and no closer to a drawing that satisfied her. Looking at him now, she wondered why on earth she couldn't draw him. The light was perfect, soft bronze October light that laid a sheen of paler gold over his already golden hair and skin. His closed lids were fringed with gold a shade darker than his hair. One of his hands was draped loosely over his chest, the other open at his side. His face was relaxed and vulnerable in sleep, softer and less angular than when he was awake. Perhaps that was the problem. He was so rarely relaxed and vulnerable, it was hard to capture the lines of him when he was. It felt . . . unfamiliar.

At that precise moment he moved. He had begun making little gasping sounds in his sleep, his eyes darting back and forth behind his shut eyelids. His hand jerked, tightened against his chest, and he sat up, so suddenly that he nearly knocked Clary over. His eyes flew open. For a moment he looked simply dazed; he had gone startlingly pale.

"Jace?" Clary couldn't hide her surprise.

His eyes focused on her; a moment later he had drawn her toward him with none of his customary gentleness; he pulled her onto his lap and kissed her fiercely, his hands winding into her hair. She could feel the hammering of his heart with hers, and she felt her cheeks flush. They were in a public park, she thought, and people were probably staring.

"Whoa," he said, drawing back, his lips curving into a smile. "Sorry. You probably weren't expecting that."

"It was a nice surprise." Her voice sounded low and throaty to her own ears. "*What* were you dreaming about?"

"You." He twisted a lock of her hair around his finger. "I always dream about you."

Still on his lap, her legs straddling his, Clary said, "Oh, yeah? Because I thought you were having a nightmare."

He tipped his head back to look at her. "Sometimes I dream you're gone," he said. "I keep wondering when you'll figure out how much better you could do and leave me."

She touched his face with her fingertips, delicately running them over the planes of his cheekbones, down to the curve of his mouth. Jace never said things like that to anyone else but her. Alec and Isabelle knew, from living with him and loving him, that underneath the protective armor of humor and pretended arrogance, the ragged shards of memory and childhood still tore at him. But she was the only one he said the words out loud to. She shook her head; her hair fell forward across her forehead, and she pushed it away impatiently. "I wish I could say things the way you do," she said. "Everything you say, the words you choose, they're so perfect. You always find the right quote, or the right thing to say to make me believe you love me. If I can't convince you that I'll never leave you—"

He caught her hand in his. "Just say it again."

"I'll never leave you," she said.

"No matter what happens, what I do?"

"I'd never give up on you," she said. "Never. What I feel about you—" She stumbled over the words. "It's the most important thing I've ever felt."

Dammit, she thought. That sounded completely stupid. But Jace didn't seem to think so; he smiled wistfully and said, "'*L'amor che move il sole e l'altre stelle.*'"

"Is that Latin?"

"Italian," he said. "Dante."

She ran her fingertips over his lips, and he shivered. "I don't speak Italian," she said, very softly.

"It means," he said, "that love is the most powerful force in the world. That love can do anything."

She drew her hand out of his, aware as she did that he was watching her through half-lidded eyes. She locked both hands around the back of his neck, leaned forward, and touched his lips with hers—not a kiss this time, just a brush of lips against each other. It was enough; she felt his pulse speed up, and he leaned forward, trying to capture her mouth with his, but she shook her head, shaking her hair around them like a curtain that would hide them from the eyes of everyone else in the park. "If you're tired, we could go back to the Institute," she said in a half whisper. "Take a nap. We haven't slept together in the same bed since—since Idris."

Their gazes locked, and she knew he was remembering the same thing she was. The pale light filtering in through the window of Amatis's small spare bedroom, the desperation in his voice. *I just want to lie down with you and wake up with you, just once, just once ever in my life.* That whole night, lying side by side, only their hands touching. They had touched much more since that night, but had never spent the night together. He knew she was offering him more than a nap in one of the Institute's unused bedrooms, too. She was sure he could see it in her eyes—even if she herself wasn't exactly sure how much she *was* offering. But it didn't matter. Jace would never ask her for anything she didn't want to give.

"I want to." The heat she saw in his eyes, the ragged edge to his voice, told her he wasn't lying. "But—we can't." He took her wrists firmly, and drew them down, holding their hands between them, making a barrier.

Clary's eyes widened. "Why not?"

He took a deep breath. "We came here to train, and we should train. If we just spend all the time we're supposed to be training making out instead, they'll quit letting me help train you at all."

"Aren't they supposed to be hiring someone else to train me full-time *anyway*?"

"Yes," he said, getting up and pulling her to her feet along with him, "and I'm worried that if you get into the habit of making out with your instructors, you'll wind up making out with him, too."

"Don't be sexist. They could find me a female instructor."

"In that case you have my permission to make out with her, as long as I can watch."

"Nice." Clary grinned, bending down to fold up the blanket they'd brought to sit on. "You're just worried they'll hire a male instructor and he'll be hotter than you."

Jace's eyebrows went up. "Hotter than *me*?"

"It could happen," Clary said. "You know, theoretically."

"Theoretically the planet could suddenly crack in half, leaving me on one side and you on the other side, forever and tragically parted, but I'm not worried about that, either. Some things," Jace said, with his customary crooked smile, "are just too unlikely to dwell upon."

He held out his hand; she took it, and together they crossed the meadow, heading for a copse of trees at the edge of the East Meadow that only Shadowhunters seemed to know about. Clary suspected it was glamoured, since she and Jace trained there fairly often and no one had ever interrupted them there except Isabelle or Maryse.

Central Park in autumn was a riot of color. The trees lining the meadow had put on their brightest colors and circled the green in blazing gold, red, copper, and russet orange. It was a beautiful day to take a romantic walk through the park and kiss on one of the stone bridges. But *that* wasn't going to happen. Obviously, as far as Jace was concerned, the park was an outside extension of the Institute's training room, and they were there to run Clary through various exercises involving terrain navigation, escape and evasion techniques, and killing things with her bare hands.

Normally she would have been excited to learn how to kill things with her bare hands. But there was still something bothering her about Jace. She couldn't rid herself of the nagging feeling that something was seriously wrong. If only there were a rune, she thought, that would make him tell her what he was really feeling. But she would never create a rune like that, she reminded herself hastily. It would be unethical to use her power to try to control someone else. And besides, since she'd created the binding rune in Idris, her power had lain seemingly dormant. She had felt no urge to draw old runes, nor had she had any visions of new runes to create. Maryse had told her that they would be trying to bring in a specialist in runes to tutor her, once training really got underway, but so far that hadn't materialized. Not that she minded, really. She had to admit she wasn't sure she would be entirely sorry if her power had vanished forever.

"There are going to be times when you encounter a demon and you don't have a fighting weapon," Jace was saying as they passed under a row of trees laden with low-hanging leaves whose colors ran the gamut from green to brilliant gold. "At that point, you can't panic. First, you have to remember that anything can be a weapon. A tree branch, a handful of coins— they make great brass knuckles—a shoe, anything. And second, keep in mind that *you* are a weapon. In theory, when you're done with training, you should be able to kick a hole in a wall or knock out a moose with a single punch."

"I would never hit a moose," said Clary. "They're endangered."

Jace smiled slightly, and swung to face her. They had reached the copse, a small, cleared area in the center of a stand of trees. There were runes carved into the trunks of the trees that surrounded them, marking it as a Shadowhunter place.

"There's an ancient fighting style called Muay Thai," he said. "Have you heard of it?"

She shook her head. The sun was bright and steady, and she was almost too hot in her track pants and warm-up jacket. Jace took off his jacket and turned back to her, flexing his slim pianist's hands. His eyes were intensely gold in the autumn light. Marks for speed, agility, and strength trailed like a pattern of vines from his wrists up and over the swell of each bicep, disappearing under the sleeves of his T-shirt. She wondered why he'd bothered Marking himself up as if she were a foe to be reckoned with.

"I heard a rumor that the new instructor we're getting next

week is a master of Muay Thai," he said. "And sambo, lethwei, tomoi, krav maga, jujitsu, and another one that frankly I don't remember the name of, but it involves killing people with small sticks or something. My *point* is, he or she isn't going to be used to working with someone your age who's as inexperienced as you are, so if we teach you a few of the basics, I'm hoping it'll make them feel a little more generously toward you." He reached out to put his hands on her hips. "Now turn and face me."

Clary did as instructed. Facing each other like this, her head came to the bottom of his chin. She rested her hands lightly on his biceps.

"Muay Thai is called 'the art of eight limbs.' That's because you use not just your fists and feet as strike points, but also your knees and elbows. First you want to pull your opponent in, then pummel him with every one of your strike points until he or she collapses."

"And that works on demons?" Clary raised her eyebrows.

"The smaller ones." Jace moved closer to her. "Okay. Reach your hand around and grip the back of my neck."

It was just possible to do as he instructed without going up on her toes. Not for the first time, Clary cursed the fact that she was so short.

"Now you raise your other hand and do the same thing again, so your hands are looped around the back of my neck."

She did it. The back of his neck was warm from the sun, and his soft hair tickled her fingers. Their bodies were pressed up against each other; she could feel the ring she wore on a chain around her neck pressed between them like a pebble pressed between two palms.

"In a real fight you'd do that move much faster," he said.

Unless she was imagining it, his voice was a little unsteady. "Now that grip on me gives you leverage. You're going to use that leverage to pull yourself forward and add momentum to your upward knee kicks—"

"My, my," said a cool, amused voice. "Only six weeks, and already at each other's throats? How swiftly mortal love does fade."

Releasing her hold on Jace, Clary whirled, though she already knew who it was. The Queen of the Seelie Court stood in the shadows between two trees. If Clary had not known she was there, she wondered if she would have seen her, even with the Sight. The Queen wore a gown as green as grass, and her hair, falling around her shoulders, was the color of a turning leaf. She was as beautiful and awful as a dying season. Clary had never trusted her.

"What are you doing here?" It was Jace, his eyes narrow. "This is a Shadowhunter place."

"And I have news of interest to Shadowhunters." As the Queen stepped gracefully forward, the sun lanced down through the trees and sparked off the circlet of golden berries she wore around her head. Clary sometimes wondered if the Queen planned these dramatic entrances, and if so, how. "There has been another death."

"What sort of death?"

"Another one of you. Dead Nephilim." There was a certain relish to the way the Queen said it. "The body was found this dawn beneath Oak Bridge. As you know, the park is my domain. A human killing is not of concern to me, but the death did not seem to be one of mundane origins. The body was brought to the Court to be examined by my physicians. They pronounced the dead mortal one of yours."

Clary looked quickly at Jace, remembering the news of the dead Shadowhunter two days before. She could tell Jace was thinking the same thing; he had paled. "Where is the body?" he asked.

"Are you concerned about my hospitality? He bides in my court, and I assure you that we afford his body all the respect we would give a living Shadowhunter. Now that one of my own has a place on the Council beside you and yours, you can hardly doubt our good faith."

"As always, good faith and my Lady go hand in hand." The sarcasm in Jace's voice was clear, but the Queen just smiled. She liked Jace, Clary had always thought, in that way that faeries liked pretty things because they were pretty. She did not think the Queen liked her, and the feeling was mutual. "And why are you giving this message to us, instead of to Maryse? Custom would indicate—"

"Oh, custom." The Queen waved away convention with a flip of her hand. "You were here. It seemed expedient."

Jace gave her another narrow look and flipped his cell phone open. He gestured at Clary to stay where she was, and walked a little ways away. She could hear him saying, "Maryse?" as the phone was answered, and then his voice was swallowed up by shouts from the playing fields nearby.

With a feeling of cold dread, she looked back at the Queen. She had not seen the Lady of the Seelie Court since her last night in Idris, and then Clary had not exactly been polite to her. She doubted the Queen had forgotten or forgiven her for that. *Would you truly refuse a favor from the Queen of the Seelie Court?*

"I heard Meliorn got a seat on the Council," Clary said now. "You must be pleased about that."

"Indeed." The Queen looked at her with amusement. "I am sufficiently delighted."

"So," Clary said. "No hard feelings, then?"

The Queen's smile turned icy around the edges, like frost riming the sides of a pond. "I suppose you refer to my offer, which you so rudely declined," she said. "As you know, my objective was accomplished regardless; the loss there, I imagine most would agree, was yours."

"I didn't want your deal." Clary tried to keep the sharpness from her voice, and failed. "People can't do what you want all the time, you know."

"Do not presume to lecture me, child." The Queen's eyes followed Jace, who was pacing at the edge of the trees, phone in hand. "He is beautiful," she said. "I can see why you love him. But did you ever wonder what draws him to you?"

Clary said nothing to that; there seemed nothing to say.

"The blood of Heaven binds you," said the Queen. "Blood calls to blood, under the skin. But love and blood are not the same."

"Riddles," Clary said angrily. "Do you even *mean* anything when you talk like that?"

"He is bound to you," said the Queen. "But does he love you?"

Clary felt her hands twitch. She longed to try out on the Queen some of the new fighting moves she'd learned, but she knew how unwise that would be. "Yes, he does."

"And does he want you? For love and desire are not always as one."

"That's none of your business," Clary said shortly, but she could see that the Queen's eyes on her were as sharp as pins.

"You want him like you have never wanted anything else. But does he feel the same?" The Queen's soft voice was inexorable.

"He could have anything or anyone he pleases. Do you wonder why he chose you? Do you wonder if he regrets it? Has he changed toward you?"

Clary felt tears sting the backs of her eyes. "No, he hasn't." But she thought of his face in the elevator that night, and the way he had told her to go home when she'd offered to stay.

"You told me that you did not wish to make a compact with me, for there was nothing I could give you. You said there was nothing in the world you wanted." The Queen's eyes glittered. "When you imagine your life without him, do you still feel the same?"

Why are you doing this to me? Clary wanted to scream, but she said nothing, for the Faerie Queen glanced past her, and smiled, saying, "Wipe your tears, for he returns. It will do you no good for him to see you cry."

Clary rubbed hastily at her eyes with the back of her hand, and turned; Jace was walking toward them, frowning. "Maryse is on her way to the Court," he said. "Where did the Queen go?"

Clary looked at him, surprised. "She's right here," she began, turning—and broke off. Jace was right. The Queen was gone, only a swirl of leaves at Clary's feet to show where she had stood.

Simon, his jacket wadded up under his head, was lying on his back, staring up at the hole-filled ceiling of Eric's garage with a sense of grim fatality. His duffel bag was at his feet, his phone pressed against his ear. Right now the familiarity of Clary's voice on the other end of it was the only thing keeping him from falling apart completely.

"Simon, I'm so sorry." He could tell she was somewhere in the city. The loud blare of traffic sounded behind her, muffling her voice. "Are you seriously in Eric's *garage?* Does he know you're there?"

"No," Simon said. "No one's home at the moment, and I've got the garage key. It seemed like a place to go. Where are you, anyway?"

"In the city." To Brooklynites, Manhattan was always "the city." No other metropolis existed. "I was training with Jace, but then he had to go back to the Institute for some kind of Clave business. I'm headed back to Luke's now." A car honked loudly in the background. "Look, do you want to stay with us? You could sleep on Luke's couch."

Simon hesitated. He had good memories of Luke's. In all the years he'd known Clary, Luke had lived in the same ratty but pleasant old row house over the bookstore. Clary had a key, and she and Simon had whiled away a lot of pleasant hours there, reading books they'd "borrowed" from the store downstairs, or watching old movies on the TV.

Things were different now, though.

"Maybe my mom could talk to your mom," Clary said, sounding worried by his silence. "Make her understand."

"Make her understand that I'm a *vampire?* Clary, I think she does understand that, in a weird kind of way. That doesn't mean she's going to accept it or ever be okay with it."

"Well, you can't just keep making her forget it, either, Simon," Clary said. "It's not going to work forever."

"Why not?" He knew he was being unreasonable, but lying on the hard floor, surrounded by the smell of gasoline and the whisper of spiders spinning their webs in the corners of the garage, feeling lonelier than he ever had, reasonable seemed very far away.

"Because then your whole relationship with her is a lie. You can't never go home—"

"So what?" Simon interrupted harshly. "That's part of the curse, isn't it? 'A fugitive and a wanderer shalt thou be.'"

Despite the traffic noises and the sound of chatter in the background, he could hear Clary's sudden indrawn breath.

"You think I should tell her about that, too?" he said. "How you put the Mark of Cain on me? How I'm basically a walking curse? You think she's going to want *that* in her house?"

The background sounds quieted; Clary must have ducked into a doorway. He could hear her struggling to hold back tears as she said, "Simon, I'm so sorry. You *know* I'm sorry—"

"It's not your fault." He suddenly felt bone-tired. *That's right, terrify your mother and then make your best friend cry. A banner day for you, Simon.* "Look, obviously I shouldn't be around people right now. I'm just going to stay here, and I'll crash with Eric when he gets home."

She made a snuffling laughing-through-tears sound. "What, doesn't Eric count as people?"

"I'll get back to you on that later," he said, and hesitated. "I'll call you tomorrow, all right?"

"You'll *see* me tomorrow. You promised to come to that dress fitting with me, remember?"

"Wow," he said. "I must really love you."

"I know," she said. "I love you, too."

Simon clicked off the phone and lay back, holding it against his chest. It was funny, he thought. Now he could say "I love you" to Clary, when for years he'd struggled to say those words and had not been able to get them out of his mouth. Now that he no longer meant them the same way, it was easy.

Sometimes he did wonder what would have happened if there had never been a Jace Wayland. If Clary had never found out she was a Shadowhunter. But he pushed the thought away—pointless, don't go down that road. You couldn't change the past. You could only go forward. Not that he had any idea what forward entailed. He couldn't stay in Eric's garage forever. Even in his current mood, he had to admit it was a miserable place to stay. He wasn't cold—he no longer felt either cold or heat in any real way—but the floor was hard, and he was having trouble sleeping. He wished he could dull his senses. The loud noise of traffic outside was keeping him from resting, as was the unpleasant stench of gasoline. But it was the gnawing worry about what to do next that was the worst.

He'd thrown away most of his blood supply and stashed the rest in his knapsack; he had about enough for a few more days, and then he'd be in trouble. Eric, wherever he was, would certainly let Simon stay in the house if he wanted, but that might result in Eric's parents calling Simon's mom. And since she thought he was on a school field trip, that would do him no good at all.

Days, he thought. That was the amount of time he had. Before he ran out of blood, before his mother started to wonder where he was and called the school looking for him. Before she started to remember. He was a vampire now. He was supposed to have eternity. But what he had was days.

He had been so careful. Tried so hard for what he thought of as a normal life—school, friends, his own house, his own bedroom. It had been strained, but that was what life *was*. Other options seemed so bleak and lonely that they didn't bear thinking about. And yet Camille's voice rang in his head. *What about in ten years, when you are supposed to be twenty-six? In twenty years? Thirty? Do you think no one will notice that as they age and change, you do not?*

The situation he had created for himself, had carved so carefully in the shape of his old life, had never been permanent, he thought now, with a sinking in his chest. It never could have been. He'd been clinging to shadows and memories. He thought again of Camille, of her offer. It sounded better now than it had before. An offer of a community, even if it wasn't the community he wanted. He had only about three more days before she'd come looking for his answer. And what would he tell her when she did? He'd thought he knew, but now he wasn't so sure.

A grinding noise interrupted his reverie. The garage door was ratcheting upward, bright light spearing into the dark interior of the space. Simon sat up, his whole body suddenly on the alert.

"Eric?"

"Nah. It's me. Kyle."

"Kyle?" Simon said blankly, before he remembered—the guy they'd agreed to take on as a lead singer. Simon almost flopped back down onto the ground again. "Oh. Right. None of the other guys are here right now, so if you were hoping to practice . . ."

"It's cool. That's not why I came." Kyle stepped into the garage, blinking in the darkness, his hands in the back pockets of his jeans. "You're whatshisname, the bassist, right?"

Simon got to his feet, brushing garage floor dust off his clothes. "I'm Simon."

Kyle glanced around, a perplexed furrow between his brows. "I left my keys here yesterday, I think. Been looking for them everywhere. Hey, there they are." He ducked behind the drum set and emerged a second later, rattling a set of keys triumphantly in his hand. He looked much the same as he had the day before. He had a blue T-shirt on today under a leather jacket, and a gold saint's medal sparkled around his neck. His dark hair was messier than ever. "So," Kyle said, leaning against one of the speakers. "Were you, like, sleeping here? On the floor?"

Simon nodded. "Got thrown out of my house." It wasn't precisely true, but it was all he felt like saying.

Kyle nodded sympathetically. "Mom found your weed stash, huh? That sucks."

"No. No . . . weed stash." Simon shrugged. "We had a difference of opinion about my lifestyle."

"So, she found out about your two girlfriends?" Kyle grinned. He was good-looking, Simon had to admit, but unlike Jace, who seemed to know exactly how good-looking he was, Kyle looked like someone who probably hadn't brushed his hair in weeks. There was an open, friendly puppyishness about him that was appealing, though. "Yeah, Kirk told me about it. Good for you, man."

Simon shook his head. "It wasn't that."

There was a short silence between them. Then:

"I . . . don't live at home either," Kyle said. "I left a couple of years ago." He hugged his arms around himself, hanging his head down. His voice was low. "I haven't talked to my parents since then. I mean, I'm doing all right on my own but . . . I get it."

"Your tattoos," Simon said, touching his own arms lightly. "What do they mean?"

Kyle stretched his arms out. "*Shaantih shaantih shaantih,*" he said. "They're mantras from the Upanishads. Sanskrit. Prayers for peace."

Normally Simon would have thought that getting yourself

tattooed in Sanskrit was kind of pretentious. But right now, he didn't. "*Shalom*," he said.

Kyle blinked at him. "What?"

"Means peace," said Simon. "In Hebrew. I was just thinking the words sounded sort of alike."

Kyle gave him a long look. He seemed to be deliberating. Finally he said, "This is going to sound sort of crazy—"

"Oh, I don't know. My definition of crazy has become pretty flexible in the past few months."

"—but I have an apartment. In Alphabet City. And my roommate just moved out. It's a two-bedroom, so you could crash in his space. There's a bed in there and everything."

Simon hesitated. On the one hand he didn't know Kyle at all, and moving into the apartment of a total stranger seemed like a stupid move of epic proportions. Kyle could turn out to be a serial killer, despite his peace tattoos. On the other hand he didn't know Kyle at all, which meant no one would come looking for him there. And what did it matter if Kyle did turn out to be a serial killer? he thought bitterly. It would turn out worse for Kyle than it would for him, just like it had for that mugger last night.

"You know," he said, "I think I'll take you up on that, if it's okay."

Kyle nodded. "My truck's just outside if you want to ride into the city with me."

Simon bent to grab his duffel bag and straightened with it slung over his shoulder. He slid his phone into his pocket and spread his hands wide, indicating his readiness. "Let's go."

5

HELL CALLS HELL

Kyle's apartment turned out to be a pleasant surprise.
Simon expected a filthy walk-up in an Avenue D tenement,
with roaches crawling on the walls and a bed made out of
mattress foam and milk crates. In reality it was a clean two-
bedroom with a small living area, a ton of bookshelves,
and lots of photos on the walls of famous surfing spots.
Admittedly, Kyle seemed to be growing marijuana plants
on the fire escape, but you couldn't have everything.

Simon's room was basically an empty box. Whoever had
lived there before had left nothing behind but a futon mattress. It had bare walls, bare floors, and a single window,
through which Simon could see the neon sign of the Chinese
restaurant across the street. "You like it?" Kyle inquired,

hovering in the doorway, his hazel eyes open and friendly.

"It's great," Simon replied honestly. "Exactly what I needed."

The most expensive item in the apartment was the flat-screen TV in the living room. They threw themselves down on the futon couch and watched bad TV as the sunlight dimmed outside. Kyle was cool, Simon decided. He didn't poke, didn't pry, didn't ask questions. He didn't seem to want anything in exchange for the room except for Simon to pitch in grocery money. He was just a friendly guy. Simon wondered if he'd forgotten what ordinary human beings were like.

After Kyle headed out to work an evening shift, Simon went into his room, collapsed on the mattress, and listened to the traffic going by on Avenue B.

He'd been haunted by thoughts of his mother's face since he'd left: the way she'd looked at him with loathing and fear, as if he were an intruder in her house. Even if he didn't need to breathe, the thought of it had still constricted his chest. But now . . .

When he was a kid, he'd always liked traveling, because being in a new place had meant being away from all his problems. Even here, just a river away from Brooklyn, the memories that had been eating at him like acid—the mugger's death, his mother's reaction to the truth of what he was—seemed blurred and distant.

Maybe that was the secret, he thought. Keep moving. Like a shark. Go to where no one can find you. *A fugitive and a wanderer shalt thou be in the earth.*

But that only worked if there was no one you cared about leaving behind.

He slept fitfully all night. His natural urge was to sleep during the day, despite his Daylighter powers, and he fought off restlessness and dreams before waking up late with the sun streaming in through the window. After throwing on clean clothes from his knapsack, he left the bedroom to find Kyle in the kitchen, frying bacon and eggs in a Teflon pan.

"Hey, roommate," Kyle greeted him cheerfully. "Want some breakfast?"

The sight of the food made Simon feel vaguely sick to his stomach. "No, thanks. I'll take some coffee, though." He perched himself on one of the slightly lopsided bar stools.

Kyle pushed a chipped mug across the counter toward him. "Breakfast is the most important meal of the day, bro. Even if it's already noon."

Simon put his hands around the mug, feeling the heat seep into his cold skin. He cast about for a topic of conversation— one that wasn't how little he ate. "So, I never asked you yesterday—what do you do for a living?"

Kyle picked a piece of bacon out of the pan and bit into it. Simon noticed that the gold medal at his throat had a pattern of leaves on it, and the words *Beati Bellicosi.* "*Beati,*" Simon knew, was a word that had something to do with saints; Kyle must be Catholic. "Bike messenger," he said, chewing. "It's awesome. I get to ride around the city, seeing everything, talking to everyone. Way better than high school."

"You dropped out?"

"Got my GED senior year. I prefer the school of life." Simon would have thought Kyle sounded ridiculous if it weren't for the fact that he said "school of life" the way he said everything else—with total sincerity. "What about you? Any plans?"

Oh, you know. Wander the earth, causing death and destruction to innocent people. Maybe drink some blood. Live forever but never have any fun. The usual. "I'm kind of winging it at the moment."

"You mean you don't want to be a musician?" Kyle asked.

To Simon's relief his phone rang before he had to answer that. He fished it out of his pocket and looked at the screen. It was Maia. "Hey," he greeted her. "What's up?"

"Are you going to be at that dress fitting with Clary this afternoon?" she asked, her voice crackling down the line. She was probably calling from pack headquarters in Chinatown, where the reception wasn't great. "She told me she was making you go to keep her company."

"What? Oh, right. Yes. I'll be there." Clary had demanded that Simon accompany her to her bridesmaid's dress fitting so afterward they could shop for comics and she could feel, in her words, like "less of a frilled-up girly-girl."

"Well, I'm going to come too, then. I have to give Luke a message from the pack, and besides, I feel like I haven't seen you in ages."

"I know. I'm really sorry—"

"It's fine," she said lightly. "But you're going to have to let me know what you're wearing to the wedding eventually, because otherwise we'll clash."

She hung up, leaving Simon staring at the phone. Clary had been right. The wedding was D-day, and he was woefully unprepared for the battle.

"One of your girlfriends?" Kyle asked curiously. "Was that red-headed chick at the garage one of them? Because she was cute."

"No. That's Clary; she's my best friend." Simon pocketed his phone. "And she has a boyfriend. Like, really, really, *really* has a boyfriend. The nuclear bomb of boyfriends. Trust me on this one."

Kyle grinned. "I was just asking." He dumped the bacon pan, now empty, into the sink. "So, your two girls. What are they like?"

"They're very, very . . . different." In some ways, Simon thought, they were opposites. Maia was calm and grounded; Isabelle lived at a high pitch of excitement. Maia was a steady light in the darkness; Isabelle a burning star, spinning through the void. "I mean, they're both great. Beautiful, and smart . . ."

"And they don't know about each other?" Kyle leaned against the counter. "Like, at all?"

Simon found himself explaining—how when he'd come back from Idris (though he didn't mention the place by name), they'd both started calling him, wanting to hang out. And because he liked them both, he went. And somehow things started to turn casually romantic with each of them, but there never seemed to be a chance to explain to either of them that he was seeing someone else, too. And somehow it had snowballed, and here he was, not wanting to hurt either of them, and not knowing how to go on, either.

"Well, if you ask me," Kyle said, turning to dump his remaining coffee out in the sink, "you ought to pick one of them and quit dogging around. I'm just saying."

Since his back was to Simon, Simon couldn't see his face, and for a moment he wondered if Kyle was actually angry. His voice sounded uncharacteristically stiff. But when Kyle turned around, his expression was as open and friendly as ever. Simon decided he must have imagined it.

"I know," he said. "You're right." He glanced back toward

the bedroom. "Look, are you sure it's okay, me staying here? I can clear out whenever . . ."

"It's fine. You stay as long as you need." Kyle opened a kitchen drawer and scrabbled around until he found what he was looking for—a set of spare keys on a rubber-band ring. "There's a set for you. You're totally welcome here, okay? I gotta go to work, but you can hang around if you want. Play Halo, or whatever. Will you be here when I get back?"

Simon shrugged. "Probably not. I have a dress fitting to get to at three."

"Cool," said Kyle, slinging a messenger bag over his shoulder and heading toward the door. "Get them to make you something in red. It's totally your color."

"So," Clary said, stepping out of the dressing room. "What do you think?"

She did an experimental twirl. Simon, balanced on one of Karyn's Bridal Shop's uncomfortable white chairs, shifted position, winced, and said, "You look nice."

She looked better than nice. Clary was her mother's only bridesmaid, so she'd been allowed to pick out whatever dress she wanted. She'd selected a very simple coppery silk with narrow straps that flattered her small frame. Her only jewelry was the Morgenstern ring, worn on a chain around her neck; the very plain silver chain brought out the shape of her collarbones and the curve of her throat.

Not that many months ago, seeing Clary dressed up for a wedding would have conjured up in Simon a mix of feelings: dark despair (she would never love him) and high excitement (or maybe she would, if he could get up the nerve to tell her how he felt). Now it just made him feel a little wistful.

"Nice?" echoed Clary. "Is that it? Sheesh." She turned to Maia. "What do *you* think?"

Maia had given up on the uncomfortable chairs and was sitting on the floor, her back against a wall that was decorated with tiaras and long gauzy veils. She had Simon's DS balanced on one of her knees and seemed to be at least partly absorbed in playing Grand Theft Auto. "Don't ask me," she said. "I hate dresses. I'd wear jeans to the wedding if I could."

This was true. Simon rarely saw Maia out of jeans and T-shirts. In that way she was the opposite of Isabelle, who wore dresses and heels at even the most inappropriate times. (Though since he'd once seen her dispatch a Vermis demon with the stiletto heel of a boot, he was less inclined to worry about it.)

The shop bell tinkled, and Jocelyn came in, followed by Luke. Both were holding steaming cups of coffee, and Jocelyn was looking up at Luke, her cheeks flushed and her eyes shining. Simon remembered what Clary had said about them being disgustingly in love. He didn't find it disgusting himself, though that was probably because they weren't *his* parents. They both seemed so happy, and he thought it was actually rather nice.

Jocelyn's eyes widened when she saw Clary. "Honey, you look gorgeous!"

"Yeah, you have to say that. You're my mother," Clary said, but she grinned anyway. "Hey, is that coffee black by any chance?"

"Yep. Consider it a sorry-we're-late gift," Luke said, handing her the cup. "We got held up. Some catering issue or other." He nodded toward Simon and Maia. "Hey, guys."

Maia inclined her head. Luke was the head of the local wolf

pack, of which Maia was a member. Though he'd broken her of the habit of calling him "Master" or "Sir," she remained respectful in his presence. "I brought you a message from the pack," she said, setting down her game console. "They have questions about the party at the Ironworks—"

As Maia and Luke fell into conversation about the party the wolf pack was throwing in honor of their alpha wolf's marriage, the owner of the bridal shop, a tall woman who had been reading magazines behind the counter while the teenagers chatted, realized that the people who were actually going to *pay* for the dresses had just arrived, and hurried forward to greet them. "I just got your dress back in, and it looks *marvelous*," she gushed, taking Clary's mother by the arm and steering her toward the back of the store. "Come and try it on." As Luke started after them, she pointed a threatening finger at him. "*You* stay here."

Luke, watching his fiancée disappear through a set of white swinging doors painted with wedding bells, looked puzzled.

"Mundanes think you're not supposed to see the bride in her wedding dress before the ceremony," Clary reminded him. "It's bad luck. She probably thinks it's weird you came to the fitting."

"But Jocelyn wanted my opinion—" Luke broke off and shook his head. "Ah, well. Mundane customs are so peculiar." He threw himself down in a chair, and winced as one of the carved rosettes poked into his back. "Ouch."

"What about Shadowhunter weddings?" Maia inquired, curious. "Do they have their own customs?"

"They do," Luke said slowly, "but this isn't going to be a classic Shadowhunter ceremony. Those specifically don't address any situation in which one of the participants is not a Shadowhunter."

"Really?" Maia looked shocked. "I didn't know that."

"Part of a Shadowhunter marriage ceremony involves tracing permanent runes on the bodies of the participants," said Luke. His voice was calm, but his eyes looked sad. "Runes of love and commitment. But of course, non-Shadowhunters can't bear the Angel's runes, so Jocelyn and I will be exchanging rings instead."

"That sucks," Maia pronounced.

At that, Luke smiled. "Not really. Marrying Jocelyn is all I ever wanted, and I'm not that bothered about the particulars. Besides, things are changing. The new Council members have made a lot of headway toward convincing the Clave to tolerate this sort of—"

"Clary!" It was Jocelyn, calling from the back of the store. "Can you come here for a second?"

"Coming!" Clary called, bolting down the last of her coffee. "Uh-oh. Sounds like a dress emergency."

"Well, good luck with that." Maia got to her feet, and dropped the DS back in Simon's lap before bending to kiss him on the cheek. "I've got to go. I'm meeting some friends at the Hunter's Moon."

She smelled pleasantly of vanilla. Under that, as always, Simon could smell the salt scent of blood, mixed with a sharp, lemony tang that was peculiar to werewolves. Every Downworlder's blood smelled different—faeries smelled like dead flowers, warlocks like burnt matches, and other vampires like metal.

Clary had once asked him what Shadowhunters smelled like.

"Sunlight," he'd said.

"See you later, baby." Maia straightened up, ruffled Simon's hair once, and departed. As the door closed behind her, Clary fixed him with a piercing glare.

"You *must* work your love life out by next Saturday," she said. "I mean it, Simon. If you don't tell them, I will."

Luke looked bewildered. "Tell who what?"

Clary shook her head at Simon. "You're on thin ice, Lewis." With which pronouncement she flounced away, holding up her silk skirts as she went. Simon was amused to note that underneath them she was wearing green sneakers.

"Clearly," said Luke, "something is going on that I don't know about."

Simon looked over at him. "Sometimes I think that's the motto of my life."

Luke raised his eyebrows. "Has something happened?"

Simon hesitated. He certainly couldn't tell Luke about his love life—Luke and Maia were in the same pack, and werewolf packs were more loyal than street gangs. It would put Luke in a very awkward position. It was true, though, that Luke was also a resource. As the leader of the Manhattan wolf pack, he had access to all sorts of information, and was well versed in Downworlder politics. "Have you heard of a vampire named Camille?"

Luke made a low whistling sound. "I know who she is. I'm surprised you do."

"Well, she's the head of the New York vampire clan. I do know *something* about them," Simon said, a little stiffly.

"I didn't realize you did. I thought you wanted to live like a human as much as you could." There was no judgment in Luke's voice, only curiosity. "Now, by the time I took over the downtown pack from the previous pack leader, she had put Raphael in charge. I don't think anyone knew where she'd gone exactly. But she is something of a legend. An extraordinarily old vampire, from everything I understand. Famously cruel and cunning. She could give the Fair Folk a run for their money."

"Have you ever seen her?"

Luke shook his head. "Don't think I have, no. Why the curiosity?"

"Raphael mentioned her," Simon said vaguely.

Luke's forehead creased. "You've seen Raphael lately?"

Before Simon could answer, the shop bell sounded again, and to Simon's surprise, Jace came in. Clary hadn't mentioned he was coming.

In point of fact, he realized, Clary hadn't mentioned Jace much lately at all.

Jace looked from Luke to Simon. He looked as if he were mildly surprised to see Simon and Luke there, although it was hard to tell. Though Simon imagined that Jace ran the gamut of facial expressions when he was alone with Clary, his default one around other people was a fierce sort of blankness. "He looks," Simon had once said to Isabelle, "like he's thinking about something deep and meaningful, but if you ask him what it is, he'll punch you in the face."

"So don't ask him," Isabelle had said, as if she thought Simon was being ridiculous. "No one says you two need to be friends."

"Is Clary here?" Jace asked, shutting the door behind him. He looked tired. There were shadows under his eyes, and he didn't seem to have bothered to put on a jacket, despite the fact that the autumn wind was brisk. Though cold no longer affected Simon much, looking at Jace in just jeans and a thermal shirt made him feel chilly.

"She's helping Jocelyn," explained Luke. "But you're welcome to wait here with us."

Jace looked around uneasily at the walls hung with veils, fans, tiaras, and seed-pearl-encrusted trains. "Everything is . . . so white."

"Of course it's white," said Simon. "It's a wedding."

"White for Shadowhunters is the color of funerals," Luke explained. "But for mundanes, Jace, it's the color of weddings. Brides wear white to symbolize their purity."

"I thought Jocelyn said her dress wasn't white," Simon said.

"Well," said Jace, "I suppose that ship *has* sailed."

Luke choked on his coffee. Before he could say—or do— anything, Clary walked back into the room. Her hair was up now, in sparkling pins, with a few curls hanging loose. "I don't know," she was saying as she came closer to them. "Karyn got her hands on me and did my hair, but I'm not sure about the sparkles—"

She broke off as she saw Jace. It was clear from her expression that she hadn't been expecting him either. Her lips parted in surprise, but she said nothing. Jace, in his turn, was staring at her, and for once in his life Simon could read Jace's expression like a book. It was as if everything else in the world had fallen away for Jace but himself and Clary, and he was looking at her with an unconcealed yearning and desire that made Simon feel awkward, as if he had somehow walked in on a private moment.

Jace cleared his throat. "You look beautiful."

"Jace." Clary looked more puzzled than anything else. "Is

everything all right? I thought you said you couldn't come because of the Conclave meeting."

"That's right," Luke said. "I heard about the Shadowhunter body in the park. Is there any news?"

Jace shook his head, still looking at Clary. "No. He's not one of the New York Conclave members, but beyond that he hasn't been identified. Neither of the bodies have. The Silent Brothers are looking at them now."

"That's good. The Brothers will figure out who they are," said Luke.

Jace said nothing. He was still looking at Clary, and it was the oddest sort of look, Simon thought—the sort of look you might give someone you loved but could never, ever have. He imagined Jace had felt like that about Clary once before, but now?

"Jace?" Clary said, and took a step toward him.

He tore his gaze away from her. "That jacket you borrowed from me in the park yesterday," he said. "Do you still have it?"

Now looking even more puzzled, Clary pointed to where the item of clothing in question, a perfectly ordinary brown suede jacket, was hanging over the back of one of the chairs. "It's over there. I was going to bring it to you after—"

"Well," said Jace, picking it up and thrusting his arms hastily into the sleeves, as if he were suddenly in a hurry, "now you don't have to."

"Jace," Luke said in that calming tone he had, "we're going to get an early dinner in Park Slope after this. You're welcome to come along."

"No," Jace said, zipping the jacket up. "I've got training this afternoon. I'd better head out."

"Training?" Clary echoed. "But we trained yesterday."

"Some of us have to train every day, Clary." Jace didn't sound angry, but there was a harshness to his tone, and Clary flushed. "I'll see you later," he added without looking at her, and practically flung himself toward the door.

As it shut behind him, Clary reached up and angrily yanked the pins out of her hair. It cascaded in tangles down around her shoulders.

"Clary," Luke said gently. He stood up. "What are you doing?"

"My hair." She yanked the last pin out, hard. Her eyes were shining, and Simon could tell she was forcibly willing herself not to cry. "I don't want to wear it like this. It looks stupid."

"No, it doesn't." Luke took the pins from her and set them down on one of the small white end tables. "Look, weddings make men nervous, okay? It doesn't mean anything."

"Right." Clary tried to smile. She nearly managed it, but Simon could tell she didn't believe Luke. He could hardly blame her. After seeing the look on Jace's face, Simon didn't believe him either.

In the distance the Fifth Avenue Diner was lit up like a star against the blue twilight. Simon walked beside Clary down the avenue blocks, Jocelyn and Luke a few steps ahead of them. Clary had changed out of her dress and was back in jeans now, a thick white scarf wound around her neck. Every once in a while she would reach up and twirl the ring on the chain around her neck, a nervous gesture he wondered if she was even aware of.

When they'd left the bridal store, he had asked her if she knew what was wrong with Jace, but she hadn't really answered him. She'd shrugged it off, and started asking him about what was going on with him, if he'd talked to his mother yet, and whether he minded staying with Eric. When he told her he was crashing with Kyle, she was surprised.

"But you hardly even know him," she said. "He could be a serial killer."

"I did have that thought. I checked the apartment out, but if he's got an ice cooler full of arms in it, I haven't seen it yet. Anyway, he seems pretty sincere."

"So what's his apartment like?"

"Nice for Alphabet City. You should come over later."

"Not tonight," Clary said, a little absently. She was fiddling with the ring again. "Maybe tomorrow?"

Going to see Jace? Simon thought, but he didn't press the point. If she didn't want to talk about it, he wasn't going to make her. "Here we are." He opened the diner door for her, and a blast of warm souvlaki-smelling air hit them.

They found a booth over by one of the big flat-screen TVs that lined the walls. They crowded into it as Jocelyn and Luke chattered animatedly with each other about wedding plans. Luke's pack, it seemed, felt insulted that they hadn't been invited to the ceremony—even though the guest list was tiny—and were insisting on holding their own celebration in a renovated factory in Queens. Clary listened, not saying anything; the waitress came around, handing out menus so stiffly laminated they could have been used as weapons. Simon set his own on the table and stared out the window. There was a gym across the street, and he could see people through the plate glass that fronted it, running on treadmills, arms pumping, headphones clamped to their ears. *All that running and getting nowhere, he thought. Story of my life.*

He tried to force his thoughts away from dark places, and almost succeeded. This was one of the most familiar scenes in his life, he thought—a corner booth in a diner, himself and Clary and her family. Luke had always been family, even when he hadn't been about to marry Clary's mom. Simon ought to feel at home. He tried to force a smile, only to realize that Clary's mother had just asked him something and he hadn't heard her. Everyone at the table was staring at him expectantly.

"Sorry," he said. "I didn't— What did you say?"

Jocelyn smiled patiently. "Clary told me you've added a new member to your band?"

Simon knew she was just being polite. Well, polite in that way parents were when they pretended to take your hobbies seriously. Still, she'd come to several of his gigs before, just to help fill up the room. She did care about him; she always had. In the very dark, tucked-away places of his mind, Simon suspected she had always known how he felt about Clary, and he wondered if she wouldn't have wanted her daughter to make a different choice, had it been something she could control. He knew she didn't entirely like Jace. It was clear even in the way she said his name.

"Yeah," he said. "Kyle. He's kind of a weird guy, but super-nice." Invited, by Luke, to expand on the topic of Kyle's weirdness, Simon told them about Kyle's apartment—careful to leave out the detail that it was now *his* apartment too—his bike messenger job, and his ancient, beat-up pickup truck. "And he grows these weird plants on the balcony," he added. "Not pot—I checked. They have sort of silvery leaves—"

Luke frowned, but before he could say anything, the waitress arrived, carrying a big silver coffee pitcher. She was young, with bleached pale hair tied into two braids. As she bent to fill Simon's coffee cup, one of them brushed his arm. He could smell sweat on her, and under that, blood. Human blood, the sweetest smell of all. He felt a familiar tightening in his stomach. Coldness spread through him. He was hungry, and all he had back at Kyle's place was room-temperature blood that was already beginning to separate—a sickening prospect, even for a vampire.

You have never fed on a human, have you? You will. And when you do, you will not forget it.

He closed his eyes. When he opened them again, the waitress was gone and Clary was staring at him curiously across the table. "Is everything okay?"

"Fine." He closed his hand around his coffee cup. It was shaking. Above them the TV was still blaring the nightly news.

"Ugh," Clary said, looking up at the screen. "Are you listening to this?"

Simon followed her gaze. The news anchor was wearing that expression news anchors tended to wear when they were reporting on something especially grim. "No one has come forward to identify an infant boy found abandoned in an alley behind Beth Israel hospital several days ago," he was saying. "The infant is white, weighs six pounds and eight ounces, and is otherwise healthy. He was discovered strapped to an infant car seat behind a Dumpster in the alley," the anchor went on. "Most disturbing, a handwritten note tucked into the child's blanket begged hospital authorities to euthanize the child because 'I don't have the strength to do it myself.' Police say it is likely that the child's mother was mentally ill, and claim they have 'promising leads.' Anyone with information about this child should call Crime Stoppers at—"

"That's so horrible," Clary said, turning away from the TV with a shudder. "I can't understand how people just dump their babies off like they're trash—"

"Jocelyn," Luke said, his voice sharp with concern. Simon looked toward Clary's mother. She was as white as a sheet and looked as if she were about to throw up. She pushed her plate away abruptly, stood up from the table, and hurried toward the bathroom. After a moment Luke dropped his napkin and went after her.

"Oh, crap." Clary put her hand over her mouth. "I can't believe I said that. I'm so stupid."

Simon was thoroughly perplexed. "What's going on?"

Clary slunk down in her seat. "She was thinking about Sebastian," she said. "I mean Jonathan. My brother. I assume you remember him."

She was being sarcastic. None of them was likely to forget Sebastian, whose real name was Jonathan and who had murdered Hodge and Max and had nearly succeeded in helping Valentine win a war that would have seen the destruction of all Shadowhunters. Jonathan, who had had burning black eyes and a smile like a razor blade. Jonathan, whose blood had tasted like battery acid when Simon had bitten him once. Not that he regretted it.

"But your mom didn't abandon him," Simon said. "She stuck with raising him even though she knew there was something horribly wrong with him."

"She hated him, though," Clary said. "I don't think she's ever gotten over that. Imagine hating your own baby. She used to take out a box that had his baby things in it and cry over it every year on his birthday. I think she was crying over the son she would have had—you know, if Valentine hadn't done what he had."

"And you would have had a brother," said Simon. "Like, an actual one. Not a murdering psychopath."

Looking close to tears, Clary pushed her plate away. "I feel sick now," she said. "You know that feeling like you're hungry but you can't bring yourself to eat?"

Simon looked over at the bleached-haired waitress, who was leaning against the diner counter. "Yeah," he said. "I know."

Luke returned to the table eventually, but only to tell Clary and Simon that he was taking Jocelyn home. He left some money, which they used to pay the bill before wandering out of the diner and over to Galaxy Comics on Seventh Avenue. Neither of them could concentrate enough to enjoy themselves, though, so they split up, with a promise to see each other the next day.

Simon rode into the city with his hood pulled up and his iPod on, blasting music into his ears. Music had always been his way of blocking everything out. By the time he got out at Second Avenue and headed down Houston, a light rain had started to fall, and his stomach was in knots.

He cut over to First Street, which was mostly deserted, a strip of darkness between the bright lights of First Avenue and Avenue A. Because he had his iPod on, he didn't hear them coming up behind him until they were nearly on him. The first intimation he had that something was wrong was a long shadow that fell across the sidewalk, overlapping his own. Another shadow joined it, this one on his other side. He turned—

And saw two men behind him. Both were dressed exactly like the mugger who had attacked him the other night—gray tracksuits, gray hoods pulled up to hide their faces. They were close enough to touch him.

Simon leaped back, with a force that surprised him. Because his vampire strength was so new, it still had the power to shock him. When, a moment later, he found himself perched on the stoop of a brownstone, several feet away from the muggers, he was so astonished to be there that he froze.

The muggers advanced on him. They were speaking the same guttural language as the first mugger—who, Simon was beginning to suspect, had not been a mugger at all. Muggers, as far as he knew, didn't work in gangs, and it was unlikely that the first mugger had criminal friends who had decided to take revenge on him for their comrade's demise. Something else was clearly going on here.

They had reached the stoop, effectively trapping him on the steps. Simon tore his iPod headphones from his ears and hastily held his hands up. "Look," he said, "I don't know what this is about, but you really want to leave me alone."

The muggers just looked at him. Or at least he thought they were looking at him. Under the shadows of their hoods, it was impossible to see their faces.

"I'm getting the feeling someone sent you after me," he said. "But it's a suicide mission. Seriously. I don't know what they're paying you, but it's not enough."

One of the tracksuited figures laughed. The other had reached into his pocket and drawn something out. Something that shone black under the streetlights.

A gun.

"Oh, man," Simon said. "You really, really don't want to do that. I'm not kidding." He took a step back, up one of the stairs. Maybe if he got enough height, he could actually jump over them, or past them. Anything but let them attack him. He didn't think he could face what that meant. Not again.

The man with the gun raised it. There was a click as he pulled the hammer back.

Simon bit his lip. In his panic his fangs had come out. Pain shot through him as they sank into his skin. *"Don't—"*

A dark object fell from the sky. At first Simon thought something had merely tumbled from one of the upper windows—an air conditioner ripping loose, or someone too lazy to drag their trash downstairs. But the falling thing, he saw, was a person—falling with direction, purpose, and grace. The person landed on the mugger, knocking him flat. The gun skittered out of his hand, and he screamed, a thin, high sound.

The second mugger bent and seized the gun. Before Simon could react, the guy had raised it and pulled the trigger. A spark of flame appeared at the gun's muzzle.

And the gun blew apart. It blew apart, and the mugger blew apart along with it, too fast to even scream. He had intended a quick death for Simon, and an even quicker death was what he got in return. He shattered apart like glass, like the outward-flying colors in a kaleidoscope. There was a soft explosion—the sound of displaced air—and then nothing but a soft drizzle of salt, falling onto the pavement like solidified rain.

Simon's vision blurred, and he sank down onto the steps. He was aware of a loud humming in his ears, and then someone grabbed him roughly by the wrists and shook him, hard. "Simon. Simon!"

He looked up. The person grabbing him and shaking him was Jace. The other boy wasn't in gear, but was still wearing his jeans and the jacket he'd taken back from Clary. He was disheveled, his clothes and face streaked with dirt and soot. His hair was wet from the rain.

"What the hell was that?" Jace asked.

Simon looked up and down the street. It was still deserted. The asphalt shone, black and wet and empty. The second mugger was gone.

"*You*," he said, a little groggily. "You jumped the muggers—"

"Those weren't muggers. They were following you since you got off the subway. Someone sent those guys." Jace spoke with complete surety.

"The other one," Simon said. "What happened to him?"

"He just vanished." Jace snapped his fingers. "He saw what happened to his friend, and he was gone, like that. I don't know what they were, exactly. Not demons, but not exactly human, either."

"Yeah, I figured that part out, thanks."

Jace looked at him more closely. "That—what happened to the mugger—that was you, wasn't it? Your Mark, here." He pointed at his forehead. "I saw it burn white before that guy just . . . dissolved."

Simon said nothing.

"I've seen a lot," Jace said. There was no sarcasm in his voice, for a change, or any mockery. "But I've never seen anything like that."

"I didn't do it," Simon said softly. "I didn't do anything."

"You didn't have to," said Jace. His golden eyes burned in his soot-streaked face. "'*For it is written, Vengeance is mine; I will repay, saith the Lord.*'"

6

WAKE THE DEAD

Jace's room was as neat as ever—bed made perfectly, the books that lined the shelves arranged in alphabetical order, notes and textbooks stacked carefully on the desk. Even his weapons were lined up along the wall in order of size, from a massive broadsword to a set of small daggers.

Clary, standing in the doorway, held back a sigh. The neatness was all very well. She was used to it. It was, she had always thought, Jace's way of exerting control over the elements of a life that otherwise might seem overwhelmed with chaos. He had lived so long not knowing who—or even what—he really was, she could hardly begrudge him the careful alphabetization of his poetry collection.

She could, however—and did—begrudge the fact that he

wasn't there. If he hadn't gone back home after leaving the bridal shop, where *had* he gone? As she looked around the room, a feeling of unreality came over her. It wasn't possible that any of this was happening, was it? She knew how breakups went from hearing other girls complain about them. First the pulling away, the gradual refusal to return notes or phone calls. The vague messages saying nothing was wrong, that the other person just wanted a little space. Then the speech about how "It's not you, it's me." Then the crying part.

She'd never thought any of that would ever apply to her and Jace. What they had wasn't ordinary, or subject to the ordinary rules of relationships and breakups. They belonged to each other totally, and always would, and that was that.

But maybe everyone felt that way? Until the moment they realized they were just like everyone else, and everything they'd thought was real shattered apart.

Something that glittered silver across the room caught her eye. It was the box Amatis had given Jace, with its delicate design of birds around the sides. She knew he had been working his way through it, reading the letters slowly, going through the notes and photos. He hadn't said much about it to her, and she hadn't wanted to pry. His feelings about his biological father were something he was going to have to come to terms with on his own.

She found herself drawn to the box now, though. She remembered him sitting on the front steps of the Accords Hall in Idris, holding the box in his lap. *As if I could stop loving you,* he'd said. She touched the lid of the box, and her fingers found the clasp, which sprung open easily. Inside were scattered papers, old photographs. She drew one out, and stared at it, fascinated. There were two people in the photograph, a young woman and a young man. She recognized the woman immediately as Luke's sister, Amatis. She was gazing up at the young man with all the radiance of first love. He was handsome, tall and blond, though his eyes were blue, not gold, and his features less angular than Jace's . . . and yet still, knowing who he was—Jace's father—was enough to make her stomach tighten.

She set the photo of Stephen Herondale down hastily, and nearly cut her finger on the blade of a slim hunting dagger that lay crosswise in the box. Birds were carved along the handle. The blade of it was stained with rust, or what looked like rust. It must not have been cleaned properly. She shut the box quickly, and turned away, guilt like a weight on her shoulders.

She had thought about leaving a note, but, deciding it would be better to wait until she could talk to Jace in person, she left and went down the hall to the elevator. She had knocked on Isabelle's door earlier, but it didn't look like she was home either. Even the witchlight torches in the hallways seemed to be burning at a lower level than usual. Feeling utterly depressed, Clary reached for the elevator call button—only to realize it was already lit. Someone was heading up from the ground floor to the Institute.

Jace, she thought immediately, her pulse jumping. But of course it might not be him, she told herself. It could be Izzy, or Maryse, or—

"Luke?" she said in surprise as the elevator door opened. "What are you doing here?"

"I might ask you the same thing." He stepped out of the elevator, pulling the gate shut behind him. He was wearing a fleece-lined zip-up flannel jacket that Jocelyn had been trying to get him to throw away since they'd first started dating. It was rather nice, Clary thought, that just about nothing seemed to change Luke, no matter what happened in his life. He liked what he liked, and that was that. Even if it was a ratty-looking old coat. "Except I think I can guess. So, is he here?"

"Jace? No." Clary shrugged, trying to look unconcerned. "It's fine. I'll see him tomorrow."

Luke hesitated. "Clary—"

"Lucian." The cool voice that came from behind them was Maryse's. "Thank you for coming on such short notice."

He turned to nod at her. "Maryse."

Maryse Lightwood stood in the doorway, her hand lightly on the frame. She was wearing gloves, pale gray gloves that matched her tailored gray suit. Clary wondered if Maryse ever wore jeans. She had never seen Isabelle and Alec's mother in anything but power suits or gear. "Clary," she said. "I didn't realize you were here."

Clary felt herself flush. Maryse didn't seem to mind her coming and going, but then, Maryse had never really acknowledged Clary's relationship with Jace at all. It was hard to blame her. Maryse was still coping with Max's death, which had been only six weeks ago, and she was doing it alone, with Robert Lightwood still in Idris. She had bigger things on her mind than Jace's love life.

"I was just leaving," Clary said.

"I'll give you a ride back home when I'm done here," Luke said, putting a hand on her shoulder. "Maryse, is it a problem if Clary remains while we talk? Because I'd prefer to have her stay."

Maryse shook her head. "No problem, I suppose." She sighed, raking her hands through her hair. "Believe me, I wish

I didn't need to bother you at all. I know you're getting married in a week—congratulations, by the way. I don't know if I told you that before."

"You didn't," said Luke, "but it's appreciated. Thank you."

"Only six weeks." Maryse smiled faintly. "Quite a whirlwind courtship."

Luke's hand tightened on Clary's shoulder, the only sign of his annoyance. "I don't suppose you called me over here to congratulate me on my engagement, did you?"

Maryse shook her head. She looked very tired, Clary thought, and there were strands of gray in her upswept dark hair that hadn't been there before. "No. I assume you've heard about the bodies we've been finding for the past week or so?"

"The dead Shadowhunters, yes."

"We found another one tonight. Stuffed in a Dumpster near Columbus Park. Your pack's territory."

Luke's eyebrows went up. "Yes, but the others—"

"The first body was found in Greenpoint. Warlock territory. The second floating in a pond in Central Park. The domain of the fey. Now we have werewolf territory." She fixed her gaze on Luke. "What does that make you think?"

"That someone who isn't very pleased about the new Accords is trying to set Downworlder against Downworlder," Luke said. "I can assure you my pack didn't have anything to do with this. I don't know who's behind it, but it's a very clumsy attempt, if you ask me. I hope the Clave can see through it."

"There's more," Maryse said. "We've identified the first two bodies. It took some time, since the first was burned nearly beyond recognition and the second was badly decomposed. Can you guess who they might have been?"

"Maryse—"

"Anson Pangborn," she said, "and Charles Freeman. Neither of whom, I might note, had been heard from since Valentine's death—"

"But that's not possible," Clary interrupted. "Luke killed Pangborn, back in August—at Renwick's."

"He killed Emil Pangborn," said Maryse. "Anson was Emil's younger brother. They were both in the Circle together."

"As was Freeman," said Luke. "So someone is killing not just Shadowhunters but former Circle members? And leaving their bodies in Downworlder territory?" He shook his head. "It sounds like someone's trying to shake up some of the more . . . recalcitrant members of the Clave. Get them to rethink the new Accords, perhaps. We should have expected this."

"I suppose," Maryse said. "I've met with the Seelie Queen already, and I have a message out to Magnus. Wherever he is." She rolled her eyes; Maryse and Robert seemed to have accepted Alec's relationship with Magnus with surprisingly good grace, but Clary could tell that Maryse, at least, didn't take it seriously. "I just thought, perhaps—" She sighed. "I've been so exhausted lately. I feel like I can hardly think straight. I hoped you might have some idea about who might be doing this, some idea that hadn't occurred to me."

Luke shook his head. "Someone with a grudge against the new system. But that could be anyone. I suppose there's no evidence on the bodies?"

Maryse sighed. "Nothing conclusive. If only the dead could talk, eh, Lucian?"

It was as if Maryse had lifted a hand and yanked a curtain across Clary's vision; everything went dark, except for a single symbol, hanging like a glowing sign against a blank night sky.

It seemed her power had not vanished, after all.

"What if . . . ," she said slowly, raising her eyes to look at Maryse. "What if they could?"

Staring at himself in the bathroom mirror in Kyle's small apartment, Simon couldn't help but wonder where that whole business about vampires not being able to see themselves in mirrors had come from. He was able to see himself perfectly well in the dinged surface—tousled brown hair, wide brown eyes, white, unmarked skin. He had sponged off the blood from his cut lip, though his skin had already healed over.

He knew, objectively speaking, that becoming a vampire had made him more attractive. Isabelle had explained to him that his movements had become graceful and that, whereas before he had seemed disheveled, somehow now he looked attractively rumpled, as if he had just gotten out of bed. "Someone *else's* bed," she had noted, which, he'd told her, he had already figured out was what she meant, thank you.

When he looked at himself, though, he didn't see any of that. The poreless whiteness of his skin, as it always did, disturbed him, as did the dark, spidering veins that showed at his temples, evidence of the fact that he had not fed today. He looked alien and not like himself. Perhaps the whole business about not being able to see yourself in a mirror once you had become a vampire was wishful thinking. Maybe it was just that you no longer recognized the reflection looking back at you.

Cleaned up, he headed back into the living room, where Jace was sprawled out on the futon couch, reading Kyle's beaten-up copy of *The Lord of the Rings*. He dropped it onto the coffee table as Simon came in. His hair looked newly wet, as if he'd splashed water on his face from the kitchen sink.

"I can see why you like it here," he said, making a sweeping gesture that encompassed Kyle's collection of movie posters and science fiction books. "There's a thin layer of nerd all over everything."

"Thanks. I appreciate that." Simon gave Jace a hard look. Up close, under the bright light of the unshaded overhead bulb, Jace looked—ill. The shadows Simon had noticed under his eyes before were more pronounced than ever, and his skin seemed tight over the bones of his face. His hand shook a little as he pushed his hair away from his forehead in a characteristic gesture.

Simon shook his head as if to clear it. Since when did he know Jace well enough to be able to identify which gestures of his were characteristic? It wasn't as if they were friends. "You look lousy," he said.

Jace blinked. "Seems an odd time to start an insult contest, but if you insist, I could probably think up something good."

"No, I mean it. You don't look good."

"This from a guy who has all the sex appeal of a penguin. Look, I realize you may be jealous that the good Lord didn't deal you the same chiseled hand he dealt me, but that's no reason to—"

"I am *not trying to insult you*," Simon snapped. "I mean you look *sick*. When was the last time you ate anything?"

Jace looked thoughtful. "Yesterday?"

"You ate something yesterday. You're sure?"

Jace shrugged. "Well, I wouldn't swear on a stack of Bibles. I think it was yesterday, though."

Simon had investigated the contents of Kyle's fridge earlier when he'd been searching the place, and there hadn't been much to find. A withered-up old lime, some soda cans, a pound of ground beef, and, inexplicably, a single Pop-Tart in the freezer. He grabbed his keys off the kitchen counter. "Come on," he said. "There's a supermarket on the corner. Let's get you some food."

Jace looked as if he were in the mood to object, then shrugged. "Fine," he said, in the tone of someone who didn't much care where they went or what they did there. "Let's go."

Outside on the front steps Simon locked the door behind them with the keys he was still getting used to, while Jace examined the list of names next to the apartment doorbell buzzers. "That one's yours, huh?" he asked, pointing to 3A. "How come it just says 'Kyle'? Doesn't he have a last name?"

"Kyle wants to be a rock star," Simon said, heading down the stairs. "I think he's working the one-name thing. Like Rihanna."

Jace followed him, hunching his shoulders slightly against the wind, though he made no move to zip up the suede jacket he'd retrieved from Clary earlier that day. "I have no idea what you're talking about."

"I'm sure you don't."

As they rounded the corner onto Avenue B, Simon looked at Jace sideways. "So," he said. "Were you *following* me? Or is it just an amazing coincidence that you happened to be on the roof of a building I was walking by when I got attacked?"

Jace stopped at the corner, waiting for the light to turn.

Apparently even Shadowhunters had to obey traffic laws. "I was following you."

"Is this the part where you tell me you're secretly in love with me? Vampire mojo strikes again."

"There's no such thing as vampire mojo," said Jace, rather eerily echoing Clary's earlier comment. "And I was following Clary, but then she got into a cab, and I can't follow a cab. So I doubled back and followed you instead. Mostly for something to do."

"You were following Clary?" Simon echoed. "Here's a hot tip: Most girls don't like being stalked."

"She left her phone in the pocket of my jacket," Jace said, patting his right side, where, presumably, the phone was stashed. "I thought if I could figure out where she was going, I could leave it where she'd find it."

"Or," Simon said, "you could call her at home and tell her you had her phone, and she could come and get it from you."

Jace said nothing. The light changed, and they headed across the street toward the C-Town supermarket. It was still open. Markets in Manhattan never closed, Simon thought, which was a nice change from Brooklyn. Manhattan was a good place to be a vampire. You could do all your shopping at midnight and no one would think it was weird.

"You're avoiding Clary," Simon observed. "I don't suppose you want to tell me why?"

"No, I don't," Jace said. "Just count yourself lucky I *was* following you, or—"

"Or what? Another mugger would be dead?" Simon could hear the bitterness in his own voice. "You saw what happened."

"Yes. And I saw the look on your face when it did." Jace's

tone was neutral. "That wasn't the first time you've seen that happen, was it?"

Simon found himself telling Jace about the tracksuited figure who had attacked him in Williamsburg, and how he had assumed it was just a mugger. "After he died, he turned into salt," he finished. "Just like the second guy. I guess it's a biblical thing. Pillars of salt. Like Lot's wife."

They had reached the supermarket; Jace shoved the door open, and Simon followed him in, grabbing a miniature wheeled silver cart from the line near the front door. He started to push it down one of the aisles, and Jace followed him, clearly lost in thought. "So I guess the question is," Jace said, "do you have any idea who might want to kill you?"

Simon shrugged. The sight of all the food around him was making his stomach twist, reminding him how hungry he was, though not for anything they sold here. "Maybe Raphael. He seems to hate me. And he wanted me dead before—"

"It's not Raphael," said Jace.

"How can you be so sure?"

"Because Raphael knows about your Mark and wouldn't be stupid enough to strike at you directly like that. He'd know exactly what would happen. Whoever's after you, it's someone who knows enough about you to know where you're likely to be, but they don't know about the Mark."

"But that could be anyone."

"Exactly," said Jace, and grinned. For a moment he almost looked like himself again.

Simon shook his head. "Look, do you know what you want to eat, or do you just want me to keep pushing this cart up and down aisles because it amuses you?"

"That," said Jace, "and I'm not really familiar with what they sell in mundane grocery stores. Maryse usually cooks or we order in food." He shrugged, and picked up a piece of fruit at random. "What's this?"

"That's a mango." Simon stared at Jace. Sometimes it really was like Shadowhunters were from an alien planet.

"I don't think I've ever seen one of those that wasn't already cut up," Jace mused. "I like mangoes."

Simon grabbed the mango and tossed it into the cart. "Great. What else do you like?"

Jace pondered for a moment. "Tomato soup," he said finally.

"Tomato soup? You want tomato soup and a mango for dinner?"

Jace shrugged. "I don't really care about food."

"Fine. Whatever. Stay here. I'll be right back." *Shadowhunters.* Simon seethed quietly to himself as he rounded the corner of an aisle lined with soup cans. They were a sort of bizarre amalgam of millionaires—people who never had to consider the petty parts of life, like how to shop for food, or use MetroCard machines in the subway—and soldiers, with their rigid self-discipline and constant training. Maybe it was easier for them, going through life with blinders on, he thought as he grabbed a soup can off the shelf. Maybe it helped you keep your focus on the big picture—which, when your job was basically keeping the world safe from evil, was a pretty big picture indeed.

He was feeling nearly sympathetic toward Jace as he neared the aisle where he'd left him—then paused. Jace was leaning against the cart, turning something over in his hands. From this distance Simon couldn't see what it was, and he couldn't get closer, either, because two teenage girls were blocking his way, standing in the middle of the aisle giggling and crowding up against each other to whisper the way girls did. They were obviously dressed to pass for twenty-one, in high heels and short skirts, push-up bras and no jackets to keep the chill away.

They smelled like lip gloss. Lip gloss and baby powder and blood.

He could hear them, of course, despite the whispering. They were talking about Jace, how hot he was, each daring the other to go up and talk to him. There was a great deal of discussion of his hair and also his abs, although how they could really see his abs though his T-shirt, Simon wasn't sure. *Blech*, he thought. *This is ridiculous.* He was about to say "Excuse me" when one of them, the taller and darker-haired of the two, broke away and sauntered over to Jace, wobbling a little on her platform heels. Jace looked up as she approached him, his eyes wary, and Simon had the sudden panicked thought that maybe Jace would mistake her for a vampire or some kind of succubus and whip out one of his seraph blades on the spot, and then they'd both be arrested.

He needn't have worried. Jace just arched an eyebrow. The girl said something to him breathlessly; he shrugged; she pressed something into his hand, and then dashed back to her friend. They wobbled out of the store, giggling together.

Simon went over to Jace and dropped the soup can into the cart. "So what was all that about?"

"I think," Jace said, "that she asked if she could touch my mango."

"She *said* that?"

Jace shrugged. "Yeah, then she gave me her number." He

showed Simon the piece of paper with an expression of bland indifference, then tossed it into the cart. "Can we go now?"

"You're not going to call her, are you?"

Jace looked at him as if he were insane.

"Forget I said that," said Simon. "This sort of thing happens to you all the time, doesn't it? Girls just coming up to you?"

"Only when I'm not glamoured."

"Yes, because when you are, girls can't see you, because you're *invisible*." Simon shook his head. "You're a public menace. You shouldn't be allowed out on your own."

"Jealousy is such an ugly emotion, Lewis." Jace grinned a crooked grin that normally would have made Simon want to hit him. Not this time, though. He had just realized what it was that Jace had been playing with, turning over and over in his fingers as if it were something precious or dangerous or both. It was Clary's phone.

"I'm still not sure that this is a good idea," said Luke.

Clary, her arms crossed over her chest to ward off the chill of the Silent City, looked sideways at him. "Maybe you should have said that *before* we got here."

"I'm fairly sure I did. Several times." Luke's voice echoed off the stone pillars that rose overhead, striped with bands of semiprecious stone—black onyx, green jade, rose carnelian, and blue lapis. Silvery witchlight burned in torches attached to the pillars, lighting the mausoleums that lined each wall to a bright white that was almost painful to look at.

Little had changed in the Silent City since the last time Clary had been here. It still felt alien and strange, though now the sweeping runes that stretched across the floors in carved whorls and etched patterns teased her mind with the edges of their meanings, instead of being totally incomprehensible. Maryse had left her and Luke here in this entry chamber the moment they had arrived, preferring to go and confer with the Silent Brothers herself. There was no guarantee they'd let the three of them in to see the bodies, she'd warned Clary. Nephilim dead were the province of the Bone City's guardians, and no one else had jurisdiction over them.

Not that there were many such guardians left. Valentine had killed nearly all of them while searching for the Mortal Sword, leaving alive only the few who had not been in the Silent City at the time. New members had been added to their order since then, but Clary doubted there were more than ten or fifteen Silent Brothers left in the world.

The harsh clack of Maryse's heels on the stone floor alerted them to her return before she actually appeared, a robed Silent Brother trailing in her wake. "Here you are," she said, as if Clary and Luke weren't exactly where she'd left them. "This is Brother Zachariah. Brother Zachariah, this is the girl I was telling you about."

The Silent Brother pushed his hood back very slightly from his face. Clary held back a start of surprise. He didn't look like Brother Jeremiah had, with his hollowed eyes and stitched mouth. Brother Zachariah's eyes were closed, his high cheekbones each marked with the scar of a single black rune. But his mouth wasn't stitched shut, and she didn't think his head was shaved, either. It was hard to tell, with the hood up, whether she was seeing shadows or dark hair.

She felt his voice touch her mind. *You truly believe you can do this thing, Valentine's daughter?*

She felt her cheeks flush. She hated being reminded of whose daughter she was.

"Surely you've heard of the other things she's done," said Luke. "Her rune of binding helped us end the Mortal War."

Brother Zachariah raised his hood to hide his face. *Come with me to the Ossuarium.*

Clary looked at Luke, hoping for a supportive nod, but he was staring straight ahead and fiddling with his glasses the way he did when he was anxious. With a sigh she set off after Maryse and Brother Zachariah. He moved as silently as fog, while Maryse's heels sounded like gunshots on the marble floors. Clary wondered if Isabelle's propensity for unsuitable footwear was genetic.

They followed a winding path through the pillars, passing the great square of the Speaking Stars, where the Silent Brothers had first told Clary about Magnus Bane. Beyond the square was an arched doorway, set with a pair of enormous iron doors. Into their surfaces had been burned runes that Clary recognized as runes of death and peace. Over the doors was written an inscription in Latin that made her wish she had her notes with her. She was woefully behind in Latin for a Shadowhunter; most of them spoke it like a second language.

Taceant Colloquia. Effugiat risus. Hic locus est ubi mors gaudet succurrere vitae.

"*Let conversation stop. Let laughter cease,*" Luke read aloud. "*Here is the place where the dead delight to teach the living.*"

Brother Zachariah laid a hand on the door. *The most recent of the murdered dead has been made ready for you. Are you prepared?*

Clary swallowed hard, wondering exactly what it was she had gotten herself into. "I'm ready."

The doors swung wide, and they filed through. Inside was a large, windowless room with walls of smooth white marble. They were featureless save for hooks on which hung silvery instruments of dissection: shining scalpels, things that looked like hammers, bone saws, and rib spreaders. And beside them on shelves were even more peculiar instruments: massive corkscrew-like tools, sheets of sandpapery material, and jars of multicolored liquid, including a greenish one labeled "Acid" that actually seemed to be steaming.

The center of the room featured a row of high marble tables. Most were bare. Three were occupied, and on two of those three, all Clary could see was a human shape concealed by a white sheet. On the third table lay a body, the sheet pulled down to just below the rib cage. Naked from the waist up, the body was clearly male, and just as clearly a Shadowhunter. The corpse-pale skin was inked all over with Marks. The dead man's eyes had been bound with white silk, as per Shadowhunter custom.

Clary swallowed back her rising nausea and moved to stand beside the corpse. Luke came with her, his hand protectively on her shoulder; Maryse stood opposite them, watching everything with her curious blue eyes, the same color as Alec's.

Clary drew her stele from her pocket. She could feel the chill of the marble through her shirt as she leaned over the dead man. This close, she could see details—that his hair had been reddish brown, and that his throat had been torn clean through in strips, as if by a massive claw.

Brother Zachariah reached out and removed the silk binding from the dead man's eyes. Beneath it, they were closed. *You may begin.*

Clary took a deep breath and set the tip of the stele to the skin of the dead Shadowhunter's arm. The rune she had visualized before, in the entryway of the Institute, came back to her as clearly as the letters of her own name. She began to draw.

The black Mark lines spiraled out from the tip of her stele, much as they always did—but her hand felt heavy, the stele itself dragging slightly, as if she were writing in mud rather than on skin. It was as if the implement were confused, skittering over the surface of the dead skin, seeking the living spirit of the Shadowhunter that was no longer there. Clary's stomach churned as she drew, and by the time she was done and had retracted her stele, she was sweating and nauseated.

For a long moment nothing happened. Then, with a terrible suddenness, the dead Shadowhunter's eyes flicked open. They were blue, the whites flecked red with blood.

Maryse let out a long gasp. It was clear she hadn't really believed the rune would work. "By the Angel."

A rattling breath came from the dead man, the sound of someone trying to breathe through a cut throat. The ragged skin of his neck fluttered like a fish's gills. His chest rose, and words came from his mouth.

"It hurts."

Luke swore, and glanced toward Zachariah, but the Silent Brother was impassive.

Maryse moved closer to the table, her eyes suddenly sharp, almost predatory. "Shadowhunter," she said. "Who are you? I demand your name."

The man's head thrashed from side to side. His hands rose and fell convulsively. *"The pain ... Make the pain stop."*

Clary's stele nearly dropped from her hand. This was much more awful than she had imagined. She looked toward

Luke, who was backing away from the table, his eyes wide with horror.

"Shadowhunter." Maryse's tone was imperious. "Who did this to you?"

"*Please...*"

Luke whirled around, his back to Clary. He seemed to be rummaging among the Silent Brother's tools. Clary stood frozen as Maryse's gray-gloved hand shot out, and closed on the corpse's shoulder, her fingers digging in. "In the name of the Angel, I command you to answer me!"

The Shadowhunter made a choking sound. "*Downworlder... vampire...*"

"Which vampire?" Maryse demanded.

"*Camille. The ancient one—*" The words choked off as a gout of black clotted blood poured from the dead mouth.

Maryse gasped and jerked her hand back. As she did so, Luke reappeared, carrying the jar of green acid liquid that Clary had noticed earlier. With a single gesture he yanked the lid off and sloshed the acid over the Mark on the corpse's arm, eradicating it. The corpse gave a single scream as the flesh sizzled—and then it collapsed back against the table, eyes blank and staring, whatever had animated it for that brief period clearly gone.

Luke set the empty jar of acid down on the table. "Maryse." His voice was reproachful. "This is not how we treat our dead."

"I will decide how we treat *our* dead, Downworlder." Maryse was pale, her cheeks spotted with red. "We have a name now. Camille. Perhaps we can prevent more deaths."

"There are worse things than death." Luke reached a hand out for Clary, not looking at her. "Come on, Clary. I think it's time for us to go."

* * *

"So you really can't think of anyone else who might want to kill you?" Jace asked, not for the first time. They'd gone over the list several times, and Simon was getting tired of being asked the same questions over and over. Not to mention that he suspected Jace was only partly paying attention. Having already eaten the soup Simon had bought—cold, out of the can, with a spoon, which Simon couldn't help thinking was disgusting—he was leaning against the window, the curtain pulled aside slightly so that he could see the traffic going by on Avenue B, and the brightly lit windows of the apartments across the street. Through them Simon could see people eating dinner, watching television, and sitting around a table talking. Ordinary things that ordinary people did. It made him feel oddly hollow.

"Unlike in your case," said Simon, "there aren't actually all that many people who dislike me."

Jace ignored this. "There's something you're not telling me."

Simon sighed. He hadn't wanted to say anything about Camille's offer, but in the face of someone trying to kill him, however ineffectually, maybe secrecy wasn't such a priority. He explained what had happened at his meeting with the vampire woman, while Jace watched him with an intent expression.

When he was done, Jace said, "Interesting, but she's not likely to be the one trying to kill you either. She knows about your Mark, for one thing. And I'm not sure she'd be keen to get caught breaking the Accords like that. When Downworlders are that old, they usually know how to stay out of trouble." He set his soup can down. "We could go out again," he suggested.

"See if they try to attack a third time. If we could just capture one of them, maybe we—"

"No," Simon said. "Why are you always trying to get yourself killed?"

"It's my job."

"It's a *hazard* of your job. At least for most Shadowhunters. For you it seems to be the purpose."

Jace shrugged. "My father always said—" He broke off, his face hardening. "Sorry. I meant Valentine. By the Angel. Every time I call him that, it feels like I'm betraying my real father."

Simon felt sympathetic toward Jace despite himself. "Look, you thought he was your father for what, sixteen years? That doesn't just go away in a day. And you never met the guy who was really your father. And he's dead. So you can't really betray him. Just think of yourself as someone who has two fathers for a while."

"You can't have two fathers."

"Sure you can," Simon said. "Who says you can't? We can buy you one of those books they have for little kids. *Timmy Has Two Dads*. Except I don't think they have one called *Timmy Has Two Dads and One of Them Was Evil*. That part you're just going to have to work through on your own."

Jace rolled his eyes. "It's fascinating," he said. "You know all these words, and they're all English, but when you string them together into sentences, they just don't make any sense." He tugged lightly on the window curtain. "I wouldn't expect you to understand."

"My father's dead," said Simon.

Jace turned to look at him. "What?"

"I figured you didn't know," said Simon. "I mean, it's not

like you were going to *ask*, or are particularly interested in anything about me. So, yeah. My father's dead. So we do have that in common." Suddenly exhausted, he leaned back against the futon. He felt sick and dizzy and tired—a deep tiredness that seemed to have sunk into his bones. Jace, on the other hand, seemed possessed of a restless energy that Simon found a little disturbing. It hadn't been easy watching him eat that tomato soup, either. It had looked too much like blood for his comfort.

Jace eyed him. "How long has it been since *you* . . . ate? You look pretty bad."

Simon sighed. He supposed he couldn't say anything, after pestering Jace to eat something. "Hang on," he said. "I'll be right back."

Peeling himself off the futon, he went into his bedroom and retrieved his last bottle of blood from under the bed. He tried not to look at it—separated blood was a sickening sight. He shook the bottle hard as he headed into the living room, where Jace was still staring out the window.

Leaning against the kitchen counter, Simon unscrewed the bottle of blood and took a swig. Normally he didn't like drinking the stuff in front of other people, but this was Jace, and he didn't care what Jace thought. Besides, it wasn't as if Jace hadn't seen him drink blood before. At least Kyle wasn't home. That would be a hard one to explain to his new roommate. Nobody liked a guy who kept blood in the fridge.

Two Jaces eyed him—one the real Jace, the other his reflection in the windowpane. "You can't just skip feeding, you know."

Simon shrugged. "I'm eating now."

"Yeah," Jace said, "but you're a vampire. Blood isn't like food for you. Blood is . . . blood."

"That's very illuminating." Simon flung himself into the armchair across from the TV; it had probably once been a pale gold velvet but was now worn to the grayish pile. "Do you have a lot of other profound thoughts like that? Blood is blood? A toaster is a toaster? A Gelatinous Cube is a Gelatinous Cube?"

Jace shrugged. "Fine. Ignore my advice. You'll be sorry later."

Before Simon could answer, he heard the sound of the front door opening. He looked daggers at Jace. "That's my roommate. Kyle. Be nice."

Jace smiled charmingly. "I'm always nice."

Simon had no chance to respond to this the way he would have liked, for a moment later Kyle bounded into the room, looking bright-eyed and energetic. "Man, I was all over town today," he said. "I almost got lost, but you know what they say. Bronx up, Battery down—" He looked at Jace, registering belatedly that there was someone else in the room. "Oh, hey. I didn't know you had a friend over." He held out a hand. "I'm Kyle."

Jace did not respond in kind. To Simon's surprise, Jace had gone rigid all over, his pale yellow eyes narrowing, his whole body displaying that Shadowhunter watchfulness that seemed to transform him from an ordinary teenage boy into something very much other than that.

"Interesting," he said. "You know, Simon never mentioned that his new roommate was a werewolf."

Clary and Luke drove most of the way back to Brooklyn in silence. Clary stared out the window as they went, watching

Chinatown slide past, and then the Williamsburg Bridge, lit up like a chain of diamonds against the night sky. In the distance, out over the black water of the river, she could see Renwick's, illuminated as it always was. It looked like a ruin again, empty black windows gaping like the eye holes in a skull. The voice of the dead Shadowhunter whispered in her mind:

The pain . . . Make the pain stop.

She shuddered and drew her jacket more tightly around her shoulders. Luke glanced at her briefly but said nothing. It wasn't until he had pulled up in front of his house and killed the engine of the truck that he turned to her and spoke.

"Clary," he said. "What you just did—"

"It was wrong," she said. "I know it was wrong. I was there too." She swiped at her face with the edge of her sleeve. "Go ahead and yell at me."

Luke stared through the windshield. "I'm not going to yell at you. You didn't know what was going to happen. Hell, I thought it might work too. I wouldn't have gone with you if I hadn't."

Clary knew this ought to have made her feel better, but it didn't. "If you hadn't thrown acid on the rune—"

"But I did."

"I didn't even know you could do that. Destroy a rune like that."

"If you disfigure it enough, you can minimize or destroy its power. Sometimes in battle the enemy will try to burn or slice off a Shadowhunter's skin, just to deprive them of the power of their runes." Luke sounded distracted.

Clary felt her lips tremble, and pressed them together, hard, to stop the shaking. Sometimes she forgot the more nightmarish aspects of being a Shadowhunter—*This life of scars and killing*, as Hodge had said to her once. "Well," she said, "I won't do it again."

"Won't do what again? Make that particular rune? I have no doubt you won't, but I'm not sure that addresses the problem." Luke drummed his fingers on the steering wheel. "You have an ability, Clary. A great ability. But you have absolutely no idea what it means. You're totally untrained. You know almost nothing about the history of runes, or what they have meant to Nephilim through the centuries. You can't tell a rune designed to do good from one designed to do harm."

"You were happy enough to let me use my power when it was the binding rune," she said angrily. "You didn't tell me not to create runes then."

"I'm not telling you not to use your power now. In fact, I think the problem is that you so rarely do use it. It's not as if you're using your power to change your nail polish color or make the subway come when you want it. You use it only in these occasional life-and-death moments."

"The runes only come to me in those moments."

"Maybe that's because you haven't yet been trained in how your power *works*. Think of Magnus; his power is a part of him. You seem to think of yours as separate from you. Something that happens to you. It's not. It's a tool you need to learn to use."

"Jace said Maryse wants to hire a rune expert to work with me, but it hasn't happened yet."

"Yes," said Luke, "I imagine Maryse has other things on her mind." He took the key out of the ignition and sat for a moment in silence. "Losing a child the way she lost Max," he said. "I can't imagine it. I should be more forgiving of her behavior. If something happened to you, I . . ."

His voice trailed off.

"I wish Robert would come back from Idris," said Clary. "I don't see why she has to deal with all this alone. It must be horrible."

"Many marriages break up when a child dies. The married couple can't stop blaming themselves, or each other. I imagine Robert is gone precisely because he needs space, or Maryse does."

"But they love each other," Clary said, appalled. "Isn't that what love means? That you're supposed to be there for the other person to turn to, no matter what?"

Luke looked toward the river, at the dark water moving slowly under the light of the autumn moon. "Sometimes, Clary," he said, "love just isn't enough."

7
PRAETOR LUPUS

The bottle slid out of Simon's hand and crashed to the floor, where it shattered, sending shards flying in all directions. "Kyle's a werewolf?"

"Of course he's a werewolf, you moron," said Jace. He looked at Kyle. "Aren't you?"

Kyle said nothing. The relaxed good humor had gone out of his expression. His hazel eyes were as hard and flat as glass. "Who's asking?"

Jace moved away from the window. There was nothing overtly hostile in his demeanor, and yet everything about him implied a clear threat. His hands were loose at his sides, but Simon remembered the way he had seen Jace, before, explode into action with almost nothing, it seemed, between thought and response. "Jace Lightwood," he said. "Of the Lightwood Institute. What pack are you sworn to?"

"Jesus," said Kyle. "You're a Shadowhunter?" He looked at Simon. "The cute redheaded girl who was with you in the garage—she's a Shadowhunter too, isn't she?"

Taken aback, Simon nodded.

"You know, some people think Shadowhunters are just myths. Like mummies and genies." Kyle grinned at Jace. "Can you grant wishes?"

The fact that Kyle had just called Clary cute did not seem to have endeared him to Jace, whose face had tightened alarmingly. "That depends," he said. "Do you wish to be punched in the face?"

"My, my," said Kyle. "And I thought you all were so gung ho for the Accords these days—"

"The Accords apply to vamps and lycanthropes with clear alliances," interrupted Jace. "Tell me what pack you're sworn to, or I'll have to assume you're rogue."

"All right, that's enough," Simon said. "Both of you, stop acting like you're about to hit each other." He looked at Kyle. "You should have told me you were a werewolf."

"I didn't notice you telling me you're a vampire. Maybe I thought it was none of your business."

Simon's whole body jerked with surprise. "What?" He glanced down at the shattered glass and blood on the floor. "I didn't—I don't—"

"Don't bother," Jace said quietly. "He can sense you're a vampire. Just like you'll be able to sense werewolves and other Downworlders when you've had a bit more practice. He's known what you are since he met you. Isn't that true?" He met

Kyle's icy hazel eyes with his own. Kyle said nothing. "And that stuff he's growing on the balcony, by the by? That's wolfsbane. Now you know."

Simon crossed his arms over his chest and glared at Kyle. "So what they hell is this? Some sort of setup? Why did you ask me to live with you? Werewolves hate vampires."

"I don't," said Kyle. "I'm not too fond of their kind, though." He jabbed a finger at Jace. "They think they're better than everyone else."

"No," said Jace. "I think *I'm* better than everyone else. An opinion that has been backed up with ample evidence."

Kyle looked at Simon. "Does he always talk like this?"

"Yes."

"Does anything shut him up? Other than getting the crap beaten out of him, of course."

Jace moved away from the window. "I would *love* for you to try."

Simon stepped between them. "I'm not going to let you fight with each other."

"And what are you going to do about it if . . . Oh." Jace's gaze trailed up to Simon's forehead, and he grinned reluctantly. "So basically you're threatening to turn me into something you can sprinkle on popcorn if I don't do what you say?"

Kyle looked baffled. "What are you—"

"I just think you two should talk," Simon interrupted. "So Kyle's a werewolf. I'm a vampire. And you're not exactly the boy next door either," he added to Jace. "I say we figure out what's going on and proceed from there."

"Your trusting idiocy knows no bounds," Jace said, but he sat down on the windowsill, crossing his arms. After a moment

Kyle sat down too, on the futon couch. They both glared at each other. *Still,* Simon thought. *Progress.*

"Fine," Kyle said. "I'm a werewolf. I'm not part of a pack, but I *do* have an alliance. Have you heard of the Praetor Lupus?"

"I've heard of lupus," said Simon. "Isn't it a kind of disease?"

Jace gave him a withering look. "'*Lupus*' means 'wolf,'" he explained. "And the praetorians were an elite Roman military force. So I guess the translation is 'Wolf Guardians.'" He shrugged. "I've run across mentions of them, but they're a pretty secretive organization."

"And the Shadowhunters aren't?" said Kyle.

"We have good reasons."

"So do we." Kyle leaned forward. The muscles in his arms flexed as he propped his elbows on his knees. "There are two kinds of werewolves," he explained. "The kind that are born werewolves, with werewolf parents, and the kind that get infected with lycanthropy through a bite." Simon looked at him in surprise. He wouldn't have thought Kyle, slacker-stoner bike messenger, would have known the word "lycanthropy," much less how to pronounce it. But this was a very different Kyle—focused, intent, and direct. "For those of us who are turned by a bite, those first few years are key. The demon strain that causes lycanthropy causes a whole raft of other changes—waves of uncontrollable aggression, inability to control rage, suicidal anger and despair. The pack can help with that, but a lot of the newly infected aren't lucky enough to fall in with a pack. They're on their own, trying to deal with all this overwhelming stuff, and a lot of them turn violent—against others or against themselves. There's a high suicide rate and a high rate of domestic violence." He looked at Simon. "The same goes for vampires, except it can be even worse. An orphaned fledgling has literally no idea what's happened to it. With no guidance, it doesn't know how to feed safely, or even to stay out of sunlight. That's where we come in."

"And do what?" Simon asked.

"We track down 'orphaned' Downworlders—vampires and werewolves who've just been Turned and don't know what they are yet. Sometimes even warlocks—some of them don't realize what they are for years. We intervene, try to get them into a pack or a clan, try to help them control their powers."

"Good Samaritans, aren't you." Jace's eyes glittered.

"We are, actually." Kyle sounded like he was trying to keep his voice neutral. "We intervene before the new Downworlder can get violent and hurt themselves or other people. I know what would have happened to me if it hadn't been for the Guard. I've done bad things. Really bad."

"How bad?" asked Jace. "Illegal bad?"

"Shut up, Jace," said Simon. "You're off duty, okay? Stop being a Shadowhunter for a second." He turned to Kyle. "So how did you end up auditioning for my crappy band, then?"

"I didn't realize you knew it was crappy."

"Just answer the question."

"We got a report of a new vampire—a Daylighter, living on his own, not with a clan. Your secret's not as secret as you think. Fledgling vampires without a clan to help them can be very dangerous. I got dispatched to keep an eye on you."

"So, what you're saying," said Simon, "is not just that you don't want me to move out now that I know you're a werewolf, but that you won't let me move out?"

"Right," said Kyle. "I mean, you can move out, but I'll come with you."

"That's not necessary," said Jace. "I can keep a perfectly good eye on Simon, thank you. He's *my* neophyte Downworlder to mock and boss around, not yours."

"Shut up!" Simon yelled. "Both of you. Neither of you were around when someone tried to kill me earlier today—"

"I was," said Jace. "You know, eventually."

Kyle's eyes shone, like a wolf's eyes at night. "Someone tried to kill you? What happened?"

Simon's gaze met Jace's across the room. A silent agreement not to mention the Mark of Cain passed between them. "Two days ago, and today, I was followed and attacked by some guys in gray tracksuits."

"Humans?"

"We're not sure."

"And you have no idea what they want with you?"

"They definitely want me dead," said Simon. "Beyond that, I don't really know, no."

"We have some leads," said Jace. "We'll be investigating."

Kyle shook his head. "Fine. Whatever it is you're not telling me, I'll find out eventually." He got to his feet. "And now, I'm beat. I'm going to sleep. I'll see you in the morning," he said to Simon. "You," he said to Jace, "well, I guess I'll see you around. You're the first Shadowhunter I've ever met."

"That's too bad," said Jace, "since all the ones you meet from now on will be a terrible letdown."

Kyle rolled his eyes and left, banging his bedroom door shut behind him.

Simon looked at Jace. "You're not going back to the Institute," he said, "are you?"

Jace shook his head. "You need protecting. Who knows when someone might try to kill you again?"

"This avoiding Clary thing of yours has truly taken an epic turn," Simon said, standing up. "Are you ever going home?"

Jace looked at him. "Are you?"

Simon stalked into the kitchen, retrieved a broom, and swept up the broken glass from the smashed bottle. It had been his last. He dumped the shards into the trash and walked past Jace into his own small bedroom, where he stripped off his jacket and shoes and flung himself down onto the mattress.

A moment later Jace came into the room. He looked around, his light eyebrows raised, his expression a mask of amusement. "Quite a space you've got here. Minimalist. I like it."

Simon rolled onto his side and stared at Jace in disbelief. "Please tell me you're not actually planning on staying in my *room*."

Jace perched on the windowsill and looked down at him. "You really don't get this bodyguard thing, do you?"

"I didn't even think you liked me all that much," said Simon. "Is this one of those keep-your-friends-close-and-your-enemies-closer things?"

"I thought it was keep your friends close so you have someone to drive the car when you sneak over to your enemy's house at night and throw up in his mailbox."

"I'm pretty sure that's not it. And this protecting me thing is less touching than creepy, just so you know. I'm *fine*. You've seen what happens if someone tries to hurt me."

"Yes, I have," said Jace. "But eventually the person who's

trying to kill you is going to figure out about the Mark of Cain. And then they're either going to give up or find some other way to come at you." He leaned against the window frame. "And that's why I'm here."

Despite his exasperation Simon could find no holes in this argument, or at least not one big enough to bother with. He rolled onto his stomach and buried his face in his arms. Within minutes he was asleep.

He was walking through the desert, over burning sands, past bones whitening in the sun. He had never been so thirsty. When he swallowed, his mouth felt as if it were coated with sand, his throat lined with knives.

The sharp buzzing of his cell phone woke Simon. He rolled over and clawed tiredly at his jacket. By the time he'd pried the cell phone loose from the pocket, it had stopped ringing.

He turned it over and looked to see who had called. It was Luke.

Crap. I bet my mom called Clary's house looking for me, he thought, sitting up. His brain was still fuzzy from sleep, and it took a moment for him to remember that when he had fallen asleep in this room, he hadn't been alone.

He looked quickly toward the window. Jace was still there, but he was clearly asleep—sitting up, his head leaning against the window glass. Pale blue dawn light filtered past him. He looked very young like that, Simon thought. No mockery in his expression, no defensiveness or sarcasm. It was almost possible to imagine what Clary saw in him.

It was pretty clear he wasn't taking his bodyguard duties all that seriously, but that had been obvious from the beginning.

Simon wondered, not for the first time, what the hell was going on between Clary and Jace.

The phone started buzzing again. Propelling himself to his feet, Simon padded out into the living room, pressing the talk button just before the call went to voice mail again. "Luke?"

"Sorry to wake you up, Simon." Luke was, as always, unfailingly polite.

"I was awake anyway," Simon lied.

"I need you to meet me in Washington Square Park in half an hour," said Luke. "At the fountain."

Now Simon was seriously alarmed. "Is everything okay? Is Clary all right?"

"She's fine. This isn't about her." There was a rumbling sound in the background. Simon guessed that Luke was starting up his truck. "Just meet me in the park. And don't bring anyone with you."

He clicked off.

The sound of Luke's truck pulling out of the driveway woke Clary out of uneasy dreams. She sat up, and winced. The chain around her neck had gotten caught in her hair while she slept, and she drew it off over her head, carefully pulling it free of the tangles.

She dropped the ring into her palm, the chain pooling around it. The little silver circlet, stamped with its pattern of stars, seemed to wink up at her mockingly. She remembered when Jace had given it to her, wrapped in the note he'd left behind when he'd gone off to hunt down Jonathan. *Despite everything, I can't bear the thought of this ring being lost forever, any more than I can bear the thought of leaving you forever.*

That had been almost two months ago. She had been sure that he loved her, so sure that the Queen of the Seelie Court had not been able to tempt her. How could there be anything else she wanted, when she had Jace?

But maybe you never really had someone, she thought now. Maybe, no matter how much you loved them, they could slip through your fingers like water, and there was nothing you could do about it. She understood why people talked about hearts "breaking"; she felt as if hers were made of cracked glass, and the shards were like tiny knives inside her chest when she breathed. *Imagine your life without him*, the Seelie Queen had said—

The phone rang, and for a moment Clary felt only relieved that something, anything, had cut through her misery. Her second thought was, *Jace*. Maybe he couldn't reach her on her cell phone and was calling her house. She dropped the ring on her bedside table and reached to lift the receiver out of its cradle. She was about to voice a greeting when she realized that the phone had already been picked up, by her mother.

"Hello?" Her mother sounded anxious, and surprisingly awake for so early in the morning.

The voice that answered was unfamiliar, faintly accented. "This is Catarina from Beth Israel hospital. I'm looking for Jocelyn."

Clary froze. The hospital? Had something happened, maybe to Luke? He had pulled out of the driveway awfully fast—

"This is Jocelyn." Her mother didn't sound frightened, but rather as if she'd expected the call. "Thank you for calling me back so soon."

"Of course. I was glad to hear from you. You don't often

see people recover from a curse like the one you were suffering from." Right, Clary thought. Her mother had been in Beth Israel, comatose from the effects of the potion she'd taken to prevent Valentine from interrogating her. "And any friend of Magnus Bane's is a friend of mine."

Jocelyn sounded strained. "Did my message make sense? You know what I was calling about?"

"You wanted to know about the child," said the woman on the other end of the line. Clary knew she ought to hang up, but she couldn't. What child? What was going on? "The one who was abandoned."

There was a catch in Jocelyn's voice. "Y-yes. I thought—"

"I'm sorry to say this, but he's dead. He died last night."

For a moment Jocelyn was silent. Clary could feel her mother's shock through the phone line. "Died? How?"

"I'm not sure I understand it myself. The priest came last night to baptize the child, and—"

"Oh, my God." Jocelyn's voice shook. "Can I— Could I please come down and look at the body?"

There was a long silence. Finally the nurse said, "I'm not sure about that. The body's in the morgue now, awaiting transfer to the medical examiner's office."

"Catarina, I think I know what happened to the boy." Jocelyn sounded breathless. "And if I could confirm it, maybe I could prevent it from happening again."

"Jocelyn—"

"I'm coming down," Clary's mother said, and hung up the phone. Clary gazed blankly at the receiver for a moment before hanging up herself. She scrambled to her feet, ran a brush through her hair, tossed on jeans and a sweater, and was out her bedroom door just in time to catch her mother in the living room, scribbling a note on the pad of paper by the telephone. She looked up as Clary came in, and gave a guilty start.

"I was just running out," she said. "A few last-minute wedding things have come up, and—"

"Don't bother lying to me," Clary said without preamble. "I was listening on the phone, and I know exactly where you're going."

Jocelyn paled. Slowly she set her pen down. "Clary—"

"You have to stop trying to protect me," Clary said. "I bet you didn't say anything to Luke, either, about calling the hospital."

Jocelyn pushed her hair back nervously. "It seems unfair on him. With the wedding coming up and everything—"

"Right. The wedding. You're having a wedding. And why is that? Because you're getting *married*. Don't you think it's time you started trusting Luke? And trusting me?"

"I do trust you," Jocelyn said softly.

"In that case you won't mind me coming with you to the hospital."

"Clary, I don't think—"

"I know what you think. You think this is just like what happened to Sebastian—I mean Jonathan. You think maybe someone's out there doing to babies what Valentine did to my brother."

Jocelyn's voice shook slightly. "Valentine's dead. But there are others who were in the Circle who have never been caught."

And they never found Jonathan's body. It wasn't something Clary liked to think about. Besides, Isabelle had been there and had always been adamant that Jace had severed

Jonathan's spine with the blade of a dagger and that Jonathan had been quite, quite dead as a result. She had gone down into the water and checked, she'd said. There had been no pulse, no heartbeat.

"Mom," Clary said. "He was *my brother*. I have a right to come with you."

Very slowly Jocelyn nodded. "You're right. I suppose you do." She reached for her purse where it hung on a peg by the door. "Well, come on, then, and get your coat. The weather forecast says it might rain."

Washington Square Park in the early morning was mostly deserted. The air was crisp and morning-clean, the leaves already thickly covering the pavement in sheets of red, gold, and dark green. Simon kicked them aside as he made his way under the stone archway at the south end of the park.

There were few other people around—a couple of homeless men sleeping on benches, wrapped in sleeping bags or threadbare blankets, and some guys in green sanitation uniforms emptying the trash cans. There was a guy pushing a cart through the park, selling doughnuts and coffee and pre-sliced bagels. And in the center of the park, by the big circular stone fountain, was Luke. He was wearing a green zip-up Windbreaker and waved when he saw Simon.

Simon waved back, a little tentatively. He still wasn't sure he wasn't in some kind of trouble. Luke's expression, as Simon drew closer, only intensified Simon's foreboding. Luke looked tired and more than a little stressed out. His gaze, as it fell on Simon, was full of concern.

"Simon," he said. "Thanks for coming."

"Sure." Simon wasn't cold, but he stuck his hands into the pockets of his jacket anyway, just to give them something to do. "What's wrong?"

"I didn't say anything was wrong."

"You wouldn't drag me out here at the crack of dawn if nothing was wrong," Simon pointed out. "If it isn't about Clary, then . . . ?"

"Yesterday, in the bridal shop," Luke said. "You asked me about someone. Camille."

A flock of birds rose, cawing, from the nearby trees. Simon remembered a rhyme his mother used to recite to him, about magpies. You were supposed to count them and say: *One for sorrow, two for mirth, three for a wedding, four for a birth; five for silver, six for gold, seven for a secret that's never been told.*

"Right," Simon said. He had already lost count of the number of birds there were. Seven, he guessed. A secret that's never been told. Whatever that was.

"You know about the Shadowhunters who have been found murdered around the city this past week or so," Luke said. "Don't you?"

Simon nodded slowly. He had a bad feeling about where this was going.

"It seems Camille may be responsible," said Luke. "I couldn't help but remember you had asked about her. Hearing her name twice, in a single day, after years of never hearing it at all—it seemed like quite a coincidence."

"Coincidences happen."

"On occasion," said Luke, "but they are rarely the most likely answer. Tonight Maryse will be summoning Raphael to interrogate him about Camille's role in these murders. If it comes out that you knew something about Camille—that you've had contact with her—I don't want you to be blind-sided, Simon."

"That makes two of us." Simon's head had started pounding again. Were vampires even supposed to get headaches? He couldn't remember the last time he'd had one, before the events of these past few days. "I met Camille," he said. "About four days ago. I thought I was being summoned by Raphael, but it turned out to be her. She offered to make me a deal. If I came to work for her, she'd make me the second most important vampire in the city."

"Why did she want you to work for her?" Luke's tone was neutral.

"She knows about my Mark," Simon said. "She said Raphael betrayed her and she could use me to get back control of the clan. I got the feeling she wasn't enormously fond of Raphael."

"That's very curious," said Luke. "The story as I've heard it is that Camille took an indefinite leave of absence from heading up the clan about a year ago and made Raphael her temporary successor. If she chose him to lead in her place, why would she move against him?"

Simon shrugged. "I don't know. I'm just telling you what she said."

"Why didn't you tell us about her, Simon?" Luke said very quietly.

"She told me not to." Simon realized how stupid this sounded. "I've never met a vampire like her before," he added. "Just Raphael, and the others at the Dumont. It's hard to explain what she was like. Everything she said, you wanted to believe. Everything she asked you to do, you wanted to do. I wanted to please her even though I knew she was just messing around with me."

The man with the coffee and doughnut cart was passing by again. Luke bought coffee and a bagel and sat down on the edge of the fountain. After a moment Simon joined him.

"The man who gave me Camille's name called her 'the ancient one,'" Luke said. "She is, I think, one of the very, very old vampires of this world. I imagine she would make most people feel fairly small."

"She made me feel like a bug," Simon said. "She did promise that if in five days I didn't want to work for her, she'd never bother me again. So I told her I'd think about it."

"And have you? Thought about it?"

"If she's killing Shadowhunters, I don't want anything to do with her," said Simon. "I can tell you that much."

"I'm sure Maryse will be relieved to hear it."

"Now you're just being sarcastic."

"I am not," said Luke, looking very serious. It was at moments like this that Simon could put aside his memories of Luke—Clary's sort-of stepfather, the guy who was always around, who was always willing to give you a ride home from school or lend you ten bucks for a book or a movie ticket—and remember that Luke led the biggest wolf pack in the city, that he was someone to whom, at crucial times, the whole Clave had listened. "You forget what you are, Simon. You forget the power you have."

"I wish I could forget it," Simon said bitterly. "I wish if I didn't use it, it would just go away."

Luke shook his head. "Power is a magnet. It draws those who desire it. Camille is one of them, but there will be others. We've been lucky, in a way, that it's taken this long." He looked at Simon. "Do you think that if she summons you again, you could get word to me, or to the Conclave, letting us know where to find her?"

"Yes," Simon said slowly. "She gave me a way to contact her. But it's not like she's just going to show up if I blow a magic whistle. Last time she wanted to talk to me, she had her minions surprise me and then bring me to her. So just having people hang around with me while I try to contact her isn't going to work. Otherwise you'll get her subjugates, but you won't get her."

"Hmm." Luke looked considering. "We'll have to think of something clever, then."

"Better think fast. She said she'd give me five days, so that means by tomorrow she's going to expect some kind of signal from me."

"I imagine she will," said Luke. "In fact, I'm counting on it."

Simon opened the front door of Kyle's apartment cautiously. "Hey there," he called, coming into the entryway and hanging up his jacket. "Is anyone home?"

No one answered, but from the living room Simon could hear the familiar *zap-bang-crash* sounds of a video game being played. He headed into the room, holding in front of him like a peace offering the white bag of bagels he'd picked up from Bagel Zone on Avenue A. "I brought breakfast. . . ."

His voice trailed off. He wasn't sure what he'd expected would happen when his self-appointed bodyguards realized he'd sneaked out of the apartment behind their backs. It had definitely involved some form of the phrase "Try that again, and I'll kill you." What it hadn't involved was Kyle and Jace sitting on the futon couch side by side, looking for all the world like newly minted best friends. Kyle had a video game controller in his hands, and Jace was leaning forward, his elbows on his knees, watching intently. They barely seemed to notice Simon's entrance.

"That guy over there in the corner is totally looking the other way," Jace observed, pointing at the TV screen. "A spinning wheel kick would put him out of commission."

"I can't kick people in this game. I can only shoot them. See?" Kyle mashed some buttons.

"That's stupid." Jace looked over and seemed to see Simon for the first time. "Back from your breakfast meeting, I see," he said without much welcome in his tone. "I bet you thought you were very clever, sneaking off like that."

"Medium clever," Simon acknowledged. "Like a cross between George Clooney in *Ocean's Eleven* and those *MythBusters* guys, but, you know, better-looking."

"I'm always so glad I have no idea what you're vacantly chattering about," said Jace. "It fills me with a sense of peace and well-being."

Kyle set his controller down, leaving the screen frozen on a close-up of an enormous needle-tipped gun. "I'll take a bagel."

Simon tossed him one, and Kyle headed into the kitchen, which was separated from the living room by a long counter, to toast and butter his breakfast. Jace looked at the white bag and waved a dismissive hand. "No, thanks."

Simon sat down on the coffee table. "You ought to eat something."

"Look who's talking."

"I'm out of blood right now," Simon said. "Unless you're offering."

"No, thanks. We've been down that road before, and I think we're better off as just friends." Jace's tone was as lightly sarcastic as ever, but this close up, Simon could see how pale he looked, and that his eyes were ringed with gray shadows. The bones of his face seemed to be sticking out more prominently than they had before.

"Really," Simon said, pushing the bag across the table toward Jace. "You should eat something. I'm not kidding."

Jace glanced down at the bag of food, and winced. The lids of his eyes were grayish blue with exhaustion. "The thought makes me sick, to be honest."

"You fell asleep last night," Simon said. "When you were supposed to be guarding me. I know this bodyguard thing is mostly a joke to you, but still. How long has it been since you slept?"

"As in, through the night?" Jace considered. "Two weeks. Maybe three."

Simon's mouth opened. "Why? I mean, what's going on?"

Jace offered the ghost of a smile. "'I could be bounded in a nut shell and count myself a king of infinite space, were it not that I have bad dreams.'"

"I actually know that one. *Hamlet*. So you're saying you can't sleep because you're having *nightmares*?"

"Vampire," said Jace, with a tired certainty, "you have no idea."

"Hey." Kyle came back around the counter and flung himself down in the nubby armchair. He took a bite out of his bagel. "What's going on?"

"I went to meet Luke," Simon said, and explained what had happened, seeing no reason to hide it. He left out any mention of Camille wanting him not just because he was a Daylighter, but also because of the Mark of Cain. Kyle nodded when he was done. "Luke Garroway. He's the head of the downtown pack. I've heard of him. He's kind of a big shot."

"His real name isn't Garroway," said Jace. "He used to be a Shadowhunter."

"Right. I heard that, too. And now he's been instrumental with all the new Accords stuff." Kyle glanced at Simon. "You know some important people."

"Important people are a lot of trouble," Simon said. "Camille, for instance."

"Once Luke tells Maryse what's going on, the Clave will take care of her," said Jace. "There are protocols for dealing with rogue Downworlders." At that, Kyle looked at him sideways, but Jace didn't seem to notice. "I already told you I don't think she's the one trying to kill you. She knows—" Jace broke off. "She knows better than that."

"And besides, she wants to use you," Kyle said.

"Good point," said Jace. "No one's going to off a valuable resource."

Simon looked from one of them to the other, and shook his head. "When did you two get so buddy-buddy? Last night it was all, 'I'm the most elite warrior!' 'No, *I'm* the most elite warrior!' And today you're playing Halo and giving each other props for good ideas."

"We realized we have something in common," said Jace. "You annoy us both."

"In that vein, I had a thought," Simon said. "I don't think either of you are going to like it, though."

Kyle raised his eyebrows. "Let's hear it."

"The problem with you guys watching me all the time," Simon said, "is that if you do, the guys trying to kill me won't try it again, and if they don't try it again, then we won't know who they are, and plus, you'll have to watch me all the time. And I assume you have other things you'd rather be doing. Well," he added in Jace's direction, "possibly *you* don't."

"So?" said Kyle. "What's your suggestion?"

"We lure them out. Get them to attack again. Try to capture one of them and find out who sent them."

"If I recall," said Jace, "I had this idea the other day, and you didn't like it much."

"I was tired," Simon said. "But now I've been thinking. And so far, in my experience with evildoers, they don't go away just because you ignore them. They keep on coming in different ways. So either I make these guys come to me, or I spend forever waiting for them to attack again."

"I'm in," Jace said, though Kyle still looked dubious. "So do you just want to go out and wander around until they show up again?"

"I thought I'd make it easy for them. Show up somewhere everyone knows I'm supposed to be."

"You mean . . . ?" said Kyle.

Simon pointed to the flyer taped to the fridge. MILLENNIUM LINT, OCTOBER 16, THE ALTO BAR, BROOKLYN. 9 P.M. "I mean the gig. Why not?" His headache was still there, full force; he pushed it back, trying not to think about how exhausted he was, or how he'd push himself through the gig. He had to get more blood somehow. Had to.

Jace's eyes were shining. "You know, that's actually a pretty good idea there, vampire."

"You want them to attack you *onstage*?" Kyle asked.

"It'll make for an exciting show," said Simon, with more bravado than he really felt. The idea of being attacked one more time was almost more than he could stand, even if he didn't fear for his personal safety. He wasn't sure he could bear to watch the Mark of Cain do its work again.

Jace shook his head. "They don't attack in public. They'll wait till after the show. And we'll be there to deal with them."

Kyle shook his head. "I don't know . . ."

They went a few more rounds, Jace and Simon on one side of the argument and Kyle on the other. Simon felt a little guilty. If Kyle knew about the Mark, he'd be a lot easier to persuade. Eventually he cracked under the pressure and reluctantly agreed to what he continued to insist was "a stupid plan."

"But," he said finally, getting to his feet and brushing bagel crumbs off his shirt, "I'm only doing this because I realize that you'll both just do it whether I agree or not. So I might as well be there." He looked at Simon. "Who would have thought protecting you from yourself would be so hard?"

"I could have told you that," Jace said, as Kyle threw a jacket on and headed to the door. He had to work, he'd explained to them. It appeared he really was a bike messenger; the Praetor Lupus, despite having a badass name, didn't pay that well. The door closed behind him, and Jace turned back to Simon. "So, the gig's at nine, right? What do we do with the rest of the day?"

"We?" Simon looked at him in disbelief. "Are you *ever* going home?"

"What, bored with my company already?"

"Let me ask you something," Simon said. "Do you find me fascinating to be around?"

"What was that?" Jace said. "Sorry, I think I fell asleep for a moment. Do, continue with whatever mesmerizing thing you were saying."

"Stop it," Simon said. "Stop being sarcastic for a second. You're not eating, you're not sleeping. You know who else isn't? Clary. I don't know what's going on with you and her, because frankly she hasn't said anything about it. I assume she doesn't want to talk about it either. But it's pretty obvious you're having a fight. And if you're going to break up with her—"

"Break up with her?" Jace stared at him. "Are you insane?"

"If you keep avoiding her," Simon said, "she's going to break up with *you.*"

Jace got to his feet. His easy relaxation was gone; he was all tension now, like a prowling cat. He went to the window and twitched the curtain back restlessly; the late-morning light came through the gap, bleaching the color in his eyes. "I have reasons for the things I do," he said finally.

"Great," Simon said. "Does Clary know them?"

Jace said nothing.

"All she does is love you and trust you," said Simon. "You owe her—"

"There are more important things than honesty," said Jace. "You think I like hurting her? You think I like knowing that I'm making her angry, maybe making her hate me? Why do you think I'm *here?*" He looked at Simon with a bleak sort of rage. "I can't be with her," he said. "And if I can't be with her, it doesn't really matter to me where I am. I might as well be with you, because at least if she knew I was trying to protect you, that might make her happy."

"So you're trying to make her happy despite the fact that the reason she's unhappy in the first place is you," said Simon, not very kindly. "That seems contradictory, doesn't it?"

"Love is a contradiction," said Jace, and turned back to the window.

8

WALK IN DARKNESS

Clary had forgotten how much she hated the smell of hospitals until they walked through the front doors of Beth Israel. Sterility, metal, old coffee, and not enough bleach to cover up the stench of sickness and misery. The memory of her mother's illness, of Jocelyn lying unconscious and unresponsive in her nest of tubes and wires, hit her like a slap in the face, and she sucked in a breath, trying not to taste the air.

"Are you all right?" Jocelyn pulled the hood of her coat down and looked at Clary, her green eyes anxious.

Clary nodded, hunching her shoulders into her jacket, and looked around. The lobby was all cold marble, metal, and plastic. There was a big information desk behind which several women, probably nurses, were milling; signs pointed the way to the ICU, Radiation, Surgical Oncology, Pediatrics, and so on. She could probably have found the cafeteria in her sleep; she'd brought Luke enough tepid cups of coffee from there to fill the Central Park reservoir.

"Excuse me." A slender nurse pushing an old man in a wheelchair went past them, nearly rolling the wheels over Clary's toes. Clary looked after her—there had been something—a shimmer—

"Don't stare, Clary," Jocelyn said under her breath. She put her arm around Clary's shoulders, turning them both so that they faced the doors that led to the waiting room for the lab where people got their blood taken. Clary could see herself and her mother reflected in the dark glass of the doors. Though she was still half a head shorter than her mother, they really *did* look alike, didn't they? In the past she'd always shrugged it off when people said that. Jocelyn was beautiful, and she wasn't. But the shape of their eyes and mouths were the same, as were their red hair and green eyes and slight hands. How had she gotten so little of Valentine's looks, Clary wondered, when her brother had gotten them all? He had had their father's fair hair and startling dark eyes. Though maybe, she thought, if she looked closely, she could see a little of Valentine in the stubborn set of her jaw. . . .

"Jocelyn." They both turned. The nurse who had been pushing the old man in the wheelchair was standing in front of them. She was slim, young-looking, dark-skinned, and dark-eyed—and then, as Clary looked at her, the glamour peeled away. She was still a slight, youthful-looking woman, but now her skin was dark blue, and her hair, twisted up into a knot at the back of her head, was snowy white. The blue of her skin contrasted shockingly with her pale pink scrubs.

"Clary," Jocelyn said. "This is Catarina Loss. She took care of me while I was here. She's also a friend of Magnus's."

"You're a warlock." The words came out of Clary's mouth before she could stop them.

"*Shhh.*" The warlock woman looked horrified. She glared at Jocelyn. "I don't remember you saying you were going to bring your daughter along. She's just a kid."

"Clarissa can behave herself." Jocelyn looked sternly at Clary. "Can't you?"

Clary nodded. She'd seen warlocks before, other than Magnus, at the battle in Idris. All warlocks had some feature that marked them out as not human, she'd learned, like Magnus's cat eyes. Some had wings or webbed toes or taloned fingers. But having entirely blue skin was something it would be hard to hide with contacts or oversize jackets. Catarina Loss must have had to glamour herself every day just to go outside—especially working in a mundane hospital.

The warlock jerked her thumb toward the elevators. "Come on. Come with me. Let's get this done fast."

Clary and Jocelyn hurried after her to the bank of elevators and into the first one whose doors opened. As the doors slid shut behind them with a hiss, Catarina pressed a button marked simply M. There was an indentation in the metal beside it that indicated that floor M could be reached only with an access key, but as she touched the button, a blue spark leaped from her finger and the button lit up. The elevator began to move downward.

Catarina was shaking her head. "If you weren't a friend of Magnus Bane's, Jocelyn Fairchild—"

"Fray," Jocelyn said. "I go by Jocelyn Fray now."

"No more Shadowhunter names for you?" Catarina smirked; her lips were startlingly red against her blue skin. "What about you, little girl? You going to be a Shadowhunter like your dad?"

Clary tried to hide her annoyance. "No," she said. "I'm going to be a Shadowhunter, but I'm not going to be like my father. And my name's Clarissa, but you can call me Clary."

The elevator came to a stop; the doors slid open. The warlock woman's blue eyes rested on Clary for a moment. "Oh, I know your name," she said. "Clarissa Morgenstern. Little girl who stopped a big war."

"I guess so." Clary walked out of the elevator after Catarina, her mother close behind. "Were you there? I don't remember seeing you."

"Catarina was here," said Jocelyn, a little breathless from hurrying to keep up. They were walking down an almost totally featureless hallway; there were no windows, and no doors along the corridor. The walls were painted a sickly pale green. "She helped Magnus use the Book of the White to wake me up. Then she stayed behind to watch over it while he returned to Idris."

"To watch over the book?"

"It's a very important book," said Catarina, her rubber-soled shoes slapping against the floor as she hurried ahead.

"I thought it was a very important war," Clary muttered under her breath.

They had finally reached a door. There was a square of frosted glass set in it, and the word "morgue" was painted on it in large black letters. Catarina turned with her hand on the knob, a look of amusement on her face, and gazed at Clary. "I learned early on in my life that I had a healing gift," she said. "It's the kind of magic I do. So I work here, for crap pay, at this hospital, and I do what I can to heal mundanes who would scream if they knew what I really looked like. I could make a fortune selling my skills to Shadowhunters and dumb mundanes who think they know what magic is, but I don't. I work here. So don't get all high-and-mighty on me, little redheaded girl. You're no better than me, just because you're famous."

Clary's cheeks flamed. She had never thought of herself as famous before. "You're right," she said. "I'm sorry."

The warlock's blue eyes flicked to Jocelyn, who looked white and tense. "You ready?"

Jocelyn nodded, and looked at Clary, who nodded as well. Catarina pushed the door open, and they followed her into the morgue.

The first thing that struck Clary was the chill. It was freezing inside the room, and she hastily zipped her jacket. The second was the smell, the harsh stench of cleaning products overlaying the sweetish odor of decay. Yellowish light flooded down from the fluorescent lights overhead. Two large, bare exam tables stood in the center of the room; there was a sink as well, and a metal stand with a scale on it for weighing organs. Along one wall was a bank of steel compartments, like safe-deposit boxes in a bank, but much bigger. Catarina crossed the room to one, took hold of the handle, and pulled it; it slid out on rollers. Inside, lying on a metal slab, was the body of an infant.

Jocelyn made a little noise in her throat. A moment later she had hurried to Catarina's side; Clary followed more slowly. She had seen dead bodies before—she had seen Max Lightwood's dead body, and she had known him. He had been only nine years old. But a baby—

Jocelyn put her hand over her mouth. Her eyes were very

large and dark, fixed on the body of the child. Clary looked down. At first glance the baby—a boy—looked normal. He had all ten fingers and all ten toes. But looking closer—looking the way she would look if she wanted to see past a glamour—she saw that the child's fingers were not fingers at all, but claws, curving inward, sharply pointed. The child's skin was gray, and its eyes, wide open and staring, were absolutely black—not just the irises, but the whites as well.

Jocelyn whispered, "That's how Jonathan's eyes were when he was born—like black tunnels. They changed later, to look more human, but I remember. . . ."

And with a shudder she turned and hurried from the room, the morgue door swinging shut behind her.

Clary glanced at Catarina, who looked impassive. "The doctors couldn't tell?" she asked. "I mean, his eyes—and those hands—"

Catarina shook her head. "They don't see what they don't want to see," she said, and shrugged. "There's some kind of magic at work here I haven't seen much of before. Demon magic. Bad stuff." She slipped something out of her pocket. It was a swatch of fabric, tucked into a plastic Ziploc bag. "This is a piece of what he was wrapped in when they brought him in. It stinks of demon magic too. Give it to your mother. Maybe she can show it to the Silent Brothers, see if they can get something from it. Find out who did this."

Numbly, Clary took it. As her hands closed over the bag, a rune rose up behind her eyes—a matrix of lines and swirls, the whisper of an image that was gone as soon as she slid the Baggie into the pocket of her coat.

Her heart was pounding, though. *This isn't going to the Silent Brothers*, she thought. *Not till I see what that rune does to it.*

"You'll talk to Magnus?" said Catarina. "Tell him I showed your mama what she wanted to see."

Clary nodded mechanically, like a doll. Suddenly all she wanted was to get out of there, out of the yellow-lit room, away from the smell of death and the tiny defiled body lying still on its slab. She thought of her mother, every year on Jonathan's birthday taking out that box and crying over the lock of his hair, crying over the son she should have had, replaced by a *thing* like this one. *I don't think this was what she wanted to see,* Clary thought. *I think this was what she was hoping was impossible.* But "Sure," was all she said. "I'll tell him."

The Alto Bar was your typical hipster dive, located partially under the Brooklyn-Queens Expressway overpass in Greenpoint. But it had an all-ages night every Saturday, and Eric was friends with the owner, so they let Simon's band play pretty much any Saturday they wanted, despite the fact that they kept changing their name and couldn't be counted on to draw a crowd.

Kyle and the other band members were already onstage, setting up their equipment and doing final checks. They were going to run through one of their old sets, with Kyle on vocals; he learned lyrics fast, and they were feeling pretty confident. Simon had agreed to stay backstage until the show started, which seemed to relieve some of Kyle's stress. Now Simon peered around the dusty velvet curtain at the back of the stage, trying to get a glimpse of who might be out there.

The interior of the bar had once been stylishly decorated, with pressed-tin walls and ceiling, reminiscent of an old speakeasy, and frosted art deco glass behind the bar. It was a lot grungier now than it had been when it opened, with permanent smoke stains on the walls. The floor was covered in sawdust that had formed into clumps as a result of beer spills and worse.

On the plus side, the tables that lined the walls were mostly full. Simon saw Isabelle sitting at a table by herself, dressed in a short silver mesh dress that looked like chain mail, and her demon-stomping boots. Her hair was pulled up into a messy bun, stuck through with silver chopsticks. Simon knew each of those chopsticks was razor sharp, able to slice through metal or bone. Her lipstick was bright red, like fresh blood.

Get a grip, Simon told himself. *Stop thinking about blood.*

More tables were taken up by other friends of the band. Blythe and Kate, the respective girlfriends of Kirk and Matt, were at a table together sharing a plate of pallid-looking nachos. Eric had various girlfriends scattered at tables around the room, and most of his friends from school were there too, making the place look a lot more full. Sitting off in the corner, at a table all by herself, was Maureen, Simon's one fan—a tiny waifish blond girl who looked about twelve but claimed she was sixteen. He figured she was probably actually about fourteen. Seeing him sticking his head around the curtain, she waved and smiled vigorously.

Simon pulled his head back in like a turtle, yanking the curtains closed.

"Hey," said Jace, who was sitting on an overturned speaker, looking at his cell phone, "do you want to see a photo of Alec and Magnus in Berlin?"

"Not really," said Simon.

"Magnus is wearing lederhosen."

"And yet, still no."

Jace shoved the phone into his pocket and looked at Simon quizzically. "Are you okay?"

"Yes," Simon said, but he wasn't. He felt light-headed and nauseated and tense, which he put down to the strain of worrying about what was going to happen tonight. And it didn't help that he hadn't fed; he was going to have to deal with that, and soon. He wished Clary were here, but he knew she couldn't come. She had some wedding responsibility to attend to, and had told him a long time ago that she wasn't going to be able to make it. He'd passed that on to Jace before they'd gotten here. Jace had seemed both miserably relieved and also disappointed, all at the same time, which was impressive.

"Hey, hey," Kyle said, ducking through the curtain. "We're just about ready to go." He looked at Simon closely. "You sure about this?"

Simon looked from Kyle to Jace. "Did you know you two match?"

They glanced down at themselves, and then at each other. Both were wearing jeans and long-sleeved black T-shirts. Jace tugged on his shirt hem with slight self-consciousness. "I borrowed this from Kyle. My other shirt was pretty filthy."

"Wow, you're wearing each other's clothes now. That's, like, best-friend stuff."

"Feeling left out?" said Kyle. "I suppose you want to borrow a black T-shirt too."

Simon did not state the obvious, which was that nothing that fit Kyle or Jace was likely to fit his skinny frame. "As long as everyone's wearing their own pants."

"I see I have come in on a fascinating moment in the con-versation." Eric poked his head through the curtain. "Come on. It's time to start."

As Kyle and Simon headed for the stage, Jace got to his feet. Just below the hem of his borrowed shirt, Simon could see the glittering edge of a dagger. "Break a leg up there," Jace said with a wicked grin. "And I'll be down here, hopefully breaking someone else's."

Raphael had been supposed to come at twilight, but he kept them waiting almost three hours past the appointed time before his Projection appeared in the Institute library.

Vampire politics, thought Luke dryly. The head of the New York vampire clan would come, if he must, when the Shadowhunters called; but he would not be summoned, and he would not be punctual. Luke had spent the past few hours whiling away the time by reading several of the library's books; Maryse hadn't been interested in talking and had spent most of the time standing by the window, drinking red wine out of a cut-crystal glass and staring at the traffic going by on York Avenue.

She turned as Raphael appeared, like a white chalk drawing on the darkness. First the pallor of his face and hands became visible, and then the darkness of his clothes and hair. Finally he stood, filled in, a solid-looking Projection. He looked at Maryse hurrying toward him and said, "You called, Shadowhunter?" He turned then, his gaze sweeping over Luke. "And the wolf-human is here too, I see. Have I been summoned to a sort of Council?"

"Not exactly." Maryse set her glass down on the desk-top. "You have heard about the recent deaths, Raphael? The Shadowhunter bodies that have been found?"

Raphael raised expressive eyebrows. "I have. I did not think to make note of it. It has nothing to do with my clan."

"One body found in warlock territory, one in wolf territory, one in faerie territory," said Luke. "I imagine your folk will be next. It seems a clear attempt to foment discord among Downworlders. I am here in good faith, to show you that I do not believe that you are responsible, Raphael."

"What a relief," Raphael said, but his eyes were dark and watchful. "Why would there be any suggestion that I was?"

"One of the dead was able to tell us who attacked him," said Maryse carefully. "Before he—died—he let us know that the person responsible was Camille."

"Camille." Raphael's voice was careful, but his expression, before he schooled it into blankness, showed fleeting shock. "But that is not possible."

"Why is it not possible, Raphael?" Luke asked. "She is the head of your clan. She is very powerful and famously quite ruthless. And she seems to have disappeared. She never came to Idris to fight with you in the war. She never agreed to the new Accords. No Shadowhunter has seen or heard tell of her in months—until now."

Raphael said nothing.

"There is something going on," Maryse said. "We wanted to give you the chance to explain it to us before we told the Clave of Camille's involvement. A show of good faith."

"Yes," said Raphael. "Yes, it is certainly a show."

"Raphael," said Luke, not unkindly. "You don't have to protect her. If you care for her—"

"Care for her?" Raphael turned aside and spat, though as he was a Projection, this was more for show than result.

"I hate her. I despise her. Every evening when I rise, I wish her dead."

"Oh," said Maryse delicately. "Then, perhaps—"

"She led us for years," said Raphael. "She was the clan head when I was made a vampire, and that was fifty years ago. Before that, she came to us from London. She was a stranger to the city but ruthless enough to rise to head the Manhattan clan in only a few short months. Last year I became her second in command. Then, some months ago, I discovered that she had been killing humans. Killing them for sport, and drinking their blood. Breaking the Law. It happens sometimes. Vampires go rogue and there is nothing that can be done to stop them. But for it to happen to the head of a clan—they are supposed to be better than that." He stood still, his dark eyes inward-looking, lost in his memories. "We are not like the wolves, those savages. We do not kill one leader to find another. For a vampire to raise a hand against another vampire is the worst of crimes, even if that vampire has broken the Law. And Camille has many allies, many followers. I could not risk ending her. Instead I went to her and told her she had to leave us, to get out, or I would go to the Clave. I didn't want to do that, of course, because I knew that if it were discovered, it would bring wrath down on the entire clan. We would be distrusted, investigated. We would be shamed and humiliated in front of other clans."

Maryse made an impatient noise. "There are more important things than loss of face."

"When you are a vampire, it can mean the difference between life and death." Raphael's voice dropped. "I gambled that she would believe I would do it, and she did. She agreed to go. I sent her away, but it left behind a conundrum. I could not take her place, for she had not abdicated it. I could not explain her departure without revealing what she had done. I had to pose it as a long absence, a need to travel. Wanderlust is not unheard of in our kind; it comes upon us now and then. When you can live forever, staying in one place can come to seem a dull prison after many, many years."

"And how long did you think you could keep up the charade?" Luke inquired.

"As long as I could," said Raphael. "Until now, it seems." He looked away from them, toward the window and the sparkling night outside.

Luke leaned back against one of the bookshelves. He was vaguely amused to notice that he seemed to be in the shape-shifter section, lined with volumes on the topics of werewolves, naga, kitsunes, and selkies. "You might be interested to know she has been telling much the same story about you," he said, neglecting to mention whom she had been telling it to.

"I thought she had left the city."

"Perhaps she did, but she has returned," said Maryse. "And she is no longer satisfied only with human blood, it seems."

"I do not know what I can tell you," said Raphael. "I was trying to protect my clan. If the Law must punish me, then I will accept punishment."

"We aren't interested in punishing you, Raphael," said Luke. "Not unless you refuse to cooperate."

Raphael turned back to them, his dark eyes burning. "Cooperate with what?"

"We would like to capture Camille. Alive," said Maryse. "We want to question her. We need to know why she has been killing Shadowhunters—and these Shadowhunters in particular."

"If you sincerely hope to accomplish this, I hope you have a very clever plan." There was a mixture of amusement and scorn in Raphael's voice. "Camille is cunning even for our kind, and we are very cunning indeed."

"I have a plan," said Luke. "It involves the Daylighter. Simon Lewis."

Raphael made a face. "I dislike him," he said. "I would rather not be a part of a plan that relies upon his involvement."

"Well," said Luke, "isn't that too bad for you."

Stupid, Clary thought. *Stupid not to bring an umbrella.* The faint drizzle that her mother had told her was coming that morning had turned into nearly full-blown rain by the time she reached the Alto Bar on Lorimer Street. She pushed past the knot of people smoking out on the sidewalk and ducked gratefully into the dry warmth of the bar inside.

Millennium Lint was already onstage, the guys whaling away on their instruments, and Kyle, at the front, growling sexily into a microphone. Clary felt a moment of satisfaction. It was largely down to her influence that they'd hired Kyle at all, and he was clearly doing them proud.

She glanced around the room, hoping to see either Maia or Isabelle. She knew it wouldn't be both of them, since Simon carefully invited them only to alternating gigs. Her gaze fell on a slender figure with black hair, and she moved toward that table, only to stop midway. It wasn't Isabelle at all, but a much older woman, her face made up with dark outlined eyes. She was wearing a power suit and reading a newspaper, apparently oblivious to the music.

"Clary! Over here!" Clary turned and saw the actual Isabelle, seated at a table close to the stage. She wore a dress that shone like a silver beacon; Clary navigated toward it and flung herself down in the seat opposite Izzy. "Got caught in the rain, I see," Isabelle observed.

Clary pushed her damp hair back from her face with a rueful smile. "You bet against Mother Nature, you lose."

Isabelle raised her dark eyebrows. "I thought you weren't coming tonight. Simon said you had some wedding blah-blah to deal with." Isabelle was not impressed with weddings or any of the trappings of romantic love, as far as Clary could tell.

"My mom wasn't feeling well," Clary said. "She decided to reschedule."

This was true, up to a point. When they'd come home from the hospital, Jocelyn had gone into her room and shut the door. Clary, feeling helpless and frustrated, had heard her crying softly through the door, but her mom had refused to let her in or to talk about it. Eventually Luke had come home, and Clary had gratefully left the care of her mother to him and headed out to kick around the city before going to see Simon's band. She always tried to come to his gigs if she could, and besides, talking to him would make her feel better.

"Huh." Isabelle didn't inquire further. Sometimes her almost total lack of interest in other people's problems was something of a relief. "Well, I'm sure Simon will be glad you came."

Clary glanced toward the stage. "How's the show been so far?"

"Fine." Isabelle chewed thoughtfully on her straw. "That new lead singer they have is hot. Is he single? I'd like to ride *him* around town like a bad, bad pony—"

"Isabelle!"

"What?" Isabelle glanced over at her and shrugged. "Oh, whatever. Simon and I aren't exclusive. I told you that."

Admittedly, Clary thought, Simon didn't have a leg to stand on in this particular situation. But he was still her friend. She was about to say something in his defense when she glanced toward the stage again—and something caught her eye. A familiar figure, emerging from the stage door. She would have recognized him anywhere, at any time, no matter how dark the room or how unexpected the sight of him.

Jace. He was dressed like a mundane: jeans, a tight black T-shirt that showed the movement of the slim muscles in his shoulders and back. His hair gleamed under the stage lights. Covert gazes watched him as he moved toward the wall and leaned against it, looking intently toward the front of the room. Clary felt her heart begin to pound. It felt like it had been forever since she'd last seen him, though she knew it had been only about a day. And yet, already, watching him seemed like watching someone distant, a stranger. What was he even doing here? He didn't like Simon! He'd never come to a single one of the band's performances before.

"Clary!" Isabelle sounded accusing. Clary turned to see that she'd accidentally upset Isabelle's glass, and water was dripping off the other girl's lovely silver dress.

Isabelle, grabbing a napkin, looked at her darkly. "Just talk to him," she said. "I know you want to."

"I'm sorry," Clary said.

Isabelle made a shooing gesture in her direction. "Go."

Clary got up, smoothing down her dress. If she'd known Jace was going to be here, she would have worn something other than red tights, boots, and a vintage hot-pink Betsey Johnson dress of hers she'd found hanging in Luke's spare closet. Once, she'd thought the flower-shaped green buttons that ran all the way up the front were funky and cool, but now she just felt less put-together and sophisticated than Isabelle.

She pushed her way across the floor, which was now crowded with people either dancing or standing in place, drinking beer, and swaying a little to the music. She couldn't help but remember the first time she'd ever seen Jace. It had been in a club, and she'd watched him across the floor, watched his bright hair and the arrogant set of his shoulders. She'd thought he was beautiful, but not in any way that applied to her. He wasn't the sort of boy you could have dated, she'd thought. He existed apart from that world.

He didn't notice her now until she was nearly standing in front of him. Up close, she could see how tired he looked, as if he hadn't slept in days. His face was tight with exhaustion, the bones sharp-looking under the skin. He was leaning against the wall, his fingers hooked in the loops of his belt, his pale gold eyes watchful.

"Jace," she said.

He started, and turned to look at her. For a moment his eyes lit, the way they always did when he saw her, and she felt a wild hope rise in her chest.

Almost instantly the light went out of them, and the remaining color drained out of his face. "I thought—Simon said you weren't coming."

A wave of nausea passed over her, and she put her hand out to steady herself against the wall. "So you only came because you thought I wouldn't be here?"

He shook his head. "I—"

"Were you ever planning on talking to me again?" Clary felt her voice rise, and forced it back down with a vicious effort. Her hands were now tight at her sides, her nails cutting hard into her palms. "If you're going to break it off, the least you could do is tell me, not just stop talking to me and leave me to figure it out on my own."

"Why," Jace said, "does everyone keep goddamn asking me if I'm going to break up with you? First Simon, and now—"

"You talked to *Simon* about us?" Clary shook her head. "Why? Why aren't you talking to me?"

"Because I can't talk to you," Jace said. "I can't talk to you, I can't be with you, I can't even look at you."

Clary sucked her breath in; it felt like breathing battery acid. "What?"

He seemed to realize what he had said, and lapsed into an appalled silence. For a moment they simply looked at each other. Then Clary turned and darted back through the crowd, pushing her way past flailing elbows and knots of chatting people, blind to everything but getting to the door as quickly as she could.

"And now," Eric yelled into his microphone, "we're going to sing a new song—one we just wrote. This one's for my girl-friend. We've been going out for three weeks, and, damn, our love is true. We're gonna be together forever, baby. This one's called 'Bang You Like a Drum.'"

There was laughter and applause from the audience as the music started up, though Simon wasn't sure if Eric realized they thought he was joking, which he wasn't. Eric was always in love with whatever girl he'd just started dating, and he always wrote an inappropriate song about it. Normally Simon wouldn't have cared, but he'd really hoped they were going to get off the stage after the previous song. He felt worse than ever—dizzy, sticky and sick with sweat, his mouth tasting metallic, like old blood.

The music crashed around him, sounding like nails being pounded into his eardrums. His fingers slipped and slid on the strings as he played, and he saw Kirk look over at him quizzically. He tried to force himself to focus, to concentrate, but it was like trying to start a car with a dead battery. There was an empty grinding noise in his head, but no spark.

He stared out into the bar, looking—he wasn't even quite sure why—for Isabelle, but he could see only a sea of white faces turned toward him, and he remembered his first night in the Dumont Hotel and the faces of the vampires turned toward him, like white paper flowers unfolding against a dark emptiness. A surge of gripping, painful nausea seized him. He staggered back, his hands falling away from the guitar. The ground under his feet felt as if it were moving. The other members of the band, caught up in the music, didn't seem to notice. Simon tore the strap of the guitar off his shoulder and pushed past Matt to the curtain at the back of the stage, ducking through it just in time to fall to his knees and retch.

Nothing came up. His stomach felt as hollow as a well. He stood up and leaned against the wall, pressing his icy hands against his face. It had been weeks since he'd felt either cold or hot, but now he felt feverish—and scared. What was happening to him?

He remembered Jace saying, *You're a vampire. Blood isn't like food for you. Blood is . . . blood.* Could all this be because he hadn't eaten? But he didn't feel hungry, or even thirsty, really. He felt as sick as if he were dying. Maybe he'd been poisoned. Maybe the Mark of Cain didn't protect against something like that?

He moved slowly toward the fire door that would take him out onto the street in back of the club. Maybe the cold air outside would clear his head. Maybe all this was just exhaustion and nerves.

"Simon?" A little voice, like a bird's chirp. He looked down with dread, and saw that Maureen was standing at his elbow. She looked even tinier close up—little birdlike bones and a lot of very pale blond hair, which cascaded down her shoulders from beneath a knitted pink cap. She wore rainbow-stripe arm warmers and a short-sleeved white T-shirt with a screen print of Strawberry Shortcake on it. Simon groaned inwardly.

"This really isn't a good time, Mo," he said.

"I just want to take a picture of you on my camera phone," she said, pushing her hair back behind her ears nervously. "So I can show it to my friends, okay?"

"Fine." His head was pounding. This was ridiculous. It wasn't like he was overwhelmed with fans. Maureen was literally the band's only fan, that he knew about, and was Eric's little cousin's friend, to boot. He supposed he couldn't really afford to alienate her. "Go ahead. Take it."

She raised her phone and clicked, then frowned. "Now one with you and me?" She sidled up to him quickly, pressing herself against his side. He could smell strawberry lip gloss on her, and under that, the smell of salt sweat and saltier human blood. She looked up at him, holding the phone up and out with her free hand, and grinned. She had a gap between her two front teeth, and a blue vein in her throat. It pulsed as she drew a breath.

"Smile," she said.

Twin jolts of pain went through Simon as his fangs slid free, digging into his lip. He heard Maureen gasp, and then her phone went flying as he caught hold of her and spun her toward him, and his canine teeth sank into her throat.

Blood exploded into his mouth, the taste of it like nothing else. It was as if he had been starving for air and now was breathing, inhaling great gasps of cold, clean oxygen, and Maureen struggled and pushed at him, but he barely noticed. He didn't even notice when she went limp, her dead weight dragging him to the floor so that he was lying on top of her, his hands gripping her shoulders, clenching and unclenching as he drank.

You have never fed on someone purely human, have you? Camille had said. *You will.*

And when you do, you will never forget it.

9

FROM FIRE UNTO FIRE

Clary reached the door and burst out into the rain-drenched evening air. It was coming down in sheets now, and she was instantly soaked. Choking on rainwater and tears, she darted past Eric's familiar-looking yellow van, rain sheeting off its roof into the gutter, and was about to race across the street against the light when a hand caught her arm and spun her around.

It was Jace. He was as soaked as she was, the rain sticking his fair hair to his head and plastering his shirt to his body like black paint. "Clary, didn't you hear me calling you?"

"Let go of me." Her voice shook.

"No. Not until you talk to me." He looked around, up and down the street, which was deserted, the rain exploding off the black pavement like fast-blooming flowers. "Come on."

Still holding her by the arm, he half-dragged her around the van and into a narrow alley that bordered the Alto Bar. High windows above them let through the blurred sound of the music that was still being played inside. The alley was brick-walled, clearly a dumping ground for old bits of no longer usable musical equipment. Broken amps and old mikes littered the ground, along with shattered beer glasses and cigarette butts.

Clary jerked her arm out of Jace's grasp and turned to face him. "If you're planning to apologize, don't bother." She pushed her wet, heavy hair back from her face. "I don't want to hear it."

"I was going to tell you that I was trying to help out Simon," he said, rainwater running off his eyelashes and down his cheeks like tears. "I've been at his place for the past—"

"And you couldn't tell me? Couldn't text me a single line letting me know where you were? Oh, wait. You couldn't, because you still have my *goddamned phone*. Give it to me."

Silently he reached into his jeans pocket and handed it to her. It looked undamaged. She jammed it into her messenger bag before the rain could ruin it. Jace watched her as she did it, looking as if she'd hit him in the face. It only made her angrier. What right did he have to be hurt?

"I think," he said slowly, "that I thought that the closest thing to being with you was being with Simon. Watching out for him. I had some stupid idea that you'd realize I was doing it for you and forgive me—"

All of Clary's rage rose to the surface, a hot, unstoppable tide. "I don't even know what you think I'm supposed to forgive you *for*," she shouted. "Am I supposed to forgive you for not loving me anymore? Because if that's what you want, Jace Lightwood, you can go right ahead and—" She took a step back, blindly, and nearly tripped over an abandoned speaker. Her bag slid to the ground as she put her hand out to right herself, but Jace was already there. He moved forward to catch her, and kept moving, until her back hit the alley wall, and his arms were around her, and he was kissing her frantically.

She knew she ought to push him away; her mind told her it was the sensible thing to do, but no other part of her cared about what was sensible. Not when Jace was kissing her like he thought he might go to hell for doing it, but it would be worth it.

She dug her fingers into his shoulders, into the damp fabric of his T-shirt, feeling the resistance of the muscles underneath, and kissed him back with all the desperation of the past few days, all the not knowing where he was or what he was thinking, all the feeling like a part of her heart had been ripped out of her chest and she could never get enough air. "Tell me," she said between kisses, their wet faces sliding against each other. "Tell me what's wrong— Oh," she gasped as he drew away from her, only far enough to reach his hands down and put them around her waist. He lifted her up so she stood on top of a broken speaker, making them almost the same height. Then he put his hands on either side of her head and leaned forward, so their bodies almost touched—but not quite. It was nerve-wracking. She could feel the feverish heat that came off him; her hands were still on his shoulders, but it wasn't enough. She wanted him wrapped around her, holding her tight. "W-why," she breathed, "can't you talk to me? Why can't you look at me?"

He ducked his head down to look into her face. His eyes, surrounding by lashes darkened with rainwater, were impossibly gold.

"Because I love you."

She couldn't stand it anymore. She took her hands off his shoulders, hooked her fingers through his belt loops, and pulled him against her. He let her do it with no resistance, his hands flattening against the wall, folding his body against hers until they were pressed together everywhere—chests, hips, legs—like puzzle pieces. His hands slid down to her waist and he kissed her, long and lingering, making her shudder.

She pulled away. "That doesn't make any sense."

"Neither does this," he said, "but I don't care. I'm sick of trying to pretend I can live without you. Don't you understand that? Can't you see it's killing me?"

She stared at him. She could see he meant what he said, could see it in the eyes she knew as well as her own, in the bruised shadows under those eyes, the pulse pounding in his throat. Her desire for answers battled the more primal part of her brain, and lost. "Kiss me then," she whispered, and he pressed his mouth against hers, their hearts slamming together through the thin layers of wet fabric that divided them. And she was drowning in it, in the sensation of him kissing her; of rain everywhere, running off her eyelashes; of letting his hands slide freely over the wet, crumpled fabric of her dress, made thin and clinging by the rain. It was almost like having his hands on her bare skin, her chest, her hips, her stomach; when he reached the hem of her dress, he gripped her legs, pressing her harder back against the wall while she wrapped them around his waist.

He made a noise of surprise, low in his throat, and dug his fingers into the thin fabric of her tights. Not unexpectedly, they ripped, and his wet fingers were suddenly on the bare skin of her legs. Not to be outdone, she slid her hands under the hem of his soaked shirt, and let her fingers explore what was underneath: the tight, hot skin over his ribs, the ridges of his abdomen, the scars on his back, the angle of his hipbones above the waistband of his jeans. This was uncharted territory for her, but it seemed to be driving him crazy: he was moaning softly against her mouth, kissing her harder and harder, as if it would never be enough, not quite enough—

And a horrific clanging noise exploded in Clary's ears, shattering her out of her dream of kissing and rain. With a gasp she pushed Jace away, hard enough that he let go of her and she tumbled off the speaker to land unsteadily on her feet, hastily straightening her dress. Her heart was slamming against her rib cage like a battering ram, and she felt dizzy.

"Dammit." Isabelle, standing in the mouth of the alley, her wet black hair like a cloak around her shoulders, kicked a trash can out of her way and glowered. "Oh, for goodness' sake," she said. "I can't believe you two. Why? What's wrong with bedrooms? And privacy?"

Clary looked at Jace. He was utterly drenched, water running off him in sheets, his fair hair, plastered to his head, nearly silver in the faint glow of the distant streetlights. Just looking at him made Clary want to touch him again, Isabelle or no Isabelle, with a longing that was nearly painful. He was staring at Izzy with the look of someone who had been slapped out of a dream—bewilderment, anger, dawning realization.

"I was just looking for Simon," Isabelle said defensively, seeing Jace's expression. "He ran offstage, and I've no idea where he went." The music had stopped, Clary realized, at some point; she hadn't noticed when. "Anyway, he's obviously not here. Go back to what you were doing. What's the point in wasting a perfectly good brick wall when you have someone to throw against it, that's what I always say." And she stalked off, back toward the bar.

Clary looked at Jace. At any other time they would have laughed together at Isabelle's moodiness, but there was no humor in his expression, and she knew immediately that whatever they had had between them—whatever had blossomed out of his momentary lack of control—it was gone now. She could taste blood in her mouth and wasn't sure if she had bitten her own lip or he had.

"Jace—" She took a step toward him.

"Don't," he said, his voice very rough. "I can't."

And then he was gone, running as fast as only he could run, a blur that vanished into the distance before she could even take a breath to call him back.

"Simon!"

The angry voice exploded in Simon's ears. He would have released Maureen then—or so he told himself—but he didn't get the chance. Strong hands grabbed him by the arms, hauling him off her. He was dragged to his feet by a white-faced Kyle, still tousled and sweaty from the set they'd just finished. "What the hell, Simon. What the hell—"

"I didn't mean to," Simon gasped. His voice sounded blurry to his own ears; his fangs were still out, and he hadn't learned to talk around the goddamn things yet. Past Kyle, on the floor, he could see Maureen lying in a crumpled heap, horribly still. "It just happened—"

"I told you. I *told* you." Kyle's voice rose, and he pushed Simon, hard. Simon stumbled back, his forehead burning, as an invisible hand seemed to lift Kyle and fling him hard against the wall behind him. He hit it and slid to the ground, landing in a wolflike crouch, on his hands and knees. He staggered to his feet, staring. "Jesus Christ. Simon—"

But Simon had dropped to his knees beside Maureen, his hands on her, frantically feeling at her throat for a pulse. When it fluttered under his fingertips, faint but steady, he nearly wept with relief.

"Get away from her." Kyle, sounding strained, moved to stand over Simon. "Just get up and move away."

Simon got up reluctantly and faced Kyle over Maureen's limp form. Light was lancing through the gap in the curtains that led to the stage; he could hear the other band members out there, chattering to one another, starting the teardown. Any minute they'd be coming back here.

"What you just did," Kyle said. "Did you—push me? Because I didn't see you move."

"I didn't mean to," Simon said again, wretchedly. It seemed to be all he said these days.

Kyle shook his head, his hair flying. "Get out of here. Go wait by the van. I'll deal with her." He bent down and lifted Maureen in his arms. She looked tiny against the bulk of him, like a doll. He fixed Simon with a glare. "Go. And I hope you feel really goddamn terrible."

Simon went. He moved to the fire door and shoved it open. No alarm went off; the alarm had been busted for months. The door swung shut behind him, and he leaned up against the back wall of the club as every part of his body began to tremble.

The club backed onto a narrow street lined with warehouses. Across the way was a vacant lot blocked off with a sagging chain-link fence. Ugly scrub grass grew up through the cracks in the pavement. Rain was sheeting down, soaking the garbage that littered the street, floating old beer cans on the runoff-filled gutters.

Simon thought it was the most beautiful thing he'd ever seen. The whole night seemed to have exploded with prismatic light. The fence was a linked chain of brilliant silver wires, each raindrop a platinum tear.

I hope you feel really goddamn terrible, Kyle had said. But this was much worse. He felt fantastic, alive in a way he never had before. Human blood was clearly somehow the perfect, the ideal food for vampires. Waves of energy were running through him like electric current. The pain in his head, his stomach, was gone. He could have run ten thousand miles.

It was awful.

"Hey, you. Are you all right?" The voice that spoke was cultured, amused; Simon turned and saw a woman in a long black trench coat, a bright yellow umbrella open over her head. With his brand-new prismatic vision, it looked like a glimmering sunflower. The woman herself was beautiful—though everything looked beautiful to him right now—with gleaming black hair and a red-lipsticked mouth. He dimly recalled seeing her sitting at one of the tables during the band's performance.

He nodded, not trusting himself to speak. He must have looked pretty shell-shocked, if total strangers were coming up to inquire about his well-being.

"You look like maybe you got banged on the head there," she said, indicating his forehead. "That's a nasty bruise. Are you sure I can't call anyone for you?"

He reached up hastily to move his hair across his forehead, hiding the Mark. "I'm fine. It's nothing."

"Okay. If you say so." She sounded a little doubtful. She reached into her pocket, pulled out a card, and handed it to him. It had a name on it, Satrina Kendall. Underneath the name was a title,

BAND PROMOTER, in small capitals, and a phone number and address. "That's me," she said. "I liked what you guys did in there. If you're interested in making it a little more big-time, give me a call."

And with that, she turned and sashayed away, leaving Simon staring after her. Surely, he thought, there was no way this night could get any more bizarre.

Shaking his head—a move that sent water drops flying in all directions—he squelched around the corner to where the van was parked. The door of the bar was open, and people were streaming out. Everything still looked unnaturally bright, Simon thought, but his prismatic vision was beginning to fade slightly. The scene in front of him looked ordinary—the bar emptying out, the side doors open, and the van with its back doors open, already being loaded up with gear by Matt, Kirk, and a variety of their friends. As Simon drew closer, he saw that Isabelle was leaning against the side of the van, one leg drawn up, the heel of her boot braced against the van's blistered side. She could have been helping with the teardown, of course—Isabelle was stronger than anyone else in the band, with the possible exception of Kyle—but she clearly couldn't be bothered. Simon would hardly have expected anything else.

She looked up as he came closer. The rain had slowed, but she had clearly been out in it for some time; her hair was a heavy, wet curtain down her back. "Hey there," she said, pushing off from the side of the van and coming toward him. "Where have you been? You just ran offstage—"

"Yeah," he said. "I wasn't feeling well. Sorry."

"As long as you're better now." She wrapped her arms around him and smiled up into his face. He felt a wave of relief that he didn't feel any urge to bite her. Then another wave of guilt as he remembered why.

"You haven't seen Jace anywhere, have you?" he asked.

She rolled her eyes. "I ran across him and Clary making out," she said. "Although they're gone now—home, I hope. Those two epitomize 'get a room.'"

"I didn't think Clary was coming," Simon said, though it wasn't that odd; he supposed the cake appointment had been canceled or something. He didn't even have the energy to be annoyed about what a terrible bodyguard Jace had turned out to be. It wasn't as if he'd ever thought Jace took his personal safety all that seriously. He just hoped Jace and Clary had worked it out, whatever it was.

"Whatever." Isabelle grinned. "Since it's just us, do you want to go somewhere and—"

A voice—a very familiar voice—spoke out of the shadows just beyond the reach of the nearest streetlight. "Simon?"

Oh, no, not now. Not right now.

He turned slowly. Isabelle's arm was still loosely clasped around his waist, though he knew that wouldn't last much longer. Not if the person speaking was who he thought it was.

It was.

Maia had moved into the light, and was standing looking at him, an expression of disbelief on her face. Her normally curly hair was pasted to her head with rain, her amber eyes very wide, her jeans and denim jacket soaked. She was clutching a rolled-up piece of paper in her left hand.

Simon was vaguely aware that off to the side the band members had slowed down their movements and were openly gawking. Isabelle's arm slid off his waist. "Simon?" she said. "What's going on?"

"You told me you were going to be busy," Maia said, looking

at Simon. "Then someone shoved this under the station door this morning." She thrust the rolled-up paper forward; it was instantly recognizable as one of the flyers for the band's performance tonight.

Isabelle was looking from Simon to Maia, recognition slowly dawning on her face. "Wait a second," she said. "Are you two *dating*?"

Maia set her chin. "Are you?"

"Yes," Isabelle said. "For quite a few weeks now."

Maia's eyes narrowed. "Us, too. We've been dating since September."

"I can't believe it," Isabelle said. She genuinely looked as if she couldn't. "Simon?" She turned to him, her hands on her hips. "Do you have an explanation?"

The band, who had finally shoved all the equipment into the van—the drums packing out the back bench seat and the guitars and basses in the cargo section—were hanging out the back of the car, openly staring. Eric put his hands around his mouth to make a megaphone. "Ladies, ladies," he intoned. "There is no need to fight. There is enough Simon to go around."

Isabelle whipped around and shot a glare at Eric so terrifying that he fell instantly silent. The back doors of the van slammed shut, and it took off down the road. *Traitors*, Simon thought, though to be fair, they probably assumed he would catch a ride home in Kyle's car, which was parked around the corner. Assuming he lived long enough.

"I can't believe you, Simon," Maia said. She was standing with her hands on her hips as well, in a pose identical to Isabelle's. "What were you thinking? How could you lie like that?"

"I didn't lie," Simon protested. "We never said we were

exclusive!" He turned to Isabelle. "Neither did we! And I know you were dating other people—"

"Not people you *know*," Isabelle said, blisteringly. "Not your *friends*. How would you feel if you found out I was dating Eric?"

"Stunned, frankly," said Simon. "He really isn't your type."

"That's not the point, Simon." Maia had moved closer to Isabelle, and the two of them faced him down together, an immovable wall of female rage. The bar had finished emptying out, and aside from the three of them, the street was deserted. He wondered about his chances if he made a break for it, and decided they weren't good. Werewolves were fast, and Isabelle was a trained vampire hunter.

"I'm really sorry," Simon said. The buzz from the blood he'd drunk was beginning to wear off, thankfully. He felt less dizzy with overwhelming sensation, but more panicked. To make things worse, his mind kept returning to Maureen, and what he'd done to her, and whether she was all right. *Please let her be all right.* "I should have told you guys. It's just—I really like you both, and I didn't want to hurt either of your feelings."

The moment it was out of his mouth, he realized how stupid he sounded. Just another jerkish guy making excuses for his jerk behavior. Simon had never thought of himself like that. He was a nice guy, the kind of guy who got overlooked, passed up for the sexy bad boy or the tortured artist type. For the self-involved kind of guy who would think nothing of dating two girls at once while maybe not exactly *lying* about what he was doing, but not telling the truth about it either.

"Wow," he said, mostly to himself. "I am a *huge* asshole."

"That's probably the first true thing you've said since I got here," said Maia.

"Amen," said Isabelle. "Though if you ask me, it's too little, too late—"

The side door of the bar opened, and someone came out. It was Kyle. Simon felt a wave of relief. Kyle looked serious, but not as serious as Simon thought he would look if something awful had happened to Maureen.

He started down the steps toward them. The rain was barely a drizzle now. Maia and Isabelle had their backs to him; they were glaring at Simon with the laser focus of rage. "I hope you don't expect *either* of us to speak to you again," Isabelle said. "And I'm going to have a talk with Clary—a very, very serious talk about her choice of friends."

"Kyle," Simon said, unable to keep the relief out of his voice as Kyle came into earshot. "Uh, Maureen—is she—"

He had no idea how to ask what he wanted to ask without letting Maia and Isabelle know what had happened, but as it turned out, it didn't matter, because he never managed to get the rest of the words out. Maia and Isabelle turned; Isabelle looked annoyed and Maia surprised, clearly wondering who Kyle was.

As soon as Maia really saw Kyle, her face changed; her eyes went wide, the blood draining from her face. And Kyle, in his turn, was staring at her with the look of someone who has woken up from a nightmare only to discover that it is real and continuing. His mouth moved, shaping words, but no sound came out.

"Whoa," Isabelle said, looking from one of them to the other. "Do you two—know each other?"

Maia's lips parted. She was still staring at Kyle. Simon had time only to think that she had never looked at him with anything like that intensity, when she whispered *"Jordan"*—and lunged for Kyle, her claws out and sharp, and sank them into his throat.

Part Two
For Every Life

———✦———

Nothing is free. Everything has to be paid for.
For every profit in one thing, payment in some other thing.
For every life, a death. Even your music, of which we have
heard so much, that had to be paid for. Your wife was the
payment for your music. Hell is now satisfied.
—Ted Hughes, "The Tiger's Bones"

10

232 RIVERSIDE DRIVE

Simon sat in the armchair in Kyle's living room and stared at the frozen image on the TV screen in the corner of the room. It had been paused on the game Kyle had been playing with Jace, and the image was one of a dank-looking underground tunnel with a heap of collapsed bodies on the ground and some very realistic-looking pools of blood. It was disturbing, but Simon didn't have either the energy or the inclination to bother to turn it off. The images that had been running through his head all night were worse.

The light streaming into the room through the windows had strengthened from watery dawn light to the pale illumination of early morning, but Simon barely noticed. He kept seeing Maureen's limp body on the ground, her blond hair stained with blood. His own staggering progress out into the night, her blood singing through his veins. And then Maia lunging at Kyle, tearing into him with her claws. Kyle had lain there, not lifting a hand to defend himself. He probably would have let her kill him if Isabelle hadn't interfered, pulling Maia bodily off him and rolling her onto the pavement, holding her there until her rage dissolved into tears. Simon had tried to go to her, but Isabelle had held him off with a furious glare, her arm around the other girl, her hand up to ward him off.

"Get *out* of here," she'd said. "And take him with you. I don't know what he did to her, but it must have been pretty bad."

And it was. Simon knew that name, Jordan. It had come up before, when he'd asked her how she'd been turned into a werewolf. Her ex-boyfriend had done it, she'd said. He'd done it with a savage and vicious attack, and he'd run off afterward, leaving her to deal with the aftermath alone.

His name had been Jordan.

That was why Kyle had only one name next to his door buzzer. Because it was his *last* name. His full name must have been Jordan Kyle, Simon realized. He'd been stupid, unbelievably stupid, not to have figured it out before. Not that he needed another reason to hate himself right now.

Kyle—or rather, Jordan—was a werewolf; he healed fast. By the time Simon had hauled him, none too gently, to his feet and had led him back over to his car, the deep slashes in his throat and under the torn rags of his shirt had healed to crusted-over scars. Simon had taken his keys from him and driven them back to Manhattan mostly in silence, Jordan sitting almost motionless in the passenger seat, staring down at his bloody hands.

"Maureen's fine," he'd said finally as they drove over the Williamsburg Bridge. "It looked worse than it was. You're not that good at feeding off humans yet, so she hadn't lost too much blood. I put her in a cab. She doesn't remember anything. She thinks she fainted in front of you, and she's really embarrassed."

Simon knew he ought to thank Jordan, but he couldn't bring himself to do it. "You're Jordan," he said. "Maia's old boyfriend. The one who turned her into a werewolf."

They were on Kenmare now; Simon turned north, heading up the Bowery with its flophouses and lighting stores. "Yeah," Jordan said at last. "Kyle's my last name. I started to go by it when I joined the Praetor."

"She would've killed you if Isabelle had let her."

"She has a perfect right to kill me if she wants to," said Jordan, and fell silent. He didn't say anything else as Simon found parking and they trudged up the stairs to the apartment. He'd gone into his room without even taking off his bloody jacket, and slammed the door.

Simon had packed his things into his backpack and had been about to leave the apartment when he'd hesitated. He wasn't sure why, even now, but instead of leaving he'd dropped his bag by the door and come back to sit in this chair, where he'd stayed all night.

He wished he could call Clary, but it was too early in the morning, and besides, Isabelle had said she and Jace had gone off together, and the thought of interrupting some special moment of theirs wasn't appealing. He wondered how his mother was. If she could have seen him last night, with Maureen, she would have thought he was every bit the monster she'd accused him of being.

Maybe he was.

He looked up as Jordan's door cracked open and Jordan emerged. He was barefoot, still in the same jeans and shirt he'd been wearing yesterday. The scars on his throat had faded to red lines. He looked at Simon. His hazel eyes, normally so bright and cheerful, were darkly shadowed. "I thought you would leave," he said.

"I was going to," Simon said. "But then I figured I ought to give you a chance to explain."

"There's nothing to explain." Jordan shuffled into the kitchen and dug around in a drawer until he produced a coffee filter. "Whatever Maia said about me, I'm sure it was true."

"She said you hit her," Simon said.

Jordan, in the kitchen, went very still. He looked down at the filter as if he were no longer quite sure what it was for.

"She said you guys went out for months and everything was great," Simon went on. "Then you turned violent and jealous. When she called you on it, you hit her. She broke up with you, and when she was walking home one night, something attacked her and nearly killed her. And you—you took off out of town. No apology, no explanation."

Jordan set the filter down on the counter. "How did she get here? How did she find Luke Garroway's pack?"

Simon shook his head. "She hopped a train to New York and tracked them down. She's a survivor, Maia. She didn't let what you did to her wreck her. A lot of people would have."

"Is this why you stayed?" asked Jordan. "To tell me I'm a bastard? Because I already know that."

"I stayed," Simon said, "because of what I did last night. If I'd found out about you yesterday, I would have left. But after what I did to Maureen . . ." He chewed his lip. "I thought I had control over what happened to me and I didn't, and I hurt someone who didn't deserve it. So that's why I'm staying."

"Because if I'm not a monster, then you're not a monster."

"Because I want to know how to go on, now, and maybe you can tell me." Simon leaned forward. "Because you've been a good guy to me since I met you. I've never seen you be mean or get angry. And then I thought about the Wolf Guard, and how you said you joined it because you'd done bad things. And I thought Maia was maybe the bad thing you'd done that you were trying to make up for."

"I was," said Jordan. "She is."

Clary sat at her desk in Luke's small spare room, the scrap of cloth she'd taken from the Beth Israel morgue spread out in front of her. She'd weighted it down on either side with pencils and was hovering over it, stele in hand, trying to remember the rune that had come to her in the hospital.

It was hard to concentrate. She kept thinking about Jace, about last night. Where he might have gone. Why he was so unhappy. She hadn't realized until she had seen him that he was as miserable as she was, and it tore at her heart. She wanted to call him, but had held herself back from doing so several times since she'd gotten home. If he was going to tell her what the problem was, he'd have to do it without being asked. She knew him well enough to know that.

She closed her eyes, and tried to force herself to picture the rune. It wasn't one she'd invented, she was pretty sure. It was one that actually existed, though she wasn't sure she'd seen it in the Gray Book. Its shape spoke to her less of translation than of revelation, of showing the shape of something hidden belowground, blowing the dust away from it slowly to read the inscription beneath. . . .

The stele twitched in her fingers, and she opened her eyes to find, to her surprise, that she'd managed to trace a small pattern on the edge of the fabric. It looked almost like a blot, with odd bits going off every which way, and she frowned, wondering if she was losing her skill. But the fabric began to shimmer, like heat rising off hot blacktop. She stared as words unfolded across the cloth as if an invisible hand was writing them:

Property of the Church of Talto. 232 Riverside Drive.

A hum of excitement went through her. It was a clue, a real clue. And she'd found it herself, without any help from anyone else.

232 Riverside Drive. That was on the Upper West Side, she thought, by Riverside Park, just across the water from New Jersey. Not that long a trip at all. The Church of Talto. Clary set the stele down with a worried frown. Whatever that was, it sounded like bad news. She scooted her chair over to Luke's old desktop computer and pulled up the Internet. She couldn't say she was surprised that typing in "Church of Talto" produced no comprehensible results. Whatever had been written there on the corner of the cloth had been in Purgatic, or Cthonian, or some other demon language.

One thing she was sure of: Whatever the Church of Talto was, it was secret, and probably bad. If it was mixed up with turning human babies into *things* with claws for hands, it wasn't any kind of a real religion. Clary wondered if the mother who'd dumped her baby near the hospital was a member of the church, and if she knew what she'd gotten herself into before her baby was born.

She felt cold all over as she reached for her phone—and paused with it in hand. She had been about to call her mother, but she couldn't call Jocelyn about this. Jocelyn had only just stopped crying and agreed to go out, with Luke, to look at rings. And while Clary thought her mother was strong enough to handle whatever the truth turned out to be, she'd doubtless get in massive trouble with the Clave for having taken her investigation this far without informing them.

Luke. But Luke was with her mother. She couldn't call him.

Maryse, maybe. The mere idea of calling her seemed alien and intimidating. Plus, Clary knew—without quite wanting to admit to herself that it was a factor—that if she let the Clave take this over, she'd be benched. Pushed off to the sidelines of a mystery that seemed intensely personal. Not to mention that it felt like betraying her mother to the Clave.

But to go running off on her own, not knowing what she'd find . . . Well, she had training, but not *that* much training. And she knew she had a tendency to act first, think later. Reluctantly she pulled the phone toward her, hesitated a moment—and sent a quick text: 232 RIVERSIDE DRIVE. YOU NEED TO MEET ME THERE RIGHT AWAY. IT'S IMPORTANT. She hit the send button and sat for a moment until the screen lit up with an answering buzz: OK.

With a sigh Clary set down the phone, and went to get her weapons.

"I loved Maia," Jordan said. He was sitting on the futon now, having finally managed to make coffee, though he hadn't drunk any of it. He was just holding the mug in his hands, turning it around and around as he talked. "You have to know that, before I tell you anything else. We both came from this dismal hellhole of a town in New Jersey, and she got endless crap because her dad was black and her mom was white. She had a brother, too, who was a total psychopath. I don't know if she told you about him. Daniel."

"Not much," Simon said.

"With all that, her life was pretty hellish, but she didn't let it get her down. I met her in a music store, buying old records. Vinyl, right. We got to talking, and I realized she was basically the coolest girl for miles around. Beautiful, too. And sweet." Jordan's eyes were distant. "We went out, and it was fantastic. We were totally in love. The way you are when you're sixteen. Then I got bit. I was in a fight one night, at a club. I used to get into fights a lot. I was used to getting kicked and punched, but bitten? I thought the guy who'd done it was crazy, but whatever. I went to the hospital, got stitched up, forgot about it.

"About three weeks later it started to hit. Waves of uncontrollable rage and anger. My vision would just black out, and I wouldn't know what was happening. I punched my hand through my kitchen window because a drawer was stuck shut. I was crazy jealous about Maia, convinced she was looking at other guys, convinced . . . I don't even know what I thought. I just know I snapped. I hit her. I want to say I don't remember doing it, but I do. And then she broke up with me. . . ." His voice trailed off. He took a swallow of coffee; he looked sick, Simon thought. He must not have told this story much before. Or ever. "A couple nights later I went to a party and she was there. Dancing with another guy. Kissing him like she wanted to prove to me it was over. It was a bad night for her to choose, not that she could have known that. It was the first full moon since I'd been bitten." His knuckles were white where he gripped the cup. "The first time I ever Changed. The transformation ripped through my body and tore my bones and skin apart. I was in agony, and not just because of that. I wanted her, wanted her to come back, wanted to explain, but all I could do was howl. I took off running through the streets, and that was when I saw her, crossing the park near her house. She was going home. . . ."

"And you attacked her," Simon said. "You bit her."

"Yeah." Jordan stared blindly into the past. "When I woke up the next morning, I knew what I'd done. I tried to go to her house, to explain. I was halfway there when a big guy stepped into my path and stared me down. He knew who I was, knew everything about me. He explained he was a member of the Praetor Lupus and he'd been assigned to me. He wasn't too happy that he'd gotten there too late, that I'd already bitten someone. He wouldn't let me go anywhere near her. He said I'd just make it worse. He promised the Wolf Guard would be watching over her. He told me that since I'd bitten a human already, which was strictly forbidden, the only way I'd evade punishment was to join the Guard and get trained to control myself.

"I wouldn't have done it. I would have spit on him and taken whatever punishment they wanted to hand out. I hated myself that much. But when he explained that I'd be able to help other people like me, maybe stop what had happened to me and Maia from happening again, it was like I saw a light in the darkness, way off in the future. Like maybe it was a chance to fix what I'd done."

"Okay," Simon said slowly. "But isn't it kind of a weird

coincidence that you wound up assigned to me? A guy who was dating the girl you once bit and turned into a werewolf?"

"No coincidence," Jordan said. "Your file was one of a bunch I got handed. I picked you *because* Maia was mentioned in the notes. A werewolf and a vampire dating. You know, it's kind of a big deal. It was the first time I realized she'd become a werewolf after I—after what I did."

"You never checked up to find out? That seems kind of—"

"I tried. The Praetor didn't want me to, but I did what I could to find out what happened to her. I knew she ran away from home, but she had a crappy home life anyway, so that didn't tell me anything. And it's not like there's some national registry of werewolves where I could look her up. I just . . . hoped she hadn't Turned."

"So you took my assignment because of Maia?"

Jordan flushed. "I thought maybe if I met you, I could find out what happened to her. If she was okay."

"That's why you told me off for two-timing her," said Simon, thinking back. "You were being protective."

Jordan glared at him over the rim of the coffee cup. "Yeah, well, it was a jerk move."

"And you're the one who shoved the flyer for the band performance under her door. Aren't you?" Simon shook his head. "So, was messing with my love life part of the assignment, or just your personal extra touch?"

"I screwed her over," Jordan said. "I didn't want to see her screwed over by someone else."

"And it didn't occur to you that if she showed up at our performance she'd try to rip your face off? If she hadn't been late, maybe she even would have done it while you were onstage.

That would have been an exciting extra for the audience."

"I didn't know," Jordan said. "I didn't realize she hated me so much. I mean, I don't hate the guy who Turned me; I kind of understand that he might not have been in control of himself."

"Yeah," said Simon, "but you never *loved* that guy. You never had a relationship with him. Maia loved you. She thinks you bit her and then you ditched and never thought about her again. She's going to hate you as much as she loved you once."

Before Jordan could reply, the doorbell rang—not the buzzer that would have sounded if someone had been downstairs, calling up, but the one that could be rung only if the visitor was standing in the hallway outside their door. The boys exchanged baffled looks. "Are you expecting someone?" Simon asked.

Jordan shook his head and put the coffee cup down. Together they went into the small entryway. Jordan gestured for Simon to stand behind him before he swung the door open.

There was no one there. Instead there was a folded piece of paper on the welcome mat, weighed down by a solid-looking hunk of rock. Jordan bent to free the paper and straightened up with a frown.

"It's for you," he said, handing it to Simon.

Puzzled, Simon unfolded the paper. Printed across the center, in childish block letters, was the message:

SIMON LEWIS. WE HAVE YOUR GIRLFRIEND. YOU MUST COME TO 232 RIVERSIDE DRIVE TODAY. BE THERE BEFORE DARK OR WE WILL CUT HER THROAT.

"It's a joke," Simon said, staring numbly at the paper. "It has to be."

Without a word Jordan grabbed Simon's arm and hauled him into the living room. Letting go of him, he rooted around for the cordless phone until he found it. "Call her," he said, slapping the phone against Simon's chest. "Call Maia and make sure she's all right."

"But it might not be her." Simon stared down at the phone as the full horror of the situation buzzed around his brain like a ghoul buzzing around the outside of a house, begging to be let in. *Focus*, he told himself. *Don't panic*. "It might be Isabelle."

"Oh, Jesus." Jordan glowered at him. "Do you have any other girlfriends? Do we have to make a list of names to call?"

Simon yanked the phone away from him and turned away, punching in the number.

Maia answered on the second ring. "Hello?"

"Maia—it's Simon."

The friendliness went out of her voice. "Oh. What do you want?"

"I just wanted to check that you were okay," he said.

"I'm fine." She spoke stiffly. "It's not like what was going on with us was all that serious. I'm not happy, but I'll live. You're still an ass, though."

"No," Simon said. "I mean I wanted to check that you were *okay*."

"Is this about Jordan?" He could hear the tense anger when she said his name. "Right. You guys went off together, didn't you? You're friends or something, right? Well, you can tell him to stay away from me. In fact, that goes for both of you."

She hung up. The dial tone buzzed down the phone like an angry bee.

Simon looked at Jordan. "She's fine. She hates us both, but it really didn't sound like anything else was wrong."

"Fine," Jordan said tightly. "Call Isabelle."

It took two tries before Izzy picked up; Simon was nearly in a panic by the time her voice came down the line, sounding distracted and annoyed. "Whoever this is, it had better be good."

Relief poured through his veins. "Isabelle. It's Simon."

"Oh, for God's sake. What do *you* want?"

"I just wanted to make sure you were okay—"

"Oh, what, I'm supposed to be devastated because you're a cheating, lying, two-timing son of a—"

"No." This was really starting to wear on Simon's nerves. "I meant, are you all right? You haven't been kidnapped or anything?"

There was a long silence. "Simon," Isabelle said finally. "This is really, seriously, the stupidest excuse for a whiny makeup call that I have ever, ever heard. What's *wrong* with you?"

"I'm not sure," Simon said, and hung up before she could hang up on him. He handed the phone to Jordan. "She's fine too."

"I don't get it." Jordan looked bewildered. "Who makes a threat like that if it's totally empty? I mean, it's so easy to check and find out it's a lie."

"They must think I'm stupid," Simon began, and then paused, a horrible thought dawning on him. He snatched the phone back from Jordan and started to dial with numb fingers.

"Who is it?" Jordan said. "Who are you calling?"

Clary's phone rang just as she turned the corner of Ninety-sixth Street onto Riverside Drive. The rain seemed to have washed away the city's usual dirt; the sun shone down from a brilliant sky onto the bright green strip of the park running alongside the river, whose water looked nearly blue today.

She dug into her bag for her phone, found it, and flipped it open. "Hello?"

Simon's voice came down the line. "Oh, thank—" He broke off. "Are you all right? You're not kidnapped or anything?"

"*Kidnapped?*" Clary peered up at the numbers of the buildings as she walked uptown. 220, 224. She wasn't entirely sure what she was looking for. Would it *look* like a church? Something else, glamoured to look like an abandoned lot? "Are you drunk or something?"

"It's a little early for that." The relief in his voice was plain. "No, I just—I got a weird note. Someone threatening to go after my girlfriend."

"Which one?"

"Har de har." Simon did not sound amused. "I called Maia and Isabelle already, and they're both fine. Then I thought of you—I mean, we spend a lot of time together. Someone might get the wrong idea. But now I don't know what to think."

"I dunno." 232 Riverside Drive loomed up in front of Clary suddenly, a big square stone building with a pointed roof. It *could* have been a church at one point, she thought, though it didn't look much like one now.

"Maia and Isabelle found out about each other last night, by the way. It wasn't pretty," Simon added. "You were right about the playing-with-fire bit."

Clary examined the facade of number 232. Most of the edifices lining the drive were expensive apartment buildings, with doormen in livery waiting inside. This one, though, had only a set of tall wooden doors with curved tops, and old-fashioned-looking metal handles instead of doorknobs. "Ooh, ouch. Sorry, Simon. Are either of them speaking to you?"

"Not really."

She took hold of one of the handles, and pushed. The door slid open with a soft hissing noise. Clary dropped her voice. "Maybe one of them left the note?"

"It doesn't really seem like their style," said Simon, sounding genuinely puzzled. "Do you think Jace would have done it?"

The sound of his name was like a punch to the stomach. Clary caught her breath and said, "I really don't think he'd do that, even if he was angry." She drew the phone away from her ear. Peering around the half-open door, she could see what looked reassuringly like the inside of a normal church—a long aisle, and flickering lights like candles. Surely it couldn't hurt just to take a peek inside. "I have to go, Simon," she said. "I'll call you later."

She flipped her phone closed and stepped inside.

"You really think it was a joke?" Jordan was prowling up and down the apartment like a tiger pacing its cage at the zoo. "I dunno. It seems like a really sick sort of joke to me."

"I didn't say it wasn't sick." Simon glanced at the note; it lay on the coffee table, the block-printed letters clearly visible even at a distance. Just looking at it gave him a lurching feeling in his stomach, even though he knew it was meaningless. "I'm just trying to think who might have sent it. And why."

"Maybe I should take the day off watching you and keep an eye on her," said Jordan. "You know, just in case."

"I assume you're talking about Maia," said Simon. "I know you mean well, but I really don't think she wants you around. In any capacity."

Jordan's jaw tightened. "I'd stay out of the way so she wouldn't see me."

"Wow. You're still really into her, aren't you?"

"I have a personal responsibility." Jordan sounded stiff. "Whatever else I feel doesn't matter."

"You can do what you want," Simon said. "But I think—"

The door buzzer sounded again. The two boys exchanged a single look before both bolting down the narrow hallway to the door. Jordan got there first. He grabbed for the coatrack that stood by the door, ripped the coats off it, and flung the door wide, the rack held above his head like a javelin.

On the other side of the door was Jace. He blinked. "Is that a coatrack?"

Jordan slammed the coatrack down on the ground and sighed. "If you'd been a vampire, this would have been a lot more useful."

"Yes," said Jace. "Or, you know, just someone with a lot of coats."

Simon stuck his head around Jordan and said, "Sorry. We've had a stressful morning."

"Yeah, well," said Jace. "It's about to get more stressful. I came to bring you to the Institute, Simon. The Conclave wants to see you, and they don't like having to wait."

The moment the door of the Church of Talto shut behind Clary, she felt that she was in another world, the noise and bustle of New York City entirely shut out. The space inside the building was big and lofty, with high ceilings soaring above. There was a narrow aisle banked by rows of pews, and fat brown candles burned in sconces bolted along the walls. The interior seemed dimly lit to Clary, but perhaps that was just because she was used to the brightness of witchlight.

She moved along the aisle, the tread of her sneakers soft against the dusty stone. It was odd, she thought, a church with no windows at all. At the end of the aisle she reached the apse, where a set of stone steps led to a podium on which was displayed an altar. She blinked up at it, realizing what else was strange: There were no crosses in this church. Instead there was an upright stone tablet on the altar, crowned by the carved figure of an owl. The words on the tablet read:

FOR HER HOUSE INCLINETH UNTO DEATH,

AND HER PATHS UNTO THE DEAD.

NONE THAT GO UNTO HER RETURN AGAIN,

NEITHER TAKE THEY HOLD OF THE PATHS OF LIFE.

Clary blinked. She wasn't too familiar with the Bible—she certainly didn't have anything like Jace's near-perfect recall of large passages of it—but while that sounded religious, it was also an odd bit of text to feature in a church. She shivered, and drew closer to the altar, where a large closed book had been left out. One of the pages seemed to be marked; when Clary reached to open the book, she realized that what she'd thought was a bookmark was a black-handled dagger carved with occult symbols. She'd seen pictures of these before in her textbooks. It was an *athame*, often used in demonic summoning rituals.

Her stomach went cold, but she bent to scan the marked page anyway, determined to learn something—only to discover that it was written in a cramped, stylized hand that would have been hard to decipher had the book been in English. It wasn't; it was in a sharp, spiky-looking alphabet that she was sure she'd never seen before. The words were below an illustration of what Clary recognized as a summoning circle—the kind of pattern warlocks traced on the ground before they enacted spells. The circles were meant to draw down and concentrate magical power. This one, splashed across the page in green ink, looked like two concentric circles, with a square in the center of them. In the space between the circles, runes were scrawled. Clary didn't recognize them, but she could feel the language of the runes in her bones, and it made her shiver. Death and blood.

She turned the page hastily, and came on a group of illustrations that made her suck in her breath.

It was a progression of pictures that started with the image of a woman with a bird perched on her left shoulder. The bird, possibly a raven, looked sinister and cunning. In the second picture the bird was gone, and the woman was obviously pregnant. In the third image the woman was lying on an altar not unlike the one Clary was standing in front of now. A robed figure was standing in front of her, a jarringly modern-looking syringe in its hand. The syringe was full of dark red liquid. The woman clearly knew she was about to be injected with it, because she was screaming.

In the last picture the woman was sitting with a baby on her lap. The baby looked almost normal, except that its eyes were entirely black, without whites at all. The woman was looking down at her child with a look of terror.

Clary felt the hairs on the back of her neck prickle. Her mother had been right. Someone was trying to make more babies like Jonathan. In fact, they already had.

She stepped back from the altar. Every nerve in her body was screaming that there was something very wrong with this place. She didn't think she could spend another second here;

better to go outside and wait there for the cavalry to arrive. She might have discovered this clue on her own, but the result was way more than she could handle on her own.

It was then that she heard the sound.

A soft susurration, like a slow tide pulling back, that seemed to come from above her. She looked up, the *athame* gripped firmly in her hand. And stared. All around the upstairs gallery stood rows of silent figures. They wore what looked like gray tracksuits—sneakers, dull gray sweats, and zip-up tops with hoods pulled down over their faces. They were utterly motionless, their hands on the gallery railing, staring down at her. At least, she assumed they were staring. Their faces were hidden entirely in shadow; she couldn't even tell if they were male or female.

"I . . . I'm sorry," she said. Her voice echoed loudly in the stone room. "I didn't mean to intrude, or . . ."

There was no answer but silence. Silence like a weight. Clary's heart began to beat faster.

"I'll just go, then," she said, swallowing hard. She stepped forward, laid the *athame* on the altar, and turned to leave. She caught the scent on the air then, a split second before she turned—the familiar stench of rotting garbage. Between her and the door, rising up like a wall, was a nightmarish mishmash of scaled skin, bladelike teeth, and reaching claws.

For the past seven weeks Clary had trained to face down a demon in battle, even a massive one. But now that it was actually happening, all she could do was scream.

11

OUR KIND

The demon lunged for Clary, and she stopped screaming abruptly and flung herself backward, over the altar—a perfect flip, and for one bizarre moment she wished Jace had been there to see it. She hit the ground in a crouch, just as something struck the altar hard, making the stone vibrate.

A howl sounded through the church. Clary scrambled to her knees and peered over the edge of the altar. The demon wasn't as big as she'd first thought, but it wasn't small, either—about the size of a refrigerator, with three heads on swaying stalks. The heads were blind, with enormous gaping jaws from which ropes of greenish drool hung. The demon seemed to have smacked its leftmost head on the altar when it grabbed for her, because it was shaking the head back and forth as if trying to clear it.

Clary glanced up wildly, but the tracksuited figures were still where they had been before. None of them had moved. They seemed to be watching what was going on with a detached interest. She spun and looked behind her, but there appeared to be no exits from the church besides the door she'd come through, and the demon was currently blocking her path back to it. Realizing she was wasting precious seconds, she scrambled to her feet and grabbed for the *athame*. She yanked it off the altar and ducked back down just as the demon came for her again. She rolled to the side as a head, swaying on a thick stalk of neck, darted over the altar, its thick black tongue flicking out, searching for her. With a scream she jammed the *athame* into the creature's neck once, then jerked it free, scrambling backward and out of the way.

The thing screamed, its head rearing back, black blood spraying from the wound she'd made. But it wasn't a killing blow. Even as Clary watched, the wound began to heal slowly, the demon's blackish green flesh knitting together like fabric being sewed up. Her heart sank. Of course. The whole reason Shadowhunters used runed weapons was that the runes prevented demons from healing.

She reached for the stele in her belt with her left hand, and yanked it free just as the demon came for her again. She leaped to the side and threw herself painfully down the stairs, rolling until she fetched up against the first row of pews. The demon turned, lumbering a bit as it moved, and made for her again. Realizing she was still clutching both the stele and the dagger—in fact, the dagger had cut her as she had rolled, and blood was quickly staining the front of her jacket—she transferred the dagger to her left hand, the stele to her right, and with a desperate swiftness, cut an *enkeli* rune into the *athame*'s hilt.

The other symbols on the hilt began to melt and run as the rune of angelic power took hold. Clary looked up; the demon was almost on her, its three heads reaching, their mouths gaping. Propelling herself to her feet, she drew her arm back and flung the dagger as hard as she could. To her great surprise, it struck the middle head right in the center of the skull, sinking in up to the hilt. The head thrashed as the demon screamed—Clary's heart lifted—and then the head simply dropped, hitting the ground with a sickening thud. The demon kept coming anyway, dragging the now-dead head on its limp neck after it as it moved toward Clary.

The sound of many footsteps came from above. Clary looked up. The tracksuited figures were gone, the gallery empty. The sight was not reassuring. Her heart doing a wild tango in her chest, Clary turned and ran for the front door, but the demon was faster than she was. With a grunt of effort it launched itself *over* her and landed in front of the doors, blocking her way out. Making a hissing noise, it moved toward her, its two living heads swaying, then rising, stretching to their full length in order to strike at her—

Something flashed through the air, a darting flame of silvery gold. The demon's heads whipped around, the hissing rising to a scream, but it was too late—the silvery thing that encircled them pulled tight, and with a spray of blackish blood, its remaining two heads sheared away. Clary rolled out of the way as flying blood splattered her, searing her skin. Then she ducked her head as the headless body swayed, fell toward her—

And was gone. As it was collapsing, the demon vanished, sucked back to its home dimension. Clary raised her head cautiously. The front doors of the church were open, and in the entranceway stood Isabelle, in boots and a black dress, her electrum whip in hand. She was winding it back slowly around her wrist, glancing around the church as she did so, her dark eyebrows drawn together in a curious frown. As her gaze fell on Clary, she grinned.

"Damn, girl," she said. "What have you gotten yourself into now?"

The touch of the vampire servants' hands on Simon's skin was cold and light, like the touch of icy wings. He shuddered a little as they unwound the blindfold from around his head, their withered skin rough on his, before they stepped back, bowing as they retreated.

He looked around, blinking. Moments ago, he had been standing in the sunlight on the corner of Seventy-Eighth Street and Second Avenue—enough of a distance from the Institute that he had judged it safe to use the grave-dirt to contact Camille without arousing her suspicions. Now he was in a dimly lit room, quite large, with a smooth marble floor and elegant marble pillars holding up a high ceiling. Along the left wall ran a row of glass-fronted cubicles, each with a brass-lettered plaque hanging over it that read TELLER. Another brass plaque on the wall proclaimed this to be the DOUGLAS NATIONAL BANK. Thick layers of dust padded the floor and the counters where people had once stood to write out checks or withdrawal slips, and the brass-bound lamps that hung from the ceiling were coated with verdigris.

In the center of the room was a high armchair, and in the chair sat Camille. Her silvery-blond hair was undone, and rained down over her shoulders like tinsel. Her beautiful face had been wiped clean of makeup, but her lips were still very red. In the dimness of the bank, they were almost the only color Simon could see.

"I would not normally agree to meet during sunlight hours,

Daylighter," she said. "But since it is you, I have made an exception."

"Thank you." He noticed no chair had been provided for him, so he continued awkwardly standing. If his heart still beat, he thought, it would have been pounding. When he had agreed to do this for the Conclave, he had forgotten how much Camille scared him. Maybe it was illogical—what could she really *do* to him?—but there it was.

"I suppose this means that you have considered my offer," said Camille. "And that you agree to it."

"What makes you think I agree?" Simon said, very much hoping that she wouldn't put down the fatuousness of the question to the fact that he was stalling for time.

She looked mildly impatient. "You would hardly deliver in person the news that you had decided to refuse me. You would be afraid of my temper."

"Should I be afraid of your temper?"

Camille sat back in the wing-back chair, smiling. The chair was modern-looking and luxurious, unlike anything else in the abandoned bank. It must have been hauled here from somewhere else, probably by Camille's servants, who were currently standing off to each side like silent statues. "Many are," she said. "But you have no reason to be. I am very pleased with you. Though you waited until the last moment to contact me, I sense you have made the right decision."

Simon's phone chose that minute to begin buzzing insistently. He jumped, feeling a trickle of cold sweat going down his back, then fished it hastily out of the pocket of his jacket. "Sorry," he said, flipping it open. "Phone."

Camille looked horrified. "Do *not* answer that."

Simon began lifting the phone to his ear. As he did, he managed to hit the camera button several times with his finger. "It'll just take a second."

"*Simon.*"

He hit the send button and then quickly flipped the phone closed. "Sorry. I didn't think."

Camille's chest was rising and falling with rage, despite the fact that she didn't actually breathe. "I demand more respect than that from my servants," she hissed. "You will never do that again, or—"

"Or what?" Simon said. "You can't hurt me, any more than anyone else can. And you told me I wouldn't be a servant. You told me I'd be your partner." He paused, letting just the right note of arrogance into his voice. "Maybe I ought to reconsider my acceptance of your offer."

Camille's eyes darkened. "Oh, for God's sake. Don't be a little fool."

"How can you say that word?" Simon demanded.

Camille raised delicate eyebrows. "Which word? Are you annoyed that I called you a fool?"

"No. Well, yes, but that's not what I meant. You said 'Oh, for—'" He broke off, his voice cracking. He still couldn't say it. *God.*

"Because I do not believe in him, silly boy," said Camille. "And you still do." She tilted her head to the side, regarding him the way a bird might regard a worm on the sidewalk that it was considering eating. "I think perhaps it is time for a blood oath."

"A . . . blood oath?" Simon wondered if he'd heard right.

"I forget that your knowledge of the customs of our kind is so limited." Camille shook her silvery head. "I will have you sign an oath, in blood, that you are loyal to me. It will prevent you from disobeying me in the future. Consider it a sort of . . .

prenuptial agreement." She smiled, and he saw the glint of her fangs. "Come." She snapped her fingers imperiously, and her minions scurried toward her, their gray heads bent. The first to reach her handed her something that looked like an old-fashioned glass pen, the kind with a whorled tip meant to catch and hold ink. "You will have to cut yourself and draw your own blood," said Camille. "Normally I would do it myself, but the Mark prevents me. Therefore we must improvise."

Simon hesitated. This was bad. Very bad. He knew enough about the supernatural world to know what oaths meant to Downworlders. They were not just empty promises that could be broken. They truly bound the promiser, like virtual mana-cles. If he signed the oath, he really would be loyal to Camille. Possibly forever.

"Come along," Camille said, a touch of impatience creeping into her voice. "There is no need to dawdle."

Swallowing, Simon took a reluctant step forward, and then another. A servant stepped in front of him, blocking his way. He was holding out a knife to Simon, a wicked-looking thing with a needle blade. Simon took it, and raised it above his wrist. Then he lowered it. "You know," he said, "I really don't like pain very much. Or knives—"

"*Do it*," Camille growled.

"There has to be some other way."

Camille rose from her chair, and Simon saw that her fangs were fully extended. She was truly enraged. "If you do not stop wasting my time—"

There was a soft implosion, a sound like something enormous tearing down the middle. A great shimmering panel appeared against the opposite wall. Camille turned toward it, her lips parting in shock as she saw what it was. Simon knew she recognized it, just as he did. There was only one thing it could be.

A Portal. And through it were pouring at least a dozen Shadowhunters.

"Okay," said Isabelle, putting away the first aid kit with a brisk gesture. They were in one of the Institute's many spare rooms, meant to house visiting Clave members. Each was plainly furnished with a bed, a dresser and a wardrobe, and a small bathroom. And, of course, each one had a first aid kit, with bandages, poultices, and even spare steles included. "You're pretty well *iratze*'d up, but it's going to take a little while for some of those bruises to fade. And these"—she ran her hand over the burn marks on Clary's forearm where the demon blood had splashed her—"probably won't go away totally till tomorrow. If you rest, they'll heal faster, though."

"That's fine. Thanks, Isabelle." Clary looked down at her hands; there were bandages around the right one, and her shirt was still torn and bloodstained, though Izzy's runes had healed the cuts beneath. She supposed she could have done the *iratzes* herself, but it was nice to have someone take care of her, and Izzy, while not the warmest person Clary knew, could be capable and kind when she felt like it. "And thanks for showing up and, you know, saving my life from whatever that was—"

"A Hydra demon. I told you. They have a lot of heads, but they're pretty dumb. And you weren't doing such a bad job with it before I showed up. I like what you did with the *athame*. Good thinking under pressure. That's as much a part of being a Shadowhunter as learning how to punch holes in things." Isabelle flopped down onto the bed next to Clary and sighed. "I should probably go look up what I can find out about the Church of Talto before the Conclave gets back. Maybe it'll help us figure out what's going on. The hospital stuff, the babies—" She shuddered. "I don't like it."

Clary had told Isabelle as much as she could about why she'd been at the church, even about the demon baby at the hospital, though she'd pretended she was the one who'd been suspicious, and had kept her mother out of the story. Isabelle had looked sick when Clary had described the way the baby had looked exactly like a normal baby except for its open black eyes and the little claws it had instead of hands. "I think they were trying to make another baby like—like my brother. I think they experimented on some poor mundane woman," Clary said. "But she couldn't take it when the baby was born, and she lost her mind. It's just—who would do something like that? One of Valentine's followers? The ones who never got caught, maybe trying to carry on what he was doing?"

"Maybe. Or just some demon-worshipping cult. There are plenty of them. Although I can't imagine why anyone would want to make more creatures like Sebastian." Her voice gave a little jump of hatred when she said his name.

"His name's really Jonathan—"

"Jonathan is Jace's name," said Isabelle tightly. "I won't call that monster by the same name my brother has. He's always going to be Sebastian to me."

Clary had to admit Isabelle had a point. She had a hard time thinking of him as Jonathan too. She supposed it wasn't fair to the true Sebastian, but none of them had really known him. It was easier to slap a stranger's name onto Valentine's vicious son than call him something that made him feel closer to her family, closer to her life.

Isabelle spoke lightly, but Clary could tell that her mind was working, ticking over various possibilities: "Anyway, I'm glad you texted me when you did. I could tell from your message that something weird was going on, and frankly I was bored. Everyone's off doing some secret thing with the Conclave, and I didn't want to go, because Simon was going to be there, and I hate him now."

"Simon is with the Conclave?" Clary was astonished. She had noticed that the Institute had seemed even more empty than usual when they'd arrived. Jace, of course, wasn't there, but she hadn't expected him to be—though she hadn't known why. "I talked to him this morning and he didn't say anything about doing something for them," Clary added.

Isabelle shrugged. "It has something to do with vampire politics. That's all I know."

"Do you think he's all right?"

Isabelle sounded exasperated. "He doesn't need you to protect him anymore, Clary. He has the Mark of Cain. He could get blown up, shot at, drowned, and stabbed and he'd be just fine." She looked at Clary hard. "I notice you didn't ask me why I hate Simon," she said. "I assume you knew about the two-timing thing?"

"I knew," Clary admitted. "I'm sorry."

Isabelle waved her confession away. "You're his best friend. It would have been weird if you didn't know."

"I should have told you," Clary said. "It's just—I never got the sense you were that serious about Simon, you know?"

Isabelle scowled. "I wasn't. It's just—I thought *he* would take it seriously, at least. Since I was so out of his league and everything. I guess I expected better from him than I do from other guys."

"Maybe," Clary said quietly, "Simon shouldn't be dating someone who thinks they're out of his league." Isabelle looked at her, and Clary felt herself flush. "Sorry. Your relationship is really none of my business."

Isabelle was twisting her dark hair up into a knot, something she did when she felt tense. "No, it isn't. I mean, I could ask you why you texted me to come to the church and meet you, and not Jace, but I haven't. I'm not stupid. I know something's wrong between you two, passionate alley make-out sessions notwithstanding." She looked keenly at Clary. "Have the two of you slept together yet?"

Clary felt the blood rush into her face. "What—I mean, no, we haven't, but I don't see what that has to do with anything."

"It doesn't," said Isabelle, patting her knotted hair into place. "That was just prurient curiosity. What's holding you back?"

"Isabelle—" Clary pulled up her legs, wrapped her arms around her knees, and sighed. "Nothing. We were just taking our time. I've never—you know."

"Jace has," said Isabelle. "I mean, I assume he has. I don't know for sure. But if you ever need anything . . ." She let the sentence hang in the air.

"Need anything?"

"Protection. You know. So you can be careful," Isabelle said. She sounded as practical as if she were talking about extra buttons. "You'd think the Angel would have been foresighted enough to give us a birth-control rune, but no dice."

"Of course I'd be careful," Clary spluttered, feeling her cheeks turn red. "Enough. This is awkward."

"This is girl talk," said Isabelle. "You just think it's awkward because you've spent your whole life with Simon as your only friend. And you can't talk to him about Jace. That *would* be awkward."

"And Jace really hasn't said anything to you? About what's bothering him?" Clary said, in a small voice. "You promise?"

"He didn't have to," Isabelle said. "The way you've been acting, and with Jace going around looking like someone just died, it's not like I wouldn't notice something was wrong. You should have come to talk to me sooner."

"Is he at least all right?" Clary asked very quietly.

Isabelle stood up from the bed and looked down at her. "No," she said. "He is very much not all right. Are you?"

Clary shook her head.

"I didn't think so," Isabelle said.

To Simon's surprise, Camille, upon seeing the Shadowhunters, didn't even try to stand her ground. She screamed and ran for the door, only to freeze when she realized that it was daylight outside, and that exiting the bank would quickly incinerate her. She gasped and cowered back against a wall, her fangs bared, a low hiss coming from her throat.

Simon stepped back as the Shadowhunters of the Conclave swarmed around him, all in black like a murder of crows; he saw Jace, his face pale and set like white marble, slide a broadsword blade through one of the human servants as he passed him, as casually as a pedestrian might swat a fly. Maryse stalked ahead, her flying black hair reminding Simon of Isabelle. She dispatched the second cowering minion with a whipsaw movement of her seraph blade, and advanced on Camille, her shining blade outstretched. Jace was beside her, and another Shadowhunter—a tall man with black runes twining his forearms like vines—was on her other side.

The rest of the Shadowhunters had spread out and were canvassing the bank, sweeping it with those odd things they used—Sensors—checking every corner for demon activity. They ignored the bodies of Camille's human servants, lying motionless in their pools of drying blood. They ignored Simon as well. He might as well have been another pillar, for all the attention they paid him.

"Camille Belcourt," said Maryse, her voice echoing off the marble walls. "You have broken the Law and are subject to the Law's punishments. Will you surrender and come with us, or will you fight?"

Camille was crying, making no attempt to cover her tears, which were tinged with blood. They streaked her white face with red lines as she choked, "Walker—and my Archer—"

Maryse looked baffled. She turned to the man on her left. "What is she saying, Kadir?"

"Her human servants," he replied. "I believe she is mourning their deaths."

Maryse flipped her hand dismissively. "It is against the Law to make servants of human beings."

"I made them before Downworlders were subject to your accursed laws, you bitch. They have been with me two hundred years. They were like children to me."

Maryse's hand tightened on the hilt of her blade. "What would you know of children?" she whispered. "What does your kind know of anything but destroying?"

Camille's tear-streaked face flashed for a moment with triumph. "I knew it," she said. "Whatever else you might say, whatever lies you tell, you hate our kind. Don't you?"

Maryse's face tightened. "Take her," she said. "Bring her to the Sanctuary."

Jace moved swiftly to one side of Camille and took hold of her; Kadir seized her other arm. Together, they pinioned her between them.

"Camille Belcourt, you stand accused of the murder of

humans," Maryse intoned. "And of the murder of Shadowhunters. You will be taken to the Sanctuary, where you will be questioned. The sentence for the murder of Shadowhunters is death, but it is possible that if you cooperate with us, your life will be spared. Do you understand?" asked Maryse.

Camille tossed her head defiantly. "There is only one man I will answer to," she said. "If you do not bring him to me, I will tell you nothing. You can kill me, but I will tell you nothing."

"Very well," said Maryse. "What man is that?"

Camille bared her teeth. "Magnus Bane."

"*Magnus Bane?*" Maryse looked flabbergasted. "The High Warlock of Brooklyn? Why do you want to talk to him?"

"I will answer to him," Camille said again. "Or I will answer to no one."

And that was that. She said not another word. As she was dragged away by Shadowhunters, Simon watched her go. He did not feel, as he had thought he would, triumphant. He felt hollow, and strangely sick to his stomach. He looked down at the bodies of the slain servants; he hadn't liked them much either, but they hadn't asked to be what they were, not really. In a way, maybe neither had Camille. But she was a monster to Nephilim anyway. And maybe not just because she had killed Shadowhunters; maybe there was no way, really, for them to think of her as anything else.

Camille had been pushed through the Portal; Jace stood on the other side of it, gesturing impatiently for Simon to follow. "Are you coming or not?" he called.

Whatever else you might say, whatever lies you tell, you hate our kind.

"Coming," Simon said, and moved reluctantly forward.

12

SANCTUARY

"What do you think Camille wants to see Magnus for?" Simon asked.

He and Jace were standing against the back wall of the Sanctuary, which was a massive room attached to the main body of the Institute through a narrow passageway. It wasn't *part* of the Institute per se; it had been left deliberately unconsecrated in order that it might be used as a holding place for demons and vampires. Sanctuaries, Jace had informed Simon, had gone out of fashion somewhat since Projecting had been invented, but every once in a while they found a use for theirs. Apparently, this was one of those times.

It was a big room, stone-bound and pillared, with an equally stone-bound entryway beyond a wide set of double doors; the entryway led to the corridor connecting the room to the Institute. Huge gouges in the stone floor indicated that whatever had been caged here over the years had been pretty nasty—and big. Simon couldn't help wondering how many enormous rooms full of pillars he was going to have to spend time in. Camille was standing against one of the pillars, her arms behind her, guarded on either side by Shadowhunter warriors. Maryse was pacing back and forth, occasionally conferring with Kadir, clearly trying to sort out some kind of plan. There were no windows in the room, for obvious reasons, but witchlight torches burned everywhere, giving the whole scene a peculiar whitish cast.

"I don't know," Jace said. "Maybe she wants fashion tips."

"Ha," Simon said. "Who's that guy, with your mother? He looks familiar."

"That's Kadir," said Jace. "You probably met his brother. Malik. He died in the attack on Valentine's ship. Kadir's the second most important person in the Conclave, after my mom. She relies on him a lot."

As Simon watched, Kadir pulled Camille's arms behind her back, so they circled the pillar, and chained them at her wrists. The vampire gave a little scream.

"Blessed metal," said Jace without a flicker of emotion. "It burns them."

Them, Simon thought. *You mean "you." I'm just like her. I'm not different just because you know me.*

Camille was whimpering. Kadir stood back, his face impassive. Runes, dark against his dark skin, twined the entirety of his arms and throat. He turned to say something to Maryse; Simon caught the words "Magnus" and "fire-message."

"Magnus again," said Simon. "But isn't he traveling?"

"Magnus and Camille are both really old," said Jace. "I suppose it's not that odd that they know each other." He shrugged, seemingly uninterested in the topic. "Anyway, I'm pretty sure they're going to wind up summoning Magnus back here. Maryse wants information, and she wants it bad. She knows Camille wasn't killing those Shadowhunters just for blood. There are easier ways to get blood."

Simon thought fleetingly of Maureen, and felt sick. "Well," he said, trying to sound unconcerned. "I guess that means Alec will be back. So that's good, right?"

"Sure." Jace's voice sounded lifeless. He didn't look all that great either; the whitish light in the room cast the angles of his cheekbones into a new and sharper relief, showing that he'd lost weight. His fingernails were bitten down to bloody stumps, and there were dark shadows under his eyes.

"At least your plan worked," Simon added, trying to inject some cheer into Jace's misery. It had been Jace's idea to have Simon take a picture with his cell phone and send it to the Conclave, which would allow them to Portal to where he was. "It was a good idea."

"I knew it would work." Jace sounded bored by the compliment. He looked up as the double doors to the Institute swung open, and Isabelle came through them, her black hair swinging. She looked around the room—giving Camille and the other Shadowhunters barely a glance—and came toward Jace and Simon, her boots clattering against the stone floor.

"What's all this about yanking poor Magnus and Alec back from their vacation?" Isabelle demanded. "They have opera tickets!"

Jace explained, while Isabelle stood with her hands on her hips, ignoring Simon completely.

"Fine," she said when he was done. "But the whole thing's ridiculous. She's just stalling for time. What could she possibly have to say to Magnus?" She glanced back over her shoulder at Camille, who was now not just manacled but bound to the pillar with lengths of silvery-gold chain. It crisscrossed her body across her torso, her knees, and even her ankles, holding her totally immobile. "Is that blessed metal?"

Jace nodded. "The manacles are lined to protect her wrists, but if she moves too much . . ." He made a sizzling sound. Simon, remembering the way his hands had burned when he'd touched the Star of David in his cell in Idris, the way his skin had run with blood, had to fight the urge to snap at him.

"Well, while you were off trapping vampires, I was uptown fighting off a Hydra demon," Isabelle said. "With Clary."

Jace, who had evinced only the barest interest in anything going on around him until now, jerked upright. "With *Clary*? You took her demon-hunting with you? Isabelle—"

"Of course not. She was already well into the fight by the time I got there."

"But how did you know—?"

"She texted me," Isabelle said. "So I went." She examined her nails, which were, as usual, perfect.

"She texted *you*?" Jace grabbed Isabelle by the wrist. "Is she all right? Did she get hurt?"

Isabelle looked down at his hand gripping her wrist, and then back up at his face. If he was hurting her, Simon couldn't tell, but the look on her face could have cut glass, as could the sarcasm in her voice. "Yes, she's bleeding to death upstairs, but

I thought I'd avoid telling you right away, because I like to draw the suspense out."

Jace, as if suddenly conscious of what he was doing, let go of Isabelle's wrist. "She's here?"

"She's upstairs," Isabelle said. "Resting—"

But Jace was already gone, running for the entryway doors. He burst through them and vanished. Isabelle, looking after him, shook her head.

"You can't really have thought he was going to do anything else," said Simon.

For a moment she said nothing. He wondered if maybe she was just planning to ignore anything he said for the rest of eternity. "I know," she said finally. "I just wish I knew what was going on with them."

"I'm not sure *they* know."

Isabelle was worrying at her bottom lip. She looked very young all of a sudden, and unusually conflicted, for Isabelle. Something was clearly going on with her, and Simon waited quietly while she appeared to come to a decision. "I don't want to be like that," she said. "Come on. I want to talk to you." She started to head toward the Institute doors.

"You do?" Simon was astonished.

She spun and glared at him. "Right now I do. But I can't promise how long it'll last."

Simon held his hands up. "I want to talk to you, Iz. But I can't go into the Institute."

A line appeared between her eyebrows. "Why?" She broke off, looking from him to the doors, to Camille, and back again. "Oh. Right. How did you get in here, then?"

"Portaled," said Simon. "But Jace said there's an entryway

that leads to a set of doors that go outside. So vampires can enter here at night." He pointed to a narrow door set in the wall a few feet away. It was secured with a rusting iron bolt, as if it hadn't been used in a while.

Isabelle shrugged. "Fine."

The bolt made a screeching noise when she yanked it back, sending flakes of rust into the air in a fine red spray. Beyond the door was a small stone room, like the vestry of a church, and a set of doors that most likely led outside. There were no windows, but cold air crept around the edges of the doors, making Isabelle, in her short dress, shiver.

"Look, Isabelle," Simon said, figuring that the onus was on him to start the discussion. "I really am sorry about what I did. There's no excuse—"

"No, there isn't," Isabelle said. "And while you're at it, you might want to tell me why you're hanging around with the guy who Turned Maia into a werewolf."

Simon told her the story Jordan had recounted to him, trying to keep his explanation as evenhanded as he could. He felt like it was at least important to explain to Isabelle that he hadn't known who Jordan really was at first, and also, that Jordan regretted what he'd done. "Not that that makes it okay," he finished. "But, you know—" *We've all done bad things.* But he couldn't bring himself to tell her about Maureen. Not right now.

"I know," Isabelle said. "And I've heard of the Praetor Lupus. If they're willing to have him as a member, he can't be a complete washout, I guess." She looked at Simon a little more closely. "Although I don't get why you need someone to protect you. You have . . ." She pointed at her forehead.

"I can't go through the rest of my life with people running at me every day and the Mark blowing them up," Simon said. "I need to know who's trying to kill me. Jordan's helping with that. Jace too."

"Do you really think Jordan's helping you? Because the Clave has some pull with the Praetor. We could get him replaced."

Simon hesitated. "Yeah," he said. "I really do think he's helping. And I can't always rely on the Clave."

"Okay." Isabelle leaned back against the wall. "Did you ever wonder why I'm so different from my brothers?" she asked without preamble. "Alec and Jace, I mean."

Simon blinked. "You mean aside from the whole thing where you're a girl and they . . . aren't?"

"No. Not that, idiot. I mean, look at the two of them. They have no problem falling in love. They're both *in* love. The forever kind. They're done. Look at Jace. He loves Clary like—like there's nothing else in the world and there never will be. Alec's the same. And Max—" Her voice caught. "I don't know what it would have been like for him. But he trusted everyone. And as you might have noticed, I don't trust anyone."

"People are different," Simon said, trying to sound understanding. "It doesn't mean they're happier than you—"

"Sure it does," Isabelle said. "You think I don't know that?" She looked at Simon, hard. "You know my parents."

"Not well." They had never been terribly eager to meet Isabelle's vampire boyfriend, a situation that hadn't done much to ameliorate Simon's feeling that he was merely the latest in a long line of undesirable suitors.

"Well, you know they were both in the Circle. But I bet

you didn't know it was all my mom's idea. My dad was never really enthusiastic about Valentine or any of it. And then when everything happened, and they got banished, and they realized they'd practically wrecked their lives, I think he blamed her. But they already had Alec and were going to have me, so he stayed, even though I think he kind of wanted to leave. And then, when Alec was about nine, he found someone else."

"Whoa," Simon said. "Your dad cheated on your mom? That's—that's awful."

"She told me," said Isabelle. "I was about thirteen. She told me that he would have left her but they found out she was pregnant with Max, so they stayed together and he broke it off with the other woman. My mom didn't tell me who she was. She just told me that you couldn't really trust men. And she told me not to tell anyone."

"And did you? Tell anyone?"

"Not until now," Isabelle said.

Simon thought of a younger Isabelle, keeping the secret, never telling anyone, hiding it from her brothers. Knowing things about their family that they would never know. "She shouldn't have asked you to do that," he said, suddenly angry. "That wasn't fair."

"Maybe," said Isabelle. "I thought it made me special. I didn't think about how it might have changed me. But I watch my brothers give their hearts away and I think, *Don't you know better?* Hearts are breakable. And I think even when you heal, you're never what you were before."

"Maybe you're better," said Simon. "I know I'm better."

"You mean Clary," said Isabelle. "Because she broke your heart."

"Into little pieces. You know, when someone prefers their

own brother over you, it isn't a confidence booster. I thought maybe once she realized it would never work out with Jace, she'd give up and come back to me. But I finally figured out that she'd never stop loving Jace, whether it was going to work out with him or not. And I knew that if she was only with me because she couldn't have him, I'd rather be alone, so I ended it."

"I didn't know you broke it off with her," said Isabelle. "I assumed . . ."

"That I had no self-respect?" Simon smiled wryly.

"I thought that you were still in love with Clary," Isabelle said. "And that you couldn't be serious about anyone else."

"Because you pick guys who will never be serious about you," said Simon. "So you never need to be serious about them."

Isabelle's eyes shone when she looked at him, but she said nothing.

"I care about you," Simon said. "I always cared about you."

She took a step toward him. They were standing fairly close together in the small room, and he could hear the sound of her breathing, and the fainter pulse of her heartbeat underneath. She smelled of shampoo and sweat and gardenia perfume and Shadowhunter blood.

The thought of blood made him remember Maureen, and his body tensed. Isabelle noticed—of course she noticed, she was a warrior, her senses finely tuned to even the slightest movement in others—and drew back, her expression tightening. "All right," she said. "Well, I'm glad we talked."

"Isabelle—"

But she was already gone. He went after her into the Sanctuary, but she was moving fast. By the time the vestry door shut behind him, she was halfway across the room. He gave up and watched as she disappeared through the double doors into the Institute, knowing he couldn't follow.

Clary sat up, shaking her head to clear the grogginess. It took her a moment to remember where she was—in a spare bedroom in the Institute, the only light in the room the illumination that streamed in through the single high window. It was blue light—twilight light. She lay twisted in the blanket; her jeans, jacket, and shoes were stacked neatly on a chair near the bed. And beside her was Jace, looking down at her, as if she had conjured him up by dreaming of him.

He was sitting on the bed, wearing his gear, as if he had just come from a fight, and his hair was tousled, the dim light from the window illuminating shadows under his eyes, the hollows of his temples, the bones of his cheeks. In this light he had the extreme and almost unreal beauty of a Modigliani painting, all elongated planes and angles.

She rubbed at her eyes, blinking away sleep. "What time is it?" she said. "How long—"

He pulled her toward him and kissed her, and for a moment she froze, suddenly very conscious that all she was wearing was a thin T-shirt and underwear. Then she went boneless against him. It was the sort of lingering kiss that turned her insides to water. The sort of kiss that might have made her feel that nothing was wrong, that things were as they had been before, and he was only glad to see her. But when his hands went to lift the hem of her T-shirt, she pushed them away.

"No," she said, her fingers wrapped around his wrists. "You can't just keep grabbing at me every time you see me. It's not a substitute for actually talking."

He took a ragged breath and said, "Why did you text Isabelle instead of me? If you were in trouble—"

"Because I knew she'd come," said Clary. "And I don't know that about you. Not right now."

"If something had happened to you—"

"Then I guess you would have heard about it eventually. You know, when you deigned to actually pick up the phone." She was still holding his wrists; she let go of them now, and sat back. It was hard, physically hard, to be close to him like this and not touch him, but she forced her hands down by her sides and kept them there. "Either you tell me what's wrong, or you can get out of the room."

His lips parted, but he said nothing; she didn't think she'd spoken to him this harshly in a long time. "I'm sorry," he said finally. "I mean, I know, with the way I've been acting, you've got no reason to listen to me. And I probably shouldn't have come in here. But when Isabelle said you were hurt, I couldn't stop myself."

"Some burns," Clary said. "Nothing that matters."

"Everything that happens to you matters to me."

"Well, that certainly explains why you haven't called me back once. And the last time I saw you, you ran away without telling me why. It's like dating a ghost."

Jace's mouth quirked up slightly at the side. "Not exactly. Isabelle actually dated a ghost. She could tell you—"

"No," Clary said. "It was a metaphor. And you know exactly what I mean."

For a moment he was silent. Then he said, "Let me see the burns."

She held out her arms. There were harsh red splotches on the insides of her wrists where the demon's blood had spattered. He took her wrists, very lightly, looking at her for permission first, and turned them over. She remembered the first time he had touched her, in the street outside Java Jones, searching her hands for Marks she didn't have. "Demon blood," he said. "They'll go away in a few hours. Do they hurt?"

Clary shook her head.

"I didn't know," he said. "I didn't know you needed me."

Her voice shook. "I always need you."

He bent his head and kissed the burn on her wrist. A flare of heat coursed through her, like a hot spike that went from her wrist to the pit of her stomach. "I didn't realize," he said. He kissed the next burn, on her forearm, and then the next, moving up her arm to her shoulder, the pressure of his body bearing her back until she was lying against the pillows, looking up at him. He propped himself on his elbows so as not to crush her with his weight and looked down at her.

His eyes always darkened when they kissed, as if desire changed their color in some fundamental way. He touched the white star mark on her shoulder, the one they both had, that marked them as the children of those who had had contact with angels. "I know I've been acting strange lately," he said. "But it's not you. I love you. That never changes."

"Then what—?"

"I think everything that happened in Idris—Valentine, Max, Hodge, even Sebastian—I kept shoving it all down, trying to forget, but it's catching up with me. I . . . I'll get help. I'll get better. I promise."

"You promise."

"I swear on the Angel." He ducked his head down, kissed her cheek. "The hell with that. I swear on *us*."

Clary wound her fingers into the sleeve of his T-shirt. "Why us?"

"Because there isn't anything I believe in more." He tilted his head to the side. "If we were to get married," he began, and he must have felt her tense under him, because he smiled. "Don't panic, I'm not proposing on the spot. I was just wondering what you knew about Shadowhunter weddings."

"No rings," Clary said, brushing her fingers across the back of his neck, where the skin was soft. "Just runes."

"One here," he said, gently touching her arm, where the scar was, with a fingertip. "And another here." He slid his fingertip up her arm, across her collarbone, and down until it rested over her racing heart. "The ritual is taken from the Song of Solomon. *'Set me as a seal upon thine heart, as a seal upon thine arm: for love is strong as death.'*"

"Ours is stronger than that," Clary whispered, remembering how she had brought him back. And this time, when his eyes darkened, she reached up and drew him down to her mouth.

They kissed for a long time, until most of the light had bled out of the room and they were just shadows. Jace didn't move his hands or try to touch her, though, and she sensed he was waiting for permission.

She realized she would have to be the one to take it further, if she wanted to—and she *did* want to. He'd admitted something was wrong and that it had nothing to do with her. This was progress: positive progress. He ought to be rewarded, right? A little grin crooked the edge of her mouth. Who was she kidding; she wanted more on her own behalf. Because he was Jace, because she loved him, because he was so gorgeous that sometimes she felt the need to poke him in the arm just to make sure he was real.

She did just that.

"Ow," he said. "What was that for?"

"Take your shirt off," she whispered. She reached for the hem of it but he was already there, lifting it over his head and tossing it casually to the floor. He shook his hair out, and she almost expected the bright gold strands to scatter sparks in the darkness of the room.

"Sit up," she said softly. Her heart was pounding. She didn't usually take the lead in these sort of situations, but he didn't seem to mind. He sat up slowly, pulling her up with him, until they were both sitting among the welter of blankets. She crawled into his lap, straddling his hips. Now they were face-to-face. She heard him suck his breath in and he raised his hands, reaching for her shirt, but she pushed them back down again, gently, to his sides, and put her own hands on him instead. She watched her fingers slide over his chest and arms, the swell of his biceps where the black Marks twined, the star-shaped mark on his shoulder. She traced her index finger down the line between his pectoral muscles, across his flat washboard stomach. They were both breathing hard when she reached the buckle on his jeans, but he didn't move, just looked at her with an expression that said: *Whatever you want.*

Her heart thudding, she dropped her hands to the hem of her own shirt and pulled it off over her head. She wished she'd worn a more exciting bra—this one was plain white cotton—but when she looked up again at Jace's expression, the thought evaporated. His lips were parted, his eyes nearly black; she could see herself reflected in them and knew he didn't care if her bra was white or black or neon green. All he was seeing was her.

She reached for his hands, then, freeing them, and put

them on her waist, as if to say, *You can touch me now*. He tilted his head up, her mouth came down over his, and they were kissing again, but it was fierce instead of languorous, a hot and fast-burning fire. His hands were feverish: in her hair, on her body, pulling her down so that she lay under him, and as their bare skin slid together she was acutely conscious that there really was nothing between them but his jeans and her bra and panties. She tangled her hands in his silky, disheveled hair, holding his head as he kissed down her throat. *How far are we going? What are we doing?* a small part of her brain was asking, but the rest of her mind was screaming at that small part to shut up. She wanted to keep touching him, kissing him; she wanted him to hold her and to know that he was real, here with her, and that he would never leave again.

His fingers found the clasp of her bra. She tensed. His eyes were large and luminous in the darkness, his smile slow. "Is this all right?"

She nodded. Her breath was coming fast. No one in her entire life had ever seen her topless—no *boy*, anyway. As if sensing her nervousness, he cupped her face gently with one hand, his lips teasing hers, brushing gently across them until her whole body felt as if it were shattering with tension. His long-fingered, callused right hand stroked along her cheek, then her shoulder, soothing her. She was still on edge, though, waiting for his other hand to move back to her bra clasp, to touch her again, but he seemed to be reaching for something behind him— What was he *doing*?

Clary thought suddenly of what Isabelle had said about being careful. *Oh*, she thought. She stiffened a little and drew back. "Jace, I'm not sure I—"

There was a flash of silver in the darkness, and something cold and sharp lanced across the side of her arm. All she felt for a moment was surprise—then pain. She drew her hands back, blinking, and saw a line of dark blood beading on her skin where a shallow cut ran from her elbow to her wrist. "Ouch," she said, more in annoyance and surprise than hurt. "What—"

Jace launched himself off her, off the bed, in a single motion. Suddenly he was standing in the middle of the room, shirtless, his face as white as bone.

Hand clasped across her injured arm, Clary started to sit up. "Jace, what—"

She broke off. In his left hand he was clutching a knife—the silver-handled knife she had seen in the box that had belonged to his father. There was a thin smear of blood across the blade.

She looked down at her hand, and then up again, at him. "I don't understand. . . ."

He opened his hand, and the knife clattered to the floor. For a moment he looked as if he might run again, the way he had outside the bar. Then he sank to the ground and put his head in his hands.

"I like her," said Camille as the doors shut behind Isabelle. "She rather reminds me of me."

Simon turned to look at her. It was very dim in the Sanctuary, but he could see her clearly, her back against the pillar, her hands bound behind her. There was a Shadowhunter guard stationed near the doors to the Institute, but either he hadn't heard Camille or he wasn't interested.

Simon moved a bit closer to Camille. The bonds that constrained her held an odd fascination for him. Blessed metal.

The chain seemed to gleam softly against her pale skin, and he thought he could see a few threads of blood seeping around the manacles at her wrists. "She isn't at all like you."

"So you think." Camille tilted her head to the side; her blond hair seemed artfully arranged around her face, though he knew she couldn't have touched it. "You love them so," she said, "your Shadowhunter friends. As the falcon loves the master who binds and blinds it."

"Things aren't like that," Simon said. "Shadowhunters and Downworlders aren't enemies."

"You can't even go with them into their home," she said. "You are shut out. Yet so eager to serve them. You would stand on their side against your own kind."

"I have no kind," Simon said. "I'm not one of them. But I'm not one of you, either. And I'd rather be like them than like you."

"You *are* one of us." She moved impatiently, rattling her chains, and gave a little gasp of pain. "There is something I didn't say to you, back at the bank. But it is true." She smiled tightly through the pain. "I can smell human blood on you. You fed recently. On a mundane."

Simon felt something inside him jump. "I . . ."

"It was wonderful, wasn't it?" Her red lips curved. "The first time since you've been a vampire that you haven't been hungry."

"No," Simon said.

"You're lying." There was conviction in her voice. "They try to make us fight against our natures, the Nephilim. They will accept us only if we pretend to be other than we are—not hunters, not predators. Your friends will never accept what you are, only what you pretend to be. What you do for them, they would never do for you."

"I don't know why you're bothering with this," said Simon. "What's done is done. I'm not going to let you go. I made my choice. I don't want what you offered me."

"Maybe not now," Camille said softly. "But you will. You will."

The Shadowhunter guard stepped back as the door opened, and Maryse came into the room. She was followed by two figures immediately familiar to Simon: Isabelle's brother Alec, and his boyfriend, the warlock Magnus Bane.

Alec was dressed in a sober black suit; Magnus, to Simon's surprise, was similarly dressed, with the addition of a long white silk scarf with tasseled ends and a pair of white gloves. His hair stood up like it always did, but for a change he was devoid of glitter. Camille, upon seeing him, went very still.

Magnus didn't seem to see her yet; he was listening to Maryse, who was saying, rather awkwardly, that it was good of them to come so quickly. "We really didn't expect you until tomorrow, at the earliest."

Alec made a muffled noise of annoyance and gazed off into space. He seemed as if he wasn't happy to be there at all. Beyond that, Simon thought, he looked much the same as he always had—same black hair, same steady blue eyes—although there was something more relaxed about him than there had been before, as if he had grown into himself somehow.

"Fortunately there's a Portal located near the Vienna Opera House," Magnus said, flinging his scarf back over his shoulder with a grand gesture. "The moment we got your message, we hurried to be here."

"I still really don't see what any of this has to do with us," Alec said. "So you caught a vampire who was up to something nasty. Aren't they always?"

Simon felt his stomach turn. He looked toward Camille to see if she was laughing at him, but her gaze was fixed on Magnus.

Alec, looking at Simon for the first time, flushed. It was always very noticeable on him because his skin was so pale. "Sorry, Simon. I didn't mean you. You're different."

Would you think that if you had seen me last night, feeding on a fourteen-year-old girl? Simon thought. He didn't say that, though, just dropped Alec a nod.

"She is of interest in our current investigation into the deaths of three Shadowhunters," said Maryse. "We need information from her, and she will only talk to Magnus Bane."

"Really?" Alec looked at Camille with puzzled interest. "Only to Magnus?"

Magnus followed his gaze, and for the first time—or so it seemed to Simon—looked at Camille directly. Something crackled between them, a sort of energy. Magnus's mouth quirked up at the corners into a wistful smile.

"Yes," Maryse said, a look of puzzlement passing over her face as she caught the look between the warlock and the vampire. "That is, if Magnus is willing."

"I am," Magnus said, drawing off his gloves. "I'll talk to Camille for you."

"Camille?" Alec looked at Magnus with his eyebrows raised. "You know her, then? Or—she knows you?"

"We know each other." Magnus shrugged, very slightly, as if to say, *What can you do?* "Once upon a time she was my girlfriend."

13

GIRL FOUND DEAD

"Your *girlfriend*?" Alec looked astonished. So did Maryse. Simon couldn't say he was unastonished himself. "You dated a *vampire*? A *girl* vampire?"

"It was a hundred and thirty years ago," said Magnus. "I haven't seen her since."

"Why didn't you tell me?" Alec demanded.

Magnus sighed. "Alexander, I've been alive for hundreds of years. I've been with men, been with women—with faeries and warlocks and vampires, and even a djinn or two." He looked sideways at Maryse, who looked mildly horrified. "Too much information?"

"It's all right," she said, though she sounded a little wan. "I have to discuss something with Kadir for a moment. I'll be back." She stepped aside, joining Kadir; they disappeared through the doorway. Simon took a few steps back as well, pretending to study one of the stained-glass windows intently, but his vampire hearing was good enough that he could hear everything Magnus and Alec were saying to each other, whether he wanted to or not. Camille, he knew, could hear it too. She had her head cocked to the side as she listened, her eyes heavy-lidded and thoughtful.

"How *many other* people?" Alec asked. "Roughly."

Magnus shook his head. "I can't count, and it doesn't matter. The only thing that matters is how I feel about you."

"More than a hundred?" Alec asked. Magnus looked blank. "*Two* hundred?"

"I can't believe we're having this conversation now," Magnus said, to no one in particular. Simon was inclined to agree, and wished they weren't having it in front of him.

"Why so many?" Alec's blue eyes were very bright in the dimness. Simon couldn't tell if he was angry. He didn't *sound* angry, just very intense, but Alec was a shut-down person, and perhaps this was as angry as he ever got. "Do you get bored with people fast?"

"I live forever," Magnus said quietly. "But not everyone does."

Alec looked as if someone had hit him. "So you just stay with them as long as they live, and then you find someone else?"

Magnus didn't say anything. He looked at Alec, his eyes shining like a cat's. "Would you rather I spent all of eternity alone?"

Alec's mouth twitched. "I'm going to find Isabelle," he said, and without another word he turned and walked back into the Institute.

Magnus watched him go with sad eyes. Not a human sort of sad, Simon thought. His eyes seemed to contain the sadness of great ages, as if the sharp edges of human sadness had been worn down to something softer by the passing of years, the way sea water wore away the sharp edges of glass.

As if he could tell Simon was thinking about him, Magnus looked at him sideways. "Eavesdropping, vampire?"

"I really don't love it when people call me that," Simon said. "I have a name."

"I suppose I'd better remember it. After all, in a hundred, two hundred, years, it'll be just you and me." Magnus regarded Simon thoughtfully. "We'll be all that's left."

The thought made Simon feel as if he were in an elevator that had suddenly broken free of its moorings and started plunging toward the ground, a thousand stories down. The thought had passed through his mind before, of course, but he had always pushed it away. The thought that he would stay sixteen while Clary got older, Jace got older, everyone he knew got older, grew up, had children, and nothing ever changed for him was too enormous and horrible to contemplate.

Being sixteen forever sounded good until you really thought about it. Then it didn't seem like such a great prospect anymore.

Magnus's cat eyes were a clear gold-green. "Staring eternity in the face," he said. "Not so much fun, is it?"

Before Simon could reply, Maryse had returned. "Where's Alec?" she asked, looking around in puzzlement.

"He went to see Isabelle," said Simon, before Magnus had to say anything.

"Very well." Maryse smoothed the front of her jacket down, though it wasn't wrinkled. "If you wouldn't mind . . ."

"I'll talk to Camille," said Magnus. "But I want to do it alone. If you'd like to wait for me in the Institute, I'll join you there when I'm finished."

Maryse hesitated. "You know what to ask her?"

Magnus's gaze was unwavering. "I know how to talk to her, yes. If she is willing to say anything, she'll say it to me."

Both of them seemed to have forgotten that Simon was there. "Should I go too?" he asked, interrupting their staring contest.

Maryse looked at him, half-distracted. "Oh, yes. Thank you for your help, Simon, but you're no longer needed. Go home if you like."

Magnus said nothing at all. With a shrug Simon turned and went toward the door that led to the vestry and the exit that would take him outside. At the door he paused and looked back. Maryse and Magnus were still talking, though the guard was already holding open the Institute door, ready to leave. Only Camille seemed to remember that Simon was there at all. She was smiling at him from her pillar, her lips curved up at the corners, her eyes shining like a promise.

Simon went out, and closed the door behind him.

"It happens every night." Jace was sitting on the floor, his legs drawn up, his hands dangling between his knees. He had put the knife on the bed next to Clary; she kept one hand on it while he talked—more to reassure him than because she needed it to defend herself. All the energy seemed to have drained out of Jace; even his voice sounded empty and far away while he talked, as if he were speaking to her from a great distance. "I dream that you come into my room and we . . . start doing what we were just doing. And then I hurt you. I cut you or strangle or stab you, and you die, looking up at me with those green eyes of yours while your life bleeds away between my hands."

"They're only dreams," Clary said gently.

"You just saw that they aren't," said Jace. "I was wide awake when I picked up that knife."

Clary knew he was right. "Are you worried that you're going crazy?"

He shook his head slowly. Hair fell into his eyes; he pushed it back. His hair had gotten a little too long; he hadn't cut it in a while, and Clary wondered if it was because he couldn't be bothered. How could she not have paid more attention to the shadows under his eyes, the bitten nails, the drawn exhausted look of him? She had been so concerned about whether he still loved her that she had not thought about anything else. "I'm not so worried about that, really," he said. "I'm worried about hurting you. I'm worried that whatever poison it is that's eating its way into my dreams will bleed through into my waking life and I'll . . ." His throat seemed to close up.

"You would never hurt me."

"I had that knife *in my hand*, Clary." He looked up at her, and then away. "If I hurt you . . ." His voice trailed off. "Shadowhunters die young, a lot of the time," he said. "We all know that. And you wanted to be a Shadowhunter, and I would never stop you because it isn't my job to tell you what to do with your life. Especially when I'm taking the same kind of risks. What kind of person would I be if I told you it was all right for me to risk my life, but not for you? So I've thought about what it would be like for me if you died. I bet you've thought about the same thing."

"I know what it would be like," Clary said, remembering the lake, the sword, and Jace's blood spreading over the sand. He had been dead, and the Angel had brought him back, but those had been the worst minutes of her life. "I wanted to die. But I knew how disappointed in me you'd have been if I'd just given up."

He smiled, the ghost of a smile. "And I've thought the same thing. If you died, I wouldn't want to live. But I wouldn't kill myself, because whatever happens after we die, I want to be with you there. And if I killed myself, I know you'd never talk to me again. In any life. So I'd live, and I'd try to make something out of my life, until I could be with you again. But if *I* hurt you—if *I* was the cause of your death—there's nothing that would keep me from destroying myself."

"Don't say that." Clary felt chilled to the bone. "Jace, you should have told me."

"I couldn't." His voice was flat, final.

"Why not?"

"I thought I was Jace Lightwood," he said. "I thought it was possible that my upbringing hadn't touched me. But now I wonder if maybe people can't change. Maybe I'll always be Jace Morgenstern, Valentine's son. He raised me for ten years, and maybe that's a stain that won't ever bleach out."

"You think this is because of your father," Clary said, and the bit of story that Jace had told her once ran through her head, *to love is to destroy*. And then she thought how strange it was that she would call Valentine Jace's father, when his blood ran in her veins, not Jace's. But she had never felt about

Valentine the way you might feel about a father. And Jace had. "And you didn't want me to know?"

"You're everything I want," Jace said. "And maybe Jace Lightwood deserves to get everything he wants. But Jace Morgenstern doesn't. Somewhere inside I must know that. Or I wouldn't be trying to destroy what we have."

Clary took a deep breath, and let it out slowly. "I don't think you are."

He raised his head and blinked. "What do you mean?"

"You think this is psychological," Clary said. "That there's something wrong with you. Well, I don't. I think someone is doing this to you."

"I don't—"

"Ithuriel sent me dreams," Clary said. "Maybe someone is sending you dreams."

"Ithuriel sent you dreams to try to help you. To guide you to the truth. What's the point of these dreams? They're sick, meaningless, sadistic—"

"Maybe they have a meaning," Clary said. "Maybe the meaning just isn't what you think. Or maybe whoever's sending them is trying to hurt you."

"Who would do that?"

"Someone who doesn't like us very much," said Clary, and pushed away an image of the Seelie Queen.

"Maybe," Jace said softly, looking down at his hands. "Sebastian—"

So he doesn't want to call him Jonathan either, Clary thought. She didn't blame him. It was his own name too. "Sebastian's dead," she said, a little more sharply than she'd intended. "And if he had had this sort of power, he would have used it before."

Doubt and hope chased each other across Jace's face. "You really think someone else could be doing this?"

Clary's heart beat hard against her rib cage. She *wasn't* sure; she wanted it so badly to be true, but if it wasn't, she would have gotten Jace's hopes up for nothing. *Both* their hopes.

But then she got the feeling it had been a while since Jace had felt hopeful about anything.

"I think we should go to the Silent City," she said. "The Brothers can get into your head and find out if someone's been messing around in there. The way they did with me."

Jace opened his mouth and closed it again. "When?" he said finally.

"Now," Clary said. "I don't want to wait. Do you?"

He didn't reply, just got up off the floor and picked up his shirt. He looked at Clary, and almost smiled. "If we're going to the Silent City, you might want to get dressed. I mean, I appreciate the bra-and-panties look, but I don't know if the Silent Brothers will. There are only a few of them left, and I don't want them to die of excitement."

Clary got up off the bed and threw a pillow at him, mostly out of relief. She reached for her clothes and began to pull her shirt on. Just before it went over her head, she caught sight of the knife lying on the bedspread, gleaming like a fork of silvery flame.

"Camille," Magnus said. "It's been a long time, hasn't it?"

She smiled. Her skin looked whiter than he recalled, and dark spidery veins were beginning to show beneath its surface. Her hair was still the color of spun silver, and her eyes were still as green as a cat's. She was still beautiful. Looking at her, he was in London again. He saw the gaslight and smelled the smoke and dirt and horses, the metallic tang of fog, the flowers in Kew Gardens. He saw a boy with black hair and blue eyes like Alec's. A girl with long brown curls and a serious face. In a world where everything went away from him eventually, she was one of the few remaining constants.

And then there was Camille.

"I've missed you, Magnus," she said.

"No, you haven't." He sat down on the floor of the Sanctuary. He could feel the cold of the stone through his clothes. He was glad he had worn the scarf. "So why the message for me? Just stalling for time?"

"No." She leaned forward, the chains rattling. He could almost hear the hissing where the blessed metal touched the skin of her wrists. "I have heard things about you, Magnus. I have heard that you are under the wing of the Shadowhunters these days. I had heard that you have won the love of one of them. That boy you were just talking to, I imagine. But then your tastes were always diverse."

"You have been listening to rumors about me," Magnus said. "But you could simply have asked me. All these years I was in Brooklyn, not far away at all, and I never heard from you. Never saw you at one of my parties. There has been a wall of ice between us, Camille."

"I did not build it." Her green eyes widened. "I have loved you always."

"You left me," he said. "You made a pet out of me, and then you left me. If love were food, I would have starved on the bones you gave me." He spoke matter-of-factly. It had been a long time.

"But we had all of eternity," she protested. "You must have known I would come back to you—"

"Camille." Magnus spoke with infinite patience. "What do you *want*?"

Her chest rose and fell quickly. Since she had no need to breathe, Magnus knew this was mainly for effect. "I know you have the ear of the Shadowhunters," she said. "I want you to speak to them on my behalf."

"You want me to cut a deal for you," Magnus translated.

She cut her eyes at him. "Your diction has always been so regrettably modern."

"They're saying you killed three Shadowhunters," said Magnus. "Did you?"

"They were Circle members," she said, her lower lip trembling. "They had tortured and killed my kind in the past. . . ."

"Is that why you did it? Revenge?" When she was silent, Magnus said, "You know what they do to those who kill Nephilim, Camille."

Her eyes shone. "I need you to intercede for me, Magnus. I want immunity. I want a signed promise from the Clave that if I give them information, they will spare my life and set me free."

"They'll never set you free."

"Then they'll never know why their colleagues had to die."

"*Had* to die?" Magnus mused. "Interesting wording, Camille. Am I correct that there is more to this than meets the eye? More than blood or revenge?"

She was silent, looking at him, her chest rising and falling artfully. Everything about her was artful—the fall of her silvery hair, the curve of her throat, even the blood on her wrists.

"If you want me to speak to them for you," Magnus said, "you have to tell me at least some small thing. A show of good faith."

She smiled brilliantly. "I knew you would speak to them for me, Magnus. I knew the past was not entirely dead for you."

"Consider it undead if you like," Magnus said. "The truth, Camille?"

She ran her tongue across her lower lip. "You can tell them," she said, "that I was under orders when I killed those Shadowhunters. It did not disturb me to do it, for they had killed my kin, and their deaths were deserved. But I would not have done it unless requested to do so by someone else, someone much more powerful than myself."

Magnus's heart beat a little faster. He didn't like the sound of this. "Who?"

But Camille shook her head. "Immunity, Magnus."

"Camille—"

"They will stake me out in the sun and leave me to die," she said. "That is what they do to those who slay Nephilim."

Magnus got to his feet. His scarf was dusty from lying on the ground. He looked at the stains mournfully. "I'll do what I can, Camille. But I make no promises."

"You never would," she murmured, her eyes half-lidded. "Come here, Magnus. Come close to me."

He did not love her, but she was a dream out of the past, so he moved toward her, until he was standing close enough to touch her. "Remember," she said softly. "Remember London? The parties at de Quincey's? Remember Will Herondale? I know you do. That boy of yours, that Lightwood. They even look alike."

"Do they?" Magnus said, as if he had never thought about it.

"Pretty boys have always been your undoing," she said. "But what can some mortal child give you? Ten years, twenty, before dissolution begins to claim him. Forty years, fifty, before death takes him. I can give you all of eternity."

He touched her cheek. It was colder than the floor had been. "You could give me the past," he said a little sadly. "But Alec is my future."

"Magnus—," she began.

The Institute door opened, and Maryse stood in the doorway, outlined by the witchlight behind her. Beside her was Alec, his arms crossed over his chest. Magnus wondered if Alec had heard any of the conversation between him and Camille through the door—surely not?

"Magnus," said Maryse Lightwood. "Have you come to some agreement?"

Magnus dropped his hand. "I'm not sure I'd call it an agreement," he said, turning to Maryse. "But I do think we have some things to talk about."

Dressed, Clary went with Jace to his room, where he packed a small canvas bag with things to bring with him to the Silent City, as if, she thought, he were going to some grim sleepover party. Weapons mostly—a few seraph blades; his stele; and almost as an afterthought, the silver-handled knife, its blade now cleaned of blood. He slid on a black leather jacket, and she watched as he zipped it, pulling loose strands of blond hair free of his collar. When he turned to look at her, slinging his bag across his shoulder, he smiled faintly, and she saw the slight chip in his front left incisor that she had always thought was endearing, a little flaw in looks that would otherwise be too perfect. Her heart contracted, and for a moment she looked away from him, hardly able to breathe.

He held out his hand to her. "Let's go."

There was no way to summon the Silent Brothers to come and get them, so Jace and Clary took a taxi heading downtown toward Houston and the Marble Cemetery. Clary supposed they could just have Portaled into the Bone City—she'd been there before; she knew what it looked like—but Jace said there were rules about that sort of thing, and Clary couldn't shake the feeling that the Silent Brothers might find it rather rude.

Jace sat beside her in the back of the taxi, holding one of her hands and tracing patterns on the back of it with his fingers. This was distracting, but not so distracting that she couldn't concentrate while he filled her in on what had been going on with Simon, the story of Jordan, their capture of Camille, and her demand to speak to Magnus.

"Simon's all right?" she said worriedly. "I didn't realize. He was in the Institute, and I didn't even see him—"

"He wasn't in the Institute; he was in the Sanctuary. And he seems to be holding his own. Better than I would have thought for someone who was so recently a mundane."

"But the plan sounds dangerous. I mean Camille, she's absolutely crazy, isn't she?"

Jace traced his fingers over her knuckles. "You have to stop thinking of Simon as the mundane boy you used to know. The one who required so much saving. He's almost beyond being harmed now. You haven't seen that Mark you gave him in action. I have. Like the wrath of God being visited upon the world. I suppose you should be proud."

She shivered. "I don't know. I did it because I had to do it, but it's still a curse. And I didn't know he was going through all this. He didn't say. I knew Isabelle and Maia had found out about each other, but I didn't know about Jordan. That he was really Maia's ex, or—any of it." *Because you haven't asked. You were too busy worrying about Jace. Not good.*

"Well," Jace said, "have you been telling him what *you're* up to? Because it has to go both ways."

"No. I haven't really told anyone," Clary said, and filled Jace in on her trip to the Silent City with Luke and Maryse, what she had found at the morgue at Beth Israel, and her subsequent discovery of the Church of Talto.

"Never heard of it," Jace said. "But Isabelle's right, there are all sorts of bizarro demon-worshipping sects out there. Most of them never actually succeed in summoning up a demon. Sounds like this one did."

"Do you think the demon we killed was the one they were worshipping? Do you think now they might—stop?"

Jace shook his head. "That was just a Hydra demon, a sort of guard dog. Besides, 'Her house inclineth unto death, and her paths unto the dead.' Sounds like a female demon to me. And it's the cults that worship female demons that often do horrible stuff with babies. They have all sorts of twisted ideas about fertility and infants." He sat back against the seat, half-closing his eyes. "I'm sure the Conclave will go to the church and check it out, but twenty to one they don't find anything. You killed their guard demon, so the cult's going to clear out and ditch the evidence. We might have to wait until they set up shop again somewhere else."

"But—" Clary's stomach clenched. "That baby. And the pictures in the book I saw. I think they're trying to make more children like—like Sebastian."

"They can't," said Jace. "They shot up a human baby with demon blood, which is pretty bad, yes. But you get something like Sebastian only if what you're doing is using demon blood on Shadowhunter children. Instead the baby died." He squeezed her hand lightly, as if for reassurance. "They're not nice people, but I can't imagine they'd try the same thing again, since it didn't work."

The taxi came to a screeching halt at the corner of Houston and Second Avenue. "Meter's broken," said the cabbie. "Ten bucks."

Jace, who under other circumstances would probably have made a sarcastic remark, tossed the cabbie a twenty and got out of the car, holding the door open for Clary to follow. "You ready?" he asked as they headed toward the iron gate that led to the City.

She nodded. "I can't say my last trip here was much fun, but yes, I'm ready." She took his hand. "As long as we're together, I'm ready for anything."

The Silent Brothers were waiting for them in the entryway of the City, almost as if they had been expecting them. Clary recognized Brother Zachariah among the group. They stood in a silent line, blocking Clary and Jace's farther ingress into the City.

Why have you come here, daughter of Valentine and son of the Institute? Clary wasn't sure which of them was speaking to her inside her head, or if all of them were. *It is unusual for children to enter the Silent City unsupervised.*

The appellation "children" stung, though Clary was aware

that as far as Shadowhunters were concerned, everyone under eighteen was a child and subject to different rules.

"We need your help," Clary said when it became apparent Jace wasn't going to say anything. He was looking from one of the Silent Brothers to the other with a curious listlessness, like someone who had received countless terminal diagnoses from different doctors and now, having reached the end of the line, waited without much hope for a specialist's verdict. "Isn't that your job—helping Shadowhunters?"

And yet we are not servants, at your beck and call. Nor does every problem fall under our jurisdiction.

"But this one does," Clary said firmly. "I believe someone is reaching into Jace's mind—someone with power—and messing with his memories and dreams. Making him do things he doesn't want to do."

Hypnomancy, said one of the Silent Brothers. *The magic of dreams. That is the province of only the greatest and most powerful users of magic.*

"Like angels," said Clary, and she was rewarded by a stiff, surprised silence.

Perhaps, said Brother Zachariah finally, *you should come with us to the Speaking Stars.* This was not an invitation, clearly, but an order, for they turned immediately and began walking into the heart of the City, not waiting to see if Jace and Clary followed.

They reached the pavilion of the Speaking Stars, where the Brothers took their places behind their black basalt table. The Mortal Sword was back in its place, gleaming on the wall behind them like the wing of a silver bird. Jace moved to the center of the room and stared down at the pattern of metallic stars burned into the red and gold tiles of the floor. Clary watched him, feeling her heart ache. It was hard to see him like this, all his usual burning energy gone, like witchlight suffocating under a covering of ash.

He raised his blond head then, blinking, and Clary knew that the Silent Brothers were speaking inside his mind, saying words she couldn't hear. She saw him shake his head and heard him say, "I don't know. I thought they weren't anything but ordinary dreams." His mouth tightened then, and she couldn't help wondering what they were asking him. "Visions? I don't think so. Yes, I did encounter the Angel, but it's Clary who had the prophetic dreams. Not me."

Clary tensed. They were getting awfully close to asking about what had happened with Jace and the Angel that night by Lake Lyn. She hadn't thought about that. When the Silent Brothers pried into your mind, just what did they see? Only what they were looking for? Or everything?

Jace nodded then. "Fine. I'm ready if you are."

He closed his eyes, and Clary, watching, relaxed slightly. This must have been what it had been like for Jace to watch her, she thought, the first time the Silent Brothers had delved into her mind. She saw details she hadn't noticed then, for she had been caught inside the nets of their minds and her own, reeling back into her memories, lost to the world.

She saw Jace stiffen all over as if they had touched him with their hands. His head went back. His hands, at his sides, opened and closed, as the stars on the floor at his feet flared up with a blinding silver light. She blinked away tears from the brightness; he was a graceful dark outline against a sheet of blinding silver, as if he stood in the heart of a waterfall. All around them was noise, a soft, incomprehensible whispering.

As she watched, he went to his knees, his hands braced against the ground. Her heart tightened. Having the Silent Brothers in her head had nearly made her faint, but Jace was stronger than that, wasn't he? Slowly he doubled in on himself, hands gripped against his stomach, agony in every line of him, though he never cried out. Clary could take it no longer—she darted toward him, through the sheets of light, and went on her knees next to him, throwing her arms around his body. The whispering voices around her rose to a storm of protest as he turned his head and looked at her. The silver light had washed out his eyes, and they looked flat and as white as marble tiles. His lips shaped her name.

And then it was gone—the light, the sound, all of it, and they knelt together on the bare floor of the pavilion, silence and shadow all around them. Jace was shaking, and when his hands released each other, she saw that they were bloody where his nails had torn the skin. Still holding him by the arm, she looked up at the Silent Brothers, fighting back her anger. She knew it was like being furious at a doctor who had to administer a painful but lifesaving treatment, but it was hard—so hard—to be reasonable when it was someone that you loved.

There is something you have not told us, Clarissa Morgenstern, said Brother Zachariah. *A secret you both have been keeping.*

An icy hand closed around Clary's heart. "What do you mean?"

The mark of death is on this boy. It was another of the Brothers speaking—Enoch, she thought.

"Death?" said Jace. "Do you mean I'm going to die?" He didn't sound surprised.

We mean that you were dead. You had passed beyond the portal into the shadow realms, your soul untethered from your body.

Clary and Jace exchanged a look. She swallowed. "The Angel Raziel—," she began.

Yes, his mark is all over the boy as well. Enoch's voice was without emotion. *There are only two ways to bring back the dead. The way of necromancy, the black sorcery of bell, book, and candle. That will return a semblance of life. But only an Angel of God's own right hand could place a human's soul back into their body as easily as life was breathed into the first of men.* He shook his head. *The balance of life and death, of good and evil, is a delicate one, young Shadowhunters. You have upset it.*

"But Raziel's the Angel," said Clary. "He can do whatever he wants. You worship him, don't you? If he chose to do this—"

Did he? asked another of the Brothers. *Did he choose?*

"I . . ." Clary looked at Jace. She thought, *I could have asked for anything else in the universe. World peace, a cure to disease, to live forever. But all I wanted was you.*

We know the ritual of the Instruments, said Zachariah. *We know that he who possesses them all, who is their Lord, may request of the Angel one thing. I do not think he could have refused you.*

Clary set her chin. "Well," she said, "it's done now."

Jace gave the ghost of a laugh. "They could always kill me, you know," he said. "Bring things back into balance."

Her hands tightened on his arm. "Don't be ridiculous." But her voice was thin. She tensed further as Brother Zachariah broke away from the tight group of Silent Brothers and approached them, his feet gliding silently over the Speaking Stars. He reached Jace, and Clary had to fight the urge to push him away as he bent down and placed his long fingers under Jace's chin, raising the boy's face to his. Zachariah's fingers were slim, unlined—a young man's fingers. She had never given much thought to the ages of the Silent Brothers before, assuming them to be all some species of wizened and old.

Jace, kneeling, gazed up at Zachariah, who looked down at him with his blind, impassive expression. Clary could not help but think of medieval paintings of saints on their knees, gazing upward, their faces suffused with shining golden light. *Would that I had been here,* he said, his voice unexpectedly gentle, *when you were growing up. I would have seen the truth in your face, Jace Lightwood, and known who you were.*

Jace looked puzzled but didn't move to pull away.

Zachariah turned to the others. *We cannot and should not harm the boy. Old ties exist between the Herondales and the Brothers. We owe him help.*

"Help with what?" Clary demanded. "Can you see something wrong with him—something inside his head?"

When a Shadowhunter is born, a ritual is performed, a number of protective spells placed upon the child by both the Silent Brothers and the Iron Sisters.

The Iron Sisters, Clary knew from her studies, were the sister sect of the Silent Brothers; even more retiring than their brethren, they were in charge of crafting Shadowhunter weapons.

Brother Zachariah went on. *When Jace died and then was raised, he was born a second time, with those protections and rituals stripped away. It would have left him as open as an unlocked door— open to any kind of demonic influence or malevolence.*

Clary licked her dry lips. "Possession, you mean?"

Not possession. Influence. I suspect that a powerful demonic power whispers into your ears, Jonathan Herondale. You are strong, you fight it, but it wears you down as the sea wears down the sand.

"Jace," he whispered through white lips. "Jace Lightwood, not Herondale."

Clary, clinging to practicalities, said, "How can you be sure it's a demon? And what can we do to get it to leave him alone?"

Enoch, sounding thoughtful, said, *The ritual must be performed again, the protections laid upon him a second time, as if he had just been born.*

"Can you do it?" Clary asked.

Zachariah inclined his head. *It can be done. The preparations must be made, one of the Iron Sisters called on, an amulet crafted.* . . . He trailed off. *Jonathan must remain with us until the ritual is finished. This is the safest place for him.*

Clary looked at Jace again, searching for an expression— any expression—of hope, relief, delight, anything. But his face was impassive. "For how long?" he said.

Zachariah spread his thin hands wide. *A day, perhaps two. The ritual is meant for infants; we will have to change it, alter it to fit an adult. If he were older than eighteen, it would be impossible. As it is, it will be difficult. But he is not beyond saving.*

Not beyond saving. It was not what Clary had hoped for; she had wanted to be told that the problem was simple, easily solved. She looked at Jace. His head was bowed, his hair falling forward; the back of his neck looked so vulnerable to her, it made her heart ache.

"It's fine," she said softly. "I'll stay here with you—"

No. The Brothers spoke as a group, their voices inexorable. *He must remain here alone. For what we must do, he cannot afford to be distracted.*

She felt Jace's body tighten. The last time he had been alone in the Silent City, he had been unfairly imprisoned, present for the horrible deaths of most of the Silent Brothers, and tormented by Valentine. She could not imagine that the idea of another night alone in the City would be anything but awful for him.

"Jace," she whispered. "I'll do whatever you want me to do. If you want to go . . ."

"I'll stay," he said. He had raised his head, and his voice was strong and clear. "I'll stay. I'll do whatever I have to do to fix this. I just need you to call Izzy and Alec. Tell them—tell them I'm staying at Simon's to keep an eye on him. Tell them I'll see them tomorrow or the next day."

"But . . ."

"Clary." Gently he took both her hands and held them between his. "You were right. This isn't coming from inside me. Something is *doing* this to me. To us. You know what that means? If I can be . . . cured . . . then I don't have to be afraid of myself when I'm around you anymore. I'd spend a thousand nights in the Silent City for that."

She leaned forward, heedless of the presence of the Silent Brothers, and kissed him, a quick press of her lips against his. "I'll be back," she whispered. "Tomorrow night, after the Ironworks party, I'll come back and see you."

The hopefulness in his eyes was enough to break her heart. "Maybe I'll be cured by then."

She touched his face with her fingertips. "Maybe you will be."

Simon woke still feeling exhausted after a long night of bad dreams. He rolled onto his back and stared at the light coming in the single window in his bedroom.

He couldn't help but wonder if he'd sleep better if he did what other vampires did, and slept during the day. Despite the fact that the sun didn't harm him, he could feel the pull of the nights, the desire to be out under the dark sky and the glimmering stars. There was something in him that wanted to live in shadows, that felt the sunlight like a thin, knife-like pain—just like there was something in him that wanted blood. And look how fighting *that* had turned out for him.

He staggered upright and threw on some clothes, then made his way out into the living room. The place smelled like toast and coffee. Jordan was sitting on one of the counter stools, his hair sticking out every which way as usual, his shoulders hunched.

"Hey," Simon said. "What's up?"

Jordan looked over at him. He was pale under his tan. "We have a problem," he said.

Simon blinked. He hadn't seen his werewolf roommate since the day before. He'd come home from the Institute last night and collapsed in exhaustion. Jordan hadn't been here, and Simon had figured he was out working. But maybe something had happened. "What's wrong?"

"This was shoved under our door." Jordan pushed a folded newspaper toward Simon. It was the *New York Morning Chronicle*, folded open to one of the pages. There was a grisly picture up toward the top, a grainy image of a body sprawled on some pavement, stick-skinny limbs bent at odd angles. It hardly looked human, the way dead bodies sometimes didn't. Simon was about to ask Jordan why he had to look at this, when the text under the photo jumped out at him.

GIRL FOUND DEAD

Police say they are pursuing leads in the death of
fourteen-year-old Maureen Brown, whose body was
discovered Sunday night at eleven p.m. stuffed into a
trash can outside the Big Apple Deli on Third Avenue.
Though no official cause of death has been released
by the coroner's office, the deli owner who found the
body, Michael Garza, says her throat was cut open.
Police have not yet located a weapon . . .

Unable to read on, Simon sat down heavily in a chair. Now
that he knew, the photo was unmistakably Maureen. He recognized her rainbow arm warmers, the stupid pink hat she'd been
wearing when he'd seen her last. *My God*, he wanted to say. *Oh,
God.* But no words came out.

"Didn't that note say," Jordan said in a bleak voice, "that if you
didn't go to that address, they'd cut your girlfriend's throat?"

"No," Simon whispered. "It's not possible. No."

But he remembered.

*Eric's little cousin's friend. What's her name? The one who has a crush
on Simon. She comes to all our gigs and tells everyone she's his girlfriend.*

Simon remembered her phone, her little pink phone with
the stickers on it, the way she'd held it up to take a photo of
them. The feeling of her hand on his shoulder, as light as a
butterfly. Fourteen years old. He curled in on himself, wrapping his arms around his chest, as if he could make himself
small enough to vanish completely.

14

WHAT DREAMS MAY COME

Jace tossed uneasily on the narrow bed in the Silent City. He didn't know where the Brothers slept, and they didn't seem inclined to reveal it. The only place there seemed to be for him to lie down was in one of the cells below the City where they usually kept prisoners. They'd left the door open for him so he didn't feel too much like he was in jail, but the place couldn't by any stretch of the imagination be called pleasant.

The air was close and thick; he'd taken off his shirt and lay atop the covers in just his jeans, but he was still too hot. The walls were dull gray. Someone had carved the letters *JG* into the stone just above the bedstead, leaving him to wonder what that was about—and there was nothing else in the room but the bed, a cracked mirror that gave him back his own reflection in twisted pieces, and the sink. Not to mention the more than unpleasant memories the room stirred up.

The Brothers had been in and out of his mind all night, till he felt like a wrung-out rag. Since they were so secretive about everything, he had no idea if they were making any progress. They didn't seem pleased, but then, they never did.

The real test, he knew, was sleeping. What would he dream? *To sleep: perchance to dream.* He flipped over, burying his face in his arms. He didn't think he could stand even one more dream about hurting Clary. He thought he might actually lose his mind, and the idea frightened him. The prospect of dying had never frightened him much, but the thought of going insane was nearly the worst thing he could imagine. But going to sleep was the only way to know. He closed his eyes and willed himself to sleep.

He slept, and he dreamed.

He was back in the valley—the valley in Idris where he had fought Sebastian and nearly died. It was autumn in the valley, not high summer as it had been the last time he had been there. The leaves were exploding in gold and russet and orange and red. He was standing by the bank of the small river—a stream, really—that cut the valley in half. In the distance, coming toward him, was someone, someone he couldn't see very clearly yet, but the person's stride was direct and purposeful.

He was so sure it was Sebastian that it was not until the figure had come close enough to see clearly that he realized it couldn't possibly be. Sebastian had been tall, taller than Jace, but this person was small—the face in shadow, but a head or two shorter than Jace—and skinny, with the thin shoulders of childhood, and bony wrists sticking out of the too-short sleeves of his shirt.

Max.

The sight of his little brother hit Jace like a blow, and he went down on his knees on the green grass. The fall didn't hurt. Everything had the padded edges of the dream that it was. Max looked as he always had. A knobby-kneed boy just on the verge of growing up and out of that little-kid stage. Now he never would.

"Max," Jace said. "Max, I'm so sorry."

"Jace." Max stood where he was. A little wind had come up and lifted his brown hair off his face. His eyes, behind their glasses, were serious. "I'm not here because of me," he said. "I'm not here to haunt you or make you feel guilty."

Of course he isn't, said a voice in Jace's head. *Max has only ever loved you, looked up to you, thought you were wonderful.*

"The dreams you've been having," Max said. "They're messages."

"The dreams are a demon's influence, Max. The Silent Brothers said—"

"They're wrong," Max said quickly. "There are only a few of them now, and their powers are weaker than they used to be. These dreams are meant to tell you something. You've been misunderstanding them. They're not telling you to hurt Clary. They're warning you that you already are."

Jace shook his head slowly. "I don't understand."

"The angels sent me to talk to you because I know you," Max said, in his clear child's voice. "I know how you are with the people you love, and you'd never hurt them willingly. But you haven't destroyed all of Valentine's influence inside you yet. His voice still whispers to you, and you don't think you hear it, but you do. The dreams are telling you that until you kill that part of yourself, you can't be with Clary."

"Then I'll kill it," Jace said. "I'll do whatever I have to do. Just tell me how."

Max smiled a clear bright smile and held out something in his hand. It was a silver-handled dagger—Stephen Herondale's silver-handled dagger, the one from the box. Jace recognized it at once. "Take this," Max said. "And turn it against yourself. The part of you that is here in the dream with me must die. What will rise up afterward will be cleansed."

Jace took the knife.

Max smiled. "Good. There are many of us here on the other side who are worried about you. Your father is here."

"Not Valentine—"

"Your real father. He told me to tell you to use this. It will cut away everything rotten in your soul."

Max smiled like an angel as Jace turned the knife toward himself, blade inward. Then at the last moment Jace hesitated. It was too close to what Valentine had done to him, piercing him through the heart. He took the blade and cut a long incision into his right forearm, from elbow to wrist. There was no pain. He switched the knife to the right hand and did the same to his other arm. Blood exploded from the long cuts on his arms, brighter red than blood in real life, blood the color of rubies. It spilled down his skin and pattered onto the grass.

He heard Max breathe out softly. The boy bent down and touched the fingers of his right hand to the blood. When he raised them, they were glittering scarlet. He took a step toward Jace, and then another. This close up, Jace could see Max's face clearly—his poreless child's skin, the translucence of his eyelids, his eyes—Jace didn't remember him having such dark eyes. Max put his hand to the skin of Jace's chest, just over his heart, and with the blood he began to trace a design there, a rune. Not one Jace had ever seen before, with overlapping corners and strange angles to its shape.

Done, Max dropped his hand and stepped back, head cocked to the side, an artist examining his latest work. A sudden spear of agony went through Jace. It felt as if the skin on his chest were burning. Max stood watching him, smiling, flexing his bloody hand. "Does it hurt you, Jace Lightwood?" he said, and his voice was no longer Max's voice, but something else, high and husky and familiar.

"Max—," Jace whispered.

"As you have dealt pain, so shall you be dealt pain," said Max, whose face had begun to shimmer and change. "As you have caused grief, so shall you feel grief. You are mine now, Jace Lightwood. You are mine."

The agony was blinding. Jace crumpled forward, hands clawing at his chest, and he tumbled into darkness.

Simon sat on the couch, his face in his hands. His mind was buzzing. "This is my fault," he said. "I might as well have killed Maureen when I drank her blood. She's dead because of me."

Jordan sprawled in the armchair opposite him. He was wearing jeans and a green tee over a long-sleeved thermal shirt with holes in the cuffs; he had his thumbs stuck through them, and was worrying at the material. The gold Praetor Lupus medal around his neck glinted. "Come on," he said. "There's no way you could have known. She was fine when I put her in the cab. These guys must have grabbed her and killed her later."

Simon felt light-headed. "But I bit her. She's not going to come back, right? She's not going to be a vampire?"

"No. Come on, you know this stuff as well as I do. You'd have to have given her some of your blood for her to become a vampire. If she'd drunk *your* blood and then died, yeah, we'd be out in the graveyard on stake watch. But she didn't. I mean, I assume you'd remember something like that."

Simon tasted sour blood in the back of his throat. "They thought she was my girlfriend," he said. "They warned me they'd kill her if I didn't show up, and when I didn't come, they cut her throat. She must have waited there all day, wondering if I'd come. Hoping I'd show up . . ." His stomach revolted, and he bent over, breathing hard, trying to keep from gagging.

"Yeah," said Jordan, "but the question is, who is *they*?" He gave Simon a hard look. "I think it might be time for you to call the Institute. I don't love the Shadowhunters, but I've always heard their archives are incredibly thorough. Maybe they've got something on that address from the note."

Simon hesitated.

"Come on," Jordan said. "You do enough crap for them. Let them do something for you."

With a shrug Simon went to get his phone. Heading back to the living room, he dialed Jace's number. Isabelle picked up on the second ring. "You again?"

"Sorry," Simon said awkwardly. Apparently their little interlude in the Sanctuary hadn't softened her toward him as much as he had hoped. "I was looking for Jace, but I guess I can talk to you—"

"Charming as always," said Isabelle. "I thought Jace was with you."

"No." Simon felt a stirring of unease. "Who told you that?"

"Clary," Isabelle said. "Maybe they're sneaking some time

together or something." She sounded unworried, which made sense; the last person who'd lie about Jace's whereabouts if he was in any sort of trouble was Clary. "Anyway, Jace left his phone in his room. If you do see him, remind him he's supposed to be at the party at the Ironworks tonight. If he doesn't show, Clary will kill him."

Simon had nearly forgotten that *he* was supposed to be at the party that night.

"Right," he said. "Look, Isabelle. I've got a problem here."

"Spill. I love problems."

"I don't know if you're going to love this one," he said dubiously, and filled her in quickly on the situation. She gave a little gasp when he got to the part where he'd bitten Maureen, and he felt his throat tighten.

"Simon," she whispered.

"I know, I know," he said wretchedly. "You think I'm not sorry? I'm beyond sorry."

"If you'd killed her, you'd have broken the Law. You'd be an outlaw. I'd have to kill *you*."

"But I didn't," he said, his voice shaking a little. "I didn't do this. Jordan swears that she was fine when he put her into the cab. And the newspaper says her throat was cut. *I* didn't do that. Someone did it to get to me. I just don't know why."

"We're not done with this issue." Her voice was stern. "But first go get the note they left. Read it out to me."

Simon did as asked, and was rewarded by a sharp intake of breath on Isabelle's part.

"I thought that address sounded familiar," she said. "That's where Clary told me to meet her yesterday. It's a church, uptown. The headquarters of some sort of demon-worshipping cult."

"What would a demon-worshipping cult want with me?" Simon said, and received a curious look from Jordan, who was only hearing half the conversation.

"I don't know. You're a Daylighter. You've got crazy powers. You're going to be a target for lunatics and black magicians. That's just how it *is*." Isabelle, Simon felt, could have sounded a bit more sympathetic. "Look, you're going to the Ironworks party, right? We can meet there and talk next steps. And I'll tell my mom about what's been going on with you. They're already investigating the Church of Talto, so they can add that to the info pile."

"I guess," Simon said. The last thing in the world he felt like was going to a party.

"And bring Jordan with you," Isabelle said. "You can use a bodyguard."

"I can't do that. Maia's going to be there."

"I'll talk to her," Isabelle said. She sounded a lot more confident than Simon would have felt in her place. "See you there."

She clicked off. Simon turned to Jordan, who was lying down across the futon, his head propped against one of the woven throw pillows. "How much of that did you hear?"

"Enough to gather that we're going to a party tonight," said Jordan. "I heard about the Ironworks event. I'm not in the Garroway pack, so I wasn't invited."

"I guess you're coming as my date now." Simon shoved the phone back into his pocket.

"I'm secure enough in my masculinity to accept that," said Jordan. "We'd better get you something nice to wear, though," he called as Simon headed back into his room. "I want you to look pretty."

* * *

Years previously, when Long Island City had been a center of industry instead of a trendy neighborhood full of art galleries and coffee shops, the Ironworks was a textile factory. Now it was an enormous brick shell whose inside had been transformed into a spare but beautiful space. The floor was made up of overlapping squares of brushed steel; slender steel beams arced overhead, wrapped with ropes of tiny white lights. Ornate wrought iron staircases spiraled up to catwalks decorated with hanging plants. A massive cantilevered glass ceiling opened onto a view of the night sky. There was even a terrace outside, built out over the East River, with a spectacular view of the Fifty-Ninth Street Bridge, which loomed overhead, stretching from Queens to Manhattan like a spear of tinseled ice.

Luke's pack had outdone themselves making the place look nice. There were artfully placed huge pewter vases holding long-stemmed ivory flowers, and tables covered in white linen arranged in a circle around a raised stage on which a werewolf string quartet provided classical music. Clary couldn't help wishing Simon were there; she was pretty sure he'd think Werewolf String Quartet was a good name for a band.

Clary wandered from table to table, arranging things that didn't need arranging, fiddling with flowers and straightening silverware that wasn't actually crooked. Only a few of the guests had arrived so far, and none of them were people she knew. Her mother and Luke stood near the door, greeting people and smiling, Luke looking uncomfortable in a suit, and Jocelyn radiant in a tailored blue dress. After the events of the past few days, it was good to see her mother looking happy, though Clary wondered how much of it was real and how much was for show. There was a certain tightness about Jocelyn's mouth that made Clary worry—was she actually happy, or just smiling through the pain?

Not that Clary didn't know how she felt. Whatever else was going on, she couldn't put Jace out of her mind. What were the Silent Brothers doing to him? Was he all right? Were they going to be able to fix what was wrong with him, to block out the demon influence? She had spent a sleepless night the evening before staring into the darkness of her bedroom and worrying until she felt literally sick.

More than anything else, she wished he was here. She had picked out the dress she was wearing tonight—pale gold and more fitted to her body than anything she usually wore—with the express hope that Jace would like it; now he wasn't going to see her in it. That was a shallow thing to worry about, she knew; she'd go around dressed in a barrel for the rest of her life if it meant Jace would get better. Besides, he was always telling her she was beautiful, and he never complained about the fact that she mostly wore jeans and sneakers, but she had thought he would like this.

Standing in front of her mirror tonight, she had almost felt beautiful. Her mother had always said that she herself had been a late bloomer, and Clary, looking at her own reflection, had wondered if the same thing might happen to her. She wasn't flat as a board anymore—she'd had to go up a bra size this past year—and if she squinted, she thought she could see—yes, those were definitely hips. She had curves. Small ones, but you had to start somewhere.

She'd kept her jewelry simple—very simple.

She put her hand up and touched the Morgenstern ring on its chain around her throat. She had put it on again, for the first time in days, that morning. She felt as if it were a silent gesture of confidence in Jace, a way of signaling her loyalty, whether he knew about it or not. She had decided she would wear it until she saw him again.

"Clarissa Morgenstern?" said a soft voice at her shoulder.

Clary turned in surprise. The voice wasn't familiar. Standing there was a slim tall girl who looked about twenty. Her skin was milk-pale, threaded with veins the clear green of sap, and her blond hair had the same greenish tint. Her eyes were solid blue, like marbles, and she wore a slip of a blue dress, so thin that Clary thought she had to be freezing. Memory swam up slowly from the depths.

"Kaelie," Clary said slowly, recognizing the faerie waitress from Taki's who had served her and the Lightwoods more than once. A flicker reminded her that there had been some intimation that Kaelie and Jace had once had a fling, but the fact seemed so minor in the face of everything else that she couldn't bring herself to mind it. "I didn't realize—do you know Luke?"

"Do not mistake me for a guest at this occasion," said Kaelie, her thin hand tracing a casually indifferent gesture on the air. "My lady sent me here to find you—not to attend the festivities." She glanced curiously over her shoulder, her all-blue eyes shining. "Though I had not realized that your mother was marrying a werewolf."

Clary raised her eyebrows. "And?"

Kaelie looked her up and down with some amusement. "My lady said you were quite flinty, despite your small size. In the Court you would be looked down on for having such short stature."

"We're not in the Court," said Clary. "And we're not in

Taki's, which means *you* came to *me*, which means you have five seconds to tell me what the Seelie Queen wants. I don't like her much, and I'm not in the mood for her games."

Kaelie pointed a thin green-nailed finger at Clary's throat. "My lady said to ask you," she said, "why you wear the Morgenstern ring. Is it to acknowledge your father?"

Clary's hand stole to her throat. "It's for Jace—because Jace gave it to me," she said before she could help herself, and then cursed herself quietly. It wasn't smart to tell the Seelie Queen more than you had to.

"But he is not a Morgenstern," said Kaelie, "but a Herondale, and they have their own ring. A pattern of herons, rather than morning stars. And does that not suit him better, a soul that soars like a bird in flight, rather than falling like Lucifer?"

"Kaelie," Clary ground out between her teeth. *"What does the Seelie Queen want?"*

The faerie girl laughed. "Why," she said, "only to give you this." She held out something in her hand, a tiny silver bell pendant, with a loop at the end of the handle so that it could be strung on a chain. As Kaelie moved her hand forward, the bell chimed, light and as sweet as rain.

Clary shrank back. "I do not want the gifts of your lady," she said, "for they come freighted with lies and expectations. I will not owe the Queen anything."

"It is not a gift," Kaelie said impatiently. "It is a means of summoning. The Queen forgives you for your earlier stubbornness. She expects there is a time soon in which you will want her help. She is willing to offer it to you, should you choose to ask. Simply ring that bell, and a servant of the Court will come and bring you to her."

Clary shook her head. "I will not ring it."

Kaelie shrugged. "Then it should cost you nothing to take it."

As if in a dream Clary saw her own hand reach out, her fingers hover over the bell.

"You would do anything to save him," said Kaelie, her voice thin and as sweet as the bell's ring, "whatever it cost you, whatever you might owe to Hell or Heaven, would you not?"

Remembered voices chimed in Clary's head. *Did you ever stop to wonder what untruths might have been in the tale your mother told you, that served her purpose in telling it? Do you truly think you know each and every secret of your past?*

Madame Dorothea told Jace he would fall in love with the wrong person.

He is not beyond saving. But it will be difficult.

The bell clanged as Clary took it, folding it into her palm. Kaelie smiled, her blue eyes shining like glass beads. "A wise choice."

Clary hesitated. But before she could thrust the bell back at the faerie girl, she heard someone call her name, and turned to see her mother making her way through the crowd toward her. She turned back hastily, but was not surprised to see that Kaelie was gone, having melted away into the crowd like mist burning away in the morning sun.

"Clary," Jocelyn said, reaching her, "I was looking for you, and then Luke pointed you out, just standing over here by yourself. Is everything okay?"

Just standing over here by yourself. Clary wondered what kind of glamour Kaelie had been using; her mother ought to be able to see through most. "I'm fine, Mom."

"Where's Simon? I thought he was coming."

Of course she would think of Simon first, Clary thought, not Jace. Even though Jace had been supposed to come, and as Clary's boyfriend, he probably ought to even have been there early. "Mom," she said, and then paused. "Do you think you'll ever like Jace?"

Jocelyn's green eyes softened. "I *did* notice he wasn't here, Clary. I just didn't know if you'd want to talk about it."

"I mean," Clary went on doggedly, "do you think there's something he could do to *make* you like him?"

"Yes," Jocelyn said. "He could make you happy." She touched Clary's face lightly, and Clary clenched her own hand, feeling the bell press into her skin.

"He does make me happy," Clary said. "But he can't control everything in the world, Mom. Other things happen—" She fumbled for words. How could she explain that it wasn't *Jace* making her unhappy, but what was happening to him, without revealing what that was?

"You love him so much," Jocelyn said gently. "It scares me. I've always wanted to keep you protected."

"And look how that worked out," Clary began, and then softened her voice. This wasn't the time to blame her mother or fight with her, not now. Not with Luke looking over at them from the doorway, his face alight with love and anxiety. "If you just knew him," she said, a little hopelessly. "But I guess everyone says that about their boyfriend."

"You're right," Jocelyn said, surprising her. "I don't know him, not really. I see him, and he reminds me a little of his mother somehow. I don't know why—he doesn't look like her, except that she was also beautiful, and she had that terrible vulnerability that he has—"

"Vulnerability?" Clary was astonished. She had never thought anyone but herself thought of Jace as vulnerable.

"Oh, yes," said Jocelyn. "I wanted to hate her for taking Stephen away from Amatis, but you just couldn't help wanting to protect Céline. Jace has a little of that." She sounded lost in thought. "Or maybe it's just that beautiful things are so easily broken by the world." She lowered her hand. "It doesn't matter. I have my memories to contend with, but they're *my* memories. Jace shouldn't bear the weight of them. I will tell you one thing, though. If he didn't love you like he does—and it's written all over his face whenever he looks at you—I wouldn't tolerate him for even a moment. So keep that in mind when you're being angry with me."

She waved off Clary's protestation that she wasn't angry with a smile and a pat on the cheek, and headed back toward Luke with a last appeal for Clary to get out among the crowd and mingle. Clary nodded and said nothing, looking after her mother as she went, and feeling the bell sear against the inside of her hand where she clutched it, like the tip of a burning match.

The area around the Ironworks was mostly warehouses and art galleries, the kind of neighborhood that emptied out at night, so it didn't take too long for Jordan and Simon to find a parking space. Simon jumped down out of the truck, only to find Jordan already on the sidewalk, looking at him critically.

Simon hadn't packed any nice clothes when he'd left his house—he didn't have anything on him fancier than a bomber jacket that had once belonged to his dad—so he and Jordan had spent the afternoon prowling the East Village for a decent outfit for him to wear. They'd finally found an old Zegna suit in a consignment shop called Love Saves the Day that mostly sold glitter platform boots and sixties Pucci scarves. Simon suspected it was where Magnus got most of his clothes.

"What?" he said now, self-consciously pulling down the sleeves of his suit jacket. It was a little too small for him, though Jordan had opined that if he never buttoned it, no one would notice. "How bad do I look?"

Jordan shrugged. "You won't crack any mirrors," he said. "I was just wondering if you were armed. You want anything? Dagger, maybe?" He opened his own suit jacket just a bit, and Simon saw something long and metallic glinting against the inside lining.

"No wonder you and Jace like each other so much. You're both crazy walking arsenals." Simon shook his head in weariness and turned to head toward the Ironworks entrance. It was across the street, a wide gold awning shadowing a rectangle of sidewalk that had been decorated with a dark red carpet with the gold image of a wolf stamped into it. Simon couldn't help being slightly amused.

Leaning against one of the poles holding up the awning was Isabelle. She had her hair up and was wearing a long red dress, slit up the side to show most of her leg. Loops of gold laddered her right arm. They looked like bracelets, but Simon knew they were really her electrum whip. She was covered in Marks. They twined her arms, threaded their way up her thigh, necklaced her throat, and decorated her chest, a great deal of which was visible, thanks to the plunging neckline of her dress. Simon tried not to stare.

"Hey, Isabelle," he said.

Beside him Jordan was also trying not to stare. "Um," he said. "Hi. I'm Jordan."

"We met," Isabelle said coldly, ignoring his proffered hand. "Maia was trying to rip your face off. Quite rightly, too."

Jordan looked worried. "Is she here? Is she okay?"

"She's here," said Isabelle. "Not that how she feels is any of your business . . ."

"I feel a sense of responsibility," said Jordan.

"And where is this feeling located? In your pants, perhaps?"

Jordan looked indignant.

Isabelle waved a slim decorated hand. "Look, whatever you did in the past, it's past. I know you're Praetor Lupus now, and I told Maia what that means. She's willing to accept that you're here and ignore you. But that's all you get. Don't bother her, don't try to talk to her, don't even look at her, or I'll fold you in half so many times you'll look like a tiny little origami werewolf."

Simon snorted.

"Laugh away." Isabelle pointed at him. "She doesn't want to talk to you, either. So despite the fact that she looks totally babelicious tonight—and if I were into chicks I would completely go for her—neither of you are allowed to talk to her. Got it?"

They nodded, looking at their shoes like middle schoolers who'd just been handed detention slips.

Isabelle unpeeled herself from the pole. "Great. Let's go on in."

15

BEATI BELLICOSI

The inside of the Ironworks was alive with ropes of shimmering multicolored lights. Quite a few guests were already sitting, but just as many were milling around, carrying champagne glasses full of pale, fizzing liquid. Waiters—who were also werewolves, Simon noted; the whole event seemed to be staffed by members of Luke's pack—moved among the guests, handing out champagne flutes. Simon declined one. Ever since his experience at Magnus's party, he hadn't felt safe drinking anything that he hadn't prepared himself, and besides, he never knew which non-blood liquids were going to stay down and which would make him sick.

Maia was standing over by one of the brick pillars, talking to two other werewolves and laughing. She wore a brilliant orange satin sheath dress that set off her dark skin, and her hair was a wild halo of brown-gold curls around her face. She caught sight of Simon and Jordan and deliberately turned away. The back of her dress was a low V that showed a lot of bare skin, including a tattoo of a butterfly across her lower spine.

"I don't think she had that when I knew her," Jordan said. "That tattoo, I mean."

Simon looked at Jordan. He was goggling at his ex-girlfriend with the sort of obvious longing that, Simon suspected, was going to get him punched in the face by Isabelle if he wasn't careful. "Come on," he said, putting his hand against Jordan's back and shoving lightly. "Let's go see where we're sitting."

Isabelle, who had been watching them over her shoulder, smiled a catlike smile. "Good idea."

They made their way through the crowd to the area where the tables were, only to find that their table was already half-occupied. Clary sat in one of the seats, looking down into a champagne glass full of what was most likely ginger ale. Next to her were Alec and Magnus, both in the dark suits they'd worn when they'd come from Vienna. Magnus seemed to be playing with the fringed edges of his long white scarf. Alec, his arms crossed over his chest, was staring ferociously into the distance.

Clary, on seeing Simon and Jordan, bounced to her feet, relief evident on her face. She came around the table to greet Simon, and he saw that she was wearing a very plain gold silk dress and low gold sandals. Without heels to give her height, she looked tiny. The Morgenstern ring was around her neck, its silver glinting against the chain that held it. She reached up to hug him and muttered, "I think Alec and Magnus are fighting."

"Looks like it," he muttered back. "Where's your boyfriend?"

At that, she detached her arms from his neck. "He got held up at the Institute." She turned. "Hey, Kyle."

He smiled a little awkwardly. "It's Jordan, actually."

"So I've heard." Clary gestured toward the table. "Well, we might as well sit. I think pretty soon there's going to be toasting and stuff. And then, hopefully, food."

They all sat. There was a long, awkward silence.

"So," Magnus said finally, running a long white finger around the rim of his champagne glass. "Jordan. I hear you're in the Praetor Lupus. I see you're wearing one of their medallions. What does it say on it?"

Jordan nodded. He was flushed, his hazel eyes sparkling, his attention clearly only partly on the conversation. He was following Maia around the room with his eyes, his fingers nervously clenching and unclenching on the edge of the tablecloth. Simon doubted he was even aware of it. "*Beati bellicosi: Blessed are the warriors.*"

"Good organization," said Magnus. "I knew the man who founded it, back in the 1800s. Woolsey Scott. Respectable old werewolf family."

Alec made an ugly sound in the back of his throat. "Did you sleep with him, too?"

Magnus's cat eyes widened. "Alexander!"

"Well, I don't know anything about your past, do I?" Alec demanded. "You won't tell me anything; you just say it doesn't matter."

Magnus's face was expressionless, but there was a dark tinge of anger to his voice. "Does this mean every time I mention anyone I've ever met, you're going to ask me if I had an affair with them?"

Alec's expression was stubborn, but Simon couldn't help having a flash of sympathy; the hurt behind his blue eyes was clear. "Maybe."

"I met Napoleon once," said Magnus. "We didn't have an affair, though. He was shockingly prudish for a Frenchman."

"You met Napoleon?" Jordan, who appeared to be missing most of the conversation, looked impressed. "So it's true what they say about warlocks, then?"

Alec gave him a very unpleasant look. "*What's* true?"

"Alexander," said Magnus coldly, and Clary met Simon's eyes across the table. Hers were wide, green, and full of an expression that said *Uh-oh.* "You can't be rude to everyone who talks to me."

Alec made a wide, sweeping gesture. "And why not? Cramping your style, am I? I mean, maybe you were hoping to flirt with werewolf boy here. He's pretty attractive, if you like the messy-haired, broad-shouldered, chiseled-good-looks type."

"Hey, now," said Jordan mildly.

Magnus put his head in his hands.

"Or there are plenty of pretty girls here, since apparently your taste goes both ways. Is there anything you *aren't* into?"

"Mermaids," said Magnus into his fingers. "They always smell like seaweed."

"It's *not funny*," Alec said savagely, and kicking back his chair, he got up from the table and stalked off into the crowd.

Magnus still had his head in his hands, the black spikes of his hair sticking out between his fingers. "I just don't see," he said to no one in particular, "why the past has to matter."

To Simon's surprise it was Jordan who answered. "The past always matters," he said. "That's what they tell you when you join the Praetor. You can't forget the things you did in the past, or you'll never learn from them."

Magnus looked up, his gold-green eyes glinting through his fingers. "How old are you?" he demanded. "Sixteen?"

"Eighteen," said Jordan, looking slightly frightened.

Alec's age, thought Simon, suppressing an interior grin. He didn't really find Alec and Magnus's drama funny, but it was hard not to feel a certain bitter amusement at Jordan's expression. Jordan had to be twice Magnus's size—despite being tall, Magnus was slender to the point of skinniness—but Jordan was clearly afraid of him. Simon turned to share a glance with Clary, but she was staring off toward the front door, her face gone suddenly bone white. Dropping her napkin onto the table, she murmured, "Excuse me," and got to her feet, practically fleeing the table.

Magnus threw his hands up. "Well, if there's going to be a mass exodus . . . ," he said, and got up gracefully, flinging his scarf around his neck. He vanished into the crowd, presumably looking for Alec.

Simon looked at Jordan, who was looking at Maia again. She had her back to them and was talking to Luke and Jocelyn, laughing, flinging her curly hair back. "Don't even think about it," Simon said, and got up. He pointed at Jordan. "You stay here."

"And do what?" Jordan demanded.

"Whatever Praetor Lupus do in this situation. Meditate. Contemplate your Jedi powers. Whatever. I'll be back in five minutes, and you better still be here."

Jordan leaned back, crossing his arms over his chest in a clearly mutinous manner, but Simon had already stopped paying attention. He turned and moved into the crowd, following Clary. She was a speck of red and gold among the moving bodies, crowned with her twist of bright hair.

He caught up to her by one of the light-wrapped pillars, and put a hand on her shoulder. She turned with a startled exclamation, eyes wide, hand raised as if to fend him off. She relaxed when she saw who it was. "You scared me!"

"Obviously," Simon said. "What's going on? What are you so freaked out about?"

"I . . ." She lowered her hand with a shrug; despite her forced look of casual dismissal, the pulse was going in her neck like a hammer. "I thought I saw Jace."

"I figured," Simon said. "But . . ."

"But?"

"You look really frightened." He wasn't sure why he'd said it exactly, or what he was hoping she'd say back. She bit her lip, the way she always did when she was nervous. Her gaze for a moment was far away; it was a look familiar to Simon. One of the things he'd always loved about Clary was how easily caught up in her imagination she was, how easily she could wall herself away in illusory worlds of curses and princes and destiny and magic. Once he had been able to do the same, had been able to inhabit imaginary worlds all the more exciting for being safe—for being fictional. Now that the real and the imagined had collided, he wondered if she, like he, longed for the past, for the normal. He wondered if normalcy was something, like vision or silence, you didn't realize was precious until you lost it.

"He's having a hard time," she said in a low voice. "I'm scared for him."

"I know," Simon said. "Look, not to pry, but—has he figured out what's wrong with him? Has anyone?"

"He—" She broke off. "He's all right. He's just having a hard
time coming to terms with some of the Valentine stuff. You
know." Simon did know. He also knew she was lying. Clary,
who hardly ever hid anything from him. He gave her a hard
look.

"He's been having bad dreams," she said. "He was worried
that there was some demon involvement—"

"*Demon* involvement?" Simon echoed in disbelief. He'd
known that Jace was having bad dreams—he'd said as much—
but Jace had never mentioned demons.

"Well, apparently there are kinds of demons that try to
reach you through your dreams," Clary said, sounding as if she
were sorry she'd brought it up at all, "but I'm sure it's nothing.
Everyone has bad dreams sometimes, don't they?" She put a
hand on Simon's arm. "I'm just going to see how he is. I'll come
back." Her gaze was already sliding past him, toward the doors
that led onto the terrace; he stood back with a nod and let her
go, watching her as she moved off into the crowd.

She looked so small—small the way she had in first grade
when he'd walked her to the front door of her house and
watched her go up the stairs, tiny and determined, her lunch
box banging against her knee as she went. He felt his heart,
which no longer beat, contract, and he wondered if there was
anything in the world as painful as not being able to protect the
people you loved.

"You look sick," said a voice at his elbow. Husky, familiar.
"Thinking about what a horrible person you are?"

Simon turned and saw Maia leaning against the pillar

behind him. She had a strand of the small, glowing white lights wound around her neck, and her face was flushed with champagne and the warmth of the room.

"Or maybe I should say," she went on, "what a horrible *vampire* you are. Except that makes it sound like you're bad at being a vampire."

"I *am* bad at being a vampire," Simon said. "But that doesn't mean I wasn't bad at being a boyfriend, too."

She smiled crookedly. "Bat says I shouldn't be so hard on you," she said. "He says guys do stupid things when girls are involved. Especially geeky ones who previously haven't had much luck with women."

"It's like he can see into my soul."

Maia shook her head. "It's hard to stay mad at you," she said. "But I'm working on it." She turned away.

"Maia," Simon said. His head had started to ache, and he felt a little dizzy. If he didn't talk to her now, though, he never would. "Please. Wait."

She turned back and looked at him, both eyebrows raised questioningly.

"I'm sorry about what I did," he said. "I know I said that before, but I really do mean it."

She shrugged, expressionless, giving him nothing.

He swallowed past the pain in his head. "Maybe Bat's right," he said. "But I think there's more to it than that. I wanted to be with you because—and this is going to sound so selfish—you made me feel normal. Like the person I was before."

"I'm a werewolf, Simon. Not exactly normal."

"But you—you are," he said, stumbling over his words a little. "You're genuine and real—one of the realest people

I've ever known. You wanted to come over and play Halo. You wanted to talk about comics and check out concerts and go dancing and just do normal things. And you treated me like I was normal. You've never called me 'Daylighter' or 'vampire' or anything but Simon."

"That's all friend stuff," Maia said. She was leaning against the pillar again, her eyes glinting softly as she spoke. "Not *girl-friend* stuff."

Simon just looked at her. His headache pulsed like a heartbeat.

"And then you come around," she added, "bringing Jordan with you. *What* were you thinking?"

"That's not fair," Simon protested. "I had no idea he was your ex—"

"I know. Isabelle told me," Maia interrupted. "I just feel like giving you hell about it anyway."

"Oh, yeah?" Simon glanced over at Jordan, who was sitting alone at the round linen-draped table, like a guy whose prom date hadn't showed up. Simon suddenly felt very tired—tired of worrying about everyone, tired of feeling guilty for the things he'd done and would probably do in the future. "Well, did Izzy tell you that Jordan got himself assigned to me so he could be near you? You should hear the way he asks about you. The way he says your name, even. Man, the way he ripped into me when he thought I was cheating on you—"

"You weren't cheating. We weren't exclusively dating. Cheating is different—"

Simon smiled as Maia broke off, blushing. "I guess it's good that you dislike him so much that you'll take my side against him no matter what," he said.

"It's been years," she said. "He's never tried to get in touch with me. Not once."

"He did try," Simon said. "Did you know the night he bit you was the first time he ever Turned?"

She shook her head, her curls bouncing, her wide amber eyes very serious. "No. I thought he knew—"

"That he was a werewolf? No. He knew he was losing control in some way, but who guesses they're turning into a were-wolf? The day after he bit you he went looking for you, but the Praetor stopped him. They kept him away from you. Even then he didn't stop looking. I don't think a day's gone by in the past two years that he hasn't wondered where you were—"

"Why are you defending him?" she whispered.

"Because you should know," said Simon. "I sucked at being a boyfriend, and I owe you. You should know he didn't mean to abandon you. He only took me on as an assignment because your name was mentioned in the notes on my case."

Her lips parted. As she shook her head, the glittering lights of her necklace winked like stars. "I just don't know what I'm supposed to do with that, Simon. What am I supposed to *do*?"

"I don't know," Simon said. His head felt like nails were being pounded into it. "But I can tell you one thing. I'm the last guy in the world you should be asking for relationship advice from." He pressed a hand to his forehead. "I'm going to go out-side. Get some air. Jordan's over at that table there if you want to talk to him."

He gestured over toward the tables and then turned away, away from her questioning eyes, from the eyes of everyone in the room, the sound of raised voices and laughter, and stum-bled toward the doors.

* * *

Clary pushed open the doors that led out onto the terrace and was greeted by a rush of cold air. She shivered, wishing she had her coat but unwilling to take up any time going back to the table to get it. She stepped out onto the terrace and shut the door behind her.

The terrace was a wide expanse of flagstones, surrounded by ironwork railings. Tiki torches burned in big pewter holders, but they did little to warm the air—which probably explained why no one was out here but Jace. He was standing by the railing, looking out over the river.

She wanted to run over to him, but she couldn't help hesitating. He was wearing a dark suit, the jacket open over a white shirt, and his head was turned to the side, away from her. She had never seen him dressed like this before, and it made him look older and a little remote. The wind off the river lifted his fair hair, and she saw the little scar across the side of his throat where Simon had bitten him once, and she remembered that Jace had let himself be bitten, had risked his life, for her.

"Jace," she said.

He turned and looked at her and smiled. The smile was familiar and seemed to unlock something inside her, freeing her to run across the flagstones to him and throw her arms around him. He picked her up and held her off the ground for a long time, his face buried in her neck.

"You're all right," she said finally, when he set her down. She scrubbed fiercely at the tears that had spilled out of her eyes. "I mean—the Silent Brothers wouldn't have let you go if you weren't all right—but I thought they said the ritual was going to take a long time? Days, even?"

"It didn't." He put his hands on either side of her face and smiled down at her. Behind him the Queensboro Bridge arced out over the water. "You know the Silent Brothers. They like to make a big deal out of everything they do. But it's actually a pretty simple ceremony." He grinned. "I felt kind of stupid. It's a ceremony meant for little kids, but I just kept thinking that if I got it over with fast, I'd get to see you in your sexy party dress. It got me through." His eyes raked her up and down. "And let me tell you, I am *not* disappointed. You're gorgeous."

"You look pretty good yourself." She laughed a little through the tears. "I didn't even think you owned a suit."

"I didn't. I had to buy one." He slid his thumbs over her cheekbones where the tears had made them damp. "Clary—"

"Why did you come out here?" she asked. "It's freezing. Don't you want to go back inside?"

He shook his head. "I wanted to talk to you alone."

"So talk," Clary said in a half whisper. She took his hands away from her face and put them on her waist. Her need to be held against him was almost overwhelming. "Is something else wrong? Are you going to be okay? Please don't hold anything back from me. After everything that's happened, you should know I can handle any bad news." She knew she was nervously chattering, but she couldn't help it. Her heart felt as if it were beating a thousand miles a minute. "I just want you to be all right," she said as calmly as she could.

His gold eyes darkened. "I keep going through that box. The one that belonged to my father. I don't feel anything about it. The letters, the photos. I don't know who those people were. They don't feel real to me. Valentine was real."

Clary blinked; it wasn't what she'd expected him to say. "Remember, I said that it would take time—"

He didn't even seem to hear her. "If I really were Jace Morgenstern, would you still love me? If I were Sebastian, would you love me?"

She squeezed his hands. "You could never be like that."

"If Valentine did to me what he did to Sebastian, *would you love me?*"

There was an urgency to the question that she didn't understand. Clary said, "But then you wouldn't be you."

His breath caught, almost as if what she'd said had hurt him—but how could it have? It was the truth. He wasn't like Sebastian. He was like himself. "I don't know who I am," he said. "I look at myself in the mirror and I see Stephen Herondale, but I act like a Lightwood and talk like my father—like Valentine. So I see who I am in your eyes, and I try to be that person, because you have faith in that person and I think faith might be enough to make me what you want."

"You're already what I want. You always have been," Clary said, but she couldn't help feeling as if she were calling into an empty room. It was as if Jace couldn't *hear* her, no matter how many times she told him she loved him. "I know you feel like you don't know who you are, but I do. I know. And someday you will too. And in the meantime you can't keep worrying about losing me, because it'll never happen."

"There is a way . . ." Jace raised his eyes to hers. "Give me your hand."

Surprised, Clary reached her hand out, remembering the first time he'd ever taken her hand like that. She had the rune now, the open-eye rune, on the back of her hand, the one he'd been looking for then and hadn't found. Her first permanent rune. He turned her hand over, baring her wrist, the vulnerable skin of her forearm.

She shivered. The wind off the river felt as if it were driving into her bones. "Jace, what are you doing?"

"Remember what I said about Shadowhunter weddings? How instead of exchanging rings, we Mark each other with runes of love and commitment?" He looked at her, his eyes wide and vulnerable under their thick gold lashes. "I want to Mark you in a way that will bind us together, Clary. It's just a small Mark, but it's permanent. Are you willing?"

She hesitated. A permanent rune, when they were so young— her mother would be incensed. But nothing else seemed to be working; nothing she said convinced him. Maybe this would. Silently, she drew out her stele and handed it to him. He took it, brushing her fingers as he did. She was shivering harder now, cold everywhere except where he touched her. He cradled her arm against him and lowered the stele, touching it softly to her skin, moving it gently up and down, and then, when she didn't protest, with more force. As cold as she was, the burn of the stele was almost welcome. She watched as the dark lines spiraled out from the tip of it, forming a pattern of hard, angular lines.

Her nerves tingled with a sudden alarm. The pattern didn't speak of love and commitment to her; there was something else there, something darker, something that spoke of control and submission, of loss and darkness. Was he drawing the wrong rune? But this was Jace; surely he knew better than that. And yet a numbness was beginning to spread up her arm from the place the stele touched—a painful tingling, like nerves waking up— and she felt dizzy, as if the ground were moving under her—

"Jace." Her voice rose, tinged with anxiety. "Jace, I don't think that's right—"

He let her arm go. He held the stele balanced lightly in his hand, with the same grace with which he would hold any weapon. "I'm sorry, Clary," he said. "I do want to be bound to you. I would never lie about that."

She opened her mouth to ask him what on earth he was talking about, but no words came. The darkness was rushing up too fast. The last thing she felt was Jace's arms around her as she fell.

After what seemed like an eternity of wandering around what he considered to be an extremely boring party, Magnus finally found Alec, sitting alone at a table in a corner, behind a spray of artificial white roses. There were a number of champagne glasses on the table, most half-full, as if passing partygoers had abandoned them there. Alec was looking rather abandoned himself. He had his chin in his hands and was staring mood-ily into space. He didn't look up, even when Magnus hitched a foot around the chair opposite his, spun it toward him, and sat down, resting his arms along the back.

"Do you want to go back to Vienna?" he said.

Alec didn't answer, just stared into space.

"Or we could go somewhere else," said Magnus. "Anywhere you want. Thailand, South Carolina, Brazil, Peru— Oh, wait, no, I'm banned from Peru. I'd forgotten about that. It's a long story, but amusing if you want to hear it."

Alec's expression said that he very much did not want to hear it. Pointedly he turned and looked out over the room as if the werewolf string quartet fascinated him.

Since Alec was ignoring him, Magnus decided to amuse himself by changing the colors of the champagne in the glasses on the table. He made one blue, the next pink, and was working on green when Alec reached across the table and hit him on the wrist.

"Stop that," he said. "People are looking."

Magnus looked down at his fingers, which were spraying blue sparks. Maybe it was a bit obvious. He curled his fingers under. "Well," he said. "I have to do something to keep myself from dying of boredom, since you're not talking to me."

"I'm not," said Alec. "Not talking to you, I mean."

"Oh?" said Magnus. "I just asked you if you wanted to go to Vienna, or Thailand, or the moon, and I don't recall you saying anything in response."

"I don't know what I want." Alec, his head bent, was playing with an abandoned plastic fork. Though his eyes were defiantly cast down, their pale blue color was visible even through his lowered eyelids, which were pale and as fine as parchment. Magnus had always found humans more beautiful than any other creatures alive on the earth, and had often wondered why. Only a few years before dissolution, Camille had said. But it was mortality that made them what they were, the flame that blazed brighter for its flickering. *Death is the mother of beauty*, as the poet said. He wondered if the Angel had ever considered making his human servants, the Nephilim, immortal. But no, for all their strength, they fell as humans had always fallen in battle through all the ages of the world.

"You've got that look again," Alec said peevishly, glancing up through his lashes. "Like you're staring at something I can't see. Are you thinking about Camille?"

"Not really," Magnus said. "How much of the conversation I had with her did you overhear?"

"Most of it." Alec prodded the tablecloth with his fork. "I was listening at the door. Enough."

"Not at all enough, I think." Magnus glared at the fork, and it skidded out of Alec's grasp and across the table toward him. He slammed his hand down on top of it and said, "Stop fidgeting. What was it I said to Camille that bothered you so much?"

Alec raised his blue eyes. "Who's *Will*?"

Magnus exhaled a sort of laugh. "Will. Dear God. That was a long time ago. Will was a Shadowhunter, like you. And yes, he did look like you, but you're not anything like him. Jace is much more the way Will was, in personality at least—and my relationship with you is nothing like the one I had with Will. Is *that* what's bothering you?"

"I don't like thinking you're only with me because I look like some dead guy you liked."

"I never said that. Camille implied it. She is a master of implication and manipulation. She always has been."

"You didn't tell her she was wrong."

"If you let Camille, she will attack you on every front. Defend one front, and she will attack another. The only way to deal with her is to pretend she isn't getting to you."

"She said pretty boys were your undoing," Alec said. "Which makes it sound like I'm just one in a long line of toys for you. One dies or goes away, you get another one. I'm nothing. I'm—trivial."

"Alexander—"

"Which," Alec went on, staring down at the table again, "is especially unfair, because you are anything but trivial for me.

I changed my whole life for you. But nothing ever changes for you, does it? I guess that's what it means to live forever. Nothing ever really has to matter all that much."

"I'm telling you that you do matter—"

"The Book of the White," Alec said, suddenly. "Why did you want it so badly?"

Magnus looked at him, puzzled. "You know why. It's a very powerful spellbook."

"But you wanted it for something specific, didn't you? A spell that was in it?" Alec took a ragged breath. "You don't have to answer; I can tell by your face that you did. Was it—was it a spell for making me immortal?"

Magnus felt shaken to his core. "Alec," he whispered. "No. No, I—I wouldn't do that."

Alec fixed him with his piercing blue gaze. "Why not? Why through all the years of all the relationships you've ever had have you never tried to make any of them immortal like you? If you could have me with you forever, wouldn't you want to?"

"Of course I would!" Magnus, realizing he was almost shouting, lowered his voice with an effort. "But you don't understand. You don't get something for nothing. The price for living forever—"

"Magnus." It was Isabelle, hurrying toward them, her phone in her hand. "Magnus, I need to talk to you."

"Isabelle." Normally Magnus liked Alec's sister. Not so much at the moment. "Lovely, wonderful Isabelle. Could you please go away? Now is a really bad time."

Isabelle looked from Magnus to her brother, and back again. "Then, you don't want me to tell you that Camille's just escaped from the Sanctuary and my mother is demanding that you come back to the Institute right now to help them find her?"

"No," Magnus said. "I don't want you to tell me that."

"Well, too bad," Isabelle said. "Because it's true. I mean, I guess you don't have to go, but—"

The rest of the sentence hung in the air, but Magnus knew what she wasn't saying. If he didn't go, the Clave would be suspicious that he'd had something to do with Camille's escape, and that was the last thing he needed. Maryse would be furious, complicating his relationship with Alec even further. And yet—

"She *escaped*?" Alec said. "No one's ever escaped from the Sanctuary."

"Well," said Isabelle, "now someone has."

Alec slunk down lower in his seat. "Go," he said. "It's an emergency. Just go. We can talk later."

"Magnus . . ." Isabelle sounded half-apologetic, but there was no mistaking the urgency in her voice.

"Fine." Magnus stood up. "But," he added, pausing by Alec's chair and leaning in close to him, *"you are not trivial."*

Alec flushed. "If you say so," he said.

"I say so," said Magnus, and he turned to follow Isabelle out of the room.

Outside on the deserted street, Simon leaned against the wall of the Ironworks, against the ivy-covered brick, and stared up at the sky. The lights of the bridge washed out the stars so there was nothing to see but a sheet of velvety blackness. He wished with a sudden fierceness that he could breathe in the cold air to clear his head, that he could feel it on his face, on his skin. All he was wearing was a thin shirt, and it made no difference.

He couldn't shiver, and even the memory of what it felt like to shiver was going away from him, little by little, every day, slipping away like the memories of another life.

"Simon?"

He froze where he stood. That voice, small and familiar, drifting like a thread on the cold air. *Smile.* That was the last thing she had said to him.

But it couldn't be. She was dead.

"Won't you look at me, Simon?" Her voice was as small as ever, barely a breath. "I'm right here."

Dread clawed its way up his spine. He opened his eyes, and turned his head slowly.

Maureen stood in the circle of light cast by a streetlamp just at the corner of Vernon Boulevard. She wore a long white virginal dress. Her hair was brushed straight down over her shoulders, shining yellow in the lamplight. There was still some grave dirt caught in it. There were little white slippers on her feet. Her face was dead white, circles of rouge painted on her cheekbones, and her mouth colored a dark pink as if it had been drawn on with a felt-tip marker.

Simon's knees gave out. He slid down the wall he had been leaning against, until he was sitting on the ground, his knees drawn up. His head felt like it was going to explode.

Maureen gave a girlish little giggle and stepped out of the lamplight. She moved toward him and looked down; her face wore a look of amused satisfaction.

"I thought you'd be surprised," she said.

"You're a vampire," Simon said. "But—how? I didn't do this to you. I know I didn't."

Maureen shook her head. "It wasn't you. But it was *because* of you. They thought I was your girlfriend, you know. They took me out of my bedroom at night, and they kept me in a cage for the whole next day. They told me not to worry because you'd come for me. But you didn't come. You never came."

"I didn't know." Simon's voice cracked. "I would have come if I'd known."

Maureen flung her blond hair back over her shoulder in a gesture that reminded Simon suddenly and painfully of Camille. "It doesn't matter," she said in her girlish little voice. "When the sun went down, they told me I could die or I could choose to live like this. As a vampire."

"So you *chose* this?"

"I didn't want to die," she breathed. "And now I'll be pretty and young forever. I can stay out all night, and I never need to go home. And she takes care of me."

"Who are you talking about? Who's she? Do you mean Camille? Look, Maureen, she's crazy. You shouldn't listen to her." Simon staggered to his feet. "I can get you help. Find you a place to stay. Teach you how to be a vampire—"

"Oh, Simon." She smiled, and her little white teeth showed in a precise row. "I don't think you know how to be a vampire either. You didn't want to bite me, but you did. I remember. Your eyes went all black like a shark's, and you bit me."

"I'm so sorry. If you'll let me help you—"

"You could come with me," she said. "That would help me."

"Come with you where?"

Maureen looked up and down the empty street. She looked like a ghost in her thin white dress. The wind blew it around her body, but she clearly didn't feel the cold. "You have been chosen," she said. "Because you are a Daylighter. Those who did this to me want you. But they know you bear the Mark now. They can't get to you unless you choose to come to them. So they sent me as a messenger." She cocked her head to the side, like a bird's. "I might not be anyone who matters to you," she said, "but the next time it will be. They will keep coming for the people you love until there is no one left, so you might as well come with me and find out what they want."

"Do you know?" Simon asked. "Do you know what they want?"

She shook her head. She was so pale under the diffuse lamplight that she looked almost transparent, as if Simon could have looked right through her. The way, he supposed, he always had.

"Does it matter?" she said, and reached out her hand.

"No," he said. "No, I guess it doesn't." And he took her hand.

16

NEW YORK CITY ANGELS

"We're here," Maureen said to Simon.

She had stopped in the middle of the sidewalk and was looking up at a massive glass-and-stone building that rose above them. It was clearly designed to look like one of the luxury apartment complexes that had been built on Manhattan's Upper East Side before the Second World War, but the modern touches gave it away—the high sheets of windows, the copper roof untouched by verdigris, the banner signs draping themselves down the front of the edifice, promising LUXURY CONDOS STARTING AT $750,000. Apparently the purchase of one would entitle you to the use of a roof garden, a fitness center, a heated pool, and twenty-four-hour doorman service, starting in December. At the moment the place was still under construction, and KEEP OUT: PRIVATE PROPERTY signs were tacked to the scaffolding that surrounded it.

Simon looked at Maureen. She seemed to be getting used to being a vampire pretty fast. They had run over the Queensboro Bridge and up Second Avenue to get here, and her white slippers were shredded. But she had never slowed, and had never seemed surprised not to have gotten tired. She was looking up at the building now with a beatific expression, her small face aglow with what Simon could only guess was anticipation.

"This place is closed," he said, knowing he was stating the obvious. "Maureen—"

"Hush." She reached out a small hand to pull at a placard attached to a corner of the scaffolding. It came away with a sound of tearing plasterboard and ripped-out nails. Some of them rattled to the ground at Simon's feet. Maureen tossed the square of plasterboard aside and grinned at the hole she'd made.

An old man who'd been passing by, walking a small plaid-jacketed poodle on a leash, stopped and stared. "You ought to get a coat on your little sister there," he said to Simon. "Skinny thing like that, she'll freeze in this weather."

Before Simon could reply, Maureen turned on the man with a ferocious grin, showing all her teeth, including her needle fangs. *"I am not his sister,"* she hissed.

The man blanched, picked up his dog, and hurried away.

Simon shook his head at Maureen. "You didn't need to do that."

Her fangs had pierced her lower lip, something that had happened to Simon often before he'd gotten used to them. Thin trickles of blood ran down her chin. "Don't tell me what to do," she said peevishly, but her fangs retracted. She wiped the back of her hand across her chin, a childish gesture, smearing the blood. Then she turned back to the hole she'd made. "Come on."

She ducked through, and he followed her. They passed through an area where the construction crew had clearly dumped their junk. There were broken tools lying around, smashed bricks, old plastic bags, and Coke cans littering the ground. Maureen lifted her skirts and picked her way daintily through the wreckage, a look of disgust on her face. She hopped over a narrow trench, and up a row of cracked stone steps. Simon followed.

The steps led to a set of glass doors, propped open. Through the doors was an ornate marble lobby. A massive unlit chandelier hung from the ceiling, though there was no light to spark off its pendant crystals. It would have been too dark in the room for a human to see at all. There was a marble desk for a doorman to sit at, a green chaise longue beneath a gilt-edged mirror, and banks of elevators on either side of the room. Maureen hit the button for the elevator, and to Simon's surprise, it lit.

"Where are we going?" he asked.

The elevator pinged, and Maureen stepped in, Simon behind her. The elevator was paneled in gold and red, with frosted glass mirrors on each of the walls. "Up." She hit the button for the roof and giggled. "Up to Heaven," she said, and the doors closed.

"I can't find Simon."

Isabelle, who had been leaning against a pillar in the Ironworks and trying not to brood, looked up to see Jordan looming over her. He really was most unreasonably tall, she thought. He had to be at least six foot two. She had thought he was very attractive the first time she'd seen him, with his tousled dark hair and greenish eyes, but now that she knew he was Maia's ex, she had moved him firmly into the mental space she reserved for boys who were off-limits.

"Well, I haven't seen him," she said. "I thought you were supposed to be his keeper."

"He told me he was going to be right back. That was forty minutes ago. I figured he was going to the bathroom."

"What kind of guardian are you? Shouldn't you have gone to the bathroom *with* him?" Isabelle demanded.

Jordan looked horrified. "Dudes," he said, "do not follow other dudes to the bathroom."

Isabelle sighed. "Latent homosexual panic will do you in every time," she said. "Come on. Let's look for him."

They circled the party, moving in and out among the guests. Alec was sulking alone at a table, playing with an empty champagne glass. "No, I haven't seen him," he said in response to their question. "Though admittedly I haven't been looking."

"Well, you can search along with us," said Isabelle. "It'll give you something to do besides look miserable."

Alec shrugged and joined them. They decided to split up and fan out across the party. Alec headed upstairs to search the catwalks and the second level. Jordan went outside to check the terraces and the entryway. Isabelle took the party area. She was just wondering whether glancing under the tables would actually be ridiculous, when Maia came up behind her. "Everything all right?" she inquired. She glanced up toward Alec, and then in the direction Jordan had gone. "I know a searching formation when I see one. What are you guys looking for? Is there trouble?"

Isabelle filled her in on the Simon situation.

"I just talked to him about half an hour ago."

"So did Jordan, but he's gone now. And since people have been trying to kill him lately . . ."

Maia set her glass down on the table. "I'll help you look."

"You don't have to. I know you're not feeling super-fond of Simon right now—"

"That doesn't mean I don't want to help out if he's in *trouble*," Maia said, as if Isabelle were being ridiculous. "Wasn't Jordan supposed to be watching him?"

Isabelle threw up her hands. "Yeah, but apparently dudes don't follow other dudes to the bathroom or something. He wasn't making a lot of sense."

"Guys never do," Maia said, and followed her. They glided in and out through the crowd, though Isabelle was already pretty sure they weren't going to find Simon. She had a small cold spot in the middle of her stomach that was growing bigger and colder. By the time they'd all convened back at their original table, she felt as if she'd swallowed a glass of ice water.

"He isn't here," she said.

Jordan swore, then stared guiltily at Maia. "Sorry."

"I've heard worse," she said. "So what's the next step? Anyone tried calling him?"

"Straight to voice mail," Jordan said.

"Any idea where he might have gone?" asked Alec.

"Best-case scenario, maybe back to the apartment," said Jordan. "Worst, those people who've been after him finally got him."

"People who what?" Alec looked bewildered; while Isabelle had told Maia Simon's story, she hadn't had a chance to fill her brother in yet.

"I'm going to head back to the apartment and look for him," said Jordan. "If he's there, great. If not, that's still where I should start. They know where he lives; they've been sending us messages there. Maybe there'll be a message." He didn't sound too hopeful.

Isabelle made a split-second decision. "I'll go with you."

"You don't have to—"

"Yes, I do. I told Simon he should come here tonight; I'm responsible. Besides, I'm having a crap time at this party anyway."

"Yeah," Alec said, looking relieved at the prospect of getting out of there. "Me too. Maybe we should all go. Should we tell Clary?"

Isabelle shook her head. "It's her mom's party. It wouldn't be fair. Let's see what we can do just the three of us."

"Three of you?" Maia asked, a tone of delicate annoyance shading her voice.

"Do you want to come with us, Maia?" It was Jordan. Isabelle froze; she wasn't sure how Maia would respond to having her ex-boyfriend speak to her directly. The other girl's mouth tightened a little, and for just a moment she looked at Jordan—not as if she hated him, but thoughtfully.

"It's Simon," she said finally, as if that decided everything. "I'll go get my coat."

The elevator doors opened onto a swirl of dark air and shadows. Maureen gave another high-pitched giggle and danced out into the darkness, leaving Simon to follow her with a sigh.

They stood in a large marble windowless room. There were no lights, but the wall to the left of the elevator was fitted with a towering set of double glass doors. Through them Simon could see the flat surface of the roof, and above it the black night sky overhead pinpointed with faintly glowing stars.

The wind was blowing hard again. He followed Maureen through the doors and out into the cold, gusting air, her dress fluttering around her like a moth beating its wings against a gale. The roof garden was as elegant as the signs had promised. Smooth hexagonal stone tiles made up the flooring; there were banks of flowers blooming under glass, and carefully clipped topiary hedges in the shapes of monsters and animals. The walkway they followed was lined with tiny gleaming lights. All around them rose high glass-and-steel apartment buildings, their windows aglow with electricity.

The path dead-ended at a row of raised, tiled steps, atop which was a wide square bordered on three sides by the high wall that encircled the garden. It was clearly intended to be an area where the building's eventual residents would socialize. There was a big concrete block in the center of the square, which would probably someday hold a grill, Simon guessed, and the area was encircled by neatly clipped rosebushes that in June would bloom, just as the bare trellises adorning the walls would one day vanish under a covering of leaves. It would be an attractive space eventually, a luxury Upper East Side penthouse garden where you could relax on a lounge chair, with the East River glittering under the sunset, and the city stretched out before you, a mosaic of shimmering light.

Except. The tile floor had been defaced, splattered with some sort of black, sticky fluid that had been used to draw a rough circle, inside a larger circle. The space between the two circles was filled with scrawled runes. Though Simon wasn't a Shadowhunter, he'd seen enough Nephilim runes to recognize what came from the Gray Book. These didn't. They looked menacing and wrong, like a curse scrawled in an unfamiliar language.

In the very center of the circle was the concrete block. On top of it a bulky rectangular object sat, draped with a dark cloth. The shape of it was not unlike that of a coffin. More runes were scribbled around the base of the block. If Simon's blood had run, it would have run cold.

Maureen clapped her hands together. "Oh," she said in her elfin little voice. "It's pretty."

"*Pretty?*" Simon looked quickly at the hunched shape on top of the concrete block. "Maureen, what the hell—"

"So you brought him." It was a woman's voice that spoke, cultured, strong, and—familiar. Simon turned. Standing on the pathway behind him was a tall woman with short dark hair. She was very slender, wearing a long dark coat, belted around the middle like a femme fatale from a forties spy movie. "Maureen, thank you," she went on. She had a hard, beautiful face, sharply planed, with high cheekbones and wide dark eyes. "You've done very well. You may go now." She turned her gaze on Simon. "Simon Lewis," she said. "Thank you for coming."

The moment she said his name he recognized her. The last time he'd seen her she'd been standing in pouring rain outside the Alto Bar. "You. I remember you. You gave me your card. The music promoter. Wow, you must *really* want to promote my band. I didn't even think we were that good."

"Don't be sarcastic," the woman said. "There's no point in it." She glanced sideways. "Maureen. You may *go*." Her voice was firm this time, and Maureen, who had been hovering like a little ghost, gave a tiny squeak and darted back the way they'd come. He watched as she vanished through the doors that led to the elevators, feeling almost sorry to see her go. Maureen wasn't much company, but without her he felt very alone. Whoever this strange woman was, she gave off a clear aura of dark power he'd been too blood-drugged to notice before.

"You led me a dance, Simon," she said, and now her voice was coming from another direction, several feet away. Simon spun, and saw that she was standing beside the concrete block, in the center of the circle. The clouds were blowing swiftly across the moon, casting a moving pattern of shadows across her face. Because he was at the foot of the steps, he had to crane his head back to look up at her. "I thought getting hold of you would be easy. Dealing with a simple vampire. A newly made one, at that. Even a Daylighter is nothing I haven't encountered before, though there has not been one for a hundred years. Yes," she added, with a smile at his glance, "I am older than I look."

"You look pretty old."

She ignored the insult. "I sent my best people after you, and only one returned, with some babbled tale about holy fire and the wrath of God. He was quite useless to me after that. I had to have him put down. It was most annoying. After that I decided I ought to deal with you myself. I followed you to your silly musical show, and afterward, when I came up to you, I saw it. Your Mark. As one who knew Cain personally, I am intimately familiar with its shape."

"Knew Cain *personally*?" Simon shook his head. "You can't expect me to believe that."

"Believe it or do not believe it," she said. "It makes no difference to me. I am older than the dreams of your kind, little boy. I walked the paths of the Garden of Eden. I knew Adam before Eve did. I was his first wife, but I would not be obedient to him, so God cast me out and made for Adam a new wife, one fashioned of his own body that she might ever be subservient." She smiled faintly. "I have many names. But you may call me Lilith, first of all demons."

At that, Simon, who had not felt cold in months, finally shivered. He had heard the name Lilith before. He couldn't remember where exactly, but he knew it was a name associated with darkness, with evil and terrible things.

"Your Mark presented me with a conundrum," said Lilith. "I need you, you see, Daylighter. Your life force—your blood. But I could not force you or harm you."

She said this as if needing his blood were the most natural thing in the world.

"You—drink blood?" Simon asked. He felt dazed, as if he were trapped in a strange dream. Surely this couldn't really be happening.

She laughed. "Blood is not the food of demons, silly child. What I want from you is not for myself." She held out a slender hand. "Come closer."

Simon shook his head. "I'm not stepping inside that circle."

She shrugged. "Very well, then. I intended only to give you a better view." She moved her fingers slightly, almost negligently, the gesture of someone twitching a curtain aside. The black cloth covering the coffin-shaped object between them vanished.

Simon stared at what was revealed. He had not been wrong about the coffin shape. It was a big glass box, just long and wide enough for a person to lie down in. A glass coffin, he thought, like Snow White's. But this was no fairy tale. Inside the coffin was a cloudy liquid, and floating in that liquid—naked from the waist up, his white-blond hair drifting around him like pale seaweed—was Sebastian.

There were no messages stuck to Jordan's apartment door, nothing on or under the welcome mat, and nothing immediately obvious inside the apartment, either. While Alec stood guard downstairs and Maia and Jordan rummaged through Simon's backpack in the living room, Isabelle, standing in the doorway of Simon's bedroom, looked silently at the place he'd been sleeping for the past few days. It was so empty—just four walls, naked of any decoration, a bare floor with a futon mattress on it and a white blanket folded at the foot, and a single window that looked out onto Avenue B.

She could hear the city—the city she had grown up in, whose noises had always surrounded her, since she was a baby. She had found the quiet of Idris terribly alien without the sounds of car alarms, people shouting, ambulance sirens, and music playing that never, in New York City, quite went away, even in the dead of night. But now, standing here looking at Simon's small room, she thought about how lonely those noises sounded, how distant, and whether he had been lonely himself at night, lying here looking up at the ceiling, alone.

Then again, it wasn't as if she'd ever seen his bedroom at home, which presumably was covered with band posters, sports trophies, boxes of those games he loved to play, musical instruments, books—all the flotsam and jetsam of a normal life. She'd never asked to come over, and he'd never suggested it. She'd been gun-shy of meeting his mother, of doing anything that might bespeak a greater commitment than she was willing to make. But now, looking at this empty shell of a room, feeling the vast dark bustle of the city all around her, she felt a twinge of fear for Simon—mixed with an equal twinge of regret.

She turned back toward the rest of the apartment, but paused when she heard a low murmur of voices coming from the living room. She recognized Maia's voice. She didn't sound angry, which was surprising in and of itself, considering how much she seemed to hate Jordan.

"Nothing," she was saying. "Some keys, a bunch of papers with game stats scrawled on them." Isabelle leaned around the doorway. She could see Maia, standing on one side of the kitchen counter, her hand in the zip pocket of Simon's back-pack. Jordan, on the other side of the counter, was watching her. Watching *her*, Isabelle thought, not what she was doing—that way guys watched you when they were so into you they were fascinated by every move you made. "I'll check his wallet."

Jordan, who had changed out of his formal wear into jeans and a leather jacket, frowned. "Weird that he left it. Can I see?" He reached across the counter.

Maia jerked back so fast she dropped the wallet, her hand flying out.

"I wasn't . . ." Jordan drew his hand back slowly. "I'm sorry."

Maia took a deep breath. "Look," she said, "I talked to Simon. I know you never meant to Turn me. I know you didn't know what was happening to you. I remember what that was like. I remember being terrified."

Jordan put his hands down slowly, carefully, on the coun-tertop. It was odd, Isabelle thought, watching someone so tall try to make himself look harmless and small. "I should have been there for you."

"But the Praetor wouldn't let you be," Maia said. "And let's face it, you didn't know anything about being a werewolf; we would have been like two blindfolded people stumbling around in a circle. Maybe it's better you weren't there. It made me run away to where I could get help. From the Pack."

"At first I hoped the Praetor Lupus would bring you in," he whispered. "So I could see you again. Then I realized that was selfish and I should be wishing that I didn't pass on the disease to you. I knew it was fifty-fifty. I thought you might be one of the lucky ones."

"Well, I wasn't," she said, matter-of-factly. "And over the years I built you up in my head to be this sort of monster. I thought you knew what you were doing when you did this to me. I thought it was revenge on me for kissing that boy. So I hated you. And hating you made everything easier. Having someone to blame."

"You should blame me," he said. "It is my fault."

She ran her finger along the countertop, avoiding his eyes. "I do blame you. But . . . not the way I did before."

Jordan reached up and grabbed his own hair with his fists, tugging on it hard. "There isn't a day goes by I don't think about what I did to you. I bit you. I Turned you. I made you what you are. I raised my hand to you. I hurt you. The one person I loved more than anything else in the world."

Maia's eyes were shining with tears. "Don't *say* that. That doesn't help. You think that helps?"

Isabelle cleared her throat loudly, stepping into the living room. "So. Have you found anything?"

Maia looked away, blinking rapidly. Jordan, lowering his hands, said, "Not really. We were just about to go through his wallet." He picked it up from where Maia had dropped it. "Here." He tossed it to Isabelle.

She caught it and flicked it open. School pass, New York state nondriver's ID, a guitar pick tucked into the space that was supposed to hold credit cards. A ten-dollar bill and a receipt for dice. Something else caught her eye—a business card, shoved carelessly behind a photo of Simon and Clary, the kind of picture you might take in a cheap drugstore photo booth. They were both smiling.

Isabelle took out the card and stared at it. It had a swirling, almost abstract design of a floating guitar against clouds. Below that was a name.

Satrina Kendall. Band Promoter. Below that was a telephone number, and an Upper East Side address. Isabelle frowned. Something, a memory, tugged at the back of her mind.

Isabelle held the card up toward Jordan and Maia, who were busy not looking at each other. "What do you think of this?"

Before they could respond the apartment door opened, and Alec strode in. He was scowling. "Have you found anything? I've been standing down there for thirty minutes, and nothing even remotely threatening has come by. Unless you count the NYU student who threw up on the front steps."

"Here," Isabelle said, handing the card over to her brother. "Look at this. Does anything strike you as odd?"

"You mean besides the fact that no band promoter could possibly be interested in Lewis's sucky band?" Alec inquired, taking the card between two long fingers. Lines appeared between his eyes. "Satrina?"

"Does that name mean something to you?" Maia asked. Her eyes were still red, but her voice was steady.

"Satrina is one of the seventeen names of Lilith, the mother of all demons. She is why warlocks are called Lilith's children," said Alec. "Because she mothered demons, and they in turn brought forth the race of warlocks."

"And you have all seventeen names committed to memory?" Jordan sounded dubious.

Alec gave him a cold look. "Who are you again?"

"Oh, shut up, Alec," Isabelle said, in the tone she only ever took with her brother. "Look, not all of us have your memory for boring facts. I don't suppose you recall the *other* names of Lilith?"

With a superior look Alec rattled them off, "Satrina, Lilith, Ita, Kali, Batna, Talto—"

"Talto!" Isabelle yelped. "That's it. I knew I was remembering something. I *knew* there was a connection!" Quickly she told them about the Church of Talto, what Clary had found there, and how it connected to the dead half-demon baby at Beth Israel.

"I wish you'd told me about this before," Alec said. "Yes, Talto is another name for Lilith. And Lilith has always been associated with babies. She was Adam's first wife, but she fled from the Garden of Eden because she didn't want to obey Adam or God. God cursed her for her disobedience, though—any child she bore would die. The legend says she tried over and over to have a child, but they were all born dead. Eventually she swore she would have vengeance against God by weakening and murdering infant humans. You might say she's the demon goddess of dead children."

"But you said she was the mother of demons," said Maia.

"She was able to create demons by scattering drops of her blood on the earth in a place called Edom," said Alec. "Because they were born out of her hatred for God and mankind, they became demons." Aware that they were all staring at him, he shrugged. "It's just a story."

"All stories are true," said Isabelle. This had been a tenet of her beliefs since she was a child. All Shadowhunters believed it. There was no one religion, no one truth—and no myth lacked meaning. "You know that, Alec."

"I know something else, too," Alec said, handing her back the card. "That telephone number and that address are crap. No way they're real."

"Maybe," Isabelle said, tucking the card into her pocket. "But we don't have anywhere else to start looking. So we're going to start there."

Simon could only stare. The body floating inside the coffin—Sebastian's—didn't appear to be alive; at least, he wasn't breathing. But he clearly wasn't exactly dead, either. It had been two months. If he *were* dead, Simon was fairly sure, he'd look like he was in a lot worse shape than he did. His body was very white, like marble; one hand was a bandaged stump, but he was otherwise unmarked. He appeared to be asleep, his eyes shut, his arms loose at his sides. Only the fact that his chest wasn't rising or falling indicated that something was very wrong.

"But," Simon said, knowing he sounded ridiculous, "he's dead. Jace killed him."

Lilith placed a pale hand on the glass surface of the coffin. "Jonathan," she said, and Simon remembered that that was, in fact, his name. Her voice had an odd soft quality when she said it, as if she were crooning to a child. "He's beautiful, isn't he?"

"Um," said Simon, looking with loathing at the creature inside the coffin—the boy who had murdered nine-year-old Max Lightwood. The creature who had killed Hodge. Had tried to kill them all. "Not my type, really."

"Jonathan is unique," she said. "He is the only Shadow-hunter I have ever known of who is part Greater Demon. This makes him very powerful."

"He's *dead*," Simon said. He felt that, somehow, it was important to keep making this point, though Lilith didn't seem to quite grasp it.

Lilith, gazing down at Sebastian, frowned. "It's true. Jace Lightwood slipped up behind him and stabbed him in the back, through to the heart."

"How do you—"

"I was in Idris," said Lilith. "When Valentine opened the doorway to the demon worlds, I came through. Not to fight in his stupid battle. Out of curiosity more than anything else. That Valentine should have such hubris—" She broke off, shrugging. "Heaven smote him down for it, of course. I saw the sacrifice he made; I saw the Angel rise and turn on him. I saw what was brought back. I am the oldest of demons; I know the Old Laws. A life for a life. I raced to Jonathan. It was almost too late. That which was human about him died instantly—his heart had ceased to beat, his lungs to inflate. The Old Laws were not enough. I tried to bring him back then. He was too far gone. All I could do was this. Preserve him for this moment."

Simon wondered briefly what would happen if he made a run for it—dashed past this insane demon and threw himself off the roof of the building. He couldn't be harmed by another living creature; that was the result of the Mark, but he doubted its power extended to protecting him against the ground. Still, he was a vampire. If he fell forty stories and smashed every bone in his body, would he heal from that? He swallowed hard and found Lilith looking at him with amusement.

"Don't you want to know," she said in her cold, seductive voice, "what moment I mean?" Before he could answer, she leaned forward, her elbows on the coffin. "I suppose you know the story of the way the Nephilim came to be? How the Angel Raziel mixed his blood with the blood of men, and gave it to a man to drink, and that man became the first of the Nephilim?"

"I've heard it."

"In effect the Angel created a new race of creature. And now, with Jonathan, a new race has been born again. As Jonathan Shadowhunter led the first Nephilim, so shall this Jonathan lead the new race that I intend to create."

"The new race you intend—" Simon held up his hands. "You know what, you want to lead a new race starting off with one dead guy, you go right ahead. I don't see what this has to do with me."

"He is dead now. He need not remain so." Lilith's voice was cool, unemotional. "There is, of course, one kind of Downworlder whose blood offers the possibility of, shall we say, resurrection."

"Vampires," said Simon. "You want me to turn Sebastian into a *vampire*?"

"His name is Jonathan." Her tone was sharp. "And yes, in a sense. I want you to bite him, to drink his blood, and to give him your blood in exchange—"

"I won't do it."

"Are you so sure of that?"

"A world without Sebastian"—Simon used the name deliberately—"in it is a better world than one *with* him in it. I won't do it." Anger was rising in Simon, a swift tide. "Anyway, I couldn't if I wanted to. He's *dead*. Vampires can't bring back the dead. You ought to know that, if you know so much. Once the soul is gone from the body, nothing can bring someone back. Thankfully."

Lilith bent her gaze on him. "You really don't know, do you?" she said. "Clary never told you."

Simon was getting fed up. "Never told me what?"

She chuckled. "An eye for an eye, a tooth for a tooth, a life for a life. To prevent chaos there must be order. If a life is given to the Light, a life is owed to the Dark as well."

"I have," Simon said slowly and deliberately, "literally no idea what you're talking about. And I don't care. You villains and your creepy eugenics programs are starting to bore me. So I'm going to leave now. You're welcome to try to stop me by threatening or hurting me. I encourage you to go ahead and try."

She looked at him and chuckled. "'Cain rose up,'" she said. "You are a bit like him whose Mark you bear. He was stubborn, as you are. Foolhardy, too."

"He went up against—" Simon choked on the word. *God*. "I'm just dealing with you." He turned to leave.

"I would not turn your back on me, Daylighter," said Lilith, and there was something in her voice that made him look back at her, where she leaned on Sebastian's coffin. "You think you cannot be hurt," she said with a sneer. "And indeed I cannot lift a hand against you. I am not a fool; I have seen the holy fire of the divine. I have no wish to see it turned against me. I am not Valentine, to bargain with what I cannot understand. I am a demon, but a very old one. I know humanity better than you might think. I understand the weaknesses of pride, of lust for power, of desire of the flesh, of greed and vanity and love."

"Love isn't a weakness."

"Oh, isn't it?" she said, and glanced past him, with a look as cold and pointed as an icicle.

He turned, not wanting to, knowing he must, and looked behind him.

There on the brick walkway was Jace. He wore a dark suit and a white shirt. Standing in front of him was Clary, still in the pretty gold-colored dress she had worn to the Ironworks party. Her long, wavy red hair had come out of its knot and hung down around her shoulders. She stood very still in the circle of Jace's arms. It would almost have looked like a romantic picture if it were not for the fact that in one of his hands, Jace was holding a long and glittering bone-handled knife, and the edge of it was pressed against Clary's throat.

Simon stared at Jace in total and absolute shock. There was no emotion on Jace's face, no light in his eyes. He seemed utterly blank.

Very slightly he inclined his head.

"I brought her, Lady Lilith," he said. "Just as you asked."

17

AND CAIN ROSE UP

Clary had never been so cold.

Even when she had crawled out of Lake Lyn, coughing and sputtering its poisonous water onto the shore, she hadn't been this cold. Even when she had thought Jace was dead, she hadn't felt this terrible icy paralysis in her heart. Then she had burned with rage, rage against her father. Now she just felt ice, all the way down to her toes.

She had come back to consciousness in the marble lobby of a strange building, under the shadow of an unlit chandelier. Jace had been carrying her, one arm under her bent knees, the other supporting her head. Still dizzy and groggy, she'd buried her head against his neck for a moment, trying to remember where she was.

"What happened?" she had whispered.

They had reached the elevator. Jace pushed the button, and Clary heard the rattle that meant the machine was moving down toward them. But where were they?

"You were unconscious," he said.

"But how—" She remembered then, and fell silent. His hands on her, the sting of her stele on her skin, the wave of darkness that had come over her. Something *wrong* with the rune he had drawn on her, the way it had looked and felt. She stayed motionless in his arms for a moment, and then said:

"Put me down."

He set her down on her feet, and they looked at each other. Only a small space separated them. She could have reached out and touched him, but for the first time since she had met him, she didn't want to. She had the terrible feeling that she was looking at a stranger. He looked like Jace, and sounded like Jace when he spoke, and had felt like Jace when she was holding him. But his eyes were strange and distant, as was the tiny smile playing about his mouth.

The elevator doors opened behind him. She remembered standing in the nave of the Institute, saying "I love you" to a closed elevator door. The gap yawned behind him now, as black as the mouth of a cave. She felt for the stele in her pocket; it was gone.

"You knocked me out," she said. "With a rune. You brought me here. *Why?*"

His beautiful face was entirely, carefully blank. "I had to do it. I didn't have a choice."

She turned and ran then, going for the door, but he was faster than she was. He always had been. He swung in front of her, blocking her path, and held out his hands. "Clary, don't run," he said. "Please. For me."

She looked at him incredulously. His voice was the same—he sounded just like Jace, but not like him—like a recording of him, she thought, all the tones and patterns of his voice there, but the life that animated it gone. How had she not realized it before? She had thought he sounded remote because of stress and pain, but no. It was that he was *gone*. Her stomach turned over, and she bolted for the door again, only to have him catch her around the waist and swing her back toward him. She pushed at him, her fingers locking into the fabric of his shirt, ripping it sideways.

She froze, staring. On the skin of his chest, just over his heart, was a rune.

It wasn't one she had ever seen before. It wasn't black, like Shadowhunter runes were, but dark red, the color of blood. And it lacked the delicate grace of the runes from the Gray Book. It was scrawling, ugly, its lines sharp and cruel rather than curving and generous.

Jace didn't seem to see it. He stared down at himself as if wondering what she was gazing at, then looked at her, puzzled. "It's all right. You didn't hurt me."

"That rune—," she began, but cut herself off, hard. Maybe he *didn't* know it was there. "Let me go, Jace," she said instead, backing away from him. "You don't have to do this."

"You're wrong about that," he said, and reached for her again.

This time she didn't fight. What would happen even if she escaped? She couldn't just leave him here. Jace was still there, she thought, trapped somewhere behind those blank eyes, maybe screaming for her. She had to stay with him. Had to know what was happening. She let him pick her up and carry her into the elevator.

"The Silent Brothers will notice you left," she said, as the buttons for floor after floor lit up while the elevator rose. "They'll alert the Clave. They'll come looking—"

"I need not fear the Brothers. I wasn't a prisoner; they weren't expecting me to want to leave. They won't notice I'm gone until they wake up tomorrow morning."

"What if they wake up earlier than that?"

"Oh," he said, with a cold certainly, "they won't. It's much more likely the other partygoers at the Ironworks will notice you're missing. But what can they do about it? They'll have no idea where you went, and Tracking to this building is blocked." He stroked her hair back from her face, and she went still. "You're just going to have to trust me. No one's coming for you."

He didn't bring the knife out until they left the elevator, and then he said, "I would never hurt you. You know that, don't you?" even as he flicked her hair back with the tip of the blade and pressed the edge to her throat. The icy air hit her bare shoulders and arms as soon as they were out on the roof. Jace's hands were warm where he touched her, and she could feel the heat of him through her thin dress, but it didn't warm her, not inside. Inside she was filled with jagged slivers of ice.

She grew colder still when she saw Simon, looking at her with his huge dark eyes. His face looked scrubbed blank with shock, like a white piece of paper. He was looking at her, and Jace behind her, as if he were seeing something fundamentally *wrong*, a person with their face turned inside-out, a map of the world with all the land gone and nothing left but ocean.

She barely looked at the woman beside him, with her dark hair and her thin, cruel face. Clary's gaze had gone immediately to the transparent coffin on its pedestal of stone. It seemed to glow from within, as if lit by a milky inner light. The water that Jonathan was floating in was probably not water but some other, less natural liquid. Normal Clary, she thought dispassionately, would have screamed at the sight of her brother, floating still and dead-looking and totally unmoving in what looked like Snow White's glass coffin. But frozen Clary just stared with a remote and distant shock.

Lips as red as blood, skin as white as snow, hair as black as ebony. Well, some of that was true. When she had met Sebastian, his hair had been black, but it was white-silver now, floating around his head like albino seaweed. The same color as his father's hair. *Their* father's hair. His skin was so pale it looked as if it could be made up of luminous crystals. But his lips were colorless too, as were the lids of his eyes.

"Thank you, Jace," the woman that Jace had called Lady Lilith said. "Nicely done, and very prompt. I thought I was going to have difficulties with you at first, but it appears I worried for nothing."

Clary stared. Though the woman did not look familiar, her *voice* was familiar. She had heard that voice before. But where? She tried to pull away from Jace, but his grip on her only tightened. The edge of the knife kissed her throat. An accident, she told herself. Jace—even this Jace—would never hurt her.

"You," she said to Lilith between her teeth. "What have you done to Jace?"

"Valentine's daughter speaks." The dark-haired woman smiled. "Simon? Would you like to explain?"

Simon looked like he was going to throw up. "I have no idea." He sounded as if he were choking. "Believe me, you two were the last thing I expected to see."

"The Silent Brothers said that a demon was responsible for what's been happening with Jace," Clary said, and saw Simon look more baffled than ever. The woman, though, just watched her with eyes like flat obsidian circles. "That demon was you, wasn't it? But why Jace? What do you want from us?"

"'Us'?" Lilith pealed with laughter. "As if you mattered in this, my girl. Why you? Because you are a means to an end. Because I needed both these boys, and both of them love you. Because Jace Herondale is the one person you trust more than anyone else in the world. And *you* are someone the Daylighter loves enough to give up his own life for. Perhaps *you* cannot be harmed," she said, turning to Simon. "But *she* can be. Are you so stubborn that you will sit back and watch Jace cut her throat rather than give up your blood?"

Simon, looking like death itself, shook his head slowly, but before he could speak, Clary said, "Simon, no! Don't do it, whatever it is. Jace wouldn't hurt me."

The woman's fathomless eyes turned to Jace. She smiled. "Cut her," she said. "Just a little."

Clary felt Jace's shoulders tense, the way they had in the park when he'd been showing her how to fight. She felt something at her throat, like a stinging kiss, cold and hot at once, and felt a warm trickle of liquid spill down onto her collarbone. Simon's eyes widened.

He had cut her. He had actually done it. She thought of Jace crouched on the floor of the bedroom at the Institute, his pain clear in every line of his body. *I dream that you come into my* room. *And then I hurt you. I cut you or strangle or stab you, and you die, looking up at me with those green eyes of yours while your life bleeds away between my hands.*

She had not believed him. Not really. He was Jace. He would never hurt her. She looked down and saw the blood staining the neckline of her dress. It looked like red paint.

"You see now," said the woman. "He does what I tell him. Don't blame him for it. He is completely within my power. For weeks I have crept through his head, seeing his dreams, learning his fears and wants, his guilts and desires. In a dream he accepted my Mark, and that Mark has been burning through him ever since—through his skin, down into his soul. Now his soul is in my hands, to shape or direct as I see fit. He will do whatever I say."

Clary remembered what the Silent Brothers had said. *When a Shadowhunter is born, a ritual is performed, a number of protective spells placed upon the child by both the Silent Brothers and the Iron Sisters. When Jace died and then was raised, he was born a second time, with those protections and rituals stripped away. It would have left him as open as an unlocked door—open to any kind of demonic influence or malevolence.*

I did this, Clary thought. *I brought him back, and I wanted it kept secret. If we had only told someone what had happened, maybe the ritual could have been done in time to keep Lilith out of his head.* She felt sick with self-loathing. Behind her Jace was silent, as still as a statue, his arms around her and the knife still at her throat. She could feel it against her skin when she took a breath to speak, keeping her voice even with an effort. "I understand that you control Jace," she said. "I don't understand *why*. Surely there are other, easier ways to threaten me."

Lilith sighed as if the whole business had grown tedious. "I need you," she said, with exaggerated patience, "to get Simon to do what I want, which is give me his blood. And I need Jace not just because I needed a way to get you here, but as a counterweight. All things in magic must balance, Clarissa." She pointed at the rough black circle drawn on the tiles, and then at Jace. "He was the first. The first to be brought back, the first soul restored to this world in the name of Light. Therefore he must be present for me to successfully restore the second, in the name of the Dark. Do you understand now, silly girl? We are all needed here. Simon to die. Jace to live. Jonathan to return. And you, Valentine's daughter, to be the catalyst for it all."

The demon woman's voice had dropped to a low chant. With a shock of surprise Clary realized that she now knew where she had heard it before. She saw her father, standing inside a pentagram, a black-haired woman with tentacles for eyes kneeling at his feet. The woman said, *The child born with this blood in him will exceed in power the Greater Demons of the abysses between the worlds. But it will burn out his humanity, as poison burns the life from the blood.*

"I know," Clary said through stiff lips. "I *know* who you are. I saw you cut your wrist and drip blood into a cup for my father. The angel Ithuriel showed it to me in a vision."

Simon's eyes darted back and forth between Clary and the woman, whose dark eyes held a hint of surprise. Clary guessed she didn't surprise easily. "I saw my father summon you. I know what he called you. *My Lady of Edom.* You're a Greater Demon. *You* gave your blood to make my brother what he is. You turned him into a—a horrible *thing*. If it weren't for you—"

"Yes. All that is true. I gave my blood to Valentine

Morgenstern, and he put it in his baby boy, and this is the result." The woman placed her hand gently, almost as a caress, against the glass surface of Sebastian's coffin. There was the oddest smile on her face. "You might almost say that, in a way, I am Jonathan's mother."

"I told you that address didn't mean anything," Alec said.

Isabelle ignored him. The moment they had stepped through the doors of the building, the ruby pendant around her neck had pulsed, faintly, like the beat of a distant heart. That meant demonic presence. Under other circumstances she would have expected her brother to sense the weirdness of the place just like she did, but he was clearly too sunk in gloom about Magnus to concentrate.

"Get your witchlight," she said to him. "I left mine at home."

He shot her an irritated look. It was dark in the lobby, dark enough that a normal human wouldn't have been able to see. Maia and Jordan both had the excellent night vision of werewolves. They were standing at opposite ends of the room, Jordan examining the big marble lobby desk, and Maia leaning against the far wall, apparently examining her rings. "You're supposed to bring it with you everywhere," Alec replied.

"Oh? Did you bring your Sensor?" she snapped. "I didn't think so. At least I have this." She tapped the pendant. "I can tell you that there's *something* here. Something demonic."

Jordan's head snapped around. "There are demons here?"

"I don't know—maybe only one. It pulsed and faded," Isabelle admitted. "But it's too big a coincidence for this just to have been the wrong address. We have to check it out."

A dim light rose up all around her. She looked over and saw

Alec holding up his witchlight, its blaze contained by his fingers. It threw strange shadows across his face, making him look older than he was, his eyes a darker blue. "So let's get going," he said. "We'll take it one floor at a time."

They moved toward the elevator, Alec first, then Isabelle, Jordan and Maia dropping into line behind them. Isabelle's boots had Soundless runes carved into the soles, but Maia's heels clicked on the marble floor as she walked. Frowning, she paused to discard them, and went barefoot the rest of the way. As Maia stepped into the elevator, Isabelle noticed that she wore a gold ring around her left big toe, set with a turquoise stone.

Jordan, glancing down at her feet, said in a surprised tone, "I remember that ring. I bought that for you at—"

"Shut up," Maia said, hitting the door close button. The doors slid shut as Jordan lapsed into silence.

They paused at every floor. Most were still under construction—there were no lights, and wires hung down from the ceilings like vines. Windows had plywood nailed over them. Drop cloths blew in the faint wind like ghosts. Isabelle kept a firm hand on her pendant, but nothing happened until they reached the tenth floor. As the doors opened, she felt a flutter against the inside of her cupped palm, as if she had been holding a tiny bird there and it had beaten its wings.

She spoke in a whisper. "There's something here."

Alec just nodded; Jordan opened his mouth to say something, but Maia elbowed him, hard. Isabelle slipped past her brother, into the hall outside the elevators. The ruby was pulsing and vibrating against her hand now like a distressed insect.

Behind her, Alec whispered, "*Sandalphon*." Light blazed up

around Isabelle, illuminating the hall. Unlike some of the other floors they had seen, this one seemed at least partly finished. Bare granite walls rose around her, and the floor was smooth black tile. A corridor led in two directions. One ended in a heap of construction equipment and tangled wires. The other ended in an archway. Beyond the archway, black space beckoned.

Isabelle turned to look back at her companions. Alec had put away his witchlight stone and was holding a blazing seraph blade, lighting the interior of the elevator like a lantern. Jordan had produced a large, brutal-looking knife and was gripping it in his right hand. Maia seemed to be in the process of putting her hair up; when she lowered her hands, she was holding a long, razor-tipped pin. Her nails had grown, too, and her eyes held a feral, greenish gleam.

"Follow me," Isabelle said. "Quietly."

Tap, tap went the ruby against Isabelle's throat as she went down the hall, like the prodding of an insistent finger. She didn't hear the rest of them behind her, but she knew they were there from the long shadows cast against the dark granite walls. Her throat was tight, her nerves singing, the way they always did before she walked into battle. This was the part she liked least, the anticipation before the release of violence. During a fight nothing mattered but the fight itself; now she had to struggle to keep her mind on the task at hand.

The archway loomed above them. It was carved marble, oddly old-fashioned for such a modern building, its sides decorated with scrollwork. Isabelle glanced up briefly as she passed through, and almost started. The face of a grinning gargoyle was carved into the stone, leering down at her. She made a face at it and turned to look at the room she had entered.

It was vast, high-ceilinged, clearly meant to someday be a full loft apartment. The walls were floor-to-ceiling windows, giving out onto a view of the East River with Queens in the distance, the Coca-Cola sign flashing blood-red and navy blue down onto the black water. The lights of surrounding buildings hovered glittering in the night air like tinsel on a Christmas tree. The room itself was dark, and full of odd, humped shadows, spaced at regular intervals, low to the ground. Isabelle squinted, puzzled. They weren't animate; they appeared to be chunks of square, blocky furniture, but what—?

"Alec," she said softly. Her pendant was writhing as if alive, its ruby heart painfully hot against her skin.

In a moment her brother was beside her. He raised his blade, and the room was full of light. Isabelle's hand flew to her mouth. "Oh, dear God," she whispered. "Oh, by the Angel, no."

"You're not his mother." Simon's voice cracked as he said it; Lilith didn't even turn to look at him. She still had her hands on the glass coffin. Sebastian floated inside it, silent and unaware. His feet were bare, Simon noticed. "He has a mother. Clary's mother. Clary's his sister. Sebastian—Jonathan—won't be too pleased if you hurt her."

Lilith looked up at that, and laughed. "A brave attempt, Daylighter," she said. "But I know better. I saw my son grow up, you know. Often I visited him in the form of an owl. I saw how the woman who had given birth to him hated him. He has no love lost for her, nor should he, nor does he care for his sister. He is more like me than he is like Jocelyn Morgenstern." Her dark eyes moved from Simon to Jace and Clary. They had not moved, not really. Clary still stood in the circle of Jace's arms, with the knife near her throat. He held it easily, carelessly, as if he were barely paying attention. But Simon knew how quickly Jace's seeming uninterest could explode into violent action.

"Jace," said Lilith. "Step into the circle. Bring the girl with you."

Obediently Jace moved forward, pushing Clary ahead of him. As they crossed the barrier of the black-painted line, the runes inside the line flashed a sudden, brilliant red—and something else lit as well. A rune on the left side of Jace's chest, just above his heart, glowed suddenly, with such brightness that Simon closed his eyes. Even with his eyes closed, he could still see the rune, a vicious swirl of angry lines, printed against the inside of his eyelids.

"Open your eyes, Daylighter," Lilith snapped. "The time has come. Will you give me your blood, or will you refuse? You know the price if you do."

Simon looked down at Sebastian in his coffin—and did a double take. A rune that was the twin of the one that had just flashed on Jace's chest was visible on his bare chest as well, just beginning to fade as Simon stared down at him. In a moment it was gone, and Sebastian was still and white again. Unmoving. Unbreathing.

Dead.

"I can't bring him back for you," Simon said. "He's *dead*. I'd give you my blood, but he can't swallow it."

Her breath hissed through her teeth in exasperation, and for a moment her eyes glowed with a harsh acidic light. "First you must bite him," she said. "You are a *Daylighter*. Angel blood runs through your body, through your blood and tears, through the fluid in your fangs. Your Daylighter blood will revive him enough that he can swallow and drink. Bite him and give him your blood, and bring him back to me."

Simon stared at her wildly. "But what you're saying—you're saying I have the power to bring back the *dead*?"

"Since you've been a Daylighter you've had that power," she said. "But not the right to use it."

"The right?"

She smiled, tracing the tip of one long red-painted nail across the top of Sebastian's coffin. "History is written by the winners, they say," she said. "There might not be so much of a difference between the side of Light and the side of Dark as you suppose. After all, without the Dark, there is nothing for the Light to burn away."

Simon looked at her blankly.

"Balance," she clarified. "There are laws older than any you can imagine. And one of them is that you cannot bring back what is dead. When the soul has left the body, it belongs to death. And it cannot be taken back without a price to pay."

"And you're willing to pay it? For *him*?" Simon gestured toward Sebastian.

"He *is* the price." She threw her head back and laughed. It sounded almost like human laughter. "If the Light brings back a soul, then the Dark has the right to bring one back as well. This is my right. Or perhaps you should ask your little friend Clary what I'm talking about."

Simon looked at Clary. She looked as if she might pass out. "Raziel," she said faintly. "When Jace died—"

"Jace *died*?" Simon's voice went up an octave. Jace, despite being the subject under discussion, remained serene and expressionless, his knife hand steady.

"Valentine stabbed him," Clary said in an almost-whisper. "And then the Angel killed Valentine, and he said I could have anything I wanted. And I said I wanted Jace back, I wanted him back, and he brought him back—for me." Her eyes were huge in her small white face. "He was dead for only a few minutes . . . hardly any time at all . . ."

"It was enough," breathed Lilith. "I was hovering near my son during his battle with Jace; I saw him fall and die. I followed Jace to the lake, I watched as Valentine slew him, and then as the Angel raised him again. I knew that was my chance. I raced back to the river and took my son's body from it. . . . I kept it preserved for just this moment." She looked fondly down at the coffin. "Everything in balance. An eye for an eye. A tooth for a tooth. A life for a life. Jace is the counterweight. If Jace lives, then so shall Jonathan."

Simon couldn't tear his eyes away from Clary. "What she's saying—about the Angel—it's true?" he said. "And you never told anyone?"

To his surprise it was Jace who answered. Brushing his cheek against Clary's hair, he said, "It was our secret."

Clary's green eyes flashed, but she didn't move.

"So you see, Daylighter," said Lilith, "I am only taking what is mine by right. The Law says that the one who was first brought back must be here in the circle when the second is returned." She indicated Jace with a contemptuous flick of her finger. "He is here. You are here. All is in readiness."

"Then you don't need Clary," said Simon. "Leave her out of it. Let her go."

"Of course I need her. I need her to motivate *you*. I cannot hurt you, Mark-bearer, or threaten you, or kill you. But I can cut out your heart when I cut out her life. And I will."

She looked toward Clary, and Simon's gaze followed hers.

Clary. She was so pale that she looked almost blue, though perhaps that was the cold. Her green eyes were vast in her pale face. A trickle of drying blood spilled from her collarbone to the neckline of her dress, now spotted with red. Her hands hung at her sides, loose, but they were shaking.

Simon saw her as she was, but also as she had been when she was seven years old, skinny arms and freckles and those blue plastic barrettes she'd worn in her hair until she was eleven. He thought of the first time he'd noticed she had a real girl's shape under the baggy T-shirt and jeans she always wore, and how he hadn't been sure if he should look or look away. He thought of her laugh and her quick pencil moving across a page, leaving intricately designed images behind: spired castles, running horses, brightly colored characters she'd made up in her head. *You can walk to school by yourself*, her mother had said, *but only if Simon goes with you*. He thought of her hand in his when they crossed the street, and his own sense of the awesome task that he had undertaken: the responsibility for her safety.

He had been in love with her once, and maybe some part of him always would be, because she had been his first. But that wasn't what mattered now. She was Clary; she was part of him; she always had been and would be forever. As he stared at her, she shook her head, very slightly. He knew what she was saying. *Don't do it. Don't give her what she wants. Let whatever happens to me happen.*

He stepped into the circle; as his feet passed over the painted line, he felt a shiver, like an electric shock, go through him. "All right," he said. "I'll do it."

"*No!*" Clary cried, but Simon didn't look at her. He was watching Lilith, who smiled a cool, gloating smile as she raised her left hand and passed it across the surface of the coffin.

The lid of it vanished, peeling back in a way that reminded Simon bizarrely of peeling back the lid of a tin of sardines. As the top layer of glass pulled away, it melted and ran, dripping down the sides of the granite pedestal, crystallizing into tiny shards of glass as the drops struck the ground.

The coffin was open now, like a fish tank; Sebastian's body drifted inside, and Simon thought he could once again see the flash of the rune on his chest as Lilith reached into the tank. As Simon watched, she took Sebastian's dangling arms and crossed them over his chest with an oddly tender gesture, tucking the bandaged one under the one that was whole. She brushed a lock of his wet hair away from his still, white forehead, and stepped back, shaking milky water from her hands.

"To your work, Daylighter," she said.

Simon moved toward the coffin. Sebastian's face was slack, his eyelids still. No pulse beat in his throat. Simon remembered how much he had wanted to drink Maureen's blood. How he had craved the feeling of his teeth sinking into her skin and freeing the salty blood beneath. But this—this was feeding off a corpse. The very thought made his stomach turn.

Though he wasn't looking at her, he was aware of Clary watching him. He could feel her breath as he bent over Sebastian. He could sense Jace, too, watching him out of blank eyes. Reaching into the coffin, he closed his hands around Sebastian's cold, slippery shoulders. Biting back the urge to be sick, he bent and sank his teeth into Sebastian's throat. Black demon blood poured into his mouth, as bitter as poison.

***

Isabelle moved silently among the stone pedestals. Alec was with her, *Sandalphon* in his hand, sending light winging through the room. Maia was in one corner of the room, bent over and retching, her hand braced against the wall; Jordan hovered over her, looking as if he wanted to reach out and stroke her back, but was afraid of being rebuffed.

Isabelle didn't blame Maia for throwing up. If she hadn't had years of training, she would have thrown up herself. She had never seen anything like what she was looking at now. There were dozens, maybe fifty, of the stone pedestals in the room. Atop each one was a low crib-like basket. Inside each basket was a baby. And every one of the babies was dead.

She had held out hope at first, as she walked up and down the rows, that she might find one alive. But these children had been dead for some time. Their skin was gray, their small faces bruised and discolored. They were wrapped in thin blankets, and though it was cold in the room, Isabelle didn't think it was cold enough for them to have frozen to death. She wasn't sure how they had died; she couldn't bear to investigate too closely. This was clearly a matter for the Clave.

Alec, behind her, had tears running down his face; he was cursing under his breath by the time they reached the last of the pedestals. Maia had straightened up and was leaning against the window; Jordan had given her some kind of cloth, maybe a handkerchief, to hold to her face. The cold white lights of the city burned behind her, cutting through the dark glass like diamond drills.

"Iz," Alec said. "Who could have done something like this? *Why* would someone—even a demon—"

He broke off. Isabelle knew what he was thinking about. Max, when he had been born. She had been seven, Alec nine. They had bent over their little brother in the cradle, amused and enchanted by this fascinating new creature. They'd played with his little fingers, laughed at the weird faces he made when they tickled him.

Her heart twisted. *Max.* As she had moved down the lines of little cribs, now turned into little coffins, a sense of overwhelming dread had begun to press down on her. She couldn't ignore the fact that the pendant around her neck was glowing with a harsh, steady glow. The sort of glow she might have expected if she were facing down a Greater Demon.

She thought of what Clary had seen in the morgue in Beth Israel. *He looked just like a normal baby. Except for his hands. They were twisted into claws.* . . .

With great care she reached into one of the cribs. Careful not to touch the baby, she twitched aside the thin blanket that wrapped its body.

She felt the breath puff out of her in a gasp. Ordinary chubby baby arms, round baby wrists. The hands looked soft and new. But the fingers—the fingers were twisted into claws, as black as burned bone, tipped with sharp little talons. She took an involuntary step back.

"What?" Maia moved toward them. She still looked sickened, but her voice was steady. Jordan followed her, hands in his pockets. "What did you find?" she asked.

"By the Angel." Alec, beside Isabelle, was looking down into the crib. "Is this—like the baby Clary was telling you about? The one at Beth Israel?"

Slowly Isabelle nodded. "I guess it wasn't just the one baby," she said. "Someone's been trying to make a lot more of them. More . . . Sebastians."

"Why would anyone want more of *him*?" Alec's voice was full of naked hatred.

"He was fast and strong," Isabelle said. It almost hurt physically to say anything complimentary about the boy who had killed her brother and tried to kill her. "I guess they're trying to breed a race of super-warriors."

"It didn't work." Maia's eyes were dark with sadness.

A noise so soft it was almost inaudible teased at the edge of Isabelle's hearing. Her head jerked up, her hand going to her belt, where her whip was coiled. Something in the thick shadows at the edge of the room, near the door, moved, just the faintest flicker, but Isabelle had already broken away from the others and was running for the door. She burst out into the hallway near the elevators. There *was* something there—a shadow that had broken free of the greater darkness and was moving, edging along the wall. Isabelle picked up speed and threw herself forward, knocking the shadow to the floor.

It wasn't a ghost. As they went down together in a heap, Isabelle surprised a very human-sounding grunt of surprise out of the shadowy figure. They hit the ground together and rolled. The figure was definitely human—slight and shorter than Isabelle, wearing a gray warm-up suit and sneakers. Sharp elbows came up, jabbing into Isabelle's collarbone. A knee dug into her solar plexus. She gasped and rolled aside, feeling for her whip. By the time she got it free, the figure was on its feet. Isabelle rolled onto her stomach, flicking the whip forward; the end of it coiled around the stranger's ankle and pulled tight.

Isabelle jerked the whip back, yanking the figure off its feet.

She scrambled to her feet, reaching with her free hand for her stele, which was tucked down the front of her dress. With a quick slash she finished the *nyx* Mark on her left arm. Her vision adjusted quickly, the whole room seeming to fill with light as the night vision rune took effect. She could see her attacker more clearly now—a thin figure in a gray warm-up suit and gray sneakers, scrambling backward until its back hit the wall. The hood of the suit had fallen back, exposing the face. The head was shaved cleanly bald, but the face was definitely female, with sharp cheekbones and big dark eyes.

"Stop it," Isabelle said, and pulled hard on the whip. The woman cried out in pain. "Stop trying to crawl away."

The woman bared her teeth. "Worm," she said. "Unbeliever. I will tell you nothing."

Isabelle jammed her stele back into her dress. "If I pull hard enough on this whip, it'll cut through your leg." She gave the whip another flick, tightening it, and moved forward, until she was standing in front of the woman, looking down at her. "Those babies," she said. "What happened to them?"

The woman gave a bubbling laugh. "They were not strong enough. Weak stock, too weak."

"Too weak for what?" When the woman didn't answer, Isabelle snapped, "You can tell me or lose your leg. Your choice. Don't think I won't let you bleed to death here on the floor. Child-murderers don't deserve mercy."

The woman hissed, like a snake. "If you harm me, She will smite you down."

"Who—" Isabelle broke off, remembering what Alec had said. *Talto is another name for Lilith. You might say she's the demon goddess of dead children.* "Lilith," she said. "You worship Lilith. You did all this . . . for her?"

"Isabelle." It was Alec, carrying the light of *Sandalphon* before him. "What's going on? Maia and Jordan are searching, looking for any more . . . children, but it looks like they were all in the big room. What's going on here?"

"This . . . person," Isabelle said with disgust, "is a cult member of the Church of Talto. Apparently they worship Lilith. And they've murdered all these babies for her."

"Not murder!" The woman struggled upright. "Not murder. Sacrifice. They were tested and found weak. Not our fault."

"Let me guess," Isabelle said. "You tried injecting the pregnant women with demon blood. But demon blood is toxic stuff. The babies couldn't survive. They were born deformed, and then they died."

The woman whimpered. It was a very slight sound, but Isabelle saw Alec's eyes narrow. He had always been the one of them that was best at reading people.

"One of those babies," he said. "It was yours. How could you inject your own child with demon blood?"

The woman's mouth trembled. "I didn't. *We* were the ones who took the blood injections. The mothers. Made us stronger, faster. Our husbands, too. But we got sick. Sicker and sicker. Our hair fell out. Our nails . . ." She raised her hands, showing the blackened nails, the torn, bloody nail beds where some had fallen away. Her arms were dotted with blackish bruises. "We're all dying," she said. There was a faint sound of satisfaction in her voice. "We will be dead in days."

"She made you take poison," Alec said, "and yet you worship her?"

"You don't understand." The woman sounded hoarse, dreamy. "I had nothing before She found me. None of us did. I was on the streets. Sleeping on subway gratings so I wouldn't freeze. Lilith gave me a place to live, a family to take care of me. Just to be in Her presence is to be safe. I never felt safe before."

"You've seen Lilith," Isabelle said, struggling to keep the disbelief from her voice. She was familiar with demon cults; she had done a report on them once, for Hodge. He had given her high marks on it. Most cults worshipped demons they had imagined or invented. Some managed to raise weak minor demons, who either killed them all when set free, or contented themselves with being served by the cult members, all their needs attended to, and little asked of them in return. She had never heard of a cult who worshipped a Greater Demon in which the members had ever actually *seen* that demon in the flesh. Much less a Greater Demon as powerful as Lilith, the mother of warlocks. "You've been in her presence?"

The woman's eyes fluttered half-shut. "Yes. With Her blood in me I can feel when She is near. As She is now."

Isabelle couldn't help it; her free hand flew to her pendant. It had been pulsing on and off since they'd entered the building; she had assumed it was because of the demon blood in the dead children, but the presence nearby of a Greater Demon would make even more sense. "She's here? Where is she?"

The woman seemed to be drifting off into sleep. "Upstairs," she said vaguely. "With the vampire boy. The one who walks by day. She sent us to fetch him for Her, but he was protected. We could not lay hands on him. Those who went to find him died. Then, when Brother Adam returned and told us the boy was guarded by holy fire, Lady Lilith was angry. She slew him where he stood. He was lucky, to die by Her hand, so lucky." Her breath rattled. "And She is clever, Lady Lilith. She found another way to bring the boy. . . ."

The whip dropped from Isabelle's suddenly limp hand. "Simon? She brought Simon here? Why?"

"'None that go unto Her,'" the woman breathed, "'return again . . .'"

Isabelle dropped to her knees, seizing up the whip. "Stop it," she said in a voice that shook. "Stop yammering and tell me where he is. Where did she take him? Where is Simon? Tell me, or I'll—"

"Isabelle." Alec spoke heavily. "Iz, there's no point. She's dead."

Isabelle stared at the woman in disbelief. She had died, it seemed, between one breath and the next, her eyes wide open, her face set in slack lines. It was possible to see now that beneath the starvation and the baldness and the bruising, she had probably been quite young, not more than twenty. "God *damn* it."

"I don't get it," Alec said. "What does a Greater Demon want with Simon? He's a vampire. Granted, a powerful vampire, but—"

"The Mark of Cain," Isabelle said distractedly. "This must have something to do with the Mark. It's got to." She moved toward the elevator and jabbed at the call button. "If Lilith was really Adam's first wife, and Cain was Adam's son, then the Mark of Cain is nearly as old as she is."

"Where are you going?"

"She said they were upstairs," Isabelle said. "I'm going to search every floor until I find him."

"She can't hurt him, Izzy," said Alec in the reasonable voice

Isabelle detested. "I know you're worried, but he's got the Mark of Cain; he's untouchable. Even a Greater Demon can't harm him. No one can."

Isabelle scowled at her brother. "So what do you think she wants him for, then? So she'll have someone to pick up her dry cleaning during the day? Really, Alec—"

There was a *ping*, and the arrow above the farthest elevator lit up. Isabelle started forward as the doors began to open. Light flooded out . . . and after the light, a wave of men and women—bald, emaciated, and dressed in gray tracksuits and sneakers—poured out. They were brandishing crude weapons culled from the debris of construction: jagged shards of glass, torn-off chunks of rebar, concrete blocks. None of them spoke. In a silence as total as it was eerie, they surged from the elevator as one, and advanced on Alec and Isabelle.

18

SCARS OF FIRE

Clouds had rolled in over the river, the way they sometimes did at night, bringing a thick mist with them. It didn't hide what was happening on the roof, just laid a sort of dimming fog over everything else. The buildings rising all around them were murky pillars of light, and the moon glowed barely, a muffled lamp, through the low scudding clouds. The broken bits of the glass coffin, scattered across the tiled ground, shone like shards of ice, and Lilith, too, shone, pale under the moon, watching Simon as he bent over Sebastian's still body, drinking his blood.

Clary could hardly bear to watch. She knew Simon hated what he was doing; she knew he was doing it for her. For her, and even, a little bit, for Jace. And she knew what the next step in the ritual would be. Simon would give up his blood, willingly, to Sebastian, and Simon would die. Vampires could die when their blood was drained. He would die, and she would lose him forever, and it would—all of it—be her own fault.

She could feel Jace behind her, his arms still tight around her, the soft, regular beat of his heart against her shoulder blades. She remembered the way he had held her on the steps of the Accords Hall in Idris. The sound of the wind in the leaves as he'd kissed her, his hands warm on either side of her face. The way she had felt his heart beating and thought that no one else's heart beat like his, like every pulse of his blood matched her own.

He *had* to be in there somewhere. Like Sebastian inside his glass prison. There had to be some way to reach him.

Lilith was watching Simon as he bent over Sebastian, her dark eyes wide and fixed. Clary and Jace might as well not have been there at all.

"Jace," Clary whispered. "Jace, I don't want to watch this."

She pressed back against him, as if she were trying to snuggle into his arms, then pretended a wince as the knife brushed the side of her throat.

"Please, Jace," she whispered. "You don't need the knife. You know I can't hurt you."

"But why—"

"I just want to look at you. I want to see your face."

She felt his chest rise and fall once, fast. A shudder went through him, as if he were fighting something, pushing against it. Then he moved, the way only he could move, so swiftly it was like a flash of light. He kept his right arm tight around her; his left hand slid the knife into his belt.

Her heart leaped wildly. *I could run*, she thought, but he would only catch her, and it was only a moment. Seconds later both arms were around her again, his hands on her arms, turning her. She felt his fingers trail over her back, her bare, shivering arms, as he spun her to face him.

She was looking away from Simon now, away from the demon woman, though she could still feel their presence at her back, shivering up her spine. She looked up at Jace. His face was so familiar. The lines of it, the way his hair fell across his forehead, the faint scar over his cheekbone, another at his temple. His eyelashes a shade darker than his hair. His eyes were the color of pale yellow glass. That was where he was different, she thought. He still looked like Jace, but his eyes were clear and blank, as if she were looking through a window into an empty room.

"I'm afraid," she said.

He stroked her shoulder, sending sparks winging through her nerves; with a feeling of sickness she realized her body still responded to his touch. "I won't let anything happen to you."

She stared at him. *You really think that, don't you? Somehow you can't see the disconnect between your actions and your intentions. Somehow she's taken that away from you.*

"You won't be able to stop her," she said. "She's going to kill me, Jace."

He shook his head. "No. She wouldn't do that."

Clary wanted to scream, but she kept her voice deliberate, careful, calm. "I know you're in there, Jace. The real you." She pressed closer to him. The buckle on his belt dug into her waist. "You could fight her. . . ."

It had been the wrong thing to say. He tensed all over, and

she saw a flash of anguish in his eyes, the look of an animal in a trap. In another instant it had turned to hardness. "I can't."

She shivered. The look on his face was awful, so awful. At her shudder his eyes softened. "Are you cold?" he said, and for a moment he sounded like Jace again, concerned about her well-being. It made her throat hurt.

She nodded, though physical cold was the furthest thing from her mind. "Can I put my hands inside your jacket?"

He nodded. His jacket was unbuttoned; she slid her arms inside, her hands touching his back lightly. Everything was eerily silent. The city seemed frozen inside an icy prism. Even the light radiating off the buildings around them was still and cold.

He breathed slowly, steadily. She could see the rune on his chest through the torn fabric of his shirt. It seemed to pulse when he breathed. It was sickening, she thought, attached to him like that, like a leech, sucking out what was good, what was *Jace*.

She remembered what Luke had said to her about destroying a rune. *If you disfigure it enough, you can minimize or destroy its power. Sometimes in battle the enemy will try to burn or slice off a Shadowhunter's skin, just to deprive them of the power of their runes.*

She kept her eyes fixed on Jace's face. *Forget about what's happening*, she thought. *Forget about Simon, about the knife at your throat. What you say now matters more than anything you've ever said before.*

"Remember what you said to me in the park?" she whispered.

He looked down at her, startled. "What?"

"When I told you I didn't speak Italian. I remember what you told me, what that quote meant. You said it meant love is the most powerful force on earth. More powerful than anything else."

A tiny line appeared between his eyebrows. "I don't . . ."

"Yes, you do." *Tread carefully,* she told herself, but she couldn't help it, couldn't help the strain that surfaced in her voice. "You remember. The most powerful force there is, you said. Stronger than Heaven or Hell. It has to be more powerful than Lilith, too."

Nothing. He stared at her as if he couldn't hear her. It was like shouting down into a black, empty tunnel. *Jace, Jace, Jace. I know you're in there.*

"There's a way you could protect me and still do what she wants," she said. "Wouldn't that be the best thing?" She pressed her body closer against his, feeling her stomach twist. It was like holding Jace and not like it, all at the same time, joy and horror mixed together. And she could feel his body react to her, the drumbeat of his heart in her ears, her veins; he had not stopped wanting her, whatever layers of control Lilith exerted over his mind.

"I'll whisper it to you," she said, brushing her lips against his neck. She breathed in the scent of him, as familiar as the scent of her own skin. "Listen."

She tilted her face up, and he leaned down to hear her—and her hand moved from his waist to clamp down on the hilt of the knife in his belt. She whipped it upward, just as he had shown her when they had trained, balancing its weight in her palm, and she slashed the blade across the left side of his chest in a wide, shallow arc. Jace cried out—more in surprise than pain, she guessed—and blood burst from the cut, spilling down his skin, obscuring the rune. He put his hand to his chest; when it came away red, he stared at her, his eyes wide, as if somehow he was genuinely hurt, genuinely unable to believe in her betrayal.

Clary spun away from him as Lilith cried out. Simon was no longer bending over Sebastian; he had straightened up and was staring down at Clary, the back of his hand jammed against his mouth. Black demon blood dripped from his chin onto his white shirt. His eyes were wide.

"Jace," Lilith's voice soared upward in astonishment. "Jace, get hold of her—I order it—"

Jace didn't move. He was staring from Clary, to Lilith, at his bloody hand, and then back again. Simon had begun to back away from Lilith; suddenly he stopped with a jerk and bent double, falling to his knees. Lilith whirled away from Jace and advanced on Simon, her hard face contorted. "Get up!" she shrieked. "Get on your feet! You drank his blood. Now he needs yours!"

Simon struggled to a sitting position, then slid limply to the ground. He retched, coughing up black blood. Clary remembered him in Idris, saying that Sebastian's blood was like poison. Lilith drew back her foot to kick him—then staggered back as if an invisible hand had pushed her, hard. Lilith screeched—not words, just a scream like the cry of an owl. It was a sound of unadulterated hatred and rage.

It was not a sound a human being could have made; it felt like jagged shards of glass being driven into Clary's ears. She cried out, "Leave Simon alone! He's sick. Can't you see he's sick?"

She was immediately sorry she'd spoken. Lilith turned slowly, her gaze sliding over Jace, cold and imperious. "I told you, Jace Herondale." Her voice rang out. "Don't let the girl leave the circle. Take her weapon."

Clary had barely realized she was still holding the knife. She felt so cold she was nearly numb, but beneath that a wash of unbearable rage at Lilith—at everything—freed the movement of her arm. She flung the knife at the ground. It skidded across the tiles, fetching up at Jace's feet. He stared down at it blindly, as if he'd never seen a weapon before.

Lilith's mouth was a thin red slash. The whites of her eyes had vanished; they were all black. She did not look human. "Jace," she hissed. "Jace Herondale, you heard me. And you *will* obey me."

"Take it," Clary said, looking at Jace. "Take it and kill either her or me. It's your choice."

Slowly Jace bent down and picked up the knife.

Alec had *Sandalphon* in one hand, a *hachiwara*—good for parrying multiple attackers—in the other. At least six cultists lay at his feet, dead or unconscious.

Alec had fought quite a few demons in his time, but there was something especially eerie about fighting the cultists of the Church of Talto. They moved all together, less like people than like an eerie dark tide—eerie because they were so silent and so bizarrely strong and fast. They also seemed totally unafraid of death. Though Alec and Isabelle shouted at them to keep back, they kept moving forward in a wordless, clustering horde, flinging themselves at the Shadowhunters with the self-destructive mindlessness of lemmings hurling themselves over a cliff. They had backed Alec and Isabelle down the hallway and into the big, open room full of stone pedestals, when the noise of the fight brought Jordan and Maia running: Jordan in wolf form, Maia still human, but with her claws fully out.

The cultists seemed barely to register their presence. They fought on, falling one after the other as Alec, Maia, and Jordan laid about themselves with knives, claws, and blades. Isabelle's whip traced shimmering patterns in the air as it sliced through bodies, sending fine sprays of blood into the air. Maia especially was acquitting herself well. At least a dozen cultists lay crumpled around her, and she was laying into another one with a blazing fury, her clawed hands red to the wrists.

A cultist streaked across Alec's path and lunged at him, hands outstretched. Its hood was up; he couldn't see its face, or guess at sex or age. He sank the blade of *Sandalphon* into the left side of its chest. It screamed—a male scream, loud and hoarse. The man collapsed, clawing at his chest, where flames were licking at the edge of the torn hole in his jacket. Alec turned away, sickened. He hated watching what happened to humans when a seraph blade pierced their skin.

Suddenly he felt a searing burn across his back, and turned to see a second cultist wielding a jagged piece of rebar. This one was hoodless—a man, his face so thin that his cheekbones seemed to be digging through his skin. He hissed and lunged again at Alec, who leaped aside, the weapon whistling harmlessly past him. He spun and kicked it out of the cultist's hand; it rattled to the floor, and the cultist backed up, nearly tripped over a body—and ran.

Alec hesitated for a moment. The cultist who had just attacked him had nearly made it to the door. Alec knew he ought to follow—for all he knew, the man might be running to warn someone or to get reinforcements—but he felt bone-weary, disgusted, and a little sick. These people might be possessed; they might barely be people anymore, but it still felt too much like killing human beings.

He wondered what Magnus would say, but to tell the truth,

he already knew. Alec had fought creatures like this before, the cult servants of demons. Almost all that was human about them had been consumed by the demon for energy, leaving nothing but a murderous yearning to kill and a human body dying slowly in agony. They were beyond help: incurable, unfixable. He heard Magnus's voice as if the warlock stood beside him. *Killing them is the most merciful thing you can do.*

Jamming the *hachiwara* back into his belt, Alec gave chase, pounding out the door and into the hall after the fleeing cultist. The hallway was empty, the farthest of the elevator doors jammed open, a weird high-pitched alarm noise sounding through the corridor. Several doorways branched off from the foyer. Shrugging inwardly, Alec picked one at random and dashed through it.

He found himself in a maze of small rooms that were barely finished—drywall had been hastily thrown up, and bouquets of multicolored wire sprouted from holes in the walls. The seraph blade threw a patchwork quilt of light across the walls as he moved cautiously through the rooms, his nerves prickling. At one point the light caught movement, and he jumped. Lowering the blade, he saw a pair of red eyes and a small gray body skittering into a hole in the wall. Alec's mouth twitched. That was New York for you. Even in a building as new as this one, there were rats.

Eventually the rooms opened out into a larger space—not as large as the room with the pedestals, but more sizeable than the others. There was a wall of glass here, too, with cardboard taped across sections of it.

A dark shape was huddled in one corner of the room, near an exposed section of piping. Alec approached cautiously. Was it a trick of the light? No, the shape was recognizably human, a bent, huddled figure in dark clothes. Alec's night vision rune twinged as he narrowed his eyes, moving forward. The shape resolved itself into a slim woman, barefoot, her hands chained in front of her to a length of pipe. She raised her head as Alec approached, and the dim light that poured through the windows illuminated her pale white-blond hair.

"Alexander?" she said, her voice rich with disbelief. "Alexander Lightwood?"

It was Camille.

"Jace." Lilith's voice came down like a whip across bare flesh; even Clary flinched at the sound of it. "I command you to—"

Jace's arm drew back—Clary tensed, bracing herself—and he flung the knife at Lilith. It whipped through the air, end over end, and sank into her chest; she staggered back, caught off balance. Lilith's heels skidded on the smooth stone; the demoness righted herself with a snarl, reaching down to pluck the knife from her ribs. Spitting something in a language Clary couldn't understand, she let it drop. It fell hissing to the ground, its blade half-eaten away, as if by a powerful acid.

She whirled on Clary. "What did you do to him? *What did you do?*" Her eyes had been all black a moment ago. Now they seemed to bulge and protrude. Small black serpents slithered from her eye sockets; Clary cried out and stepped back, almost tripping over a low hedge. This was the Lilith she had seen in Ithuriel's vision, with her slithering eyes and harsh, echoing voice. She advanced on Clary—

And suddenly Jace was between them, blocking Lilith's path. Clary stared. He was himself again. He seemed to burn with a righteous fire, as Raziel had by Lake Lyn that horrible night. He had drawn a seraph blade from his belt; the white-silver of it reflected in his eyes; blood dripped from the rent in his shirt and slicked his bare skin. The way he looked at her, at Lilith—if angels could rise up out of Hell, Clary thought, they would look like that. "*Michael*," he said, and Clary wasn't sure whether it was the strength of the name, or the rage in his voice, but the blade he held blazed up brighter than any seraph blade she'd ever seen. She looked aside for a moment, blinded, and saw Simon lying in a crumpled dark heap beside Sebastian's glass coffin.

Her heart twisted inside her chest. What if Sebastian's demon blood had poisoned him? The Mark of Cain wouldn't help him. It was something he had done willingly, to himself. For her. *Simon.*

"Ah, Michael." Lilith's voice was rich with laughter as she moved toward Jace. "The captain of the hosts of the Lord. I knew him."

Jace raised the seraph blade; it blazed like a star, so bright that Clary wondered if all the city could see it, like a searchlight piercing the sky. "Don't come any closer."

Lilith, to Clary's surprise, paused. "Michael slew the demon Sammael, whom I loved," she said. "Why is it, little Shadowhunter, that your angels are so cold and without mercy? Why do they break that which will not obey them?"

"I had no idea you were such a proponent of free will," said Jace, and the way he said it, his voice heavy with sarcasm, did more to reassure Clary that he was himself again than anything else would have. "How about letting us all walk off this roof now, then? Me, Simon, Clary? What do you say, demoness? It's over. You don't control me anymore. I won't hurt Clary, and Simon won't obey you. And that piece of filth you're trying to resuscitate—I suggest you get rid of him before he starts to rot. Because he isn't coming back, and he's way past his sell-by date."

Lilith's face twisted. She spat at Jace, and her spit was a black flame that hit the ground and became a snake that wiggled toward him, its jaws agape. He smashed it with a booted foot and lunged for the demoness, blade outstretched; but Lilith was gone like a shadow when light shone on it, vanishing and reforming just behind him. As he spun, she reached out almost lazily and slammed her open palm against his chest.

Jace went flying, Michael knocked from his hand, skittering across the stone tiles. Jace sailed through the air and struck the low roof wall with such force that splintering lines appeared in the stone. He hit the ground hard, visibly stunned.

Gasping, Clary ran for the fallen seraph blade, but never reached it. Lilith caught Clary up in two thin, icy hands and threw her with incredible force. Clary hurtled into a low hedge, the branches slashing viciously at her skin, opening up long cuts. She struggled to free herself, her dress tangled in the foliage. She heard the silk rip as she tore free and turned to see Lilith drag Jace to his feet, her hand fastened in the bloody front of his shirt.

She grinned at him, and her teeth were black too, and gleamed like metal. "I am glad you're on your feet, little Nephilim. I want to see your face when I kill you, not stab you in the back the way you did my son."

Jace wiped his sleeve across his face; he was bleeding from a long cut along his cheek, and the fabric came away red. "He's not your son. You donated some blood to him. That doesn't make him yours. Mother of warlocks—" He turned his head and spat, blood. "You're not anyone's mother."

Lilith's snake eyes darted back and forth furiously. Clary, disentangling herself painfully from the hedge, saw that each of the snake heads had two eyes of its own, glittering and red. Clary's stomach turned as the snakes moved, their gazes seeming to slither up and down Jace's body. "Cutting my rune apart. How crude," she spat.

"But effective," said Jace.

"You cannot win against me, Jace Herondale," she said. "You may be the greatest Shadowhunter this world has known, but I am more than a Greater Demon."

"Then, fight me," said Jace. "I'll give you a weapon. I'll have my seraph blade. Fight me one on one, and we'll see who wins."

Lilith looked at him, shaking her head slowly, her dark hair swirling around her like smoke. "I am the oldest of demons," she said. "I am not a *man*. I have no male pride for you to trick me with, and I am not interested in single combat. That is entirely a weakness of your sex, not mine. I am a woman. I will use any weapon and all weapons to get what I want." She let go of him them, with a half-contemptuous shove; Jace stumbled for a moment, righting himself quickly and reaching to the ground for the glittering blade of Michael.

He seized it just as Lilith laughed and raised her hands. Half-opaque shadows exploded from her open palms. Even Jace looked shocked as the shadows solidified into the forms of twin black shadowy demons with shimmering red eyes. They hit the ground, pawing and growling. They were *dogs*, Clary thought in amazement, two gaunt, vicious-looking black dogs that vaguely resembled Doberman pinschers.

"Hellhounds," breathed Jace. "Clary—"

He broke off as one of the dogs sprang toward him, its

mouth opened as wide as a shark's, a loud, baying howl erupting from its throat. A moment later the second one leaped into the air, launching itself directly at Clary.

"Camille." Alec's head was spinning. "What are you doing here?"

He immediately realized that he sounded like an idiot. He fought down the urge to smack himself in the forehead. The last thing he wanted was to look like a fool in front of Magnus's ex-girlfriend.

"It was Lilith," said the vampire woman in a small, trembling voice. "She had her cult members break into the Sanctuary. It isn't warded against humans, and they're human—barely. They cut my chains and brought me here, to her." She raised her hands; the chains binding her wrists to the pipe rattled. "They brutalized me."

Alec crouched down, bringing his eyes on a level with Camille's. Vampires didn't bruise—they healed too quickly for that—but her hair was matted with blood on the left side, which made him think she was telling the truth. "Let's say I believe you," he said. "What did she want with you? Nothing in what I know about Lilith says she has a particular interest in vampires."

"You know why the Clave was holding me," she said. "You would have heard."

"You killed three Shadowhunters. Magnus said you claimed you were doing it because someone had ordered you to—" He broke off. "Lilith?"

"If I tell you, will you help me?" Camille's lower lip trembled. Her eyes were huge, green, pleading. She was very beautiful. Alec wondered if she had once looked at Magnus like this. It made him want to shake her.

"I might," he said, astonished at the coldness in his own voice. "You don't have a lot of bargaining power here. I could go off and leave you for Lilith to have, and it wouldn't make much difference to me."

"Yes, it would," she said. Her voice was low. "Magnus loves you. He wouldn't love you if you were the sort of person who could abandon someone helpless."

"He loved *you*," Alec said.

She gave a wistful smile. "He appears to have learned better since then."

Alec rocked back on his heels slightly. "Look," he said. "Tell me the truth. If you do, I'll cut you free and bring you to the Clave. They'll treat you better than Lilith would."

She looked down at her wrists, chained to the pipe. "The Clave chained me," she said. "Lilith chained me. I see little difference in my treatment between the two."

"I guess it's your choice, then. Trust me, or trust her," Alec said. It was a gamble, he knew.

He waited for several tense moments before she said, "Very well. If Magnus trusts you, I will trust you." She raised her head, doing her best to look dignified despite torn clothing and bloody hair. "Lilith came to me, not I to her. She had heard I was looking to recover my position as head of the Manhattan clan from Raphael Santiago. She said she would help me, if I would help her."

"Help her by murdering Shadowhunters?"

"She wanted their blood," said Camille. "It was for those babies. She was injecting Shadowhunter blood and demon blood into the mothers, trying to replicate what Valentine did to his son. It didn't work, though. The babies became twisted things—and then they died." Catching his revolted look, she said, "I didn't know at first what she wanted the blood *for.* You may not think much of me, but I have no taste for murdering innocents."

"You didn't have to do it," said Alec. "Just because she offered."

Camille smiled tiredly. "When you are as old as I am," she said, "it is because you have learned to play the game correctly—to make the right alliances at the right times. To ally yourself not just with the powerful, but with those who you believe will make you powerful. I knew that if I did not agree to assist Lilith, she would kill me. Demons are not by nature trusting, and she would think that I would go to the Clave with what I knew about her plans to kill Shadowhunters, even if I promised her I would stay silent. I took a chance that Lilith was a greater danger to me than your kind were."

"And you didn't mind killing Shadowhunters."

"They were Circle members," said Camille. "They had killed my kind. And yours."

"And Simon Lewis? What was your interest in him?"

"Everyone wants the Daylighter on their side." Camille shrugged. "And I knew he had the Mark of Cain. One of Raphael's vampire underlings is still loyal to me. He passed on the information. Few other Downworlders know of it. It makes him an incalculably valuable ally."

"Is that what Lilith wants with him?"

Camille's eyes widened. Her skin was very pale, and beneath it Alec could see that her veins had darkened, the pattern of them beginning to spread across the whiteness of her face like widening cracks in china. Eventually, starving vampires became savage, then lost consciousness, once they had been without blood for too long. The older they were, the longer they could stave it off, but Alec couldn't help but wonder how long it had been since she had fed. "What do you mean?"

"Apparently she's summoned Simon to meet with her," said Alec. "They're somewhere in the building."

Camille stared a moment longer, then laughed. "A true irony," she said. "She never mentioned him to me, and I never mentioned him to her, and yet both of us were pursuing him for our own ends. If she wants him, it's for his blood," she added. "The ritual she's performing is most assuredly one of blood magic. His blood—mixed Downworlder and Shadowhunter blood—would be of great use to her."

Alec felt a flicker of unease. "But she can't hurt him. The Mark of Cain—"

"She'll find a way around that," said Camille. "She is Lilith, mother of warlocks. She's been alive a *long* time, Alexander."

Alec got to his feet. "Then I'd better find out what she's doing."

Camille's chains rattled as she tried to rise to her knees. "Wait—but you said you would free me."

Alec turned and looked down at her. "I didn't. I said I would let the Clave have you."

"But if you leave me here, nothing prevents Lilith from finding me first." She tossed her matted hair back; lines of strain showed in her face. "Alexander, please. I beg you—"

"Who's Will?" Alec said. The words came out abruptly, unexpectedly, and much to his horror.

"Will?" For a moment her face was blank; then it creased into a look of realization, and near amusement. "You heard my conversation with Magnus."

"Some of it." Alec exhaled carefully. "Will is dead, isn't he? I mean, Magnus said it was a long time ago that he knew him. . . ."

"I know what's bothering you, little Shadowhunter." Camille's voice had gone musical and soft. Behind her, through the windows, Alec could see the distant flickering lights of a plane as it flew over the city. "At first you were happy. You thought of the moment, not of the future. Now you have realized. You will grow old, and will someday die. And Magnus will not. He will continue. You will not grow old together. You will grow apart instead."

Alec thought of the people on the airplane, high up in the cold and icy air, looking down on the city like a field of glittering diamonds, far below. Of course, he had never been in an airplane himself. He was only guessing at how it would feel: lonely, distant, disconnected from the world. "You can't know that," he said. "That we'll grow apart."

She smiled pityingly. "You're beautiful now," she said. "But will you be in twenty years? In forty? Fifty? Will he love your blue eyes when they fade, your soft skin when age cuts deep furrows in it? Your hands when they wrinkle and grow weak, your hair when it grows white—"

"Shut up." Alec heard the crack in his own voice, and was ashamed. "Just shut up. I don't want to hear it."

"It doesn't have to be that way." Camille leaned toward him, her green eyes luminous. "What if I told you that you didn't have to grow old? Didn't have to die?"

Alec felt a wave of rage. "I'm not interested in becoming a vampire. Don't even bother making the offer. Not if the only other alternative was death."

For the briefest of moments her face twisted. It was gone in a flash as her control reasserted itself; she smiled a thin smile and said, "That wasn't my suggestion. What if I told you there was another way? Another way for the two of you to be together forever?"

Alec swallowed. His mouth was as dry as paper. "Tell me," he said.

Camille raised her hands. Her chains rattled. "Cut these free."

"No. Tell me first."

She shook her head. "I won't do that." Her expression was as hard as marble, as was her voice. "You said I had nothing to bargain with. But I do. And I will not give it away."

Alec hesitated. In his head he heard Magnus's soft voice. *She is a master of implication and manipulation. She always has been.*

But Magnus, he thought. *You never told me. Never warned me it would be like this, that I would wake up one day and realize that I was going somewhere you couldn't follow. That we are essentially not the same. There's no "till death do us part" for those who never die.*

He took a step toward Camille, and then another. Raising his right arm, he brought the seraph blade down, as hard as he could. It sheared through the metal of her chains; her wrists sprang apart, still in their manacles but free. She brought her hands up, her expression gloating, triumphant.

"Alec." Isabelle spoke from the doorway; Alec turned and saw her standing there, her whip at her side. It was stained with blood, as were her hands and her silk dress. "What are you doing in here?"

"Nothing. I—" Alec felt a wave of shame and horror; almost without thinking, he moved to step in front of Camille, as if he could obscure her from his sister's view.

"They're all dead." Isabelle sounded grim. "The cultists. We killed every one of them. Now come on. We have to start looking for Simon." She squinted at Alec. "Are you okay? You look really pale."

"I cut her free," Alec blurted. "I shouldn't have. It's just—"

"Cut *who* free?" Isabelle took a step into the room. The ambient city light sparked off her dress, making her shine like a ghost. "Alec, what are you blathering about?"

Her expression was blank, confused. Alec turned, following her gaze, and saw—nothing. The pipe was still there, a length of chain lying beside it, the dust on the floor only very slightly disturbed. But Camille was gone.

Clary barely had time to put her arms up before the hellhound collided with her, a cannonball of muscle and bone and hot, stinking breath. Her feet went out from under her; she remembered Jace telling her the best way to fall, how to protect yourself, but the advice flew from her mind and she hit the ground with her elbows, agony shooting through her as the skin tore. A moment later the hound was on top of her, its paws crushing her chest, its gnarled tail swishing from side to side in a grotesque imitation of a wag. The tip of its tail was spiked with nail-like protrusions like a medieval mace, and a thick growl came from its barrel-chested body, so loud and strong that she could feel her bones vibrate.

"Hold her there! Tear her throat out if she tries to get away!" Lilith snapped instructions as the second hellhound sprang at Jace; he was struggling with it, rolling over and over, a whirlwind of teeth and arms and legs and the vicious whipping tail. Painfully Clary turned her head to the other side, and saw Lilith striding toward the glass coffin and Simon, still lying in a heap beside it. Inside the coffin Sebastian floated, as motionless as a drowned body; the milky color of the water had turned dark, probably with his blood.

The hound pinning her to the ground snarled close to her ear. The sound sent a jolt of fear through her—and along with the fear, anger. Anger at Lilith, and at herself. She was a Shadowhunter. It was one thing to be taken down by a Ravener demon when she'd never heard of the Nephilim. She had some training now. She ought to be able to do better.

Anything can be a weapon. Jace had said that to her in the park. The weight of the hellhound was crushing; she made a gagging noise and reached for her throat, as if fighting for air. It barked and snarled, baring its teeth; her fingers closed on the chain holding the Morgenstern ring around her neck. She yanked it, hard, and the chain snapped; she whipped it toward the dog's face, slashing the hound brutally across the eyes. The hound reared back, howling in pain, and Clary rolled to the side, scrambling to her knees. Bloody-eyed, the dog crouched, ready to spring. The necklace had fallen out of Clary's hand, the ring rolling away; she scrabbled for the chain as the dog leaped—

A shining blade split the night, slashing down inches from Clary's face, severing the dog's head from its body. It gave a single howl and vanished, leaving behind a scorched black mark on the stone, and the stench of demon in the air.

Hands came down, lifted Clary gently to her feet. It was Jace. He had shoved the burning seraph blade through his belt, and he held her by both hands, gazing at her with a peculiar look. She couldn't have described it, or even drawn it—hope, shock, love, yearning, and anger all mixed together in his expression. His shirt was torn in several places, soaked with blood; his jacket was gone, his fair hair matted with sweat and blood. For a moment they simply stared at each other, his grip on her hands painfully tight. Then they both spoke at once:

"Are you—," she began.

"Clary." Still gripping her hands, he pushed her away from him, away from the circle, toward the walkway that led to the elevators. "Go," he said raggedly. "Get out of here, Clary."

"Jace—"

He took a shaking breath. *"Please,"* he said, and then he let her go, drawing the seraph blade from his belt as he turned back toward the circle.

"Get up," Lilith growled. "Get *up.*"

A hand shook Simon's shoulder, sending a wave of agony through his head. He had been floating in darkness; he opened his eyes now and saw night sky, stars, and Lilith's white face looming over him. Her eyes were gone, replaced by slithering black snakes. The shock of the sight was enough to propel Simon to his feet.

The moment he was upright, he retched and nearly fell to his knees again. Shutting his eyes against the nausea, he heard Lilith snarl his name, and then her hand was on his arm, guiding him forward. He let her do it. His mouth was full of the nauseating, bitter taste of Sebastian's blood; it was spreading through his veins, too, making him sick, weak, and shivery down to his bones. His head felt like it weighed a thousand pounds, and dizziness was advancing and receding in waves.

Abruptly Lilith's cold grip on his arm was gone. Simon opened his eyes and found that he was standing over the glass coffin, just as he had been before. Sebastian floated in the dark, milky liquid, his face smooth, no pulse in his neck. Two dark holes were visible at the side of his throat where Simon had bitten him.

Give him your blood. Lilith's voice echoed, not aloud but inside his head. *Do it now.*

Simon looked up dizzily. His vision was fogging. He strained to see Clary and Jace through the encroaching darkness.

Use your fangs, said Lilith. *Tear your wrist open. Give Jonathan your blood. Heal him.*

Simon raised his wrist to his mouth. *Heal him.* Raising someone from the dead was a lot more than healing them, he thought. Maybe Sebastian's hand would grow back. Maybe that's what she meant. He waited for his fangs to come, but they didn't. He was too sick to be hungry, he thought, and fought back the insane urge to laugh.

"I can't," he said, half-gasping. "I can't—"

"Lilith!" Jace's voice cut through the night; Lilith turned with an incredulous hiss. Simon lowered his wrist slowly, struggling to focus his eyes. He focused on the brightness in front of him, and it became the leaping flame of a seraph blade, held in Jace's left hand. Simon could see him clearly now, a distinct image painted onto the darkness. His jacket was gone, he was filthy, his shirt torn and black with blood, but his eyes were clear and steady and focused. He no longer looked like a zombie or someone caught sleepwalking in a terrible dream.

"Where is she?" Lilith said, her snake eyes slithering forward on their stalks. "Where is the girl?"

Clary. Simon's fogged gaze scanned the darkness around Jace, but she was nowhere to be seen. His vision was beginning to clear. He could see blood smearing the tiled ground, and bits of shredded, torn satin caught on the sharp branches of a hedge. What looked like paw prints smeared the blood. Simon felt his chest tighten. He looked quickly back at Jace. Jace looked angry—very angry indeed—but not shattered the way Simon would have expected him to look if something had happened to Clary. So where was she?

"She has nothing to do with this," Jace said. "You say I can't kill you, demoness. I say I can. Let's see which of us is right."

Lilith moved so fast, she was a blur. One moment she was beside Simon, the next she was on the step above Jace. She slashed out at him with her hand; he ducked, spinning behind her, whipping the seraph blade across her shoulder. She screamed, whirling on him, blood arcing from her wound. It was a shimmering black color, like onyx. She brought her hands together as if she meant to smash the blade between them. They struck each other with a sound like a thunderclap, but Jace was already gone, several feet away, the light of the seraph blade dancing in the air before him like the wink of a mocking eye.

If it had been any other Shadowhunter but Jace, Simon thought, he would have been dead already. He thought of Camille saying, *Man cannot contend with the divine.* Shadowhunters were human, despite their angel blood, and Lilith was more than a demon.

Pain shot through Simon. With surprise he realized his fangs had, finally, come out, and were cutting into his lower lip. The pain and the taste of blood roused him further. He began to rise to his feet, slowly, his eyes on Lilith. She certainly didn't appear to notice him, or what he was doing. Her eyes were fixed on Jace. With another sudden snarl she leaped for him. It was like watching moths flashing to and fro, watching the two of them as they battled back and forth across the rooftop. Even Simon's vampire vision had trouble keeping up as they moved, leaping over hedges, darting among the walkways. Lilith backed Jace up against the low wall that surrounded a sundial, the numbers on its face picked out in shining gold. Jace was moving so fast he was nearly a blur, the light of Michael whipping around Lilith as if she were being wrapped in a net of shining filaments. Anyone else would have been cut to ribbons in seconds. But Lilith moved like dark water, like smoke. She seemed to vanish and reappear at will, and though Jace was clearly not tiring, Simon could sense his frustration.

Finally it happened. Jace swung the seraph blade violently toward Lilith—and she caught it out of the air, her hand wrapping around the blade. Her hand was dripping black blood as she yanked the blade toward her. The drops, as they struck the ground, became tiny obsidian snakes that wiggled away into the underbrush.

Taking the blade in both hands, she raised it. Blood was running down her pale wrists and forearms like streaks of tar. With a snarling grin she snapped the blade in half; one half crumbled to a shining powder in her hands, while the other— the hilt and a jagged shard of blade—sputtered darkly, a flame half-smothered by ash.

Lilith smiled. "Poor little Michael," she said. "He always was weak."

Jace was panting, his hands clenched at his sides, his hair pasted to his forehead with sweat. "You and your name-dropping," he said. "'I knew Michael.' 'I knew Sammael.' 'The angel Gabriel did my hair.' It's like *I'm with the Band* with biblical figures."

This was Jace being brave, Simon thought, brave and snarky because he thought Lilith was going to kill him, and that was the way he wanted to go, unafraid and on his feet. Like a warrior. The way Shadowhunters did. His death song would always be this—jokes and snideness and pretend arrogance, and that look in his eyes that said, *I'm better than you.* Simon just hadn't realized it before.

"Lilith," Jace went on, managing to make the word sound like a curse. "I studied you. In school. Heaven cursed you with barrenness. A thousand babies, and they all died. Isn't that the case?"

Lilith held her darkly glowing blade, her face impassive. "Be careful, little Shadowhunter."

"Or what? Or you'll kill me?" Blood was dripping down Jace's face from the cut on his cheek; he made no move to wipe it away. "Go ahead."

No. Simon tried to take a step; his knees buckled, and he fell, slamming his hands into the ground. He took a deep breath. He didn't need the oxygen, but it helped somehow, steadying him. He reached up and grabbed the edge of the stone pedestal, using it to pull himself upright. The back of his head was pounding. There was no way there would be enough time. All Lilith had to do was drive forward the jagged blade she held—

But she didn't. Looking at Jace, she didn't move, and suddenly his eyes flashed, his mouth relaxing. *"You can't kill me,"* he said, his voice rising. "What you said before—I'm the counterweight. I'm the only thing tethering *him"*—he thrust out an arm, indicating Sebastian's glass coffin—"to this world. If I die, he dies. Isn't that true?" He took a step back. "I could jump off this roof right now," he said. "Kill myself. End this."

For the first time Lilith appeared truly agitated. Her head whipped from side to side, her serpent eyes quivering, as if they were searching the wind. "Where is she? Where's the girl?"

Jace wiped blood and sweat from his face and grinned at her; his lip was already split, and blood ran down his chin. "Forget it. I sent her back downstairs while you weren't paying attention. She's gone—safe from you."

Lilith snarled. "You lie."

Jace took another step back. A few more steps would bring him to the low wall, the edge of the building. Jace could survive a lot, Simon knew, but a fall from a forty-story building might be too much even for him.

"You forget," said Lilith. "I was *there*, Shadowhunter. I watched you fall and die. I watched Valentine weep over your body. And then I watched as the Angel asked Clarissa what she desired of him, what she wanted in the world more than she wanted anything else, and she said *you*. Thinking you could be the only people in the world who could have their dead loved one back, and that there would be *no consequences*. That *is* what you thought, isn't it, both of you? Fools." Lilith spat. "You love each other—anyone can see that, looking at you—that kind of love that can burn down the world or raise it up in glory. No, she would never leave your side. Not while she thought you were in danger." Her head jerked back, her hand shooting out, fingers curved into claws. *"There."*

There was a scream, and one of the hedges seemed to tear apart, revealing Clary, who had been crouched, hiding, in the middle of it. Kicking and clawing, she was dragged forward, her fingernails scraping the ground, seizing in vain for a purchase on something that she could grip. Her hands left bloody trails on the tiles.

"*No!*" Jace started forward, then froze as Clary was whipped up into the air, where she hovered, dangling in front of Lilith. She was barefoot, her satin dress—now so torn and filthy it looked red and black rather than gold—swirling around her, one of her shoulder straps torn and dangling. Her hair had come completely out of its sparkling combs and spilled down over her shoulders. Her green eyes fixed on Lilith with hatred.

"You *bitch*," she said.

Jace's face was a mask of horror. He really had believed it when he'd said Clary was gone, Simon realized. He'd thought she was safe. But Lilith had been right. And she was gloating now, her snake's eyes dancing as she moved her hands like a puppeteer, and Clary spun and gasped in the air. Lilith flicked her fingers, and what looked like the lash of a silver whip came down across Clary's body, slicing her dress open, and the skin under it. She screamed and clutched at the wound, and her blood pattered down on the tiles like scarlet rain.

"*Clary.*" Jace whirled on Lilith. "All right," he said. He was pale now, his bravado gone; his hands, clenched into fists, were white at the knuckles. "All right. Let her go, and I'll do what you want—so will Simon. We'll let you—"

"*Let* me?" Somehow the features of Lilith's face had rearranged themselves. Snakes wriggled in the sockets of her eyes, her white skin was too stretched and shining, her mouth too wide. Her nose had nearly vanished. "You have no choice. And more to the point, you have annoyed me. All of you. Perhaps if you had simply done as I'd ordered, I would have let you go. You will never know now, will you?"

Simon let go of the stone pedestal, swayed, and steadied himself. Then he began to walk. Putting his feet down, one after the other, felt like heaving enormous bags of packed wet sand down the side of a cliff. Each time his foot hit the ground, it sent a stab of pain through his body. He concentrated on moving forward, one step at a time.

"Maybe I can't kill you," Lilith said to Jace. "But I can torture her past the point of her endurance—torture her to madness—and make you watch. There are worse things than death, Shadowhunter."

She flicked her fingers again, and the silver whip came down, slashing across Clary's shoulder this time, opening up a wide gash. Clary buckled but didn't scream, jamming her hands into her mouth, curling in on herself as if she could protect herself from Lilith.

Jace started forward to throw himself at Lilith—and saw Simon. Their gazes met. For a moment the world seemed to hang in suspension, all of it, not just Clary. Simon saw Lilith, all her attention focused on Clary, her hand drawn back, ready to deliver an even more vicious blow. Jace's face was white with anguish, his eyes darkening as they met Simon's—and he realized—and understood.

Jace stepped back.

The world blurred around Simon. As he leaped forward, he realized two things. One, that it was impossible, he would never reach Lilith in time; her hand was already whipping forward, the air in front of her alive with whirling silver. And two, that he had never understood before quite how *fast* a vampire could move. He felt the muscles in his legs, his back, tear, the bones in his feet and ankles crack—

And he was there, sliding between Lilith and Clary as the demoness's hand came down. The long, razored silver wire struck him across the face and chest—there was a moment of shocking pain—and then the air seemed to burst apart around him like glittering confetti, and Simon heard Clary scream, a clear sound of shock and amazement that cut through the darkness. "*Simon!*"

Lilith froze. She stared from Simon, to Clary, still hanging in the air, and then down at her own hand, now empty. She drew in a long, ragged breath.

"*Sevenfold,*" she whispered—and was abruptly cut off as a blinding incandescence lit up the night. Dazed, all Simon could think of was ants burning under the concentrated beam from a magnifying glass as a great ray of fire plunged down from the sky, spearing through Lilith. For a long moment she burned white against the darkness, trapped within the blinding flame, her mouth open like a tunnel in a silent scream. Her hair lifted, a mass of burning filaments against the darkness—and then she was white gold, beaten thin against the air—and then she was salt, a thousand crystalline granules of salt that rained down at Simon's feet with a dreadful sort of beauty.

And then she was gone.

19

HELL IS SATISFIED

The unimaginable brilliance printed on the back of Clary's eyelids faded into darkness. A surprisingly long darkness that gave way slowly to an intermittent grayish light, blotched with shadows. There was something hard and cold pressing into her back, and her whole body hurt. She heard murmured voices above her, which sent a stab of pain through her head. Someone touched her gently on the throat, and the hand was withdrawn. She took a deep breath.

Her whole body was throbbing. She opened her eyes to slits, and looked around her, trying not to move very much. She was lying on the hard tiles of the rooftop garden, one of the paving stones digging into her back. She had fallen to the ground when Lilith vanished, and was covered in cuts and bruises, her shoes were gone, her knees were bleeding, and her dress was slashed where Lilith had cut her with the magical whip, blood welling through the rents in her silk dress.

Simon was kneeling over her, his face anxious. The Mark of Cain still gleamed whitely on his forehead. "Her pulse is steady," he was saying, "but come on. You're supposed to have all those healing runes. There must be something you can do for her—"

"Not without a stele. Lilith made me throw Clary's away so she couldn't grab it from me when she woke up." The voice was Jace's, low and tense with suppressed anguish. He knelt across from Simon, on her other side, his face in shadow. "Can you carry her downstairs? If we can get her to the Institute—"

"You want *me* to carry her?" Simon sounded surprised; Clary didn't blame him.

"I doubt she'd want me touching her." Jace stood up, as if he couldn't bear to remain in one place. "If you could—"

His voice cracked, and he turned away, staring at the place where Lilith had stood until a moment ago, a bare patch of stone now silvered with scattered molecules of salt. Clary heard Simon sigh—a deliberate sound—and he bent over her, his hands on her arms.

She opened her eyes the rest of the way, and their gazes met. Though she knew he realized she was conscious, neither of them said anything. It was hard for her to look at him, at that familiar face with the mark she had given him blazing like a white star above his eyes.

She had known, giving him the Mark of Cain, that she was doing something enormous, something terrifying and colossal whose outcome was almost totally unpredictable. She would have done it again, to save his life. But still, while he'd been standing there, the Mark burning like white lightning as Lilith—a Greater Demon as old as mankind itself—charred away to salt, she had thought, *What have I done?*

"I'm all right," she said. She lifted herself up onto her elbows; they hurt horribly. At some point she'd landed on them and scraped off all the skin. "I can walk just fine."

At the sound of her voice, Jace turned. The sight of him tore at her. He was shockingly bruised and bloody, a long scratch running the length of his cheek, his lower lip swollen, and a dozen bleeding rents in his clothes. She wasn't used to seeing him so damaged—but of course, if he didn't have a stele to heal her, he didn't have one to heal himself, either.

His expression was absolutely blank. Even Clary, used to reading his face as if she were reading the pages of a book, could read nothing in it. His gaze dropped to her throat, where she could still feel the stinging pain, the blood crusting there where his knife had cut her. The nothingness of his expression cracked, and he looked away before she could see his face change.

Waving away Simon's offer of a helping hand, she tried to rise to her feet. A searing pain shot through her ankle, and she cried out, then bit her lip. Shadowhunters didn't scream in pain. They bore it stoically, she reminded herself. No whimpering.

"It's my ankle," she said. "I think it might be sprained, or broken."

Jace looked at Simon. "Carry her," he said. "Like I told you."

This time Simon didn't wait for Clary's response; he slid one arm under her knees and the other under her shoulders and lifted her; she looped her arms around his neck and held on tight. Jace headed toward the cupola and the doors that led inside. Simon followed, carrying Clary as carefully as if she were breakable porcelain. Clary had almost forgotten how strong he was, now that he was a vampire. He no longer smelled like himself, she thought, a little wistfully—that Simon-smell of soap and cheap aftershave (that he really didn't need) and his favorite cinnamon gum. His hair still smelled like his shampoo, but otherwise he seemed to have no smell at all, and his skin where she touched it was cold. She tightened her arms around his neck, wishing he had some body heat. The tips of her fingers looked bluish, and her body felt numb.

Jace, ahead of them, shouldered the glass double doors open. Then they were inside, where it was mercifully slightly warmer. It was strange, Clary thought, being held by someone whose chest didn't rise and fall as they breathed. A strange electricity still seemed to cling to Simon, a remnant of the brutally shining light that had enveloped the roof when Lilith was destroyed. She wanted to ask him how he was feeling, but Jace's silence was so devastatingly total that she felt afraid to break it.

He reached for the elevator call button, but before his finger touched it, the doors slid open of their own accord, and Isabelle seemed to almost explode through them, her silvery-gold whip trailing behind her like the tail of a comet. Alec followed, hard on her heels; seeing Jace, Clary, and Simon there, Isabelle skidded to a stop, Alec nearly crashing into her from behind. Under other circumstances it would almost have been funny.

"But—," Isabelle gasped. She was cut and bloodied, her beautiful red dress torn raggedly around the knees, her black hair having come down out of its updo, strands of it matted with blood. Alec looked as if he had fared only a little better; one sleeve of his jacket was sliced open down the side, though it didn't look as if the skin beneath had been injured. "What are you *doing* here?"

Jace, Clary, and Simon all stared at her blankly, too shell-shocked to respond. Finally Jace said dryly, "We could ask you the same question."

"I didn't— We thought you and Clary were at the party," Isabelle said. Clary had rarely seen Isabelle so not self-possessed. "We were looking for Simon."

Clary felt Simon's chest lift, a sort of reflexive human gasp of surprise. "You *were*?"

Isabelle flushed. "I . . ."

"Jace?" It was Alec, his tone commanding. He had given Clary and Simon an astonished look, but then his attention went, as it always did, to Jace. He might not be in love with Jace anymore, if he ever really had been, but they were still *parabatai*, and Jace was always first on his mind in any battle. "What are you doing here? And for the Angel's sake, what happened to you?"

Jace stared at Alec, almost as if he didn't know him. He looked like someone in a nightmare, examining a new landscape not because it was surprising or dramatic but to prepare himself for whatever horrors it might reveal. "Stele," he said finally, in a cracking voice. "Do you have your stele?"

Alec reached for his belt, looking baffled. "Of course." He held the stele out to Jace. "If you need an *iratze*—"

"Not for me," Jace said, still in the same odd, cracked voice. "Her." He pointed at Clary. "She needs it more than I do." His eyes met Alec's, gold and blue. "Please, Alec," he said, the harshness gone from his voice as suddenly as it had come. "Help her for me."

He turned and walked away, toward the far side of the room, where the glass doors were. He stood, staring through them— at the garden outside or his own reflection, Clary couldn't tell.

Alec looked after Jace for a moment, then came toward Clary and Simon, stele in hand. He indicated that Simon should lower Clary to the floor, which he did gently, letting her brace her back against the wall. He stepped back as Alec knelt down over her. She could see the confusion in Alec's face, and his look of surprise as he saw how bad the cuts across her arm and abdomen were. "Who did this to you?"

"I—" Clary looked helplessly toward Jace, who still had his back to them. She could see his reflection in the glass doors, his face a white smudge, darkened here and there with bruises. The front of his shirt was dark with blood. "It's hard to explain."

"Why didn't you summon us?" Isabelle demanded, her voice thin with betrayal. "Why didn't you tell us you were coming here? Why didn't you send a fire-message, or *anything*? You know we would have come if you needed us."

"There wasn't time," Simon said. "And I didn't know Clary and Jace were going to be here. I thought I was the only one. It didn't seem right to drag you into my problems."

"D-drag me into your problems?" Isabelle sputtered. "You—," she began—and then to everyone's surprise, clearly including her own, she flung herself at Simon, wrapping her arms around his neck. He staggered backward, unprepared for the assault, but he recovered quickly enough. His arms went around her, nearly snagging on the dangling whip, and he held her tightly, her dark head just under his chin. Clary couldn't quite tell—Isabelle was speaking too softly—but it sounded like she was swearing at Simon under her breath.

Alec's eyebrows went up, but he made no comment as he bent over Clary, blocking her view of Isabelle and Simon. He touched the stele to her skin, and she jumped at the stinging pain. "I know it hurts," he said in a low voice. "I think you hit your head. Magnus ought to look at you. What about Jace? How badly is he hurt?"

"I don't know." Clary shook her head. "He won't let me near him."

Alec put his hand under her chin, turning her face from side to side, and sketched a second light *iratze* on the side of her throat, just under her jawline. "What did he do that he thinks was so terrible?"

She flicked her eyes up toward him. "What makes you think he did anything?"

Alec let go of her chin. "Because I know him. And the way he punishes himself. Not letting you near him is punishing himself, not punishing you."

"He doesn't *want* me near him," Clary said, hearing the rebelliousness in her own voice and hating herself for being petty.

"You're all he ever wants," said Alec in a surprisingly gentle tone, and he sat back on his heels, pushing his long dark hair out of his eyes. There was something different about him these days, Clary thought, a surety about himself he hadn't had when she had first met him, something that allowed him to be generous with others as he had never been generous with himself before. "How did you two wind up here, anyway? We didn't even notice you leave the party with Simon—"

"They didn't," said Simon. He and Isabelle had detached

themselves, but still stood close to each other, side by side. "I came here alone. Well, not exactly alone. I was—summoned."

Clary nodded. "It's true. We didn't leave the party with him. When Jace brought me here, I had no idea Simon was going to be here too."

"*Jace* brought you here?" Isabelle said, amazed. "Jace, if you knew about Lilith and the Church of Talto, you should have said something."

Jace was still staring through the doors. "I guess it slipped my mind," he said tonelessly.

Clary shook her head as Alec and Isabelle looked from their adoptive brother to her, as if for an explanation of his behavior. "It wasn't really Jace," she said finally. "He was . . . being controlled. By Lilith."

"Possession?" Isabelle's eyes rounded into surprised Os. Her hand tightened on her whip handle reflexively.

Jace turned away from the doors. Slowly he reached up and drew open his mangled shirt so that they could see the ugly possession rune, and the bloody slash that ran through it. "That," he said, still in the same toneless voice, "is Lilith's mark. It's how she controlled me."

Alec shook his head; he looked deeply disturbed. "Jace, usually the only way to sever a demonic connection like that is to kill the demon who's doing the controlling. Lilith is one of the most powerful demons who ever—"

"She's dead," said Clary abruptly. "Simon killed her. Or I guess you could say the Mark of Cain killed her."

They all stared at Simon. "And what about you two? How did you end up here?" he asked, his tone defensive.

"Looking for you," Isabelle said. "We found that card Lilith must have given you. In your apartment. Jordan let us in. He's with Maia, downstairs." She shuddered. "The things Lilith's been doing—you wouldn't believe—*so* horrible—"

Alec held his hands up. "Slow down, everyone. We'll explain what happened with us, and then Simon, Clary, you explain what happened on your end."

The explanation took less time than Clary thought it would, with Isabelle doing much of the talking with wide, sweeping hand gestures that threatened, on occasion, to sever one of her friends' unprotected limbs with her whip. Alec took the opportunity to go out onto the roof deck to send a fire-message to the Clave telling them where they were and asking for backup. Jace stepped aside wordlessly to let him by as he left, and again when he came back in. He didn't speak during Simon and Clary's explanation of what had happened on the rooftop either, even when they got to the part about Raziel having raised Jace from the dead back in Idris. It was Izzy who finally interrupted, when Clary began to explain about Lilith being Sebastian's "mother" and keeping his body encased in glass.

"Sebastian?" Isabelle slammed her whip against the ground with enough force to open up a crack in the marble. "*Sebastian* is out there? And he's not dead?" She turned to look at Jace, who was leaning against the glass doors, arms crossed, expressionless. "I saw him die. I saw Jace cut his spine in half, and I saw him fall into the river. And now you're telling me he's *alive* out there?"

"No," Simon hastened to reassure her. "His body's there, but he's not alive. Lilith didn't get to complete the ceremony." Simon put a hand on her shoulder, but she shook it off. She had gone a deadly white color.

"'Not really alive' isn't dead enough for me," she said. "I'm going out there and I'm going to cut him into a thousand pieces." She turned toward the doors.

"Iz!" Simon put his hand on her shoulder. "Izzy. No."

"No?" She looked at him incredulously. "Give me one good reason why I shouldn't chop him into worthless-bastard-themed confetti."

Simon's eyes darted around the room, resting for a moment on Jace, as if he expected him to chime in or add a comment. He didn't; he didn't even move. Finally Simon said, "Look, you understand about the ritual, right? Because Jace was brought back from the dead, that gave Lilith the power to raise Sebastian. And to do that, she needed Jace there and alive, as—what did she call it—"

"A counterweight," put in Clary.

"That mark that Jace has on his chest. Lilith's mark." In a seemingly unconscious gesture, Simon touched his own chest, just over the heart. "Sebastian has it too. I saw them both flash at the same time when Jace stepped into the circle."

Isabelle, her whip twitching at her side, her teeth biting into her red bottom lip, said impatiently, "And?"

"I think she was making a tie between them," said Simon. "If Jace died, Sebastian couldn't live. So if you cut Sebastian into pieces—"

"It could hurt Jace," Clary said, the words spilling out of her as she realized. "Oh, my God. Oh, Izzy, you can't."

"So we're just going to let him *live*?" Isabelle sounded incredulous.

"Cut him to pieces if you like," Jace said. "You have my permission."

"Shut up," said Alec. "Stop acting like your life doesn't matter. Iz, weren't you listening? Sebastian's not alive."

"He's not dead, either. Not dead *enough*."

"We need the Clave," said Alec. "We need to give him over to the Silent Brothers. They can sever his connection to Jace, and then you'll get all the blood you want, Iz. He's *Valentine's son*. And he's a murderer. Everyone lost someone in the battle in Alicante, or knows someone who did. You think they'll be kind to him? They'll take him apart slowly while he's still living."

Isabelle stared up at her brother. Very slowly tears welled in her eyes, spilling down her cheeks, streaking the dirt and blood on her skin. "I hate it," she said. "I hate it when you're right."

Alec pulled his sister closer and kissed the top of her head. "I know you do."

She squeezed her brother's hand briefly, then drew back. "Fine," she said. "I won't touch Sebastian. But I can't stand to be this close to him." She glanced toward the glass doors, where Jace still stood. "Let's go downstairs. We can wait for the Clave in the lobby. And we need to get Maia and Jordan; they're probably wondering where we went."

Simon cleared his throat. "Someone should stay up here just to keep an eye on—on things. I'll do it."

"No." It was Jace. "You go downstairs. I'll stay. All of this is my fault. I should have made sure Sebastian was dead when I had the chance. And as for the rest of it . . ."

His voice trailed off. But Clary remembered him touching her face in a dark hallway in the Institute, remembered him whispering, *Mea culpa, mea maxima culpa.*

My fault, my fault, my own most grievous fault.

She turned to look at the others; Isabelle had pushed the call button, which was lit. Clary could hear the distant hum of the rising elevator. Isabelle's brow creased. "Alec, maybe you should stay up here with Jace."

"I don't need help," Jace said. "There's nothing to handle. I'll be fine."

Isabelle threw her hands up as the elevator arrived with a *ping*. "Fine. You win. Sulk up here alone if you want." She stalked into the elevator, Simon and Alec crowding in after her. Clary was the last to follow, turning back to look at Jace as she went. He had gone back to staring at the doors, but she could see his reflection in them. His mouth was compressed into a bloodless line, his eyes dark.

Jace, she thought as the elevator doors began to close. She willed him to turn, to look at her. He didn't, but she felt strong hands suddenly on her shoulders, shoving her forward. She heard Isabelle say, "Alec, what on earth are you—" as she stumbled through the elevator doors and righted herself, turning to stare. The doors were closing behind her, but through them she could see Alec. He gave her a rueful little half smile and a shrug, as if to say, *What else was I supposed to do?* Clary stepped forward, but it was too late; the elevator doors had clanged shut.

She was alone in the room with Jace.

The room was littered with dead bodies—crumpled figures all in gray hooded tracksuits, flung or crumpled or slumped against the wall. Maia stood by the window, breathing hard, looking out across the scene in front of her with disbelief. She had taken part in the battle at Brocelind in Idris, and had thought that was the worst thing she would ever see. But somehow this was worse. The blood that ran from dead cult members wasn't demon ichor; it was human blood. And the babies—silent and dead in their cribs, their small taloned hands folded one over the other, like dolls . . .

She looked down at her own hands. Her claws were still out, stained with blood from tip to root; she retracted them, and the blood ran down her palms, staining her wrists. Her feet were bare and bloodstained, and there was a long scratch along one bare shoulder still oozing red, though it had already begun to heal. Despite the swift healing lycanthropy provided, she knew she'd wake up tomorrow covered in bruises. When you were a werewolf, bruises rarely lasted more than a day. She remembered when she had been human, and her brother, Daniel, had made himself an expert in pinching her hard in places where the bruises wouldn't show.

"Maia." Jordan came in through one of the unfinished doors, ducking a bundle of dangling wires. He straightened up and moved toward her, picking his way among the bodies. "Are you all right?"

The look of concern on his face knotted her stomach.

"Where are Isabelle and Alec?"

He shook his head. He had sustained much less visible damage than she had. His thick leather jacket had protected him, as had his jeans and boots. There was a long scrape along his cheek, dried blood in his light brown hair and staining the blade of the knife he held. "I've searched the whole floor. Haven't seen them. Couple more bodies in the other rooms. They might have—"

The night lit up like a seraph blade. The windows went white, and bright light seared through the room. For a moment Maia thought the world had caught on fire, and Jordan, moving toward her through the light, seemed almost to disappear, white on white, into a shimmering field of silver. She heard herself scream, and she moved blindly backward, banging her head on the plate glass window. She put her hands up to cover her eyes—

And the light was gone. Maia lowered her hands, the world swinging around her. She reached out blindly, and Jordan was there. She put her arms around him—threw them around him, the way she used to when he came to pick her up from her house, and he would swing her into his arms, winding the curls of her hair through his fingers.

He had been slighter then, narrow-shouldered. Now muscle corded his bones, and holding him was like holding on to something absolutely solid, a pillar of granite in the midst of a blowing desert sandstorm. She clung on to him, and heard the beat of his heart under her ear as his hands smoothed her hair, one rough, soothing stroke at a time, comforting and . . . familiar. "Maia . . . it's all right . . ."

She raised her head and pressed her mouth to his. He had changed in so many ways, but the feel of kissing him was the same, his mouth as soft as ever. He went rigid for a second with surprise, and then gathered her up against him, his hands stroking slow circles on her bare back. She remembered the first time they had ever kissed. She had handed him her earrings to put in the glove compartment of his car, and his hand had shaken so badly he'd dropped them and then apologized and apologized until she kissed him to shut him up. She'd thought he was the sweetest boy she'd ever known.

And then he was bitten, and everything changed.

She drew away, dizzy and breathing hard. He let her go instantly; he was staring at her, his mouth open, his eyes dazed.

Behind him, through the window, she could see the city—she had half expected it to be flattened, a blasted white desert outside the window—but everything was exactly the same. Nothing had changed. Lights blinked on and off in the buildings across the street; she could hear the faint rush of traffic below. "We should go," she said. "We should look for the others."

"Maia," he said. "Why did you just kiss me?"

"I don't know," she said. "Do you think we should try the elevators?"

"Maia—"

"I don't *know*, Jordan," she said. "I don't know why I kissed you, and I don't know if I'm going to do it again, but I do know I'm freaked out and worried about my friends and I want to get out of here. Okay?"

He nodded. He looked like there were a million things he wanted to say but had determined not to say them, for which she was grateful. He ran a hand through his tousled hair, rimed white with plaster dust, and nodded. "Okay."

Silence. Jace was still leaning against the door, only now he had his forehead pressed against it, his eyes closed. Clary wondered if he even knew she was in the room with him. She took a step forward, but before she could say anything, he pushed the doors open and walked back out into the garden.

She stood still for a moment, staring after him. She could call for the elevator, of course, ride it down, wait for the Clave in the lobby with everyone else. If Jace didn't want to talk, he didn't want to talk. She couldn't force him to. If Alec was right, and he was punishing himself, she'd just have to wait until he got over it.

She turned toward the elevator—and stopped. A little flame of anger licked its way through her, making her eyes burn. *No*, she thought. She didn't have to let him behave like this. Maybe he could be this way to everyone else, but not to her. He owed her better than that. They owed each other better than that.

She whirled and made her way to the doors. Her ankle still ached, but the *iratzes* Alec had put on her were working. Most of the pain in her body had subsided to a dull, throbbing ache. She reached the doors and pushed them open, stepping onto the roof terrace with a wince as her bare feet came into contact with the freezing tiles.

She saw Jace immediately; he was kneeling near the steps, on tiles stained with blood and ichor and glittering with salt. He rose as she approached, and he turned, something shiny dangling from his hand.

The Morgenstern ring, on its chain.

The wind had come up; it blew his dark gold hair across his face. He pushed it away impatiently and said, "I just remembered that we left this here."

His voice sounded surprisingly normal.

"Is that why you wanted to stay up here?" said Clary. "To get it back?"

He turned his hand, so the chain swung upward, his fingers closing over the ring. "I'm attached to it. It's stupid, I know."

"You could have said, or Alec could have stayed—"

"I don't belong with the rest of you," he said abruptly. "After what I did, I don't deserve *iratzes* and healing and hugs and being consoled and whatever else it is my friends are going to think I need. I'd rather stay up here with *him*." He jerked his chin toward the place where Sebastian's motionless body lay in the open coffin, on its stone pedestal. "And I sure as hell don't deserve *you*."

Clary crossed her arms over her chest. "Have you ever thought about what *I* deserve? That maybe I deserve to get a chance to talk to you about what happened?"

He stared at her. They were only a few feet apart, but it felt as if an inexpressible gulf lay between them. "I don't know why you would even want to look at me, much less talk to me."

"Jace," she said. "Those things you did—that wasn't *you*."

He hesitated. The sky was so black, the lit windows of the nearby skyscrapers so bright, it was as if they stood in the center of a net of shining jewels. "If it wasn't me," he said, "then why can I remember *everything I did?* When people are possessed, and they come back from it, they don't remember what they did when the demon inhabited them. But I remember *everything*." He turned abruptly and walked away, toward the roof garden wall. She followed him, glad for the distance it put between them and Sebastian's body, now hidden from view by a row of hedges.

"Jace!" she called out, and he turned, his back to the wall, slumping against it. Behind him a city's worth of electricity lit up the night like the demon towers of Alicante. "You remember because she wanted you to remember," Clary said, catching up with him, a little breathless. "She did this to torture you as much as she did it to get Simon to do what she wanted. She wanted you to have to watch yourself hurt the people you love."

"I was watching," he said in a low voice. "It was as if some part of me was off at a distance, watching and screaming at myself to stop. But the rest of me felt completely peaceful and like what I was doing was *right*. Like it was the only thing I could do. I wonder if that's how Valentine felt about everything he did. Like it was so easy to be right." He looked away from her. "I can't stand it," he said. "You shouldn't be here with me. You should just go."

Instead of leaving, Clary moved to stand beside him against the wall. Her arms were already wrapped around herself; she was shivering. Finally, reluctantly, he turned his head to look at her again. "Clary . . ."

"You don't get to decide," she said, "where I go, or when."

"I know." His voice was ragged. "I've always known that about you. I don't know why I had to fall in love with someone who's more stubborn than I am."

Clary was silent a moment. Her heart had contracted at those two words—"in love." "All those things you said to me," she said in a half whisper, "on the terrace at the Ironworks— did you mean them?"

His golden eyes dulled. "Which things?"

That you loved me, she almost said, but thinking back—he hadn't said that, had he? Not the words themselves. The implication had been there. And the truth of the fact, that they loved each other, was something she knew as clearly as she knew her own name.

"You kept asking me if I would love you if you were like Sebastian, like Valentine."

"And you said then I wouldn't be me. Look how wrong that turned out to be," he said, bitterness coloring his voice. "What I did tonight—"

Clary moved toward him; he tensed, but didn't move away. She took hold of the front of his shirt, leaned in closely, and said, enunciating each word clearly, "That wasn't you."

"Tell that to your mother," he said. "Tell it to Luke, when they ask where *this* came from." He touched her collarbone gently; the wound was healed now, but her skin, and the fabric of her dress, were still stained darkly with blood.

"I'll tell them," she said. "I'll tell them it was my fault."

He looked at her, gold eyes incredulous. "You can't lie to them."

"I'm not. I brought you back," she said. "You were dead, and I brought you back. *I* upset the balance, not you. I opened the door for Lilith and her stupid ritual. I could have asked for anything, and I asked for you." She tightened her grip on his shirt, her fingers white with cold and pressure. "And I would *do it again.* I love you, Jace Wayland—Herondale—Lightwood—whatever you want to call yourself. I don't care. I love you and I will always love you, and pretending it could be any other way is just a waste of time."

A look of such pain crossed his face that Clary felt her heart tighten. Then he reached out and took her face between his hands. His palms were warm against her cheeks.

"Remember when I told you," he said, his voice as soft as she had ever heard it, "that I didn't know if there was a God or not, but either way, we were completely on our own? I still don't know the answer; I only knew that there was such a thing as faith, and that I didn't deserve to have it. And then there was you. You changed everything I believed in. You know that line from Dante that I quoted to you in the park? '*L'amor che move il sole e l'altre stelle*'?"

Her lips curled a little at the sides as she looked up at him. "I still don't speak Italian."

"It's a bit of the very last verse from *Paradiso*—Dante's

Paradise. 'My will and my desire were turned by love, the love that moves the sun and the other stars.' Dante was trying to explain faith, I think, as an overpowering love, and maybe it's blasphemous, but that's how I think of the way that I love you. You came into my life and suddenly I had one truth to hold on to—that I loved you, and you loved me."

Though he seemed to be looking at her, his gaze was distant, as if fixed on something far away.

"Then I started to have the dreams," he went on. "And I thought maybe I'd been wrong. That I didn't deserve you. That I didn't deserve to be perfectly happy—I mean, God, who deserves *that?* And after tonight—"

"Stop." She had been clutching his shirt; she loosened her grip now, flattening her hands against his chest. His heart was racing under her fingertips; his cheeks flushed, and not just from the cold. "Jace. Through everything that happened tonight, I knew one thing. That it wasn't you hurting me. It wasn't you doing these things. I have an absolute incontrovertible belief that you are *good.* And that will never change."

Jace took a deep, shuddering breath. "I don't even know how to try to deserve that."

"You don't have to. I have enough faith in you," she said, "for both of us."

His hands slid into her hair. The mist of their exhaled breath rose between them, a white cloud. "I missed you so much," he said, and kissed her, his mouth gentle on hers, not desperate and hungry the way it had been the last few times he had kissed her, but familiar and tender and soft.

She closed her eyes as the world seemed to spin around her like a pinwheel. Sliding her hands up his chest, she stretched upward as far as she could, wrapping her arms around his neck, rising up on her toes to meet his mouth with hers. His fingers skimmed down her body, over skin and satin, and she shivered, leaning into him, and she was sure they both tasted like blood and ashes and salt, but it didn't matter; the world, the city, and all its lights and life seemed to have narrowed down to this, just her and Jace, the burning heart of a frozen world.

He drew away first, reluctantly. She realized why a moment later. The sound of honking cars and screeching tires from the street below was audible, even up here. "The Clave," he said resignedly—though he had to clear his throat to get the words out, Clary was pleased to hear. His face was flushed, as she imagined hers was. "They're here."

With her hand in his Clary looked over the edge of the roof wall and saw that a number of long black cars had drawn up in front of the scaffolding. People were piling out. It was hard to recognize them from this height, but Clary thought she saw Maryse, and several other people dressed in gear. A moment later Luke's truck roared up to the curb and Jocelyn leaped out. Clary would have known it was her, just from the way she moved, at a greater distance than this one.

Clary turned to Jace. "My mom," she said. "I'd better get downstairs. I don't want her coming up here and seeing—and seeing *him*." She jerked her chin toward Sebastian's coffin.

He stroked her hair back from her face. "I don't want to let you out of my sight."

"Then, come with me."

"No. Someone should stay up here." He took her hand, turned it over, and dropped the Morgenstern ring into it, the chain pooling like liquid metal. The clasp had bent when she'd torn it off, but he'd managed to push it back into shape. "Please take it."

Her eyes flicked down, and then, uncertainly, back up to his face. "I wish I understood what it meant to you."

He shrugged slightly. "I wore it for a decade," he said. "Some part of me is in it. It means I trust you with my past and all the secrets that past carries. And besides"—lightly he touched one of the stars engraved around the rim—"'the love that moves the sun and all the other stars.' Pretend that that's what the stars stand for, not Morgenstern."

In answer she dropped the chain back over her head, feeling the ring settle in its accustomed place, below her collarbone. It felt like a puzzle piece clicking back into place. For a moment their eyes locked in wordless communication, more intense in some ways than their physical contact had been; she held the image of him in her mind in that moment as if she were memorizing it—the tangled golden hair, the shadows cast by his lashes, the rings of darker gold inside the light amber of his eyes. "I'll be right back," she said. She squeezed his hand. "Five minutes."

"Go on," he said roughly, releasing her hand, and she turned and went back down the path. The moment she stepped away from him, she was cold again, and by the time she reached the doors to the building, she was freezing. She paused as she opened the door, and looked back at him, but he was only a shadow, backlit by the glow of the New York skyline. *The love that moves the sun and all the other stars*, she thought, and then, as if in answering echo, she heard Lilith's words. *The kind of love that can burn down the world or raise it up in glory.* A shiver ran through her, and not just from the cold. She looked for Jace, but he had vanished into the shadows; she turned and headed back inside, the door sliding shut behind her.

Alec had gone upstairs to look for Jordan and Maia, and Simon and Isabelle were alone together, sitting side by side on the green chaise longue in the lobby. Isabelle held Alec's witchlight in her hand, illuminating the room with a nearly spectral glow, sparking dancing motes of fire from the pendant chandelier.

She had said very little since her brother had left them together. Her head was bent, her dark hair falling forward, her gaze on her hands. They were delicate hands, long-fingered, but calloused as her brothers' were. Simon had never noticed before, but she wore a silver ring on her right hand, with a pattern of flames around the band of it, and a carved *L* in the center. It reminded him of the ring Clary wore around her neck, with its design of stars.

"It's the Lightwood family ring," she said, noticing where his gaze was fixed. "Every family has an emblem. Ours is fire."

It suits you, he thought. Izzy *was* like fire, in her flaming scarlet dress, with her moods as changeable as sparks. On the roof he'd half-thought she'd strangle him, her arms around his neck as she called him every name under the sun while clutching him like she'd never let him go. Now she was staring off into the distance, as untouchable as a star. It was all very disconcerting.

You love them so, Camille had said, *your Shadowhunter friends. As the falcon loves the master who binds and blinds it.*

"What you told us," he said, a little halting, watching Isabelle wind a strand of her hair around her forefinger, "up there on the roof—that you hadn't known that Clary and Jace were missing, that you'd come here for me—was that true?"

Isabelle looked up, tucking the strand of hair behind her ear. "Of course it's true," she said indignantly. "When we saw you were gone from the party—and you've been in danger for days, Simon, and what with Camille escaping—" She caught herself up short. "And Jordan's responsible for you. He was freaking out."

"So it was his idea to come looking for me?"

Isabelle turned to look at him for a long moment. Her eyes were fathomless and dark. "I was the one who noticed you were gone," she said. "I was the one who wanted to find you."

Simon cleared his throat. He felt oddly light-headed. "But why? I thought you hated me now."

It had been the wrong thing to say. Isabelle shook her head, her dark hair flying, and moved a little away from him on the settee. "Oh, Simon. Don't be dense."

"Iz." He reached out and touched her wrist, hesitantly. She didn't move away, just watched him. "Camille said something to me in the Sanctuary. She said that Shadowhunters didn't care about Downworlders, just used them. She said the Nephilim would never do for me what I did for them. But you did. You came for me. You came for *me*."

"Of course I did," she said, in a muffled little voice. "When I thought something had happened to you—"

He leaned toward her. Their faces were inches from each other. He could see the reflected sparks of the chandelier in her black eyes. Her lips were parted, and Simon could feel the warmth of her breath. For the first time since he had become a vampire, he could feel heat, like an electrical charge passing between them. "Isabelle," he said. Not Iz, not Izzy. *Isabelle.* "Can I—"

The elevator *pinged*; the doors opened, and Alec, Maia, and Jordan spilled out. Alec looked suspiciously at Simon and Isabelle as they sprang apart, but before he could say anything, the double doors of the lobby flew wide, and Shadowhunters poured into the room. Simon recognized Kadir and Maryse, who immediately flew across the room to Isabelle and caught her by the shoulders, demanding to know what had happened.

Simon got to his feet and edged away, feeling uncomfortable—and was nearly knocked down by Magnus, racing across the room to get to Alec. He didn't seem to see Simon at all. *After all, in a hundred, two hundred, years, it'll be just you and me. We'll be all that's left,* Magnus had said to him in the Sanctuary. Feeling unutterably lonely among the milling crowd of Shadowhunters, Simon pressed himself back against the wall in the vain hope that he wouldn't be noticed.

Alec looked up just as Magnus reached him, caught him, and pulled him close. His fingers traced over Alec's face as if checking for bruises or damage; under his breath, he was muttering, "How could you—go off like this and not even tell me—I could have helped you—"

"Stop it." Alec pulled away, feeling mutinous.

Magnus checked himself, his voice sobering. "I'm sorry," he said. "I shouldn't have left the party. I should have stayed with you. Camille's gone anyway. No one's got the slightest idea where she went, and since you can't track vampires . . ." He shrugged.

Alec pushed away the image of Camille in his mind, chained to the pipe, looking at him with those fierce green eyes. "Never mind," he said. "She doesn't matter. I know you were just trying to help. I'm not angry with you for leaving the party, anyway."

"But you were angry," said Magnus. "I knew you were. That's why I was so worried. Running off and putting yourself in danger just because you're angry with me—"

"I'm a Shadowhunter," Alec said. "Magnus, this is what I *do*. It's not about you. Next time fall in love with an insurance adjuster or—"

"Alexander," said Magnus. "There isn't going to be a next time." He leaned his forehead against Alec's, gold-green eyes staring into blue.

Alec's heartbeat sped up. "Why not?" he said. "You live forever. Not everyone does."

"I know I said that," said Magnus. "But, Alexander—"

"Stop calling me that," said Alec. "Alexander is what my parents call me. And I suppose it's very advanced of you to have accepted my mortality so fatalistically—everything dies, blah, blah—but how do you think that makes me *feel*? Ordinary couples can *hope*—hope to grow old together, hope to live long lives and die at the same time, but we can't hope for that. I don't even know what it is you want."

Alec wasn't sure what he'd expected in response—anger or defensiveness or even humor—but Magnus's voice only dropped, cracking slightly when he said, "Alex—Alec. If I gave you the impression I had accepted the idea of your death I can only apologize. I tried to, I thought I had—and yet still I pictured having you for fifty, sixty more years. I thought I might be ready then to let you go. But it's you, and I realize now that I won't be any more ready to lose you then than I am right now." He put his hands gently to either side of Alec's face. "Which is not at all."

"So what do we do?" Alec whispered.

Magnus shrugged, and smiled suddenly; with his messy black hair and the gleam in his gold-green eyes, he looked like a mischievous teenager. "What everyone does," he replied. "Like you said. Hope."

Alec and Magnus had begun kissing in the corner of the room, and Simon wasn't quite sure where to look. He didn't want them to think he was staring at them during what was clearly a private moment, but wherever else he looked, he met the glaring eyes of Shadowhunters. Despite the fact that he'd fought with them in the bank against Camille, none of them looked at him with particular friendliness. It was one thing for Isabelle to accept him and to care about him, but Shadowhunters en masse were another thing entirely. He could tell what they were thinking. "Vampire, Downworlder, enemy" was written all over their faces. It came as a relief when the doors burst open again and Jocelyn came flying in, still wearing her blue dress from the party. Luke was only a few steps behind her.

"Simon!" she cried as soon as she caught sight of him. She ran over to him, and to his surprise she hugged him fiercely before letting him go. "Simon, where's Clary? Is she—"

Simon opened his mouth, but no sound came out. How could he explain to Jocelyn, of all people, what had happened that night? Jocelyn, who would be horrified to know that so much of Lilith's evil, the children she had murdered, the blood she had spilled, had all been in the service of making more creatures like Jocelyn's own dead son, whose body even now lay entombed on the rooftop where Clary was with Jace?

I can't tell her any of this, he thought. *I can't*. He looked past her at Luke, whose blue eyes rested on him expectantly.

Behind Clary's family he could see the Shadowhunters crowding around Isabelle as she presumably recounted the events of the evening.

"I—," he began helplessly, and then the elevator doors opened again, and Clary stepped out. Her shoes were gone, her lovely satin dress in bloody rags, bruises already fading on her bare arms and legs. But she was smiling—radiant even, happier than Simon had seen her look in weeks.

"Mom!" she exclaimed, and then Jocelyn had flown at her and was hugging her. Clary smiled at Simon over her mother's shoulder. Simon glanced around the room. Alec and Magnus were still wrapped up in each other, and Maia and Jordan had vanished. Isabelle was still surrounded by Shadowhunters, and Simon could hear gasps of horror and amazement rise from the group surrounding her as she recounted her story. He suspected some part of her was enjoying it. Isabelle did love being the center of attention, no matter what the cause.

He felt a hand come down on his shoulder. It was Luke. "Are *you* all right, Simon?"

Simon looked up at him. Luke looked as he always did: solid, professorial, utterly reliable. Not even the least bit put out that his engagement party had been disrupted by a sudden dramatic emergency.

Simon's father had died so long ago that he barely remembered him. Rebecca recalled bits about him—that he had a beard, and would help her build elaborate towers out of blocks—but Simon didn't. It was one of the things he'd thought he always had in common with Clary, that had bonded them: both with dead fathers, both brought up by strong single women.

Well, at least one of those things had turned out to be true, Simon thought. Though his mother had dated, he'd never had a consistent fatherly presence in his life, other than Luke. He supposed that in a way, he and Clary had shared Luke. And the wolf pack looked up to Luke for guidance, as well. For a bachelor who'd never had children, Simon thought, Luke had an awful lot of kids to look after.

"I don't know," Simon said, giving Luke the honest answer he'd like to think he'd have given his own father. "I don't think so."

Luke turned Simon to face him. "You're covered in blood," he said. "And I'm guessing it's not yours, because . . ." He gestured toward the Mark on Simon's forehead. "But hey." His voice was gentle. "Even covered in blood and with the Mark of Cain on you, you're still Simon. Can you tell me what happened?"

"It's not my blood, you're right," Simon said hoarsely. "But it's also kind of a long story." He tilted his head back to look up at Luke; he'd always wondered if maybe he'd have another growth spurt some day, grow a few more inches than the five-ten he was now, be able to look Luke—not to mention Jace—straight in the eye. But that would never happen now. "Luke," he said. "Do you think it's possible to do something so bad, even if you didn't mean to do it, that you can never come back from it? That no one can forgive you?"

Luke looked at him for a long, silent moment. Then he said, "Think of someone you love, Simon. *Really* love. Is there anything they could ever do that would mean you would stop loving them?"

Images flashed through Simon's mind, like the pages of a flip-book: Clary, turning to smile at him over her shoulder; his sister, tickling him when he was just a little kid; his mother, asleep on the sofa with the coverlet pulled up to her shoulders; Izzy—

He shut the thoughts off hastily. Clary hadn't done anything so terrible that he needed to dredge up forgiveness for her; none of the people he was picturing had. He thought of Clary, forgiving her mother for having stolen her memories. He thought of Jace, what he had done on the roof, how he had looked afterward. He had done what he had done without volition of his own, but Simon doubted Jace would be able to forgive himself, regardless. And then he thought of Jordan—not forgiving himself for what he had done to Maia, but forging ahead anyway, joining the Praetor Lupus, making a life out of helping others.

"I bit someone," he said. The words came out of his mouth, and he wished he could swallow them back. He braced himself for Luke's look of horror, but it didn't come.

"Did they live?" Luke said. "This person that you bit. Did they survive?"

"I—" How to explain about Maureen? Lilith had ordered her away, but Simon was sure they hadn't seen the last of her. "I didn't kill her."

Luke nodded once. "You know how werewolves become pack leaders," he said. "They have to kill the old pack leader. I've done that twice. I have the scars to prove it." He drew the collar of his shirt aside slightly, and Simon saw the edge of a thick white scar that looked ragged, as if his chest had been clawed. "The second time it was a calculated move. Cold-blooded killing. I wanted to become the leader, and that was how I did it." He shrugged. "You're a vampire. It's in your nature to want to drink blood. You've held out a long time without doing it. I know you can walk in the sun, Simon, and so you pride yourself on being a normal human boy, but you're still what you are. Just like I am. The more you try to crush your true nature, the more it will control you. Be what you are. No one who really loves you will stop."

Simon said hoarsely, "My mom—"

"Clary told me what happened with your mother, and that you've been crashing with Jordan Kyle," said Luke. "Look, your mother will come around, Simon. Like Amatis did, with me. You're still her son. I'll talk to her, if you want me to."

Simon shook his head silently. His mother had always liked Luke. Dealing with the fact that Luke was a werewolf would probably make things worse, not better.

Luke nodded as if he understood. "If you don't want to go back to Jordan's, you're more than welcome to stay on my sofa tonight. I'm sure Clary would be glad to have you around, and we can talk about what to do about your mother tomorrow."

Simon squared his shoulders. He looked at Isabelle across the room, the gleam of her whip, the shine of the pendant at her throat, the flutter of her hands as she talked. Isabelle, who wasn't afraid of anything. He thought of his mother, the way she had backed away from him, the fear in her eyes. He'd been hiding from the memory, running from it, ever since. But it was time to stop running. "No," he said. "Thanks, but I think I don't need a place to crash tonight. I think . . . that I'm going to go home."

Jace stood alone on the roof, looking out over the city, the East River a silvery-black snake twining between Brooklyn and

Manhattan. His hands, his lips, still felt warm from Clary's touch, but the wind off the river was icy, and the warmth was fading fast. Without a jacket the air cut through the thin material of his shirt like the blade of a knife.

He took a deep breath, sucking the cold air into his lungs, and let it out slowly. His whole body felt tense. He was waiting for the sound of the elevator, the doors opening, the Shadowhunters flooding out into the garden. They would be sympathetic at first, he thought, worried about him. Then, as they understood what had happened—then would come the shrinking away, the meaningful looks exchanged when they thought he wasn't watching. He had been possessed—not just by a demon, but by a Greater Demon—had acted against the Clave, had threatened and hurt another Shadowhunter.

He thought about how Jocelyn would look at him when she heard what he'd done to Clary. Luke might understand, forgive. But Jocelyn. He had never been able to bring himself to speak to her honestly, to say the words he thought might reassure her. *I love your daughter, more than I ever thought it was possible to love anything. I would never hurt her.*

She would just look at him, he thought, with those green eyes that were so like Clary's. She would want more than that. She would want to hear him say what he wasn't sure was true.

I am nothing like Valentine.

Aren't you? The words seemed carried on the cold air, a whisper meant only for his ears. *You never knew your mother. You never knew your father. You gave your heart to Valentine when you were a child, as children do, and made yourself a part of him. You cannot cut that away from yourself now with one clean slice of a blade.*

His left hand was cold. He looked down and saw, to his

shock, that somehow he had picked up the dagger—his real father's etched silver dagger—and was holding it in his hand. The blade, though eaten away by Lilith's blood, was whole again, and shining like a promise. A cold that had nothing to do with the weather began to spread through his chest. *How many times had he woken up like this, gasping and sweating, the dagger in his hand? And Clary, always Clary, dead at his feet.*

But Lilith was dead. It was over. He tried to slide the dagger into his belt, but his hand didn't seem to want to obey the command his mind was giving it. He felt a sense of stinging heat across his chest, a searing pain. Looking down, he saw that the bloody line that had split Lilith's mark in half, where Clary had slashed him with the dagger, had healed. The mark gleamed redly against his chest.

Jace stopped trying to shove the dagger into his belt. His knuckles turned white as his grip tightened on the hilt, his wrist twisting, desperately trying to turn the blade on himself. His heart was pounding. He had accepted no *iratzes*. How had the mark healed so fast? If he could gash it again, disfigure it, even temporarily—

But his hand wouldn't obey him. His arm stayed stiffly at his side as his body turned, against his own will, toward the pedestal where Sebastian's body lay.

The coffin had begun to glow, with a cloudy greenish light—almost a witchlight glow, but there was something painful about this light, something that seemed to pierce the eye. Jace tried to take a step back, but his legs wouldn't move. Icy sweat trickled down his back. A voice whispered at the back of his mind.

Come here.

It was Sebastian's voice.

Did you think you were free because Lilith is gone? The vampire's bite woke me; now her blood in my veins compels you.

Come here.

Jace tried to dig in his heels, but his body betrayed him, carrying him forward, though his conscious mind strained against it. Even as he tried to hang back, his feet moved him down the path, toward the coffin. The painted circle flashed green as he moved across it, and the coffin seemed to answer with a second flash of emerald light. And then he was standing over it, looking down.

Jace bit down hard on his lip, hoping the pain might shock him out of the dream state he was in. It didn't work. He tasted his own blood as he stared down at Sebastian, who floated like a drowned corpse in the water. *Those are pearls that were his eyes.* His hair was colorless seaweed, his closed eyelids blue. His mouth had the cold, hard set of his father's mouth. It was like looking at a young Valentine.

Without his volition, absolutely against his will, Jace's hands began to rise. His left hand laid the edge of the dagger against the inside of his right palm, where life and love lines crisscrossed each other.

Words spilled from his own lips. He heard them as if from an immense distance. They were in no language he knew or understood, but he knew what they were—ritual chanting. His mind was screaming at his body to stop, but it appeared to make no difference. He left hand came down, the knife clenched in it. The blade sliced a clean, sure, shallow cut across his right palm. Almost instantly it began to bleed. He tried to draw back, tried to pull his arm away, but it was as if he were encased in cement. As he watched in horror, the first blood drops splashed onto Sebastian's face.

Sebastian's eyes flew open. They were black, blacker than Valentine's, as black as the demon's who had called herself his mother. They fixed on Jace, like great dark mirrors, giving him back his own face, twisted and unrecognizable, his mouth shaping the words of the ritual, spilling forth in a meaningless babble like a river of black water.

The blood was flowing more freely now, turning the cloudy liquid inside the coffin a darker red. Sebastian moved. The bloody water shifted and spilled as he sat up, his black eyes fixed on Jace.

The second part of the ritual. His voice spoke inside Jace's head. *It is almost complete.*

Water ran off him like tears. His pale hair, pasted to his forehead, seemed to have no color at all. He raised one hand and held it out, and Jace, against the cry inside his own mind, held out the dagger, blade forward. Sebastian slid his hand along the length of the cold, sharp blade. Blood sprang up in a line across his palm. He knocked the dagger aside and took Jace's hand, gripping it with his own.

It was the last thing Jace had expected. He couldn't move to pull away. He felt each of Sebastian's cold fingers as they wrapped his hand, pressing their bleeding cuts together. It was like being gripped by cold metal. Ice began to spread up his veins from his hand. A shudder passed over him, and then another, powerful physical tremors so painful it felt as if his body were being turned inside out. He tried to scream—

And the cry died in his throat. He looked down at his and Sebastian's hands, clenched together. Blood ran through their fingers and down their wrists, as elegant as red lacework. It glittered in the cold electric light of the city. It moved not like liquid, but like moving red wires. It wrapped their hands together in a scarlet binding.

A peculiar sense of peace stole over Jace. The world seemed to fall away, and he was standing on the peak of a mountain, the world spread out before him, everything in it his for the taking. The lights of the city around him were no longer electric, but were the light of a thousand diamond-like stars. They seemed to shine down on him with a benevolent glow that said, *This is good. This is right. This is what your father would have wanted.*

He saw Clary in his mind's eye, her pale face, the fall of her red hair, her mouth as it moved, shaping the words *I'll be right back. Five minutes.*

And then her voice faded as another spoke over it, drowning it out. The image of her in his mind receded, vanishing imploringly into the darkness, as Eurydice had vanished when Orpheus had turned to look at her one last time. Her saw her, her white arms held out to him, and then the shadows closed over her and she was gone.

A new voice spoke in Jace's head now, a familiar voice, once hated, now oddly welcome. Sebastian's voice. It seemed to run through his blood, through the blood that passed through Sebastian's hand into his, like a fiery chain.

We are one now, little brother, you and I, Sebastian said.

We are one.

Acknowledgments

As always, family provides the core of support needed to make a novel happen: my husband Josh, my mother and father, Jim Hill and Kate Connor; the Esons family; Melanie, Jonathan and Helen Lewis; Florence and Joyce. This book even more than any other was the product of intense group work, so many thanks to: Delia Sherman, Holly Black, Sarah Rees Brennan, Justine Larbalestier, Elka Cloke, Robin Wasserman, and special mention to Maureen Johnson for lending her name to the character Maureen. Thanks to Wayne Miller for helping me with Latin translations. Thanks to Margie Longoria for her support of Project Book Babe: Michael Garza, the owner of the Big Apple Deli, is named for her son, Michael Eliseo Joe Garza. My always gratitude to my agent, Barry Goldblatt; to my editor, Karen Wojtyla; to Emily Fabre, for making changes long past the time changes can be made; to Cliff Nielson and Russell Gordon, for making beautiful covers; and to the teams at Simon and Schuster and Walker Books for making the rest of the magic happen. And lastly, my thanks to Linus and Lucy, my cats, who only threw up on my manuscript once.

City of Fallen Angels was written with the program Scrivener, in San Miguel de Allende, Mexico.